WELCOME TO THE BABY PLAN!

And now, a to-do list for modern motherhood

___ Set date for gender reveal party, including color-coded cake and confetti

___ Crowdsource baby name

___ Share monthly sonograms on Facebook

___ Plan perfect diet for return to your bikini body in six weeks

___ Overshare all physical changes to every part of your body

___ Register for overpriced baby stroller and nursery furniture

___ Have a calm, rational discussion about the latest child-rearing philosophies with your partner

___ When that doesn't work, have a major fight, preferably in public

___ Nest by creating a Pinterest-worthy nursery

___ And finally . . . Relaaaaaaaaax . . . (Because once the baby gets here, you won't be able to.)

THE
BABY
PLAN

Also by Kate Rorick

The Epic Adventures of Lydia Bennet
The Secret Diary of Lizzie Bennet

THE
BABY

a novel

PLAN

KATE RORICK

WILLIAM MORROW
An Imprint of HarperCollinsPublishers

P.S.™ is a trademark of HarperCollins Publishers.

HarperCollins books may be purchased for educational, business, or sales promotional use. For information, please email the Special Markets Department at SPsales@harpercollins.com.

FIRST EDITION

Designed by Diahann Sturge

Title page and chapter opener baby stroller art © shopplaywood/Shutterstock, inc.
November part opener art © Inspiring/Shutterstock, inc.
December, January, February, March, April, and May part opener art
© toranosuke/Shutterstock, inc.

Library of Congress Cataloging-in-Publication Data has been applied for.

ISBN 978-0-06-268441-7

18 19 20 21 22   LSC   10 9 8 7 6 5 4 3 2 1

For Burr, who made me a mom.
And for Maddy, who has impeccable timing.

THE
BABY
PLAN

NOVEMBER

SUNDAY	MONDAY	TUESDAY	WEDNESDAY	THURSDAY	FRIDAY	SATURDAY

"Congratulations!"

CHAPTER 1

It was the mashed potatoes that did it.

The damned holiday mashed potatoes, made with nearly a pound of butter and cream cheese and onions and pepper and salt—and the occasional potato—that ruined Nathalie Kneller's announcement, three years in the making.

And worse, she had been the one to make the potatoes. So really it was her own fault.

Usually, the family didn't get together for Thanksgiving. Christmas was their big holiday. Ever since her dad retired and traded the house they grew up in for a condo with a parking space big enough for an RV, he'd spent more time exploring the great American roadways than not. But he would always be back in Santa Barbara for Christmas, and Nathalie and her sister would joyfully make the drive up from Los Angeles to gleefully welcome him home, and dutifully receive the gifts he'd picked up in his travels.

Never mind that Nathalie was not in need of any more turquoise jewelry, or tumbled rocks taken straight out of Carlsbad Caverns. Her dad had given her a rock tumbler when she was nine, and she'd loved it. But sometimes it seemed like she was stuck at that age, as that person, in his mind.

But this year Nathalie *begged* her father to be back by Thanksgiving. He had to be. Timing was everything.

"I don't know, kiddo," her father had hemmed on the phone. She could hear the radio playing in the background. "*. . . Listening to 104.3 KBEQ Kansas City! Stay tuned for Blake Shelton, Faith Hill, and Dierks Bentley!*"

"Kathy really wanted to go to Branson this trip, see the sights . . ."

Nathalie had to bite her tongue to keep her annoyance at her stepmother's love of anything country in check.

"Please?" she'd said on the phone. "I'll even host!" Considering the postage-stamp size of the two-bedroom house she and David had just spent their life savings on, this was a card she'd hoped she wouldn't have to play. But she had to pull out all the stops against Branson and Kathy.

"Well . . ."

"Dad, it's . . . it's important."

"Important, how?" her father had asked, suspicious. "Is everything okay?"

It took everything in her to not blurt it out over the phone. But again, timing was crucial. So instead, she just said, "Everything's great, Dad. I just . . . I'd just really love to see you. And show off the house."

She'd heard him sigh on the other end of the line. "Okay. I'll talk to Kath about it, but . . . count us in."

Nathalie had smiled and mentally fist-pumped as she said her goodbyes to her dad.

Then, cold realization settled over her: she was going to have to host Thanksgiving dinner.

At the age of thirty-three, she'd never hosted a holiday

meal. Their place had always been too small, they always had friends or family to go to . . . one way or another, it was something they'd always managed to avoid. Now, she had invited it on herself.

But there was nothing to be done about it. She needed to have her family there on Thanksgiving.

Because on Thanksgiving, she would be thirteen weeks and one day pregnant.

Thirteen weeks was the cutoff point, ending the queasiness and worry of the first trimester, and the beginning of the (supposedly) smooth-sailing second. But more importantly, it was the point at which it was universally agreed that it was safe to tell people. The chances of something going catastrophically wrong plummet, and you can tentatively share your good news—either quietly, in hushed tones over brunch with girlfriends, or by the trumpet blast of posting a sonogram pic on your Facebook wall.

Or, if you were like Nathalie, you could announce it in the Thanksgiving toast you'd had composed for three years, your family gathered around, your father sniffling away tears at the thought of his first grandchild.

So, for the next ten days, while her father took a meandering route back to California from the Midwest, and her husband David watched with silent bewilderment, Nathalie wrote lists, scoured Pinterest, and laid out a rational, detailed, and perfect plan for their very first Thanksgiving.

Number one on the list was they had to get an actual dining room table.

"What's wrong with our current table?" David asked as Nathalie dragged him through IKEA.

"The bistro table can go on the deck," *where it's supposed to,* she finished mentally. The little metal table was whimsical in their old tiny apartment, but they were well into adulthood now, in their thirties, with 401(k)s and homeowner's insurance.

Time for the black STORNÄS extendable table that showed it.

After acquiring chairs (NORRNÄS in white, for contrast), she gave David a six-pack of his favorite IPA and set him to the task of assembly while she went and bought matching fall-themed linens, serving dishes, utensils, decorations, and all the other things that people who have never had cause to entertain before might not have around the house. The gold-edged china plates she'd inherited from her mother and dragged from apartment to apartment but never used finally came out of their boxes, ready for their moment in the spotlight.

The one thing she was not worried about was the food. She had made almost every single dish, minus the turkey, having brought various sides to potluck Thanksgivings and even once, when she was eleven, doing the whole dinner on her own. Plus, she had her mother's recipe box, and knew exactly how to time the cooking to make everything in her small kitchen.

Although, she could use an extra pair of hands.

"Sorry, Nat, I can't," Lyndi said into the phone. Her little sister's regret was apparent in the tone of her voice, but it did little to appease Nathalie.

"But you said you had it covered!"

"I know, but . . ."

"It's just one little pie!" Nathalie exclaimed. It wasn't just one little pie. It was their father's favorite triple berry pie, and normally she would have done it herself, but timing the pie with cooking the turkey was tricky and good leaders knew how to delegate.

"Yeah, but our oven's totally crappy, and I don't even have, like, a pie plate. Besides, Marcus doesn't eat gluten so he doesn't want any of that stuff in our apartment."

Nathalie was glad Lyndi couldn't see the look on her face at the mention of Marcus's gluten sensitivity. It also didn't help that she was in the middle of mashing the potatoes.

And oh God, the potatoes. Her morning sickness, which usually confined itself to the mornings, decided to voice a strong objection every time the masher smushed another boiled potato. She dreaded adding the butter and cream cheese and the thick dairy smells it would create.

She had just about breathed through the worst of it when Lyndi said, "You got gluten-free stuffing for him, right?"

". . . I'm sorry?"

"For Marcus? Gluten-free stuffing?"

"You're bringing Marcus?" Nathalie asked, incredulous.

"Well, yeah. I mean, if that's okay," Lyndi said.

"I . . . I guess it is." Thank God she had bought that sixth chair. "But, surely your roommate has other places to go—friends, or a party?"

In truth, Nathalie would have rather not had Marcus there. She had met him once, when she was helping Lyndi move into the third-floor apartment in the bohemian neighborhood of Echo Park. And he was nice enough, helping Lyndi carry her bike up the stairs. But his niceness and splitting the rent with her sister didn't exactly warrant him being present at the moment of her big announcement.

"No, we're going out to our friend's pre-Thanksgiving bash tonight," Lyndi said. "And, besides . . . you know that Marcus isn't *just* my roommate, right?"

Nathalie blinked. "You're dating?"

"I mean, I guess you could call it that," she said, awkwardly.

This was news to her. And not just because she'd thought Marcus was gay.

Lyndi was twenty-four, and sometimes the years between them stood out—like when one tried to define "dating." Often Nathalie felt like a second mother, rather than a big sister. And obviously Lyndi felt the same way, because when she finally spoke her voice was small, like a little girl caught after misbehaving.

"Are you mad?"

"No, sweetie," Nathalie heard herself saying with a sigh. "But you could have told me earlier. Thanksgiving is tomorrow, and now I have to make the pie, *and* gluten-free stuffing!"

"So he can come? Yay!" Lyndi cheered through the phone. "And I'm sorry about the pie but hey, I'll bring the flowers, okay? Don't worry about that!"

Lyndi was off the phone before Nathalie could protest that she'd already got a centerpiece (a brass cornucopia she filled with tiny squashes), but as usual with her little sister, Nathalie let her get her way.

Having Lyndi there for the announcement was more important than fretting over the random guy she had with her.

Of course, what she didn't expect was Lyndi showing up the next day at noon, completely hungover.

"Oh my God, are you okay?" Nathalie said, seeing Lyndi's gray face. She tried to hide how she was feeling with a wan smile, but it didn't work when she was the same color as her flowy pale blue minidress.

"Happy Thanksgiving to you, too," Lyndi said breezily, giving her sister a quick hug and then slipping past her.

"Hey, Nathalie!" said the massive arrangement of flowers behind Lyndi. "Good to see you again!"

"Good to, er, see you, too," she replied, taking the flowers (oh God, the smell) and finally being able to actually see Lyndi's if-you-could-call-him-that boyfriend.

Marcus had a sweet smile, that was the first thing she realized. He was lean—likely from a lack of gluten—and achingly hipster, with the skinniest of skinny jeans, a narrow strip of a tie and a full sleeve of tattoos peeking out from his button-down shirt. He was also surprisingly nervous. As one hand extended to shake hers, the other went to his short dreads, twisting the dark hair tightly.

Nathalie decided to take pity on him. "Good to see you, too, Marcus," she said in the voice that she used with her shyest students. "Come on in, it's wonderful to have you."

"Hey, Marcus!" David came in from the living room, extending his hand and pulling Marcus into a bear hug. Marcus seemed only slightly surprised, considering he'd never met David before. "I've got the game on. Wanna beer?"

"Um . . . do you have any wine?" Marcus replied. "White?"

David only gave the slightest hesitation before he slapped Marcus on the back, and pulled him toward the TV. "Sure thing. Hon, can you open the wine?"

"You got it," Nathalie singsonged back. Luckily they had a bottle of white in the back of the fridge. She hadn't had a drink in three years, and she knew Lyndi was a red girl. The white was meant for Kathy, who, when confronted by a lack of Bartles & Jaymes (which Nat didn't know existed outside of, oh, the 1980s), would settle for a pinot grigio.

She put the flowers on the table. "These are gorgeous," she said to Lyndi. And they were. They put her brass cornucopia to shame. Fat seasonal blooms in earthy reds and oranges, with a trail of yellow orchids flowing out, still on the vine.

"Thanks. I designed them."

"Designed them?"

"The arrangement. It's what I'm doing at the flower co-op now."

"I thought you were a delivery girl at the shop."

"I still do some deliveries, we all do . . . but I sort of got promoted." Lyndi shrugged, then scowled. "And it's not a shop, come on. You know that."

"Of course," Nathalie replied, wanting to keep the peace. "And congrats! On the promotion." In truth, she didn't really understand what Lyndi did at her current job. It was a place that sold flowers—so that was a flower shop, right? Even if it was only online? Whatever it was, Lyndi had stuck with it for six months, so it was better than any other job she'd tried. Nathalie could only hope one of these days she'd focus on a career.

A timer dinged in the kitchen. Nathalie heeded its call like Pavlov's dog.

"Oh what is that smell?" Lyndi said, following her.

"The holiday mashed potatoes," Nathalie answered, taking them carefully out of the oven. "Can you help me with this?"

To accommodate the triple berry pie, she'd had to rearrange the timing on baking the potatoes . . . which meant she'd had to hit the pause button on cooking the turkey for an hour. But, she thought, as she and Lyndi shoved the bird back in and cranked up the heat, it would be fine in the end.

Totally fine.

"Want a glass?" Nathalie asked, as she moved to the fridge to fish out the white wine from the back.

"No, thanks," Lyndi said, looking green.

"A little hair of the dog might make you feel better."

"What?" Her sister wrinkled her nose. "I'm not hungover. I don't get hungover."

"Did you go out last night?"

"Yes."

"Do you feel like crap now?"

"Yeah, but—"

"Then you're hungover." Nathalie gave her sister a sympathetic pat. "There's a reason beer bongs are relegated to college, you know. Welcome to your midtwenties."

Lyndi gave her a dirty look. Then she glanced at the potatoes, and quickly changed the subject.

"When's Dad getting here?"

"Any minute now," she said. "He called when they hit Palm Springs, so—"

As if on cue, the sound of Dolly Parton's "Islands in the Stream" as played on an air horn wafted through the air.

"Oh thank God," Lyndi muttered, as she trotted toward the front door. Marcus and David were already on the front lawn by the time Nathalie got there, David helping to hand Kathy down from the steps of the massive beige RV that took up the whole driveway, and Marcus shaking awkward hands with their dad. She could tell Dad was eyeing the tattoos peeking out of his sleeve, bewildered by what the kids did to themselves these days.

"There they are!" Dad called out in his booming baritone when he saw both girls standing in the doorway. He came over immediately and wrapped them both in a bear hug. "How you doin' squirt?"

"Great, Daddy," Lyndi answered, giving back as good as she got.

"And you, kiddo?" he said, throwing an arm over Nathalie's shoulder. "How are you holding up?"

"I'm fine, Dad. Glad you guys made it." She nuzzled against his side, his dad-warmth.

"Yoo-hoo! Babe, can you help with this?" Kathy called out. Nathalie was released, as he trotted to his wife's side to take a four-pack of Bartles & Jaymes from Kathy's hand.

"Sweetie, you look so pale!" Kathy said, as she came up to Nathalie, air-kissing her cheek. "Do you need any help in the kitchen?"

"Nope, I've got it all covered!"

"Oh, good! I was worried, I made your father drive so fast to get here. But he said that you always have everything under control, and of course, you do!" Kathy trilled. "I'll just go see what needs doing."

"Nothing needs doing—"

But Kathy was already inside. Nathalie sighed. Maybe she could pawn Kathy off on setting the table.

"So, David," she heard her dad say as they all came inside. "Who's winning the game?"

And so the afternoon went. As Kathy kept trying to get into the kitchen to see if she could help, Nathalie would effectively redirect her to something else she could do, be it refreshing the men's drinks or finding a new place for the brass cornucopia ("What a funny thing! Why did you buy it when you have these flowers?"). Lyndi kept looking gray and wan, opting to avoid the wine and instead sipping on a ginger ale. Marcus, to his credit, was happy to play the hungover Lyndi's nursemaid, leaping up to get her some ice, or put a pillow behind her, or take her on a walk to get some air. It was, Nathalie had to admit, awfully sweet.

David was ensconced on the couch, keeping her dad company, their long-established in-law relationship comfortable and quietly spent watching sports. Although, Nathalie couldn't help but wish David would take a page out of Marcus's book—even though she told him she had everything covered, and yep, was feeling totally great and didn't need any help, she wouldn't have minded a shoulder rub, a quick walk to get some air, or, for someone thirteen weeks and one day pregnant, a chance to sit down.

Finally—*finally*—the timer dinged on the turkey.

"Don't worry, Kathy, I got it!" Nathalie said automatically, knowing that the clip of kitten heels was headed toward the kitchen. "Time to get around the table everyone!"

She heaved the turkey out of the oven, and inserted the thermometer.

The dial did not rise nearly as high as it should.

"That's not how it's supposed to be," she muttered to herself. She'd done everything right—she thought. She checked and double-checked the timing, and was sure she'd calculated correctly to allow for the potatoes, and . . .

"Hold on . . . who turned down the oven?"

"I did, sweetie," Kathy said, all shock and innocence. "You can't cook a bird that high, it'll dry out!"

Nathalie closed her eyes. "I know that, Kathy," she ground out, "it wasn't that high the whole time, I had to take the turkey out for an hour. I looked it up—it would have been fine."

"Well, I didn't know *that*," Kathy huffed.

"Now it has to go in for another . . . I don't know how long!"

And that meant that the potatoes, the beans, the stuffing, everything else was going to go cold.

"I'm sure it's *fine*," Kathy tried. "We'll cut around any pink parts."

"I'm not serving undercooked poultry for Thanksgiving!" Nathalie nearly screeched.

"I'm just trying to help!"

"Hey, Mom," came Lyndi's weak voice from the kitchen doorway. "Did you know Marcus is from near Branson?"

14 KATE RORICK

Kathy turned to her daughter with a watery smile. "Is he? Oh, Marcus, I must know everything. Who's your favorite artist? I just love the greats—Hank, and Cash, and Dolly."

". . . Yeah, Dolly's the best," Marcus said agreeably.

Nathalie caught her sister's eyes, giving a silent *thank-you*.

"I'm getting pretty hungry, kiddo," her dad then said. "Maybe we start in on the sides while the bird finishes."

"But . . ."

"Yeah," came David's voice. "There's only so many chips and guac a guy can eat. Let's sit down."

Nathalie looked from the underdone turkey to the ready-to-go everything else. She shoved the turkey back in, upped the heat, and set the timer. Maybe it wouldn't take too long.

Besides, she had a toast to give.

Her heart started fluttering as they all gathered around the table. As they put the potatoes, stuffing, beans, and cranberries on their turkey- and pumpkin-shaped trivets, she looked to David. He gave her shoulder a reassuring squeeze. They all took their seats, and Nathalie realized the empty space at the center where the turkey should go didn't matter. Nothing mattered, except that everyone was here, and she got to tell them her wonderful—

CRASH!

"Oh my God!" Lyndi cried. "Marcus, are you okay?"

"Yeah," Marcus replied from the floor. "My chair just . . . I think I broke it."

The NORRNÄS chair had come apart beneath him, its Allen bolts unscrewed, its legs lying in broken bits.

"I'm so sorry," the skinniest person there said. "It's my fault."

"I think that one's my fault," David said, pulling Marcus to his feet. "Interpreting IKEA instructions is not my strongest suit."

Suddenly everyone was looking at their chairs with apprehension.

"Let's just . . . stand, for the toast," David said, giving his wife a look. "And then we'll . . . break out the folding chairs from the garage. Honey . . . ?"

"Yes. Yes," she said, forcing a smile. Then, she launched into her speech. "I'm so glad that everyone could come to this family occasion . . . And you, too, Marcus. Friends are wonderful and welcome. But, like I was saying, Thanksgiving is all about family. And my family is so important to me. Especially now as . . ."

"I'm sorry!" Lyndi's voice broke through the toast, thin and reedy. She was no longer gray, she was pea-green. And she wasn't looking at Nathalie. She was looking at the big casserole dish of holiday mashed potatoes, which was sitting directly in front of her. "Nat, I'm so sorry . . ."

She pivoted as quickly as a ballerina, grabbing the first container she saw: the brass cornucopia, which had been placed haphazardly on the buffet table behind them.

The sound of her hurling up bile and ginger ale echoed metallically through the room.

"Oh my God!" Kathy cried, once the retching was through. "Sweetie—"

"Are you okay, squirt?"

"I'm fine! I'm fine," Lyndi said, as Marcus placed a soothing hand on her back. "I'm just . . ."

The timer dinged. The turkey was ready.

Lyndi wiped her mouth on her sleeve, and gave a sheepish smile. "I suppose now is as good a time as any to tell everyone I'm pregnant."

CHAPTER 2

"SEVENTEEN HOURS OF COOKING, AND NO one said thank you," Nathalie grumbled as she spooned the last of the gluten-free (basically mush) stuffing into the trash. "And if it was so important for Marcus to have gluten-free stuffing, the least he could have done was EATEN the gluten-free stuffing!"

David, from the couch, grunted in agreement, which only managed to make Nathalie's rage burn brighter. After days of decoration and preparation, after running out to the Whole Foods all the way in Glendale to find gluten-free bread crumbs, and after being the most agreeable, accommodating host on the planet, Marcus didn't even touch the goddamned stuffing.

Okay sure, after Lyndi destroyed Nathalie's brass cornucopia with her own announcement, the afternoon had gone slightly awry, so maybe he wasn't hungry . . . but surely, he could have taken the stuffing home.

There was at least two-thirds of the turkey left over too, not to mention all the holiday mashed potatoes. Luckily, Dad had taken the triple berry pie back to Santa Barbara with them, lest they would have had to find space for that in the fridge, too.

It turned out, after Lyndi's surprise, everyone pretty much forgot about the food. Instead, they had just stood stock-still in shock, until Kathy burst out with a screech that sounded like a Muppet being slaughtered.

"Oh, my baby is giving me a grandbaby!" she'd said as she grabbed Lyndi into a big hug, and then, Marcus with them. Lyndi, through being mobbed, barely kept a handle on that now-filled brass cornucopia. Nathalie had stepped forward to take it from her just in time.

As her father loosened Kathy's grip on Lyndi, and placed a kiss on his little girl's cheek, Nathalie moved off to the kitchen, to drain the cornucopia. Once she deposited it in the sink, she came back into the dining room.

"Um, I am, too," she'd said, barely loud enough to be heard over Kathy's mews of joy and their dad manfully trying to find something to say to Marcus—but mostly just making a lot of "Well!" and "That's . . . well!" noises.

"Pregnant, that is," she'd finished lamely. "That's what I was trying to tell you. Before."

Again the room stilled in shock. Until David—unfrozen for the first time in minutes—had stepped forward and thrown his arm around Nathalie's shoulders. "That's right!" he'd said. "We are having a baby. We're twelve weeks—"

"Thirteen," she'd mumbled.

"Thirteen weeks along, and are due in . . . May? May."

No one moved. Nathalie waited for the strangled-Muppet sound from Kathy, but . . . nothing. Just leftover sniffles from her Lyndi-based joy.

"We are . . . really excited," she'd said, forcing a smile up at David.

"Of course you are!" her dad had finally replied, coming over to kiss her on the temple and slap David on the back. "So are we, kiddo. So are we!"

And that was it. That was her big announcement. *Um, I am, too.*

Something that she'd been wanting, and preparing for, for years, reduced to an "I am, too."

And an entire massive family dinner that should have been a celebration, reduced to no one eating, the wine being gulped by the people that could, Kathy sniffling over her cranberries, and awkward glances shared between sisters at the table.

"Hon, you don't have to clean everything up now," David said from the living room.

"Yes, I do, because if I don't it will just sit out on the counter overnight and the food will go bad. And attract bugs. And then we will have to have the house fumigated and we'll have to stay at a hotel and you know I can't sleep at hotels!"

A pause before an answer of "Okay then" drifted in from the other room.

"How can you be so calm about this?" she yelled over the water filling the turkey pan. "Admit it—that was a disaster!"

"It wasn't a disaster, hon," David replied. Somewhat unconvincingly. "Your dad was super happy for you."

That was the one solace. When her dad's lips had hit her temple, he'd whispered, "You're gonna be a great mom, kiddo," in her ear. And she'd felt the warm rush of emotion across her cheeks, and tears beginning to sting her nose.

Then, he moved over to Lyndi, and placed a kiss on her temple . . . and no doubt whispered the exact same thing to her.

"You don't think Lyndi puking in the cornucopia was a

disaster?" She shut off the water just in time to hear David's whispered and obviously not-meant-to-be-heard reply.

"And there it is."

She stepped into the living room. "And there what is?"

"Nothing," David replied immediately. But instead of letting him off the hook, she watched him, her hands dripping. Eventually, he said, "I'm sure Lyndi didn't mean to ruin dinner, Nat."

"She didn't ruin it," Nathalie replied immediately. "I can't blame her for morning sickness. I mean, that's just another thing we have in common."

"But . . ."

"But . . . what is she doing?" Nathalie said finally. "She's twenty-four and can't decide on a career but she's gonna have a baby? She can't even remember to walk her dog!"

David's brow came down. "When did Lyndi get a dog?"

"It's a metaphorical dog, David!"

"Okay, okay!" David held up his hands in surrender. "I'm just saying, she didn't do this on purpose. Step on your moment."

"*Our* moment." Nathalie huffed. "And I know she didn't do it on purpose. That's the problem! Obviously this entire thing was an accident for her, but she's just going to trip into it and go 'oh well, guess I'll have a baby now!' Because that's how she is!"

She wiped the wet from her hands on the dish towel tucked into her back pocket. Lyndi, no doubt, would just have wiped her hands on her pants leg, if she even bothered to do the dishes at all.

"'I didn't like accounting, so I guess I'll take an extra year and be an art major now!'" Nathalie mimicked in a high, little-girl voice. "'I graduated so I guess I'll be a graphic designer now!' 'Didn't really dig that, so I guess I'll be a barista!' 'No, now I'll be a florist!'"

"Honey, she's twenty-four. Not everyone is like you and knows exactly what their life is going to be," David said calmly.

It was true. Nathalie had known since she was six she wanted to be a teacher. She had known since she was ten she wanted to teach literature. And she had known since she was nineteen that she was going to marry David Chen, who she met half-drunk at a college party, and they argued all night and into a 3 AM Del Taco run about the merits of Dickens's early work.

Later, he'd confessed he hadn't ever read any of *The Pickwick Papers*. He just wanted to keep Nathalie talking to him, so he took the opposite opinion of whatever she said.

No wonder he was a lawyer.

"Screwing up and figuring it out," David continued, "that's what someone's twenties are for."

"Yeah, but . . . she had only just begun screwing up. Now she won't get to anymore!" Nathalie said. "This *is* her big screwup! And once she has the baby, she can't just decide to drop it and do something else."

"You think she's making a mistake," he said. It wasn't a question.

"Yes. No." She sighed deep, suddenly tired. "But you and I . . . we know what it's going to take. We've *planned* for this. We've been trying forever!"

His brow knit. "We tried for two months before we got pregnant."

She stared at him, her eyebrows disappearing beneath her bangs. Her nose began to sting. "We've been trying for three years, David."

"I meant . . . this time," David said eventually.

But it was too late. Nathalie just held up one hand, shook her head, and headed for the bedroom before she could break down in tears in front of him.

Stupid hormones.

She'd been on the knife's edge of crying all day. All the stress of cooking, all the emotions of the announcement—then the fumble of said announcement. Add that to the funhouse ride of hormones her body was putting her through to grow a human . . . well, there was a reason she had avoided watching TV. One sappy refrigerator commercial and she would be lost.

But through it all, she thought she could count on David to be her support! To be outraged and pissed off *with* her. To be aghast at Lyndi's lack of pie making and Kathy's messing with the oven temp, and Marcus's . . . sperm's ability to bypass what she hoped was decent birth control. But instead, David sat there, his eyes forward on the TV, playing devil's advocate.

Which, considering his lawyerly ways, wasn't new for him

But if his plan was to talk her around to a more open mind, he failed utterly.

I meant . . . this time.

As if the last three years had been a fluke, easily forgotten.

Nathalie remembered precisely when they began trying. It was on her thirtieth birthday. She had just made tenure at her school the year before, David was on track to be named a junior partner at Stanis and Lowe, his old law firm. And he was only months away from paying off his student loans. So, on her thirtieth birthday, after she and David and her friends had stumbled out of the bar after last call, Nathalie went straight to her bathroom, where she flushed her birth control pills down the toilet.

She was ready.

They were ready.

All they had to do was make a baby.

Which turned out to be harder than anticipated.

After five months of trying—of tracking her periods by plugging them into an app on her phone, which dinged whenever their algorithm said she was having a fertile day—Nathalie called her doctor for an appointment. Just to "check," she'd said.

Dr. Duque—a woman a few years older than her with a mop top of wavy brown hair and an authoritative motherly vibe—gave her a cursory exam, looked at her tracking app, and said, "Hmm."

"Hmm?"

"Listen—you're very likely fine," Dr. Duque said kindly. "You're young, you're healthy. Most people conceive within the first six months of trying."

"It's been five," Nathalie replied.

"Your cycle is short," Dr. Duque said. "The average menstrual cycle is twenty-one to thirty-five days. Yours are ranging from eighteen to twenty-three." The doctor took out a pen and a little slip of paper that said "Menstrual Record Chart" and copied out the info from the app. "Your app is pretty low-tech, it's predicting your fertility based on the average cycle, not on yours. So, instead of having sex when it tells you to, I want you to have sex every other day, between days five and fifteen of your cycle."

Nathalie took the card, finding a sense of security in this scrap of paper that she hadn't in all the technology the modern world could offer. Of course the app failed her—it wasn't for *her*, it was for everyone! Now . . . now she had more than a ding on the phone telling her when to have sex.

Now she had a plan.

"If you haven't conceived after eight months of trying, you should come back in and we'll do some tests," Dr. Duque said. "But seriously, don't worry. Enjoy this time."

Nathalie hugged Dr. Duque—yes, hugged. She wasn't a super huggy person, but the relief she felt warranted it.

However, the relief was short-lived.

Nathalie and David had always enjoyed a healthy sex life, and at first David had found the novelty of having sex at the ding of a phone app kind of funny. But five months of that had taken its toll. So to be told he had to perform his husbandly duties on a more aggressive schedule was . . . not romantic, to say the least. Although, Nathalie tried! When the circled dates came up, she dolled herself up, cooked his favorite food, cued up certain scenes in *Blue is the Warmest Color* . . . but doing this every other day, on command, was a bit more challenging.

David, to his credit, was game. He just said, "We're going to do what we have to do." And so they did. For the next three months.

And then Nathalie made another doctor's appointment. This time for both of them.

"It's been eight months," she told Dr. Duque, gripping David's hand, "and still nothing's happening, I just want to know . . ."

"Okay," Dr. Duque said, nodding. "Let's do some tests."

The tests came back.

She was fertile.

David was fertile.

But for some reason his sperm kept missing her egg.

This only frustrated Nathalie more. Because there was no solution. If either she or David had fertility issues, modern medicine would be able to help. But as it was, she couldn't hand David's sperm a map of her uterus and a GPS. Instead, they just had to—

"Be patient," Dr. Duque said, soothingly. "Again, you're healthy, you're young. If we reach a year without conception, then we'll talk about more aggressive measures. But for now, keep trying. And don't forget to—"

"To enjoy this time," Nathalie repeated dully. "We know. And thank you."

And so, they went back to trying. To tracking cycles and circled days. And then . . . eleven months into this exhausting journey . . .

"Is that . . . a blue line?"

Nathalie stared at the little stick she had just peed on two minutes before.

She was a couple days later than normal. Then again, her normal was so short, she couldn't really tell if this was just a longer cycle, or something more. She might be feeling different, then again, it might just have been the Mexican food they had for dinner last night. But she had an economy pack of pregnancy tests in her closet . . . might as well use one.

Now, there was a very, very faint blue line, staring back at her.

David came and peered over her shoulder. His brow came down. "I don't know if I believe it. Is it supposed to be that light?"

"I don't know." She read and reread the box. "It says *any* line, no matter how faint . . ."

"So . . . we're pregnant." A smile broke across David's face. With his hair still sticking up from sleep and blinking behind his glasses, he looked like the most adorable befuddled man in the world. He held up his hand. "High five!"

She slapped his hand, and then gave him a kiss. And went to call her doctor.

"Congratulations!" Dr. Duque's nurse said on the phone. "We'll want you in around six weeks for an ultrasound to confirm—let's look at dates."

But she and David had a vacation planned that week—wanting to get away from the stress of baby making, and a lot of craziness going on at David's work, they'd planned a drive up the coast for Nathalie's school's spring break.

"No problem—the next week will be fine," the nurse said. "The baby's not going anywhere."

Nathalie warmed at that. *The baby.* She had so many questions. Due date? Boy or girl? Left-handed or right? Any chromosomal abnormalities? Could she go to the gym? A million little thoughts running through her head nonstop. Meanwhile, the blue line was really, *really* faint. And she didn't really feel any different—Mexican food aside.

Was this even real?

Then, she did start to feel different.

But, not *good* different.

It began with cramps. Not terrible ones, but ones that would make her think her period was coming, if she hadn't known it wasn't.

Her back hurt in a weird way . . . which answered the question of whether or not she would go to the gym.

And then she started spotting.

"Is it heavy, like a period, or lighter?" Dr. Duque asked, when Nathalie reached her on the phone.

"It's lighter."

"Okay, spotting in early pregnancy is normal. It's your body adjusting. But if you would like to come in now, we can just check and see how things are going."

". . . No," Nathalie said. They were leaving the next day for their trip up the coast. She hadn't even begun to pack. "I have an appointment in ten days, I'm sure it will be fine."

It wasn't fine.

They got all the way up to Carmel, near Monterey, checking in to their Airbnb overlooking waves crashing against the coastline. But before they could even breathe a sigh of relief, Nathalie doubled over from the cramps, curling up into a ball on the couch and staying there for the next two days.

And the bleeding got worse.

Then, she called a doctor.

Not her doctor. She called a random ob-gyn in Carmel. Sat in his waiting room for an hour before she could be squeezed in. David sat next to her, looking stricken. When they called her name, she told him to stay where he was. Patted his hand. Told him everything was going to be okay.

It wasn't.

He was an older man, and tended to keep his eyes on the papers in front of him, rather than look at her.

He gave her a pregnancy test. Her HGC levels were there, but they were low.

"What does that mean?"

The new doctor hummed under his breath. "Could mean a lot of things. Could mean you're not as far along as you think you are."

"I am," she said, and reeled the dates of her last cycle off to the blinking doctor. Then he hummed again.

"Well, then, combined with the bleeding," he said, matter-of-factly, "I think it's likely you're miscarrying."

That one word made the floor open up beneath her, and suck her in at a dizzying pace.

"You're sure?" she asked weakly. "You don't want to do an

ultrasound or listen for the heartbeat?" She eyed the ultrasound machine in the corner, covered and unplugged.

"No point," the doctor said. "Heartbeat wouldn't be detectable at this stage."

He looked at her then, and his eyes were not unkind. But this was news he must have had to give a thousand times in his career. He'd long since come to the conclusion there was no point in being sentimental about it. "The embryo will pass in the next couple days—you probably won't be able to tell. It'll just be like your period, maybe slightly heavier."

But it didn't pass. In fact, the pain only got worse. And while Nathalie writhed on the couch, David grew more and more anxious.

"When did he say the pain would pass?" David asked. "And why wouldn't he do an ultrasound?"

But Nathalie didn't have the answers. And she was kicking herself for not getting them.

Finally David had had it. *He* called Dr. Duque back in Los Angeles.

And Dr. Duque gave him a plan. Told him to bring Nathalie in, ASAP.

He threw all of their stuff into the car and drove the six hours home in less than five, delivering her to Dr. Duque's office doorstep.

Dr. Duque gave Nathalie another pregnancy test—her HGC levels were exactly the same. Meaning, she hadn't miscarried. But nor had the baby progressed.

"Let's see what's going on in there," Dr. Duque said, but her normally secure smile shifted. Her jaw became set and her eyes focused. She prepped the ultrasound—transvaginal, because the baby would be too small to see otherwise. And then, on the screen . . .

Nothing.

Her uterus was empty.

Then the doctor shifted the wand, and looked elsewhere.

"There," she said, pointing to a blob in the middle of another blob. "The embryo is in your fallopian tube. No wonder you're in so much pain. It's an ectopic pregnancy."

Ectopic pregnancy. She had spent the last several days mentally making peace with a miscarriage. Somehow, an ectopic pregnancy was so much worse.

Because the baby was there, and growing . . . it was just in the wrong place.

And there was no way to get it to the right one.

"I want you to get your first dose of medication while being observed to see if we are going to need to do surgery or if the medication is going to work. I am going to send you to the emergency room to get that all started and you may need to be admitted overnight."

Dr. Duque's eyes were kind, and sad. She knew there was nothing rote about this.

"When?" Nathalie croaked.

"Now," Dr. Duque replied. "The longer we wait, the higher the chance that your fallopian tube could rupture."

So, they went to the hospital.

There, the nurse on call wheeled her into a curtained-off area—it was the ER after all, no private rooms here—giving her a thorough questioning about her medical history while they moved. Then, the doctor came in, gave her another confirming ultrasound and she was injected with methotrexate.

Chemotherapy medication.

They let her lie there for a little while as they kept an eye on the monitors, the drugs coursing through her system.

The same poison that couldn't save her mother was now going to take her baby.

It's not a baby.

It's not a baby.

It's not a baby.

She had to keep telling herself that. It wasn't a baby. It was a ticking time bomb that could take out her fallopian tube at any minute and require major surgery to save her life. It would never be a baby.

They would never meet.

David sat next to her, listening to all the hum and bustle of an emergency room beyond the curtain, his gaze resting somewhere around her knees. They stayed that way, until the nurse came back with details for follow-up visits.

Then, they went home.

And that was that.

Oh, of course she had to deal with the next thirty-six hours of nausea and awfulness as a side effect of the chemo meds. And, they had to wait at least three months until the methotrexate cleared her system and her body had recovered before they were given the green light to start trying again. Still, even then she didn't feel normal enough to try just yet.

And . . . just as they decided to start trying again, she looked at the calendar and realized her not-a-baby's due date would have been the next week. And the sadness she had not allowed herself to feel began to creep in the edges.

And then David lost his job at Stanis and Lowe.

Laid off or quit, the result was the same. They were downsizing, and David took their piddly severance package. But the stress of the job hunt made them decide to forestall their baby-making plans.

David sat at home for three months, sending out résumés and going on interviews and watching *Top Chef* reruns before he landed a new gig, as in-house counsel at a major movie studio. A huge step up in terms of responsibility, salary, and benefits (and free theme park tickets). So much so that his signing bonus would cover his half of the down payment on a house.

Thus, they began house hunting. Another layer of stress to add to their lives, and so the baby plan was postponed once more.

It was only once they were in escrow and packing boxes that Nathalie felt she could toss her pill pack again.

And this time, it was as if her body was ready for it. She didn't even have to tell David which days were circled on the calendar. They were leaving the hardship of the past behind them and enjoying a well-earned upswing in life. Everything fell into place, and suddenly, that blue line that had been so faint the first time practically leaped out from the pee stick and did a tap routine to loudly announce their fecund state.

But Nathalie wasn't taking any chances. At six weeks on the dot she was in Dr. Duque's office for an ultrasound. She signed up for every optional genetic testing available, minus amniocentesis because holy crap was that a big needle. She refused to tell anyone—or let David tell anyone—about the pregnancy until she was thirteen weeks along, and the dangers of the first trimester were over.

And after today, she was left feeling like the only one who cared.

A creak at the door and a shaft of light falling over the bed told her that David was hesitating on the threshold.

"I'm sorry," he said.

"It's okay." She sniffled up the last of her drying tears. "Today was just horrible."

He came up behind her, and lay on the bed next to her. Wrapped an arm around her waist, curling up against her, warming her with his body heat.

"It was pretty screwed up, wasn't it?" he said, and she dissolved into giggles.

"I'm shocked the turkey wasn't raw. And that Kathy didn't scream the house down."

Then his body started shaking against hers with laughter.

After a few seconds of catharsis, Nathalie sighed. "Well, at least we still have your parents. I know it's predawn over there, but your mom is an early riser—can we call them? Give them the news?"

David's parents were an interesting set, and even after knowing them for fourteen years, Nathalie still couldn't figure them out. His father was a first generation Chinese-American, and his mother Italian, and both were academics. His father taught chemistry and his mother history. While David's paternal grandparents were thrilled by his admission to law school, his parents were livid when they found out that David was pursuing a career in something "practical" rather than his passion, no matter how often he told them he enjoyed the law and didn't have a passion beyond Nathalie. Nathalie hoped that her ambitions to teach would mollify them, but when they learned she intended to teach high school—*public* high school—their interest in her career became remote.

Normally, both Dr. Chen and Dr. Russo-Chen could be found in their cramped offices at UC Davis, but this year they had decided to take a joint sabbatical, and go to Italy. It would be about 5 AM there, Nathalie reasoned. Surely, they wouldn't mind being woken up by such good news.

But David's chuckling body stilled. "Oh . . . um."

"Too early?" she asked.

"No . . . too late," he replied sheepishly.

". . . You told them already?"

"You said Thanksgiving we could tell family. And my folks called yesterday to ask about their plants and they said they were about to take a two-week walking tour through Tuscany . . . so I told them. I figured one day wouldn't make a difference."

Nathalie felt her heart sink through the mattress. But all she said was "Oh." Then, "What did they say?"

"Dad was cool about it."

Cool. That is how one would describe the male Dr. Chen's reaction to almost anything. Tomatoes. Sharks. Grandchildren. If it wasn't a controversial stance on molecular chemistry, he didn't really show any reaction.

Back when he'd first met her jovial, accountant/history buff father and the exuberant Midwestern hospitality of Kathy, it had been an awkward afternoon of trying to find things to talk about.

They eventually settled on the Manhattan Project.

"And Mom was . . . happy. You know, for her."

Yes, for her. Dr. Russo-Chen was not the kind of Italian mother that pulled people to her bosom and spoon-fed them pasta until they were numb with love. She was the "my family is in Venice's Golden Book, little schoolteacher, so I'm writing a thousand-page history of their exploits and can't be bothered with things like food or plants" kind of person.

Although Nathalie doubted that was actually a type. Dr. Russo-Chen was highly original, as she was swift to tell you.

It just went to show how desperate she was for someone to be excited that she actually hoped David's parents would fit the bill.

"Good," Nathalie managed to say. But as his arm lifted off

of her, she knew her body couldn't hide her disappointment from him.

"I'll finish cleaning up the kitchen," David said, as he rose off the bed. "You get some rest."

As he left, she lay there in the dark, wide awake. Finally, she had exactly what she wanted, exactly what she planned for.

And she had nothing but disappointment to show for it.

CHAPTER 3

"WELL, I WAS WONDERING WHAT CRAWLED up Nat's butt to make her crazy about Thanksgiving this year. Now I know."

Lyndi threw herself on the faded striped couch that dominated their little living room. It had been Marcus's mom's, purchased sometime in the '70s. She'd been happy to gift it to Marcus when he moved halfway across the country, ready to upgrade to something from this century.

Their loss, because it was the comfiest couch Lyndi had ever lain upon. Especially after a whole day of being in Nat's perfect IKEA-catalogue-with-aspirations-of-Pottery-Barn home.

With Nat staring daggers at her the whole dinner.

"I thought it was pretty funny," Marcus said, sitting down next to her, pulling her feet onto his lap and beginning what Lyndi could only hope was an hour-long foot rub.

"I thought she was going to kill me for ruining her cornucopia—ooooohhh, right there." His thumb pressed into her arch in a way that seduced her now just the way it had seduced her six months ago, when she first moved in.

She'd gone to art school, but due to her father's worries

about her future job prospects, Lyndi had minored in business, and so knew her way around a spreadsheet. A sprawling metropolis with creativity at its core seemed like the right place to be.

She'd thought about moving to the East Coast—New York, or DC, or the exotic wilds of Buffalo—but when you're a California girl . . . there's no place like Pacific sun.

Maybe she just wasn't that brave. She didn't know anyone on the other side of the country. And stepping out into the world was hard enough—doing it in an entirely unfamiliar environment was downright crazy to her.

But, she always figured, if life took her there, she'd go.

"I don't think it was the cornucopia she was pissed about, babe," Marcus said. And Lyndi, for all the foot rubbing, couldn't ignore the tension that immediately bunched up inside her.

"She'll get over it," she replied nonchalantly. And Nat totally would, she decided. It was just today that had been sucky. Lyndi would apologize for the vomiting and the screwing up Nat's speech, and everything would be fine.

In fact, one of the reasons she felt safe moving to LA was the fact that Nat was there. She knew that she could always turn to her sister if she needed something.

Just like she always had.

Nathalie was nine years older than Lyndi—and technically her half sister, Lyndi being a product of their dad's second marriage. But from the very beginning Nat had always been Lyndi's guide through girldom, her protector from all things stupid (like ice-blue eyeliner, and boys who insist that you can't like X-Men comics), and her teacher about adult things—like how to do laundry, and how to tell Dad she blew all of her textbook money on art supplies.

Having Nat in LA (and David, too, who'd been with Nat since Lyndi was ten) made LA just a little bit safer.

So she moved. She bounced around on different friends' couches and sublets, and bounced around trying different kinds of work. But nothing ever seemed to fit.

Her degree was in design . . . but she kind of hated graphic design. Spending all day on a computer made her feel like she didn't have anything to show for her efforts beyond a jpeg file.

She decided what she wanted was something real. When what she created had form, shape, and weight. Something that she could stand back and look at, and something that would evoke a reaction.

That's why she liked working at the floral start-up. She worked with real things—stems cut just that morning, bending and molding them into an explosion of color that made people inevitably smile.

That's why she liked Marcus, too.

He felt *real* to her, in a way none of the other guys in college ever had. With his skinny build and '70s furniture, his warm eyes and excellent foot rubs, he had so much more substance than all the boys who wore only flannel shirts with mother-of-pearl buttons, and man buns, and their never-finished screenplays that they spent all day in a coffee shop theoretically working on.

Marcus was actually doing what he wanted to do. He was a writer. Not for TV or anything as striving as that. He wrote for a digital media company, one that made its money with funny listicles and gifs, but still had really awesome reporting on important subjects that affected their generation. Marcus was on the listicle beat, but just recently they published a really insightful long-form article he wrote about growing up biracial, bisexual, and in Missouri.

The article had gotten more hits than anything he'd ever written before. They commissioned more long-form articles from him, two a month, on top of his listicle duties.

The day the article came out, they'd celebrated. Three weeks later, Lyndi had taken a pregnancy test.

She remembered exactly how he had looked when she told him. She was pale and shaking, and generally freaking out. But he . . . he just smiled. Wide and warm, and wrapped his arms around her.

"I never thought I'd have the chance to have a kid," he'd said. He'd kissed her temple. "Thank you."

And suddenly it felt like everything was going to be okay.

"I think it'll be a good thing, you know?" Marcus was saying.

"Hmm?" Lyndi replied.

"You were just saying the other day that you don't have any friends who've been pregnant. Now, you have someone that you can talk to about it, and ask questions."

True, she mused. She would be able to ask Nathalie all the questions she had, because Nathalie would have gone through it too—just a month or so ahead of her.

"Maybe she can even recommend a doctor. We need to make an appointment, you know."

"I know . . ." Lyndi replied on a sigh. "I still need to get my insurance sorted out through work." She'd only been promoted a couple weeks ago, to head floral designer and full-time employee. There was still a lot of paperwork she hadn't filled out. She was going to ask David to help her with that. There were pluses to a lawyer for a brother-in-law. "I need to do that, too."

"Well, you should do it soon, okay? I want to make sure you're covered. And the baby." Marcus hesitated. "If neither of those pan out . . . we could put you under my insurance. But I think we'd have to, you know . . . get married."

Lyndi froze. There was no possible way to respond to that. As much as she liked Marcus, and loved their life, marriage was just so . . . permanent. Marriage was for people like Nat and David—pairs who only knew how to function with each other.

But babies were pretty permanent, too.

"I'm sure that I'm covered. I'm probably double covered."

"Okay, good." The relief in his voice matched her own. "Oh, I almost forgot! I got you something."

Her feet were abandoned as Marcus leaped up, and moved to their little kitchenette. He got something out of the cabinet, came back, and handed her a canister-looking package with a bow on it.

"Happy Thanksgiving," he said.

She smiled at him as she carefully unwrapped the colorful magazine pages he'd wrapped it in. Of course he got her a present. That's the kind of guy Marcus was. Always thinking of her, and what might make her smile, and . . .

"Prenatal vitamins?" she asked. The bottle marked them as organic, healthy, and of course, gluten-free.

"Yeah." He grinned wide. "You're supposed to be taking them every day now. I actually read you're supposed to be taking them even before you get pregnant, but better late than never to get your folic acid up."

"Oh. Right," Lyndi replied, her brow coming down. "I didn't even think about it."

Marcus's smile dimmed a little.

"Lynds, babe . . . you got to start thinking about this stuff, okay?"

She looked down at the vitamins, and back up at him.

"You're right," she said. "I'll start thinking about it."

THREE DAYS LATER, she was still thinking about it. The Monday after Thanksgiving was quiet as Lyndi rode to work—then again, it was always quiet at 5 AM. Biking south on Echo Park Avenue, the street lamps guiding her path, Lyndi found this to be the best time in the world. She didn't have to fight traffic. No one would bother her. She could let her mind wander.

She really hadn't been thinking much about the logistics of *being* pregnant. Only that she was. Her body was keen on reminding her that things were changing though, even more so than Marcus was. Not only was morning sickness an all-day occurrence, her boobs felt like angry, tenderized meat that should never be touched by anyone or anything ever. And there was the smell thing. Everything smelled like metal. Chocolate, coffee, the garbage on the street corner as she cruised past—if it had a smell, that smell was now "pennies."

This made life at the floral co-op a little challenging lately.

She could have called Nat, asked her about doctors, about all the amorphous unknown stuff she was staring down, but Lyndi figured Nat needed a little more time between the dropped bomb and being asked for favors. She thought about calling her mom—but that just seemed exhausting, on top of an exhausting Thanksgiving.

So she turned to where everything began and ended: Google.

That led her to various baby and pregnancy oriented websites. They were all varying shades of pastel.

Fucking pastels.

But once she got past the offending color scheme, she plugged in when her last period was (or at least approximately, she'd never really kept track) and they told her the due date.

Then they told her what was going to happen to her body.

In horrifying detail.

Oh, they tried to make it less horrifying, by reminding the reader that there was a "snuggly little bundle" at the other end of "this journey," but still . . .

. . . Was the human body really meant to function this way? This many . . . fluids? And formations?

Overwhelmed, she shut down her computer. But then, her phone dinged.

Idiotically, when she'd typed in her due date, she'd also typed in her email address. And now she was signed up for daily reminders and helpful hints, flooding her inbox with more pastel.

But this one came with headlines, like *9 Amazing Facts about Your Vagina!* and *Cord Blood Banking—Should You? (You Should.)*, and endless offers on deals if and when she made her baby registry.

Lyndi shut down her phone for the rest of the weekend after that, too.

Thank God she had work today.

She biked down past City Hall, the Disney Concert Hall . . . all the prominent buildings that were the linchpin of their wacky, diverse city. And made her way to 7th Street, where the LA flower district thrived.

She needed to get there before the shipments arrived at dawn. Their morning deliveries would go out by eight, and they usually had nearly 250 bouquets to make in that time. Usually. They were now in the post-Thanksgiving rush, and everyone—*everyone*—wanted Christmas decorations. They'd had a mad Black Friday rush from their retail and department store clients. Lyndi counted herself lucky she'd had Friday off.

Although after a weekend of pastels and prenatal vitamins, maybe not.

As she coasted her bike into the booth of the Favorite Flower, Lyndi smiled as she saw Paula already in the middle of everything, sorting greens, reading the arrangement chart for the day with the rest of the team, and frowning at a pile of white flowers.

And suddenly, Lyndi was happy to let everything go with the flow again. The baby, the pregnancy, it was all going to be okay, right? At that moment, she had flowers to arrange.

"Hey, girl!" Paula called out as Lyndi dismounted. "We can't put zinnias in this arrangement."

"What?" Lyndi said. "No zinnias today?"

"Not any that looked good enough for our purposes. I grabbed these gerbera daisies from the wholesaler instead, but . . ."

Lyndi examined the wide, flat blossoms. She'd wanted the zinnias for their fatness, for their weight. Gerbera daisies always required a stem support to hold them up, as their heavy heads dropped quickly as they wilted. At least Paula had chosen the right colors—whites and blood reds, a nod to the holidays without leaning on holly and poinsettias.

"They were five cents a stem cheaper, too," Paula said, trying to find the silver lining. And that was the difference between Lyndi and Paula. Lyndi only looked at the composition of the flowers, the bouquet as a whole and what pieces she needed. Paula had a lot of other variables to consider.

So, even though Lyndi thought the arrangements would look cheaper for the five-cent savings, she couldn't say that to Paula. After all—Paula was the boss, the founder and CEO of the Favorite Flower.

A really impressive feat for someone who was only twenty-eight.

The Favorite Flower was only founded a year ago, with a website and an idea. They would only make one arrangement a day, in a couple different sizes, out of the best the flower market had to offer that day. That would cut down on flower waste (because if you offer variety, and people don't buy them, all those other flowers will end up as compost and red on your balance book) and they would be an online-only business. You could place an order for one day, or you could make a standing order for a weekly flower delivery. They had individual clients, but also corporate clients, providing arrangements for entire buildings.

And she started the entire thing out of her van.

"I can make it work," Lyndi said. "What if we . . . used the stem as the tie for the bouquet?"

"Love it!" Paula said. "No wonder you're the artistic genius. Okay, everyone!"

The arrangers—four women of varying ages, but all older than Lyndi—brought their heads up from their flower sorting.

"Lyndi's making a quick change to the design."

Some of the women groaned, which made Lyndi's cheeks pink. She wasn't used to being in charge of things yet. Part of her wished she could just arrange flowers with everyone else like she had been up until a couple weeks ago. But even then, she would always make slight adjustments to the arrangements. Making them just a bit bolder, and brighter and interesting.

Paula had seen something in her, and gave her new responsibilities.

"I promise, it's a little one this time." And Lyndi detailed how to use the gerbera daisies, and adjust for the lack of zinnias.

Soon enough, everyone was up to date, and they went to work.

That morning, due to an influx of online orders over the weekend, they had 312 bouquets to make. The flowers were laid out on large tables, in assembly line fashion. Two people per table went down the lines and assembled the flowers into their arrangement for the day. Lyndi took her spot at the table and got to work.

There was something incredibly soothing about repetitive tasks. She could blank out everything else—the way the other women at work looked at her, worries about her sister being mad, prenatal vitamins—and just do the work. And at the end of the row, the flowers were tied together into existence as a beautiful bouquet. The satisfaction of accomplishment was real, and there for everyone to see.

The six of them working together made quick work of the 312 arrangements. At 8 AM on the dot, the couriers arrived.

Some of the couriers drove vans—but the kids on the bikes were her favorites. They were loaded down with a front basket, two saddlebags, and a backpack all bursting with flowers. They maneuvered through the streets of LA to do the geographically closest deliveries with the grace and fearlessness of extreme sport athletes.

"Hold on, where's Stan?" Lyndi said, as they loaded up one of the bike kids.

"Dunno," said the flower-laden kid, shrugging as best he could.

"I'll check my messages." Paula sighed. Sure enough there was a message from Stan, saying he was sick, with obligatory apologies and conspicuous coughs.

"What's that, the second time this month?"

"Third," Paula replied grimly. "With all these extra orders, we need all hands on deck today."

"I can take Stan's run," Lyndi said immediately. "I've done it before." Twice that month, at least.

"Are you sure? I wanted to walk the market floor with you, get a head start on tomorrow's arrangement. Also, you still have a bunch of paperwork to fill out."

"Health insurance and stuff, right," Lyndi said. "But we're short-staffed, so when needs must . . ."

Paula thought it over. "Okay, we'll walk the market when you get back."

"Awesome!" Lyndi said as she grabbed her bike, and Paula and the other women loaded her down. "I wanted to talk to you about wreaths! Maybe we open up a wreath category on the website? Just for the holidays? Use up some of the leftover branches that don't make our general arrangement."

"That's a fantastic idea!" Paula said, her face lighting up. "We could do magnolia branches, or holly, or—"

While Paula mused on the possibilities of wreaths, Lyndi lifted the bike off her kickstand and headed out.

Once out the door, Lyndi could smile and relax. Secretly, she really liked doing Stan's route. Not just because she got to get out of the flower market during her most morning-sickness-prone hours, but because she felt whimsical, a girl on a bike exploding with flowers.

Plus Stan had the best route of all the couriers.

Because it included a weekly delivery to one of the major movie studios.

Biking onto the lot of a movie studio was always a trip. The second she passed through the visitors and deliveries gate, she could feel herself smiling. It was like stepping into another world. A completely fake, immaculately curated world. The shrubbery was trimmed to perfection. Stray litter was not tolerated. Little bungalows, lining perfect streets like the most idealized neighborhoods in idealized USA Town, encircling the larger, warehouse-like buildings (the sound stages) all in varying shades of beige.

It was toward one of these sound stages she headed, but instead of going into the big, open bay doors, she headed around to the side, where a small, normal-sized door led to the production offices.

The production offices of a TV show looked like anyone else's office. There were desks, and papers, and a photocopier in the middle that didn't seem to be working right, given the young guy who was two arms deep in the machine.

But other than photocopier guy, the place was empty.

"Hi, I'm from the Favorite Flower," Lyndi said. "I have a delivery for Sophia Nunez?"

"Oh, um . . ." said the guy. "She's in the makeup trailer."

"I usually just leave them here, if you can sign for them?" Lyndi replied.

But the guy didn't move. "Well, the thing is . . . I'm stuck? And everyone is in a production meeting . . . and my other co-worker went to get help. It's my first week and apparently I didn't know the copy machine was a carnivore." He laughed weakly.

"Oh," Lyndi said. "I . . . I'll just take these to the makeup trailer then?"

"Um, sure," said the guy. "It's around the back. And if you see any of my co-workers with hand tools, can you tell them this really hurts?"

"Sure," said Lyndi, swallowing a laugh. "No problem."

So she went around to the side and back. And saw an entire parking lot filled with trailers.

Which one was the makeup trailer?

How could she tell?

She wandered around for five minutes, looking for someone to ask. Eventually, she knocked on a door labeled Waitress #1 and found an actress that she'd seen in a ketchup commercial changing into a waitress uniform. After being disappointed that the flowers in Lyndi's hands weren't for her, the ketchup actress kindly pointed her to the makeup trailer.

The door was opened by a round-faced young man in a checkered shirt with a shiny collar. His hair stood up straight from his head, revealing a comb tucked behind his ear. His eyes lit up at the sight of the flowers.

"Hi, I'm from the Favorite Flower, I have a delivery for—"

"Sophia, darling!" he called over his shoulder. "Your weekly proof of devotion has arrived!"

The young man ushered Lyndi into the trailer, which was expansive, a stylist's studio on wheels. And there, sitting in one of the well-lit chairs, having a small trail of blood painted coming out of the corner of her mouth, was Vanessa Faire.

Just about the biggest new star in Hollywood.

Lyndi nearly dropped the flowers.

"Soph, better get your flowers before they fall on the floor," Vanessa Faire said in that catlike purr she was so well known for.

"I told you no talking," the makeup artist painting the

blood singsonged. "There," she said finally, lifting her brush off of Vanessa's perfect (and now perfectly wounded) face. The makeup artist turned to Lyndi and smiled wide. Her eyes sparked with joy seeing the flowers.

"Thanks, sweetie," she said, pushing a thick strand of dark hair behind her ear. "You can put them over there. Let me get my purse."

"Oh. Oh! There's no tip. Or, er, it's already included in the bill," Lyndi said, tearing her eyes away from Vanessa and back to the person who actually received the flowers. "Enjoy your bouquet!"

"Thank you. They're gorgeous," Sophia said.

"Just like your Sebastian," the young man in the checkered shirt said, as Lyndi turned to step down from the makeup trailer.

"Just like your love," Vanessa said with emphasis. "Do they smell as nice as they look?"

Just before the door closed on Lyndi, she heard Sophia say, "Huh. That's funny. They smell kind of like pennies."

CHAPTER 4

"YOU ARE SO LUCKY," KIP, SOPHIA'S TRUSTY second in command and key hairstylist said, looking wistfully at the flowers. "When does Sebastian get back?"

"He's on tour until the ninth, then he promised that he'd take me to Baja for Christmas. Maisey's with her dad, so . . ." Sophia replied, letting the warm happiness spread across her cheeks. She wasn't used to her personal life being on display at work. But Sebastian was just so effusive, so open with his emotions that it brought their relationship into the light. Besides, they'd met through the show—through Vanessa. So the fact that he sent her flowers at work every week to brighten up her Mondays, when she sometimes had a pre-dawn call time, was just part of what made him *him*.

"Baja is *amazing* this time of year," Vanessa interjected. "I went there a few years ago, I have the best resort for you . . ." Then her eyes fell to the flowers.

And the smile dropped from her face.

"Shouldn't those go to the office? A PA should be dropping them off, not some rando," she said. "After all, we don't want the unwashed masses to know that Billie gets a bloody lip, do we?"

Billie was Vanessa's character on *Fargone*, the hottest show on TV, now in the middle of its third season—and unlike most shows that premiered big, dropped a bit, and settled into a steady viewership, *Fargone* just kept growing. Vanessa's character was a cult phenomenon. Billie was, supposedly, a superhero with impenetrable skin. Which would make a little blood coming out of her mouth quite the spoiler . . . if they hadn't had Billie lose her powers in season one. And then done flashbacks in season two to when she was mortal.

At this rate, it was more of a spoiler that Billie *wasn't* getting a bloody lip during sweeps.

But Vanessa was as protective of her character's secrets as she was of her on-screen image. She never wanted to appear imperfect. Some people might dismiss this as vanity. But after working with actors and stars for the past decade, Sophia knew it wasn't about vanity as much as it was about survival. These people lived off their faces. A bad photo could circulate for years, move them from being thought of as viable artists to has-beens, costing them work. So they had to be vigilant. Once you got past their fears about how they looked, most of them were really quite normal.

Vanessa was, all in all, pretty normal.

Except, that as the current cover girl of *Entertainment Weekly*, she had a little more power than most people . . . and sometimes felt the need to flex those muscles.

"Usually the PAs do. That was the first time they didn't go through the office," Sophia said soothingly, trying to talk Vanessa down.

"That is *not* professional," Vanessa said. "I'm going to talk to Roger about it. And Sebastian. Let him know that the flower place overstepped their bounds."

Roger was the executive producer. He didn't deal with flower deliveries. If he heard about this, Sophia would be the one getting called up to the office.

Kip shot Sophia a look. *Diva meltdown in three, two . . .*

"You're right, Vanessa, I'm absolutely appalled. Let me talk to Shana in the office," Sophia said calmly, referring to the highly efficient woman who ran the production office. "I'm sure this was a freak accident, and we'll make sure appropriate measures are taken."

Vanessa looked from the flowers, to Sophia, deciding. And Sophia could tell that Roger was about to get a phone call . . . until, a short, confident knock sounded on the trailer door.

"Come in!" Kip said with obvious relief.

A set PA, a walkie at her waist and a headset in her ear, popped her head in. "Miss Faire, they're ready for you on set."

With a metaphorical snap of her fingers, Vanessa shifted from petulant problem-solver to number one on the call sheet, the leader of the show. Her shoulders squared, she put her face forward.

"Ready! Let's go."

"Last looks!" Sophia stopped Vanessa, and inspected her makeup. Kip did a last-minute fluff on her long blond curls. Then they nodded, and Vanessa followed the set PA out the door.

And Kip and Sophia slumped in relief.

"That was close," Kip said. "She's in a mood today."

"Come on. She's holding it together pretty well for someone whose movie opened at second at the box office last weekend."

"If it was first, she'd be a nightmare."

"Give her a break, okay?" Sophia said. "It's got to be stressful."

Over the summer hiatus last year, Vanessa had done a supporting role in a little indie movie that got picked up at Sundance. Her role, while small, was critical, and she was even getting Oscar buzz.

"Well, somebody is going to get fired," Kip said, as he began sorting through his hairsprays, mousses, and teasing combs.

"As long as it's not you or me," Sophia said grimly. "I'll go down to the office, talk to Shana personally."

Chances were, there was some poor kid on his first job answering phones in the office who was about to have his or her Hollywood career cut short. But in this business, breaches of security were not tolerated—after all, how could you be trusted with intellectual property if you couldn't correctly handle a flower delivery?

Sophia took off her makeup belt—where she wore all the tools of her trade—and headed for the door. As she did, she passed the beautiful bouquet that was the cause of this little kerfuffle. And smiled.

It was really hard to be mad at flowers.

Especially considering the man who sent them.

Still . . . "We should hide these. Vanessa will be back in for new makeup after this scene."

She passed the flowers to Kip, who buried his nose in them.

"Okay, I don't know what you're on, but these do not smell like pennies."

"Says the man who is surrounded by hairspray all day."

"Seriously, maybe your allergies are kicking in."

"I don't have allergies, Kip."

"Either that or you're knocked up. My sister said everything smelled and tasted like fertilizer when she was pregnant."

Sophia shot Kip a look of mock horror. "Don't even joke about that."

Kip held up his hands. Sophia blew him a kiss as she walked out of the trailer door.

And then stopped herself at the bottom of the stairs. A memory washed over her, almost eighteen years old.

Her body shifting, feeling weird in the mornings, and her complaining to her then-boyfriend that her chocolate ice cream tasted metallic.

But no. It was impossible. She was about to get Maisey off to college. She and Sebastian were careful.

Usually.

She couldn't be pregnant.

Could she?

IT WAS ALMOST ten hours later before Sophia could return to the thought Kip had annoyingly seeded in her mind.

Once they wrapped for the day, all the frantic energy stopped, and would begin again tomorrow. And in that stillness she was left with the question that had been popping up in the background of her mind all day.

So, on the way home, she drove by a CVS, and sunglasses low over her eyes like a scared teenager, she bought a two-pack pregnancy test.

It was another twenty minutes before she got back to her apartment in North Hollywood, the CVS bag burning a hole in her peripheral vision the entire time. By the time she walked through the door, she thought she might be too nervous to pee.

The apartment was dark and quiet. Briefly she worried about where Maisey was, then she remembered that it was SAT week, and Maisey had taken an after-school job helping the juniors with SAT prep. As the person who got one of the highest scores last year, the juniors (and their parents) no doubt thought she cracked the code.

As far as Sophia could tell, the "code" her daughter cracked was constantly studying, and liking to learn.

Sometimes she marveled at how it was possible someone as bright and inquisitive as Maisey could come from her.

But at that moment, Sophia was glad she was alone in their cozy home. Because Maisey's bright inquisitiveness would have her figuring out something was wrong before Sophia even had a chance to find out if something *was* wrong.

She hightailed it to the sole bathroom in the apartment, put the CVS bag on the counter. The room was a cheery yellow—Sophia and Maisey had done the tiles themselves when they moved in, put the shelves up above the toilet. The little improvements made up for the fact that the fan didn't really work and the door never locked. But those things had never mattered. What mattered is that this place was Sophia and Maisey's home, the first place they'd lived that had been just theirs.

She took the box out of the bag. Let her eyes glaze over the instructions. There was no need for the printing to be this small, the instructions to be this detailed. There wasn't a woman in the world who didn't know how these things worked.

Turns out, having not peed in three hours superseded any nervousness she might have had. And soon enough, she set the little saturated stick on the counter . . . and began to wait.

The first time she had been pregnant, she hadn't peed on a stick. She'd had no idea it was happening. It had been her mother who had figured it out.

When Sophia was eighteen, she'd been . . . eighteen. Full of energy, of life, of that agitated need to go and do and be anything other than where she was. She'd had fun in school, but man was she glad when it was over. School for her had meant long stretches of boredom punctuated by high thrills of excitement. And most of that excitement had come courtesy of boys, and the drama that floated in their wake.

And the most dramatic of all the boys was Alan Alvarez.

They'd flirted most of their senior year. Hooked up a couple times. But once graduation and summer came, they never went a day without seeing each other. Usually, their days were spent in a heated ritual of absorbing each other, then fighting, then making up, then back to being wrapped up around each other again.

She'd had boyfriends before. She'd never not had a guy hanging around, making her mother despair for her. But Alan was the first one that Sophia felt understood her. Her desire to burst out of the world. To just try *everything*.

She had a job working at Sephora in the Sherman Oaks mall. She liked makeup, she always had. The one class she hadn't gotten Cs in was art. And she was enrolled to go to community college in the fall—much to Alan's mopey disappointment. He thought they'd grow apart, with her spending time with new college kids, not him.

She spent a lot of time persuading Alan his fears were unfounded.

And one of those persuasion times resulted in Maisey.

Sophia hadn't really had morning sickness. Just an aversion to some foods, including the metallic-tasting chocolate ice cream. And her body shifted and swelled, and one time, she slept through her alarm when she was supposed to open the store. And her mother, who did the shopping, noticed that she hadn't used the tampons she bought last month.

The doctor confirmed her mother's suspicions.

While her mother wept, and Sophia was numb, Alan was ecstatic. There would be no community college, no more fighting and making up—it was like this baby had made Sophia *his* now.

His vow to take care of her, and their baby, had made Sophia feel safe for the first time since she went to the doctor.

So, on her nineteenth birthday, four months pregnant, she and Alan Alvarez got married.

But the gravity of a baby didn't hit Alan the same way it hit her. He just thought it would grow and pop out and everything would be normal, but with a baby. But she was the one who felt every kick, every wiggle.

And she was the one who ended up in the hospital with complications, afraid for her life and that of her unborn daughter.

The marriage didn't last long after Maisey was born. Alan, for all his promises, had refused to grow up. It only took one night of him coming home drunk at 3 AM for her to pack up Maisey and go to her mother's house.

Sophia, on the other hand, had grown up fast. She spent the day with Maisey, and her mom—a fucking saint—took Maisey at night while Sophia worked part-time at Sephora and took community college classes. She built herself up. By the time Maisey was in kindergarten, Sophia was getting work doing makeup for individual clients, Beverly Hills types who threw dinner parties. That led to her being hired on as an extra makeup artist a couple of days a month for a production house. That led to her getting in the union.

And she never missed the drama. The desire to go and do and be anything other than where she was. Because she worked hard to make where she was great for her and for Maisey.

And Maisey was an *amazing* kid. Smarter than Sophia had ever hoped to be. Fascinated by everything around her, wanting to learn. It took Alan several years before he realized what he'd missed out on, and still several more before he was mature enough to have a relationship with his daughter.

He'd finally gotten his act together and remarried—this time to a very patient woman, and now had a couple of toddlers.

Sophia never missed Alan. Never missed the fights, the way his personality would overwhelm her. She might occasionally miss the physical affection, but she never missed the dramatics that came with it.

Men might screw up her life, but she'd be damned if she'd let a man screw up Maisey's.

So, while other women in their twenties were dating around, figuring themselves out, Sophia avoided men like the plague. Oh, there were a couple of fix-ups here and there that she felt obliged to not turn down, but they rarely warranted the price of the babysitter.

Until Sebastian.

She'd met Sebastian last year, at *Fargone*'s second season wrap party. Sebastian was the bassist in a band. Which would be trite, if the band wasn't actually successful. They were huge in Europe, and had just started making waves in the US with a chart-topping hit over the summer. Once they conquered the LA music scene, they were poised to take over the country.

Sebastian was a friend of Vanessa's. Vanessa had been

(and technically still was) married to the band's lead singer, Deegan. In the messy ways of Hollywood, when the band got bigger—and she got her big break on the show—their lives took separate courses. But she claimed they were all still close. In fact, the band had shown up at the bar the *Fargone* crew had taken over in West Hollywood for their revelries, and proceeded to play a set—just for fun. Then, Vanessa had steered Sebastian directly over to Sophia.

And it was like she was eighteen again.

All those feelings—the being overwhelmed by someone, pulled into the undertow of their world, the giddy delight—it came back full force.

And now, according to the piece of plastic she had peed on, the consequences of those full-force feelings were exactly the same as before.

But this time, as the new information spread through her body like soda bubbles under her skin, she didn't feel numb. She didn't even feel worried.

She felt . . . amazing.

Warm laughter caught in her throat, tears in her eyes. She found herself sitting on the floor, hugging her knees to her chest, and smiling.

She was going to have a baby.

Another beautiful baby.

But before she could absorb the joy she was feeling, Sophia heard a door slam.

"Mom!" she heard her daughter Maisey say, excitement ready in her voice. "I'm home! I've got NEWS!"

"Uh—in here!" Sophia called back. Maisey was waiting to hear back from Stanford—she'd applied for early admission and checked her email about sixty times a day. So if Maisey had news, it might be *the* news . . .

She scrambled to her feet, wiped the wet from her eyes. And her gaze rose from the pee stick sitting on the counter to her flushed reflection in the mirror.

Her inquisitive daughter would know in half a second what was going on.

"Give me a minute, okay?"

But the warning came too late. Halfway through the sentence, the door to the bathroom that never really locked swung open, with Maisey talking a mile a minute.

"So Haley from my lit class was saying that she already heard back from her early admission school, but she applied to NYU and I was thinking that the East Coast probably got things done earlier than the West Coast, because California schools have a lot more to process but then I looked up the admission totals for NYU and I was like holy crap, and now I'm wondering if I emailed my application to the right person—"

Abruptly she stopped. Sophia had moved in front of the pee stick, hiding it with her body, but Maisey wasn't looking at Sophia or the counter behind her. She was looking in the mirror behind that.

"Mom . . . why are you hiding a pregnancy test behind you?"

CHAPTER 5

"AND WHAT DOES FROST MEAN WHEN HE SAYS 'good fences make good neighbors'?"

Maisey's gaze blurred, the lines of Robert Frost's poem becoming nothing more than a swirl of ink on her desk.

It wasn't like she didn't understand the poem. She'd read Frost in tenth grade—wrote a paper on him. For extra credit.

And for fun.

But with the AP tests coming up in the spring, Maisey was more than happy to review old material (although, it was only old for her. Most of her class didn't read years ahead on the syllabus). And usually her hand would be up in the air, ready to set the record straight on Frost's sense of irony, but today . . . in fact for the past couple days . . . it just didn't seem to matter.

What the *hell* was her mom thinking?

Getting knocked up?

There was a bowl full of condoms on their health teacher's desk—she never grabbed any because her own sex life was nonexistent, but God, apparently she should have been taking some home for her mother!

"It means, boundaries make people respectful, right?" Haley, who was celebrating her obviously miraculous early admission to NYU, said.

"Hmm . . ." said their English teacher. "Is there maybe any other interpretation? Maisey?"

"What?" Maisey's eyes snapped front, and back into the present.

"What did Robert Frost mean when he said 'good fences make good neighbors'?"

Maisey knew the answer, of course. But as she had been distracted, she hesitated. And that's when the apparently unconscious form of Foz Craley jumped in.

He was the kid that you always thought was asleep in class, his arms folded over his desk, his head disappeared underneath a mop top of hair. But then, when a question came up, he would always shock the teacher and the class by having not only the right answer, but an in-depth analysis of the question itself.

It was annoying as hell. And this time was no different.

"The poem is about how people automatically put up walls, and it keeps us from engaging with each other," he said. "He put the line in the mouth of the antagonist, so the protagonist could argue against it."

"Precisely! Now, what are the arguments Frost makes against 'good fences'?"

Maisey let the classroom discussion fade into the background again. But first she sent Foz a dirty look—not that he could see it. He had gone back to sleep.

Maybe life would have been better with a couple more walls, Maisey thought. Because damn if she didn't regret the open-door bathroom policy she and her mother had always had.

Maisey had seen the pregnancy test, and despite being

seventeen years old, it took her a second to realize that it was not a thermometer, and instead the harbinger of impending doom.

And even then, she didn't quite believe it.

"But, it can't be," she'd said when her mom told her it was positive. "You're too old!"

Mom had let out a short laugh. "I'm thirty-six, Maisey. I'm not quite menopausal yet."

"Ew, Mom." She shut her eyes at the biological thoughts her mother was putting into her head. "Does Nana know?"

"Not yet." She looked from the pregnancy test to her shoes.

"Great, Nana's gonna be super pleased."

"Actually, Nana will be pleased." Her head came up, defiant. "She loves babies."

"No, she loves her book club and her Zumba class and her monthly trips to the Golden Nugget. She won't be pleased you're dropping a baby into the middle of all that. Again."

"HEY," her mom said, her tone swinging from kid-caught-out-after-curfew to full-time-parent. "It wasn't like that with you. And it won't be like that now. I'm different. And Sebastian is different."

Sebastian. At the thought of her mom's boyfriend and apparent father of the fetus, Maisey nearly puked. How her mom—her (usually) smart, steady, cautious mom—had decided this was the guy to end her dry spell for, she had no idea.

Seriously, there were a million guys who were after her mom! She'd always seen it, even when she was little. Store clerks were nicer to her, the guy who towed their car after it broke down the fourteenth time, her swimming coach. The ones on set—the grips and electrics and transpo guys—always treated her mom more gently than they did others. They stood up straighter, and spoke sweeter.

She'd even conspired once with her friend Wendy in fifth grade to get her mom and Wendy's divorced dad together. They'd seen *The Parent Trap* one too many times and thought if only they could get them on a date together, they'd automatically fall in love and Wendy's dad would buy a house and she and Maisey would totally share a room.

(It hadn't worked, which was for the best. Because the minute they hit middle school, Wendy started hanging with the track team crowd and left Maisey in her social dust.)

Her mom had always been the prettiest mom. And it wasn't just her aptitude with makeup, or the fact that she was a decade younger than most moms (although she remembered her friend Jennifer's mom making a snarky comment to that effect once). It was this light she gave off. This energy that said "isn't the world a magnificent place to be?"

But her mother always avoided men, and their entanglements. And when Maisey asked why, she'd said that she was right where she belonged, with Maisey.

Until Sebastian.

It's not that Sebastian was a bad guy. He was just . . . not mom material. He was younger, like thirty—but not young enough that he could pull off relating to a high schooler, as much as he thought he did. He was also a musician, which as far as Maisey could tell, meant he wore really expensive weathered clothes and always looked like he was wet.

She'd give him one thing—he was all about Sophia. He'd never once said anything leering to Maisey or given her a lecherous look. When he looked at her mom, it was like there was no one else in the room.

Even when there was someone else in the room. Specifically, Maisey.

The PDA was a little much to take.

All in all, he was just . . . lame. No, he was worse than lame—he was lame and he didn't know it. She'd have killed for her mom to date an actual lame person. A staid, boring accountant who told dad jokes and wore pleated pants and didn't keep her mom out until dawn at the ALT 98.7 After Party.

Seriously, who does that past thirty?

But her mom had just looked at her, standing in their tiny yellow bathroom, tears shining in her eyes.

Tears of happiness.

"Oh, baby doll," she had said, wrapping her arms around her. And Maisey let it happen, this sweet folding that had become rarer and rarer as she'd gotten older. "This is not a scary thing. This . . . this is a wonderful thing. You were the most wonderful thing to happen to me, Maisey. And this little boy or girl, they'll be the most wonderful thing to happen to us." She pulled back, held her daughter by the shoulders and looked in her eyes. "We are going on an adventure. I'll show you."

And as her mother had enveloped her in her arms again, she thought she could feel the stretch and push of the baby growing between them. And she could only think, that while her mother looked on this as a good thing, as an adventure . . . Maisey could only see the mess.

"Yes. Lives are messy," her English teacher said, snapping Maisey back to the present. "Lives intertwine. And we do ourselves an injustice when we fight against that."

Maisey audibly scoffed. But the scoff was heard by only one person—got-into-NYU-early-admission-Haley. For everyone else, it was covered by the shrill cry of the school bell, and the immediate commotion thereafter.

Haley shot her a look of pity—practicing her New York attitude, no doubt—as she packed up her bag. That Foz kid disappeared into the crowd like a ghost. But Maisey didn't care. She had bigger things to worry about than Haley Baumgarten or Foz Craley.

"You were very quiet today," her teacher said, as she walked past her desk. "I figured you knew Frost backward and forward."

"Sorry, Ms. Kneller," Maisey said automatically. "I mean, I do know Frost. I did the reading. I just . . . I have a lot of other stuff—"

"I can imagine," Ms. Kneller said, as she reached into her desk and pulled out a package of crackers. "Still haven't heard from Stanford?"

Maisey's stomach leaped at the mention of her top choice college. "No, not yet."

"Don't worry," Ms. Kneller said, her blue eyes twinkling. "It won't be long now. I'm told California schools send out their early admission acceptance packets this week."

"Oh." That in no way made Maisey feel better. "Thanks."

"Saltine?"

"Oh." She looked at the proffered cracker. "No thanks. I have lunch next."

"Well, enjoy your lunch, then." Ms. Kneller smiled, and Maisey took that as her cue to head out the door, as the next class began to dribble in.

Maisey glanced back at her English teacher before she left. And thought for a brief second that the flash of worry that crossed Ms. Kneller's face matched her own.

Whatever, she thought to herself. She had her own shit to worry about. And her mom's reproductive system shouldn't be anywhere on that list.

DECEMBER

SUNDAY   MONDAY   TUESDAY   WEDNESDAY   THURSDAY   FRIDAY   SATURDAY

CHAPTER 6

NATHALIE CLOSED THE CAR DOOR AFTER AN-other long day on her feet. No one ever seemed to realize how much standing went into teaching. She knew one teacher in the math department that developed the habit of giving out weekly quizzes to his classes on staggered days, so he could guarantee he would get to sit for at least twenty minutes every day. Of course, he then had to grade the quizzes, but there were trade-offs in everything.

Today's trade-off for Nathalie was, after a long day on her feet, to attend a disconcerting doctor's appointment.

Not that it was a *bad* appointment. But, as Nathalie was finding out, every step of this baby business had . . . bumps.

It always felt soothing to walk into Dr. Duque's world. It was clinical, clean, and straightforward. Like the logical part of the brain, but with pictures of happy, healthy babies on the walls. Nothing here was chaotic, or even in disarray. The admin nurse worked diligently and quietly behind the desk, and even the other patients were as docile as cows. Nothing to do but be patient.

Because, as Dr. Duque often said, there's no rushing a baby.

Soon enough Nathalie was led back to the intake area. The nurse asked the usual questions: *How are you feeling? Any odd symptoms?* She was weighed (oof), her blood pressure taken (not too bad, considering her long day at school), and her urine collected.

She was getting really good at peeing into a cup.

But the soothing blues of the waiting room and the calming routine of the doctor's office were overridden, when the doctor finally walked into the room.

Who was not Dr. Duque.

Bump number one.

"Hello, I'm Dr. Keen," said the chipper woman who entered the office. Really, she was a girl—younger than Nathalie, younger than possibly Lyndi, with multiple earrings and the side-shaved head look that Nathalie saw on some of her cooler students and that she secretly envied. "Dr. Duque had a family emergency, so I'm covering for her today."

"You're a doctor?" Nathalie blurted out.

"Yup!" Dr. Keen grinned. Thank God she didn't have braces. "Went to school and everything."

"When?"

". . . Recently. So, Mrs. Kneller . . . Nathalie?"

She pronounced the *h* in Nathalie, like "path" or "wrath" . . . and causing the usual twinge of annoyance that Nathalie had endured her entire life.

"It's Ms. Kneller," she corrected. No need to get into the long debate about how she was really Mrs. Kneller-Chen and how fun that was to always explain. "And it's Nathalie," she said, pronouncing the hard *t*. "My mother's French-Canadian, so the spelling . . ."

She let the sentence drift off, as Dr. Keen nodded, and

diligently marked it on her chart. In fact, she was marking everything down on her chart.

"So, your blood pressure looks good. Your weight gain normal. How are you feeling?"

"Oh, you know . . ." Nathalie shrugged, mildly amused by getting the banal question for the second time that visit. "Fine."

"Because if you have any odd symptoms, now's the time."

"Well . . ." Nathalie said. "How would I know what's odd? And what's normal for pregnancy? This is my first, and everybody responds differently, right?"

"True." Dr. Keen nodded enthusiastically, her eyes wide. "For a basic, general rule—any 'odd' symptom would be 'pain.' Of any kind. But as for everybody being different, there's a lot of evidence that pregnancy symptoms are often genetic."

"Genetic?"

"Sure—your mother, grandmother. Your pregnancy is likely to have similarities to theirs." When Nathalie didn't say anything, Dr. Keen jumped in with a rush of words. "Morning sickness for instance, if your mother wasn't much affected, you're less likely to be, too. Water retention, even some food cravings are passed generation to generation. So if you're curious about the 'oddity' of a symptom, you could ask your mother—"

And another bump. And this was a big one.

"No. I can't," Nathalie replied immediately. "She's not with us anymore."

"Oh," Dr. Keen said, blushing to her multipierced ears. Then she made another note on her clipboard. "Well, why don't we run through some regular symptoms, you can tell me if you have them, and we'll decide what's odd?"

Nathalie nodded, happy to move away from the topic of her mother.

Dr. Keen then proceeded down a massive checklist of pregnancy symptoms that even Nathalie, in her extensive research and planning, had not encountered.

"Spotting?"

"No."

"Swelling of the ankles or legs?"

"No."

"Flatulence?"

"Not . . . more than normal."

"Moles or dark spots growing?"

"They do that?"

She would give this to the young doctor: she certainly was thorough.

Once she was done, Dr. Keen looked up from her clipboard with a big bright smile. "Let's see what's going on in there!"

This was Nathalie's favorite part of these monthly appointments. She unbuttoned her pants, shrugged them down just enough to expose her lower stomach. Cold jelly was smeared, as Dr. Keen flicked on the ultrasound machine. Then, she gently ground the detector (wand? Is that what it was called?) into Nathalie's belly, watching the screen patiently for an image.

"There we are," Dr. Keen said finally, and turned the monitor so Nathalie could see.

And there it was. At fifteen weeks, the head of the baby was enormous compared to the rest of the body—but for the first time, it looked like a baby. Previously, it was far more peanut-shaped. She'd even taken to calling it "the Peanut" in her head. Guess that would have to change now, she thought, enjoying that sharp thrill of relief at seeing the image of her baby. Proof that something was really going on in there, and holiday pie wasn't the only cause of her pants getting tighter.

Proof that everything was okay, and that the baby was exactly where it was supposed to be.

Dr. Keen hit a couple buttons, and the ultrasound machine printed out a small photo. She handed it to Nathalie.

"Thank goodness," she breathed.

"Thank goodness?"

"Just . . . I had a bad experience with my previous pregnancy, thank goodness everything looks normal."

Dr. Keen's youthful enthusiasm dropped, as her eyes fell to the clipboard. "Right, I see you had a tubal pregnancy. That must have been hard."

"Yes," was Nathalie's only throaty reply.

"Your chances of miscarriage go down dramatically in the second trimester, but again, if you have concerns, or if there's a family history of later miscarriage—"

Nathalie just shook her head. And surprisingly wise beyond her years, Dr. Keen closed her mouth. She made a last few marks on her clipboard as Nathalie wiped away the jelly residue and buttoned up her pants.

"Last thing—your blood test results from last time are back. The results for the baby are normal—you'll still want to do the nuchal fold screening, I assume, just to be safe?" Nathalie nodded. A check went onto the chart. "Aaaand do you want to know the sex?"

"Yes . . . wait, no!" Nathalie replied. "Um . . . can you put it in an envelope? So my husband and I can find out at the same time?"

Dr. Keen nodded, her earrings jingling. "Well, then let's get you a printout of the results, and something to put it in."

As Nathalie left the building, clutching the ultrasound photo in one hand, and the burning envelope that contained her baby's sex in the other, her mind reeled with Dr. Keen's litany of questions.

She had all the books. All the information available in the world. But she still had questions. And apparently, she would never get answers to those questions, because they had left the world with her mother. Nathalie's grandmother had passed a long time ago, and hadn't had any children other than her mom. There were second cousins somewhere in the wilds of Montreal, but Nathalie had never met any of them. Finding them on Facebook and then asking personal questions about their pregnancies—if they'd had any—seemed a bit rude.

Maybe her dad would remember, she thought. He went through the pregnancy, too—albeit slightly removed. Yes, Nathalie thought, as she pulled into her driveway. She'd ask Dad. If anyone would know, it would be him.

So, she had a smile on her face as she walked into the dark house. It always felt good to have a plan. She flipped on the light, and called out a "hello?" just as a matter of form. David obviously wasn't there. He was working late again.

Normally, Nathalie appreciated the quiet. She would curl up with a book, or start dinner, or she could pour a glass of wine (well, now ginger ale) and do some grading. But at that moment, the quiet loomed.

But before she could combat the quiet by running straight ahead with her plan, the plan came to her, as her phone rang, her dad's number popping up on the phone.

"I was just thinking about you," she said, all smiles as she answered.

"You were?" Kathy's voice answered back. "How sweet!"

Nathalie's smile froze. She hadn't really spoken to Kathy since Thanksgiving, almost two weeks ago now. Not for lack of trying on Kathy's part—seriously, Nathalie's voice mail was maxed out by her stepmother's high-pitched, fast-talking messages that she could barely discern, and gave up trying to do so after a couple seconds.

She always intended to call Kathy back, but everything got so hectic in the stuffed few weeks between holidays.

At least, that's what she told herself.

"Sorry I'm using your dad's phone—mine's getting checked out at the store. I swear I haven't been getting any of my calls."

Yes. That was obviously exactly what was going on here.

Kathy's voice singsonged in her ear. "Sooo . . . how are you feeling?"

"Oh. You know. Fine," Nathalie replied. Kathy never asked after her health. Ever since she'd been a kid and was the only one to avoid the sixth-grade mono epidemic (mostly because she was diligent about hand washing and not because she hadn't kissed a boy yet) her father and Kathy viewed her as indestructible.

However, this was the third time today she'd been asked, and was beginning to suspect "how are you feeling?" was the new "hello." At least for the foreseeable future.

And as Kathy seemed to be waiting for more, Nathalie added, "I haven't had any morning sickness in the past couple weeks, so . . . you know. Pretty good."

"Wonderful!" Kathy exclaimed. "So you should be in good shape for Christmas!"

"Yes, of course I will," she replied as she put her bag down at the table. "David and I are looking forward to it."

In truth, she was far behind on her Christmas shopping. It might only be the first week of December, but usually by this time she had her cards done, their place decorated, and most everything but stocking stuffers purchased. But she would absolutely have everything done by Christmas Day. She'd just been a little distracted.

This time of year was also crazy at school. What with shortened attention spans for the holidays, midterms, and she was assigning a big paper tomorrow that none of her students would be happy about, save the overachievers. And her overachieving seniors were all worried about what college they were going to get into.

And oh yeah, she was currently growing a fetus. She needed to set up a nursery. And a 529 plan for the baby's college. And talk to David about getting a will and trust.

If he ever got home from the office, what with all their pre-end-of-term work. There was a company his company was in negotiations to buy, and he was killing himself over it.

Come the Christmas break, everything would be better. They would drive up to Santa Barbara, spend Christmas Day with her family, and then continue up the coast for their real vacation, and Nathalie's surprise gift to David—taking that trip to Monterey that they missed the first time around.

". . . And so you'll be able to stay an extra couple days for the party!" Kathy was saying.

"What party?"

"The gender reveal party!" Kathy's chipper voice was making her wish for a glass of wine instead of the ginger ale she went to the fridge to pour herself.

"Gender reveal party?"

"Yes! I'm inviting everyone. All your old friends from school, any friends you want to have from work, and of course my book club." Then a pause. "You do know what a gender reveal party is, right?"

"Of course I do," she replied. And she did. Vaguely. In theory. She'd never been to one, but she'd been lurking in pregnancy and mommy forums enough for the past three years to know what this latest fad in prenatal celebrations was.

A gender reveal party was when instead of just having the doctor tell you "it's a boy/girl!" when they A.) Got test results back, B.) Saw—or didn't see—a penis on the ultrasound, or C.) Pulled the child out of you kicking and screaming, they would send the gender results to a bakery. Yes, a bakery.

Which would bake a cake with either a pink or blue center, so when you cut into it, you would discover—along with everyone else with you at the time—the gender of your baby.

"You want to throw me a gender reveal party?" she said, her voice cracking a little, as she sat down at the table, ginger ale in hand. Indeed, she was even getting a little misty. "I . . . I don't know what to say."

She never expected that Kathy would want to throw her a party like this. They had never been close. Kathy had come into Nathalie's life less than a year after her mom's death. And they'd tried to find a footing then, but Nathalie was still a kid who was processing the stages of grief, and Kathy was a woman who'd never really dealt with a child before.

Then, within a year of marrying her dad, Lyndi was born, and suddenly Kathy had a baby that she could learn to parent from the ground up, not someone halfway to adulthood that required more complex interactions. Thus, theirs had always been a cordial coexistence. Kathy tried to guide Nathalie, Nathalie tolerated it, but basically figured out how to raise herself.

But now . . . maybe with the baby coming, they would finally find a way to bridge the gap between them.

"You just get your doctor to put the gender results in an

envelope and give it to me," Kathy was saying, "and I'll do the rest."

"Right," she said, looking down at the envelope on the table, with the gender results in it. The prescience of her stepmother was, at times, astounding.

On the one hand, she'd really been looking forward to sharing this moment with David today. Something to hold between them.

But on the other hand, Kathy was reaching out . . . and it's not like she and David wouldn't be together when they found out the sex—they would just also be surrounded by friends and family.

"So, what do you say?" Kathy asked, breathless.

"Um . . . sure."

"Wonderful!" Kathy trilled. "I have to call your sister, let her know you're in!"

"In?"

"Of course, sweetie—Lyndi's as excited as you are about the party for you two! Don't forget to mark your calendar!"

As Kathy hung up, a shot of cold settled into Nathalie's stomach. Of course. The party wasn't for *her*. It was for them. For Nathalie, and for Lyndi.

As if they were having a baby together, instead of one of them planning their lives around this momentous occasion, and the other one falling on her apparently-not-gay roommate's penis and ending up pregnant.

Nathalie hadn't spoken to Lyndi since Thanksgiving either. She could once again blame this on the hecticness of the postturkey/pre–candy cane life, but the truth was, she didn't really know what to say.

What she *wanted* to say was . . . a hundred different things. All variations on "what the hell are you doing?" but she knew she couldn't say that. Not with the fact that she was pregnant, too.

Except, she was pregnant with a husband, a mortgage, and a plan for how to care for the child for the next two decades. She was *ready* for this baby. There was no way Lyndi could say the same thing.

She knew it wasn't fair. But it was all she could think about when it came to her sister at the moment. Just how completely crazy the situation was. How totally unfair.

But then again, her sister was the one person she knew in a similar boat to hers. And not just the pregnancy.

So she texted a number whose last conversation was listed as almost two weeks ago.

> A gender reveal party?

It was a couple seconds before Lyndi wrote back.

> It sounded like fun. What do you think?

> Could be nice. I guess. Don't want Kathy going overboard though.

Another long pause while Lyndi typed.

> Mom's going to do what she's going to do anyway. Let her be enthusiastic.

> True. I almost let my doctor tell me the sex today. Good thing Kathy called beforehand.

> Hah.:) I have to get on that.

Finding out the sex?

Yeah, and doctors in general.

Nathalie's eyes nearly bugged out of her head.

You haven't seen a doctor yet??????

The dots loaded slow again, in an annoyingly huffy manner, or so Nathalie perceived.

I'm only 10 weeks.

I mean, 11. And a half.

You should have seen a doctor by now. You should have been seen TWICE.

Okay, okay. Sheesh. It's on my to-do list.

Nathalie resisted the urge to throw her phone across the room.

What's your insurance?

More dots. Rage-inducing dots.

Blue Cross. Just got my cards in the mail.

"Well, thank goodness for that," Nathalie grumbled to herself.

> Ok, hold on.

She quickly switched the phone into phone mode, and called up Dr. Duque's office. It took her three minutes to explain the situation. It took the nurse another two to fit Lyndi into a recently abandoned appointment slot. Five minutes Lyndi couldn't find in her busy schedule to, you know, attend to her growing child.

> You have an appointment with Dr. Keen at 3 PM tomorrow.

She texted the address and phone number while the loading dots anticipated Lyndi's response.

> You didn't have to do that.

> Apparently I did.

> I have work, you know.

> You're done by 3, you know.

> Okay, fine.

> Thanks.

> And the doc will be able to determine the sex?

> Not at 11 weeks. You'll need to take a blood test. An NIPT (noninvasive prenatal test), which you'll

> want to anyway to rule out some of the most prevalent genetic abnormalities. That test will also tell you the baby's sex.

> Oh. Ok. I hadn't really thought about that stuff.

> Stuff?

> Abnormalities.

And all of a sudden, Nathalie found her heart breaking a little bit for her sister. Lyndi hadn't even thought about "that stuff." She just assumed everything was going to be fine. Because that's who she was. Everything was always fine for Lyndi. But now, she was facing the same uncertainty that Nathalie had for the past three years.

Her response came by rote. By twenty-four years of being the protective older sister.

> It'll be okay. Dr. Keen is really nice. Young. But she'll be thorough. Your baby will be in good hands.

> Okay. And don't worry about Mom and the gender reveal party stuff. Just let her enjoy herself.

> I couldn't stop her if I tried.

And the phone fell silent.

But the silence didn't remain. Because it was only a few

ticktocks of the clock on the mantel before Nathalie was pleasantly surprised to hear the key slide in the front door.

"Oh," David said as he came in and saw her sitting at their newish IKEA table. (The chairs had been taken back. Until she chose a replacement they were using the folding chairs from the garage.) "Hey—I didn't think you'd be home."

"I didn't think you'd be home yet either," she said, rising and smiling.

"Yeah, I have to wait for signatures from Japan before I can proceed on to the next thing, so I decided to come home at a normal hour." He placed a perfunctory kiss on her nose. "I thought you had a thing."

"If by 'thing' you mean a doctor's appointment, yes I did."

"Gotcha." He nodded, looking askance, like his eyes couldn't focus on anything that wasn't paperwork. "How'd that go?"

"All good," she said. "Baby is still in there. Test results came back normal from last time."

"Great," he said on a sigh. Then he wrapped an arm around her shoulders and just held her there for a second. Her head in the crook of his neck, his body lined up against hers.

It felt wonderful. *This*, she thought. *This is what I needed.* And David, somehow had known it.

They stood there for a little bit, until David leaned back.

Not willing to let the closeness she'd been missing go quite yet, Nathalie held on to his arm.

"So what do you want for dinner? I can make anything—or call anyone. Thai? Also, I was hoping to talk to you about setting up the 529 plan. I can do it myself but I wanted to get your opinion on which one was best. Also, who should we talk to about a will—should we get an estate-planning lawyer or do you know someone in that field? And you're not going to believe this, but Kathy called, and she wants to throw us a gender reveal party over Christmas. I couldn't quite figure out how to say no—"

"Honey," David said, his eyes falling toward the dormant TV in the living room. "I know we have to talk about this stuff, but do you mind if I just . . . de-stress a little first?"

"Xbox?" Nathalie said, nodding. "Sure. No problem."

"I've been on the phone half the day talking, I just want to shoot aliens for a little while. Do whatever you want for dinner."

"Got it," Nathalie said, stepping back. Then her eyes fell to the table. Where the envelope with the gender of the baby sat next to the ultrasound photo.

She picked one up.

"Here's the ultrasound picture. Looking less and less like the Peanut and more and more like a baby."

She handed it to him, and then crossed to what was currently the office and would soon be the baby's room, letting the door slip shut behind her.

It was only a couple of seconds before she heard the Xbox start up and the theme music of David's current favorite game.

Then, she slid in front of the desktop computer, and opened up the internet.

Maybe someone on here could show her comparative models of various 529 plans and which one was the best.

But somehow her fingers took her not to college savings plans, but to the mommy forums she'd lurked in for so long.

And for once, unlurked.

Does anyone know about gender reveal parties? My family wants to throw one, I'd like to know what to expect.

And she waited. It was thirty seconds before the first response popped up. Then another and another and another.

- *OMG my gender reveal party was AMAZING. It was super fun the first of many celebrations for you and your LO! We had the most delicious cake—here's the bakery's link.*

- *Ugh, total waste of time and money. I wanted one but everyone else was not enthusiastic. So when the cake came out blue, everyone was like . . . so? Big disappointment.*

- *Enthusiasm matters. If your family wants to do it for you, consider yourself lucky. It's for them anyway, not really for you. Enjoy it!*

- *DON'T DO A CAKE! It's so passé now it's almost rotro. Besides, not everyone can eat it, with dietary restrictions. My friend had the best gender reveal, setting up exploding glitter balls on a timer, so everyone was drenched in pink sparkles at the same time. Here's a website with a ton of ideas!*

Tentatively, Nathalie clicked on the link. And her eyes bugged out of her head.

Anything that could be pink or blue was pink or blue. And some things that really, really shouldn't have been.

There were baked goods, of course: cakes, cupcakes, cake pops with centers dyed the color associated with your child's genitalia. There were also stuffed croissants, stuffed donuts, stuffed pork tenderloin—anything that could be stuffed, basically, could be cut into and presto! The big reveal.

There were things that exploded, too—glitter balls. Confetti that could be loaded into a cannon and shot at the crowd (Where was this crowd? A stadium?). You could put balloons in a box and then open it, releasing them to the sky where they would inevitably end up in the gullet of some poor bird. You could load up squirt guns with colored water and have guests shoot each other, while wearing white T-shirts. Or if the party had a younger contingent (or the young at heart! the website exclaimed) you could use Silly String. There was something Nathalie couldn't exactly determine, but they looked like colored roadside flares.

There was even one couple featured who filled a box with colored chalk, and shot the box with a sniper rifle, revealing the gender in a cloud of dust, while the event was photographed in diffused natural light.

Nathalie closed the computer window. For a moment, she was afraid that the pink or blue glitter had somehow leaked out of the computer and spilled onto the desk.

As she brushed nonexistent glitter off the keyboard, Nathalie knew one thing was clear:

Kathy must never, ever know about anything on that site.

CHAPTER 7

LYNDI HAD HAD BETTER WEEKS. OH, IT started out great! The wreath idea went over well. So well in fact, that Paula gave her the lead on the product—design, pricing, everything. It was a rush to get that kind of responsibility, and Lyndi came home from work smiling ear to ear.

Marcus was very happy to let her exercise her joy on him. Enthusiastic, even.

Then, the wreaths went over with the public so well that it crashed the Favorite Flower website. Lyndi had spent several nail-biting hours on the phone with their hosting company while Paula paced behind her, trying to get the website back up. Meanwhile, Paula tweeted and Facebooked maniacally, trying to put out an air of calm about their website's problems, and assuring their customers they would be back online and taking orders imminently.

Then of course, they had to construct the wreaths.

When Lyndi had thought of the idea, she hadn't taken packaging in with the cost. Because they usually didn't worry about packaging with their bouquets—they simply went out rolled up in paper. But the wreaths were ungainly enough to require boxing, which made their costs go up. And so the wreaths were actually something of a loss leader—bringing them business, but not enough to justify their existence.

Paula and the other arrangers had looked at her like she was some poor pitiful kid when she figured that out.

She was less enthusiastic going home that day, and ended up sniffling on the big couch while Marcus gave her blankets and noncaffeine tea.

On the one hand, she was glad Marcus was willing and able to ride the emotional roller coaster with her. On the other, she'd really appreciate it if he didn't assume her mental state was baby-related.

Although it could be—who knows? She'd definitely been feeling weirder lately. She forgot things sometimes (i.e.: wreath packaging), and her boobs were crazy sensitive. The morning sickness remained throughout the day and what she wouldn't give for a nap!

But none of that meant any of her feelings about work weren't valid. To be petted and cosseted was exactly what she didn't want—and yet she was so grateful every time Marcus brought her a steaming mug of ginger tea.

So, she thought she deserved a night out of the house.

Honestly, she didn't get together with her friends enough. So when she walked into Ora Café, the hip bistro she'd chosen for this month's get-together, she felt the familiar sense of anticipation that came with seeing all her girls. She spotted them at a back table, and waved big to get their attention.

"Heeeeeeeeyyyyy!" they all cried in unison. "There you are!"

"Sorry I'm late!" she said, air-kissing and hugging as she went. "I got stuck on the phone with my mom."

"What's Mom up to these days?" Allison, one of her oldest friends from high school, asked.

"Oh . . . you know," Lyndi hedged. "Some party she wants to throw over Christmas."

"Ohhhhh," Olivia cooed from the other side of the table. "Are we invited?"

"Are you going home for Christmas?"

As Olivia and Allison started in on their Christmas plans—wherein Olivia talked about a planned trip to Hawaii and Allison adamantly one-upped her with her spring break in Europe plans, Lyndi turned her attention to the other friend at the table, Elizabeth, and gave her a soft smile.

"What are you doing for the holidays?" she asked.

"Oh you know—making unnecessary runs to Target to avoid my family," Elizabeth replied, with her trademark sarcasm. "Actually, I'll probably be working over the break. Lots to read."

Elizabeth, Olivia, and Allison had all been friends in school in Santa Barbara. They all had vowels as their first initial and apparently decided that made them cool sometime around fourth grade. Lyndi joined their group in eighth, when they expanded their social circle to allow consonants. When everyone graduated from college, they all gravitated to Los Angeles . . . as people their age in Southern California tended to do. And when they all found each other again, their daily group texts and weekly hangout sessions were born.

Of the three, Olivia and Allison were always the go-getters. The ones who wanted to be at the center of everything, be it soccer camp or the school play or the world. They both got marketing degrees and were immersed in the middle of their corporate worlds, selling things and branding and doing online multilevel . . . something. Lyndi and Elizabeth had been the artistic, dreamy types. Lyndi with her painting and graphic design, and Elizabeth always wanting to tell stories.

So while LA was the natural place to go for Olivia and Allison, as it was the center of everything, it was the *only* place to go for Elizabeth, who loved the movies more than Lyndi had ever known anyone could.

Seriously, when they were in high school, Elizabeth watched that movie from the '80s, *Bill and Ted's Excellent Adventure*. Nineteen times. In a row. To study the structure, she said.

Yeah, Elizabeth was a little different from the rest of them.

At the moment, Elizabeth worked as a freelance script reader for a small film production company. It was, as she said, super entry level, but it allowed her to do two of her favorite things—reading and being judgmental—and let her set her own schedule, so she could hold down a receptionist job to make ends meet, and write on her own in the wee small hours.

"Nothing like family to give one fodder for story." Elizabeth smirked, and Lyndi smiled right back. "But what about you? Anything new and interesting?"

"Well . . ." There certainly was plenty that was new and interesting, she thought, as her hand automatically went to her still flat and toned belly. "I got a promotion at work."

"Oh my goooooooooddddd!!!!" Olivia squealed. "Congratulations!"

"Seriously! You've been working at that place, what—six months? God, it took me nearly that long to get my first promotion, too," Allison piped up. "So, what's the position? Stats? Do they upgrade you to a car from that little bike?"

"Um . . . no. The bike is mine, and I love it, you know?"

"Right." Olivia nodded, elbowing Allison in the side. "It's better for the environment."

"That's Lyndi—our little social conscience," Allison added. "I mean, who else would choose an, er, *awesome* vegan place like this?"

"Vegan can be really healthy," Elizabeth added in her dry drawl. "So you two might actually be able to eat something other than vodka."

Allison quirked her head to the side, as if she were a cocker spaniel that didn't understand, but Olivia blinked at Elizabeth with a frozen smile on her face and a steely look in her eyes.

Allison and Olivia had come to Los Angeles and thrown themselves into its winner-take-all lifestyle. Being perfect was as important as being hip, and so they often subscribed to the latest in elimination dieting. Unlike Marcus, who kept gluten-free for health reasons, Allison and Olivia seemed to practice whatever would keep them the thinnest, the leanest, the hungriest, as if it were a badge of honor.

Elizabeth wasn't wrong—the last two times they'd had their girls' night out, Olivia and Allison had only ordered vodka/zero calorie mixer drinks. Secretly, Lyndi was a little worried about them.

Elizabeth worried about them not so secretly. She just showed her love with a side of acid.

"Speaking of, should we order?" Lyndi said, hoping to clear the tension.

"Yes, and you with your promotion and raise can get the first round!" Allison cheered, and waved madly at the waiter.

Lyndi opened her menu, so as to avoid giving any answer. She would be expected to drink. Ora Café was even known for making its own beer and wine. This would be the first time she would have to figure out how to avoid alcohol since

Thanksgiving, and she was a little nervous that the lie she had ready to go would come off as sounding like she was six and caught stealing her older sister's lipstick.

Obviously she looked a little nervous about it, because she heard Elizabeth whisper from behind her own menu. "Don't let Allison and Olivia get you down. You know that Allison's promotion was from answering phones on one person's desk to answering phones on a different person's desk, right?"

Lyndi sent a grateful look Elizabeth's way.

"Besides," Elizabeth continued, "I like vegan food. What made you choose this place? Marcus introduce you?"

"Um, yeah. We went here a couple weeks ago, I loved their polenta cakes."

Actually, while she did enjoy their polenta cakes, Lyndi had chosen Ora Café for far more nefarious reasons. Being vegan, she knew it would not have the one thing on the menu that she really wanted, but was on the No-Pregnant-Lady food list: eggs.

Not that *all* eggs were on the No-Pregnant-Lady food list, just the ones that tasted good. Runny, slightly undercooked eggs—over easy, poached, any form by which the yolk became a delicious, rich sauce for whatever else was on your plate.

Scrambled and hardboiled eggs were allowed. Boring and chewy, but allowed.

She could kill someone for an eggs Benedict.

In fact there were a lot of strange foods that were on the No-Pregnant-Lady food list, at least according to the daily pastel-colored emails she'd been getting. At first she was miffed that her repeated opting-out of the subscriber list was being ignored, but then, she saw their advantages. Along with being a good way to know exactly how far along she was (today was eleven weeks, five days exactly) she sort of got sucked in by all the new information.

It turned out, there were a lot more things outlawed than just alcohol. Foods on the list included but were not limited to:

- high mercury fish (goodbye beloved Tuna Fish Sandwich)
- raw or undercooked fish (goodbye beloved Spicy Tuna Roll)
- raw shellfish like oysters (gross anyway, no biggie)
- undercooked meat (no more medium rare steak, only dry pieces of gray blahness)
- deli meat (what counts as deli meat? Does it have to come in the Oscar Mayer packaging or is meat cut right off the turkey considered death on a kaiser roll? What about pepperoni?)
- soft cheeses (why?)
- bean sprouts (WHY?)

and of course,

- any egg that normal humans would consider edible.

So far, Lyndi felt like she was dealing with these new restrictions like any sane person would—whining reluctance. But, much like the prenatal vitamins Marcus had given her, she was doing what needed to be done. So if that meant avoiding the temptation of an undercooked egg, so be it.

She once held her breath underwater for six minutes. She could pull this off for the next thirty weeks or so.

The waiter came around and Allison and Olivia ordered

something vodka-based and froofy. Elizabeth ordered a beer (the cheapest on the menu) and all eyes turned expectantly to Lyndi.

"Just sparkling water for me," she replied. Then, to the group—"I'm on antibiotics."

It was the easiest and absolute best lie. It had actually been recommended to her by one of those pastel-colored emails. Seriously, they had tips on "how to avoid questions when you're not quite ready to tell the world"—aka, "how to lie to friends and loved ones." Hooray for subterfuge!

But the antibiotics lie 1. Had the benefit of being hard to question, and 2. Kept people from convincing you to drink anyway, like they would if you said you were just cutting back.

"Eggghhh," Olivia said, wrinkling her nose. "Infections are not very festive."

"Seriously, what did Marcus give you?" Allison said, causing Olivia to smirk.

"Nothing!" Lyndi protested. Well, actually, he had given her something, but it didn't require antibiotics. "I . . . I had strep last week, and I'm finishing up the medication . . . But I'm not contagious!"

She could feel the words falling off her tongue too fast, too muddled. Elaborating on a lie was never the way to go—all it brings is more questions, and recalling all the details of that one bout of strep Lyndi had when she was a sophomore in college was not going to cut it if Olivia or Allison decided to dig deeper.

Luckily, however, they didn't. They just shrugged, as if to say "your loss," and went back to their menus.

"So that means you have health insurance now?" Elizabeth asked. "You know, from your promotion? My freelance-ass is beyond jealous."

"Oh—yeah! Don't be too jealous—the paperwork made it almost not worth it," she said, trying to appease with a little self-deprecation. She had actually gotten that all sorted with Paula last week, finally. Just got her membership card in the mail that afternoon, too. Now she just had to find an OB, set up some appointments . . . between this and the prenatal vitamins she was taking religiously, she was halfway to nailing this pregnancy thing.

Then her phone dinged with a text.

"Sorry," she said to Elizabeth, glancing at her phone. Her heart fluttered as she read who it was. "My sister."

She hadn't spoken to Nathalie in nearly two weeks—which was forever for them, and forever-forever considering the current circumstances. Both of them being pregnant . . . you would have thought they'd have a lot to talk about. Even though she was determined to give Nathalie time, Lyndi still didn't think it would have taken her this long to reach out.

"She's . . . we haven't spoken in a while, can you give me a sec?"

Elizabeth nodded eagerly, while Olivia and Allison both shrugged and went back to their menus and their conversation about the best pics to post on your online dating profile (the consensus was you needed one looking amazeballs in your best LBD, one looking sporty while hiking, and one at a party surrounded by people who enjoy your company—thus hitting the hot, healthy, happy trifecta).

A gender reveal party?

Lyndi hid a smile. She had no idea what a gender reveal party was, but her mom was so enthusiastic. And if there was anything that was going to bring Nathalie out of her funk, it would be bewilderment over something their mom did. Hence half the reason Lyndi agreed to the party.

Sometimes little sisters had to be nefarious.

> It sounded like fun. What do you think?

> Could be nice. I guess. Don't want Kathy going overboard though.

> Mom's going to do what she's going to do anyway. Let her be enthusiastic.

Lyndi grinned. She could practically hear Nathalie's deep sigh of acquiescence.

> True. I almost let my doctor tell me the sex today. Good thing Kathy called beforehand.

> Hah.:) I have to get on that.

> Finding out the sex?

> Yeah, and doctors in general.

The next text came fast and furious. Basically, if this were *Harry Potter*, Nathalie was typing out a howler.

> You haven't seen a doctor yet??????

> I'm only 10 weeks.

Crap, her thumb slipped and autocorrected to 10!

> I mean, 11. And a half.

Great, now she sounded like she didn't know how far along she was. Even though the pastel emails reminded her daily of the countdown.

> You should have seen a doctor by now. You should have been seen TWICE.

> Okay, okay. Sheesh. It's on my to-do list.

Seriously, Nat, she wanted to say, chill out. Her health care only kicked in a couple days ago; she couldn't have made an appointment before now. It wasn't like she was avoiding it.
Sort of.

> What's your insurance?

Lyndi told her. And made sure to mention that she had ONLY JUST gotten her cards in the mail.

> Ok, hold on.

"Hold on?" Lyndi grumbled to herself. "For what?"

"Are you going to be on your phone all night?" Allison asked, taking a big sip of the froofy drink (that was Christmas themed, Lyndi realized). "I thought girls' night out had a strict no-phone policy."

"Give her a break, okay?" Elizabeth said. "She's got some family stuff to deal with."

Once again, she sent Elizabeth a grateful look. Out of all her friends, she knew she could count on Elizabeth to understand. Not because she'd ever been through anything like this before—Elizabeth was an only child, so sibling politics was unheard of, and never dated anyone so she could be a virgin for all she knew—but because she always had this amazing ability to see what the other person was feeling.

Lyndi guessed it was because she loved stories so much—and spent her time living in characters' heads.

"Oh my God, speaking of family stuff," Olivia began, smiling with relish. "Did I tell you all that my brother Steve knocked up his girlfriend?"

"No!" gasped Allison. Elizabeth's head whipped around, and Lyndi . . . Lyndi just blinked.

"Yeah. They've only been dating a little while. My mom thinks she totally did it on purpose, to trap him."

"I . . . I don't think . . . I mean, who would do that on purpose?" Lyndi found herself asking.

"You don't know this chick. Apparently, she's totally flaky, never had a real job. And now she'll have my brother taking care of her forever."

Lyndi could feel her cheeks turning bright red. Thank God for the low lights.

Is this what Marcus's family would think of her? That she got pregnant to trap him?

Right then, her phone dinged once more.

> You have an appointment with Dr. Keen at 3 PM tomorrow.

"Of course, we can't say that in front of my brother. He's, like, over the moon about it. Meanwhile, my parents are trying to gently convince him to have a paternity test. This is going to be the most fun Christmas ever!"

Suddenly, it was all too much for Lyndi. Her sister overstepping via text. The way Olivia was salivating over every juicy word of her own story. She began to feel the familiar nausea creeping up.

"Excuse me for a second, guys."

She stood up, and before anyone could say anything (not that they would, they were all on tenterhooks for Olivia's story) she stepped out the front door of Ora Café, taking a deep breath of the chilled winter air.

God, did she really think three minutes ago that she had this pregnancy thing down? Not according to her older sister, who no doubt had been to the doctor's once a week since conception, was strictly following nutritional advice, and didn't need a daily pastel email to remind her how far along she was.

She wanted to cry. She wanted to let her emotions get the best of her and just let it out. But she had three friends inside who would see right through her, and so, she made the only other emotional choice she could. She got angry.

Well, as angry as Lyndi tended to get, anyway.

> You didn't have to do that.

There, she thought. That'll show Nathalie.

> Apparently I did.

Okay, maybe not so much. What she wanted to type back was that it was utterly presumptuous of Nathalie to think she knew what was best for Lyndi—vis-à-vis her body, her baby, or her schedule.

Instead, what she wrote was . . .

> I have work, you know.

> You're done by 3, you know.

> Okay, fine.

Fine. Felt snappish. Felt good to say. After all, everyone knows that *fine* doesn't mean *fine*.

But . . . Nathalie had helped her out. She meant well. So after a couple seconds, she added . . .

> Thanks.

> And the doc will be able to determine the sex?

> Not at 11 weeks. You'll need to take a blood test. An NIPT (noninvasive prenatal test), which you'll want to anyway to rule out some of the most prevalent genetic abnormalities. That test will also tell you the baby's sex.

Lyndi felt her body go slightly numb. And it wasn't from the cold air whipping around her.

> Oh. Ok. I hadn't really thought about that stuff.

> Stuff?

> Abnormalities.

Because she hadn't thought about that. She'd mostly been thinking about how to sign up for health insurance and how to avoid drinking alcohol when out with her friends and why on earth she couldn't have eggs Benedict with delicious hollandaise sauce.

And she suddenly felt stupid, and cold, and sad.

Luckily, she had her sister, who weirdly, knew how to make her feel better, even while they were fighting via text.

> It'll be okay. Dr. Keen is really nice. Young. But she'll be thorough. Your baby will be in good hands.

> Okay. And don't worry about Mom and the gender reveal party stuff. Just let her enjoy herself.

> I couldn't stop her if I tried.

Feeling slightly better, and much less nauseous, Lyndi straightened her shoulders and marched right back inside.

She put that same big smile on her face as she had when she approached the table earlier, although this time it took a little more effort.

"Sorry about that," she said.

"No worries!" Elizabeth said. "Olivia was just spreading her brother's dirty laundry all over the restaurant."

If Olivia had been sober, she might have taken offense at that. As it was she was buzzed and there was now a second froofy Christmas drink in front of her, so she just snickered and sipped.

"Everything okay with you?"

"Sure," she said, putting on a brave face. "My sister is just freaking out about this gender reveal party my mom wants to have."

"Gender reveal party?" Allison asked. "Wait . . . is your sister pregnant?"

". . . yes."

"Oh, congratulations! You're going to be an auntie!" Allison cried and clapped.

Even Elizabeth looked a little starry-eyed at the idea. Lyndi swung her gaze between her three friends.

"You guys are . . . good with that?"

"Well, of course!" Olivia replied. "Why wouldn't we be?"

"But . . . your brother."

"Your sister is very different from my idiot brother. She's been with her husband forever. God, I remember when we were in high school and she and her husband came and picked us up from that corner store after your car broke down—"

"The thing is, the gender reveal party . . . it's not just for her." At all their quizzical expressions, she took a deep breath, and continued.

"I'm pregnant, too."

She could have dropped a nuclear bomb in the middle of Ora Café, and no one at their table would have moved.

"Marcus and I are very excited."

It took a minute for her friends to find their footing. Unsurprisingly, the most buzzed found it first.

"Oh . . . my God!" Olivia cried, her voice pitched light, trying to sound happy. "That's just . . . congratulations! Right? Congratulations?"

"Yes," said Allison immediately. "Absolutely. Congratulations. That's amazing news. So you're going to . . . um . . . keep it?"

Ice ran through Lyndi's veins. "Obviously."

Then they fell silent again.

Lyndi turned to Elizabeth. Hoping for something. For her usual quiet, snarky support. For her ability to give light to the other side of things. For someone, anyone to be on her side.

Instead, Elizabeth just stuttered. "Well, okay. Um . . . hey, so, Allison, you know that new digital media lab your company is running? I'm thinking of applying—"

"Oh, you should—it would be right up your alley! I'll send you all the info . . ."

"Ohh, my company is thinking of putting together a digital media team," Olivia added. "I wouldn't be surprised if they asked me to head it."

And Lyndi was left mute, alone, sipping her sparkling water, while her friends did everything in their power to avoid talking to her.

CHAPTER 8

THERE WAS NOTHING LIKE A TELEVISION show's holiday party to remind you that glamour was relative, Sophia thought, as she walked into the West Hollywood bar/bowling alley that the production had rented out for the evening.

Most people, if they were reading *Us Weekly* or *People*, would think that a television show would go all out for their company party. There would be photographers, step-and-repeats, waiters with hors d'oeuvres sliding past on trays, and possibly a celebrity MC.

In reality, there were no photographers—no one was particularly interested in documenting the antics of 200 people who don't appear on-screen. And while there was food, it was of the deep-fried bar food variety, set up on a buffet table. And the attached bowling alley blasting music you could spin a disco ball to really didn't make for a glamorous atmosphere. But it did make for a fun one.

Sophia walked into the bar and was immediately hugged by two wardrobe girls, a grip, and two of the writers. There was plenty of alcohol in the signature cocktail the bar had made just for the *Fargone* crew (called The Never Too Far Gone, which was bourbon-based, and set off Sophia's smell-o-vision). When 200 people who worked together day in and day out finally have permission to blow off steam together (on the company dime, too!) the more alcohol goes in, the more love comes out. As evidenced when Kip rushed over to greet her.

"Soppppphhhhhiiieee!" he said, picking her up and spinning her around. Kip might have been delicate and precise when it came to doing hair, but when he'd had a signature cocktail or two, his high school wrestling team self came out.

"Hey, uh, put her down, man, would you?" a mellifluous voice from behind Sophia said, causing her spine to tingle, as always.

"And you brought Sebastian! The flower man himself!"

Kip put Sophia down and she stepped aside to allow Kip to assault Sebastian. Sebastian put a wide grin on his face as he shook hands with Kip . . . who wasted no time pulling Sebastian into a bear hug.

"She told me," Kip whispered into Sebastian's ear. "Congratulations."

A look of surprise crossed Sebastian's face, but he had the grace (and now, the media training) to hold it together, and accept Kip's clap on the back with a grin and a nod.

"Have you seen Vanessa yet?" Kip asked Sophia. "She's high as a kite."

"She's high?" Sebastian interjected. He'd known Vanessa longer than any of them, and his concern was justified.

"Not on drugs," Kip replied. "On the Golden Globe noms."

The Golden Globe nominations had come out just that morning, and in a complete and utter surprise (or as totally expected, given the amount of press attention it had been getting), Vanessa's little indie movie from over the summer garnered three nominations—and one of those was for Vanessa herself as supporting actress.

Sophia was incredibly happy and proud of her friend. When she heard the news this morning, she immediately texted Vanessa her congratulations. But she hadn't seen her in the flesh yet, and couldn't wait to tell her in person.

Although, judging from the crowd surrounding her at the bar, Vanessa was currently swamped with congratulations.

"I'll brave the crowd and get us some drinks. Don't worry, I'll make sure yours is a virgin," Kip said with a wink. "Let you guys get all your hellos in. Then we are getting shoes and We. Are. Bowling. Did I tell you I was on the bowling team in high school?"

"You were on every team in high school," Sophia yelled after him as he moved off.

"You told him?" Sebastian murmured in her ear. Sophia could tell he was upset.

"He's my trailer mate," she replied. "I can't exactly keep it from him why the hairspray is making me nauseous."

"No, I get it," Sebastian said quickly. His tone slid from angry to worried. "Thing is, if he knows . . . Kip definitely shouldn't be picking you up and twirling you like that—what about the baby?"

Sophia bit her lip. Kip was a cuddle bunny, his ministrations had never been jarring or dangerous. But it was so cute to have Sebastian be all concerned with her welfare. It made her feel . . . protected. And since she'd spent so long protecting herself, it gave her a kind of glow to be protected by someone else.

Her first pregnancy, she'd never had that. She hadn't had it in nearly eighteen years.

"I know, you're right. I'll talk to him," she said, her placating bearing fruit when Sebastian's brow cleared and he slung a long arm around her waist.

"I just worry, is all," Sebastian said, running his other hand through his lanky hair. "Ever since you told me about the— you know."

Sophia let her head fall on his shoulder. "I know."

She did know. And he wasn't talking about the baby. The baby news, he had taken extremely well. Ecstatically, even.

She'd told him at his place. The band leased a house in the Hollywood Hills, and kept it even when they were on the road six months out of the year. It was owned by some director who had purchased it after he had made it big with a cult favorite movie, and before his divorce.

It looked like barely anyone lived there, because all of the furniture was midcentury modern and precise and came with the house. None of the guys' possessions were there, beyond a number of shredded black T-shirts and a Mr. Coffee. The only area that looked like people actually *lived* there was the garage, which had been converted to studio space.

It was one of the reasons Sebastian had said he preferred to spend their time at Sophia and Maisey's house. Because it felt like a home.

And because there weren't five other guys underfoot.

But Sophia had known she had to do this on his turf. Because . . . because she didn't really know. Maybe because she wanted him to feel safe, surrounded by all his stuff . . . , er, all his T-shirts. Or maybe because she didn't want her own home marred with a bad memory if he reacted poorly.

But maybe, it was because she didn't want him to think that this baby would only exist in her world. It would exist in both of theirs.

Luckily none of her fears were realized, because when

the words "I'm pregnant," popped out of her mouth, after the initial shock passed, she got to witness the biggest grin spread over Sebastian's face. Then, he grabbed her hand and rushed out of his bedroom and into the living room, where one of his bandmates—Mick, the drummer—was busy banging out a rhythm on the back of an Arne Jacobsen swan chair worth more than all the furniture in Sophia's house.

"Dude," Sebastian stated firmly. "We're having a baby."

Then Mick's face split into a wide grin. Sophia knew she always liked him.

"Awesome!" Mick said, abandoning the Arne Jacobsen to squeeze Sophia in a hug, and then immediately back off. "Sorry—should I do that? I shouldn't do that."

"I'm fine," she'd assured him.

"Dude, it's our first band baby!" Mick cried. "We'll have to get him or her those noise-canceling headphones so they can come to our concerts! Oh, God," Mick said, looking down at his drumsticks, "I shouldn't have been drumming so loud."

"Mick, the thing doesn't have ears yet," Sebastian said. Then a worried look crossed his face. "Does the thing have ears yet?"

"The thing is a baby and no, it doesn't." She laughed.

"Are you sure?"

"Yes, but I go to the doctor in three days for my first appointment, and I'll make sure to verify with her."

"We'll ask her," he'd said, squeezing her hand. "But no drumming until then," he warned Mick, who nodded vehemently. Then, "C'mon."

He tugged her back toward his bedroom. She bit her lip in anticipation and let herself be pulled away.

"Hey, where are you guys going?" Mick asked.

"To celebrate," Sebastian said.

"Can I come?"

Sophia met Sebastian's eyes. Saw their heat. "No," she replied with a laugh.

The next three days were a whirlwind of affection. They still had a couple of days' worth of work on the show until they were officially on Christmas hiatus, but it was tough to concentrate. Sebastian was texting every hour on the hour. Checking in with little messages of love. His flower deliveries went from weekly to daily. Honestly, it was this, more than anything that clued Kip in to the fact that something was up.

Kip's reply had been a lot more practical than Sebastian's. After he asked how Sebastian took the news, he asked, "How did Maisey?"

Sophia had just pressed her lips together. "Like a teenager."

"Good," Kip said. "Let her act like a teenager once in her life, I almost forgot she was one."

But Maisey constantly surprised Sophia. Because when it turned out that the band's recording company wanted them to come in for an emergency meeting the same day as Sophia's first appointment and Sebastian couldn't come, Maisey gamely stepped in.

"Really?" Sophia had said. "You want to come?"

Maisey just shrugged. "It'll get my mind off Stanford."

Maisey still hadn't heard from Stanford's early admissions office. Every day after school she rushed home and checked the mailbox. And then her email. And then the mailbox again. At least the girl was smart enough to know she needed out of the house.

It was at the doctor's office that they had gotten the news that had sent Sebastian's protective instincts into overdrive, and had him worrying (even more) about Sophia's new fragile state of being.

"The baby looks great!" the doctor had said, moving the

wand around inside Sophia. The first ultrasound was trans-vaginal, which was a surprise to Sophia, and a complete shock to Maisey. The poor girl kept looking up to the corner of the room, muttering to herself "I'm never having sex, I'm never having sex." Which, to be honest, Sophia was totally fine with. Nothing like the realities of the human body to act as the most effective sex deterrent.

"Aw, honey, look—it looks like a little wiggly bean."

Maisey glanced down at the screen. Then her eyes fell somewhere in the region of her mom's knee, and she looked right back up at the ceiling again.

The doctor gave Sophia a conspiratorial wink.

Once the ultrasound was over, and Sophia could sit up again, Maisey's eyes returned to a more horizon level stare.

"So, we have you coming back in next month, to moderate a high-risk pregnancy," the doctor had said, marking things down on her chart.

"High-risk?" Sophia's brow came down.

"Because you're over thirty-five. That's considered advanced maternal age."

From her chair next to the wall, Maisey snorted. "I told you, you're old."

Sophia shot her daughter a look that she hadn't often had to employ with her firstborn. "I'm *barely* over thirty-five," she retorted.

"Don't worry," the doctor said. "Everything looks normal, it's just a categorization that means you'll get a little extra monitoring. No big deal."

When the doctor had said "no big deal," it actually had a quelling effect on Sophia's nerves. That is, until the doctor continued.

"What is more concerning is your pregnancy history."

"What history?" Maisey asked, her eyes flying to her mom's.

"You," Sophia replied. "You are my pregnancy history."

"Yes . . ." the doctor said, examining the chart. "And you were hospitalized for preeclampsia?"

"I was. For four weeks."

"Wait—you were hospitalized? For a month?" Maisey asked. "What's preeclampsia?"

"It's uncontrolled high blood pressure. It can lead to a lot of complications, threats to internal organs, and threaten the vitality of the pregnancy itself."

Maisey went pale.

"But everything turned out fine, sweetie," Sophia placated.

But the truth was a little more complicated.

After seventeen years, her first pregnancy was a bit of a blur, but she'd remembered that the warning signs had begun with headaches. She'd sailed through the first two trimesters, full of energy and excited to be starting her life with Alan. Once they got married, they moved into Alan's parents' guesthouse (really, their converted garage) in the backyard.

Where Alan's mother could make sure that Sophia was treating her boy the way he deserved to be treated. For his mother, this seemed to mean waiting on him hand and foot.

Alan didn't know how to do his own laundry. He didn't know how to cook. Neither, Sophia came to learn, did Alan's father. His mother had dedicated her life to upholding the more traditional marriage roles, and as Sophia was now Alan's wife, Sophia had been fully expected to do the same.

And Sophia, at the time, was eager to please. Part of it had been being young and in love. Part of it had been Alan's mother was terrifying.

So when she started getting crazy headaches, she brushed it off, even though her own mother told her to listen to her body and take it easier, let Alan help her. But Alan's expectations aligned with his mother's, and so Sophia focused on keeping their little guesthouse/garage clean, Alan's meals hot, and still working at Sephora so they could save money to get their own place someday.

Then she had gone to the doctor for her third trimester checkup.

Her blood pressure had been crazy high. Sophia thought it must have been the stress. The doctor saw things differently.

She had been admitted to the hospital with preeclampsia at thirty weeks pregnant. Her emotions hugely conflicted. On the one hand, she felt like a failure. Like she couldn't do everything she needed to do to be a wife and a mother and build the life she was trying to build. On the other hand . . . she was relieved. Because she was tired. She needed to rest. She needed to concentrate on having a healthy baby, and that wasn't easy to do when your mother-in-law burst into your little guesthouse at 7:30 in the morning and criticized you for not having the bed made or the breakfast dishes put away yet, while you were trying to get ready for work.

She'd hoped that Alan would take the situation as seriously as she did. But mostly he seemed confused. Now, not only did he have to go to work every day, but instead of coming home to a clean house and a cooked meal, he had to go sit in an uncomfortable chair in his wife's hospital room and spend his money on bad takeout or hospital food?

His mother of course, was of the same opinion. It took a little while for Sophia to realize that it was actually his mother's opinions that were coming out of Alan's mouth. It took only a little longer for Sophia to understand that Alan's mother blamed her for "trapping" her baby boy before he could even start out in the world.

This realization came when Alan actually said those words. Never mind how trapped Sophia was, in her body, in that bed, in the hospital.

Sophia hoped things would change when Maisey arrived. And they did. For Sophia. Because when that tiny baby, weighing less than five pounds, emerged loudly into the world at thirty-four weeks, the entire world shifted for Sophia. Everything was going to be about protecting and raising her child. And everything else—her recalcitrant mother-in-law, her immature husband, her unmade bed—was secondary.

But Alan didn't feel the same way. He felt put-upon, aggrieved. Like this was something done to him, not something that happened to all of them, that had to be dealt with. Like the preeclampsia—hell, even the pregnancy—were her fault, and her fault alone.

But this time—this new baby, this new pregnancy—would be different. It already was. Because after that doctor's appointment, when she had dinner with Sebastian that night and told him everything the doctor said, he wasn't angry   he was worried.

About her.

About the baby.

"That—what's it called—preeclampsia? That sounds really serious, babe." Sebastian's brow furrowed under a sweep of his hair.

"It can be," she had admitted. "But I don't have it yet, and I might not get it—they say that the babies having different fathers has an impact on whether or not I develop it again. But the doctors are going to be vigilant, and so am I, about my blood pressure and my health."

"Okay," he'd said, taking a calming breath. "But we should talk to another doctor, right? Like, I'm sure Vanessa knows the best ob-gyn in the city. And we should get you one of those blood pressure machines, just so we can keep tabs on it at home, right? We can do that."

She gently put a hand on his arm. "Right now, all I have to do is go about life as normal. This isn't something that develops this early in pregnancy, it comes later."

"Oh, you're not going about life as normal!" he'd said. "We're getting you a cooking service, and a maid, and you are not moving off the couch for the next nine months!"

She'd laughed then, but the look in his eyes said he was at least half-serious.

"And maybe you should move into my place—it's bigger, you'll have more space."

"Yes, but you're never there," Sophia said, reeling a little bit. "And you share it with the band." She'd never even considered giving up her little apartment. It was her home. Her and Maisey's.

"That's just more people to take care of you. And I'll make sure I'm here more often. I'll cancel our spring tour dates if I have to!"

"I still have Maisey."

"Oh," he said, calming. "Right."

Eventually, Sophia talked him down a little, and allowed him to go online and research home blood pressure machines. Men, in Sophia's limited experience, were never really good at the "wait and see" parts of life. They always wanted to be doing. And if a blood pressure machine made him feel like he had some control over the situation, it was the very least she could do for him.

Even now, as they stood in the bar/bowling alley, the music pumping and the atmosphere festive as they laced up tacky bowling shoes at the *Fargone* Season 3 Holiday Party, she could sense that Sebastian's mind wasn't on trying to beat her 150 bowling average, nor was it on the *Fargone* signature cocktail, or the fact that they were currently playing his least favorite album over the loudspeakers, Bowie's *Ziggy Stardust* (who didn't like Ziggy? she often wondered, but never said). No, Sebastian's mind was on her. And making sure she was okay.

"You didn't tell Vanessa yet, did you?" he asked in a low whisper as he selected a neon-green bowling ball from the rack. His fingers too slim for the holes, he moved to an electric-blue one.

"No," Sophia whispered back. Why was that a concern? "Did you?"

"Didn't tell me what?" Vanessa's bright voice came from behind them.

Sophia spun around so quickly that she almost dropped the purple bowling ball she had chosen on her foot. As it was, she dropped it on the floor, causing a loud *thud* and everyone in a twenty-foot radius to stare at her.

"Babe, be careful," Sebastian said, bending to pick up the ball.

"Seriously." Vanessa laughed. "I know a Golden Globe nom is shocking, but nothing to break your toes over! Besides, I'm going to need you on your feet."

"A Golden Globe nom is not a surprise!" Sophia said with a big bright smile on her face. "At least not to me. You were amazing in that movie. Congratulations!"

Vanessa squeezed Sophia hard, and Sophia prayed that Sebastian wouldn't try to stop her enthusiastic hug.

"Why do you need my toes intact?" Sophia asked when they finally pulled away.

"Because I'm going to need someone to do makeup for awards season! I've already cleared it with the studio publicity department," Vanessa cried, her eyes bright and shining. Maybe Kip was right—maybe she was only high on the congratulations. But given the size of her pupils she could easily be high on something else. But Sophia couldn't think about that—because her jaw had dropped at what Vanessa had said.

"Of *course* I'll do your makeup! I'd be honored!"

Yes, she'd gotten her start doing makeup for ladies-who-lunched, but awards season was different. It was international—your work would be seen (and hopefully it would be done so flawlessly it would go unnoticed) by tens of millions of people when it ended up in glossy magazines. It was an entirely new market, and it was a lucrative one.

With a kid about to go into college and another one on the way, money would never go out of style.

"Excellent, I'll put you in touch with the publicity department, you'll need to coordinate with the stylist and—"

"Hey, Nessa, hold on a sec," Sebastian said, interrupting their planning. Then, he pulled Sophia aside and said in a quiet undertone, "Babe—are you sure you should do this?"

"Why shouldn't I?"

"The stress of it," he said. "I've been to a couple of these awards things and they're just madness."

"It's fine. I can absolutely handle it," Sophia said. Honestly, his overprotectiveness was endearing, but tonight, it was getting a little thick. "It won't be any different than being on set, seriously."

"Of course she can handle it, Bass," Vanessa said, using Sebastian's nickname in the band. "Why wouldn't she?"

"Because . . ." Sebastian started, then hesitated.

Sophia bit her lip, and did what Sebastian couldn't.

"Because I'm pregnant," she said. "And Sebastian thinks I can't grow a baby and do your makeup at the same time."

Vanessa's eyes, already wide, seemed to jump out of her head. "You're . . . oh! Oh wow!"

"Thanks," Sebastian said, slinging his arm over Sophia's shoulder, and pulling Vanessa into an awkward three-way hug with his other arm. "You know it's all due to you, right?"

Vanessa gently extracted herself. A second later, the smile on her face became exuberant. "Well, I guess we both have things to celebrate then, don't we?"

Relief washed over Sophia. She'd been oddly worried about telling Vanessa—more so than telling the executive producers, her bosses. But of course Vanessa would be supportive. She'd set up Sebastian and Sophia, for goodness' sake. And obviously she could see how happy they were.

"And I will happily do your makeup for awards season, Vanessa—I'm honored you want me to."

"Hmm," Vanessa purred in agreement. Then, she pulled on Sebastian's arm. "Oh my God, I almost forgot—there's karaoke! And you know what you said about always being my karaoke buddy!"

As Sebastian let himself get pulled away, he sent Sophia a shrug of "you gotta do what you gotta do." She gave a rueful smile and waved him off. Let him karaoke with her blessing. But then, she looked down at her shoes, at the purple bowling ball in her hands. She'd lost her bowling partner.

No worries, she thought, rolling her shoulders back. Time to find Kip. There was always a bowling partner in the wings when you needed one.

IT WAS NEARLY midnight by the time Sophia and Sebastian got back to Sophia's apartment.

And oddly, they hadn't spoken the entire Uber ride home.

Until they walked through the door.

"You didn't have to do that, you know," Sebastian said.

"Do what?" she replied, bewildered. She was tired, sleepy, her feet hurt after those pinching bowling shoes and Kip made her go for a third round to break their tie. She was hoping for a nice shoulder rub on the couch before she guided Sebastian to bed, but instead, he was lurking in the doorway.

"Say I didn't think you could do two things at once," he said. "To Vanessa. That wasn't fair, babe. She mocked me all night for that."

"I'm sorry," Sophia said immediately. "I didn't realize that hurt you. But I can do things. I'm not on bed rest. In fact, it's better if I do continue to be active."

"I know . . ." Sebastian ran that hand through his hair again, a gesture that made him look vexed and vulnerable all at once. "I just hate when she teases, man. I don't need that. And, of course . . . I just care about you. I care about you so much."

Sophia wrapped her arms around her chest, pressed her head into his jacket. She knew he cared about her. She knew he loved her—even if those words weren't the ones he used. It was all so difficult to navigate, this new place they found themselves. They'd been going about their relationship like crazy kids. Now, they suddenly had to grow up.

But, they could still be a little crazy.

"Come inside," she purred, letting her eyes become hooded and coy. "I borrowed a little something from the wardrobe department I think you'll enjoy."

But Sebastian didn't respond with his usual eyebrow waggle and display of libido. Instead he pulled back. "I've got an early day tomorrow, babe."

"Oh. So . . . you're not staying?"

"Wish I could. And wish I could see that thing from wardrobe." He leaned down and gave her a kiss—a kiss she felt zing through her body, straight to her toes. It was the kind of kiss that made her fall for Sebastian in the first place . . . and made her really, really wish he didn't have an early day tomorrow.

"The thing from wardrobe can wait until Baja," she said, once she could find her voice again.

"Yeah," Sebastian replied, letting her go. "Baja—are you sure you still want to go? With the—"

"I think a stress-free Mexican vacation is exactly what I want."

"Alright then." He gave his media-trained smile. He reached out and bopped the tip of his finger against her nose. "Sleep well."

And he slunk off into the night, whistling as he walked down the block.

"Did you have to let him shove his tongue down your throat, for like, twenty minutes?" Maisey's voice came from behind her. Sophia whirled around. Her daughter was leaning against the living room door frame, her arms crossed in front of her, defiant.

"You didn't have to watch," Sophia replied.

"No, but the whole neighborhood did," Maisey countered as she walked over and shut the door behind her mother.

Sophia reached out to her daughter for a side-arm hug. "One day, sweetie, you are going to know what a kiss like that feels like, and then, you can tell me how much you care about the neighbors seeing."

But Maisey shrugged out of her mom's embrace. And something—her demeanor, how pale she was, the fact that she hadn't smiled—turned off Sophia's lust-brain and kick-started her mom-brain.

"What's wrong?"

"Nothing," her daughter said, walking back to the kitchen. "Just doing some stuff."

Sophia followed her, and was immediately hit by the smell of "burnt" pervading the kitchen.

"Oh God, what did you make?"

"Make?" Maisey said innocently. Too innocently. "Nothing."

"Kid, the kitchen window is open. In December. You're obviously airing out the place."

"I didn't make anything. It's no big deal."

Maisey settled in at the table, piles of papers spread out in front of her. Judiciously ignoring her mother.

"You can't have schoolwork—today was the last day before Christmas break."

"It's not schoolwork." Head down. Scribble, scribble, scribble.

Uh-huh. Mom-alarms going off in seven different directions.

But Sophia knew better than to pry—at least, not directly. Instead, she let Maisey keep her diligent focus on her papers, and followed her nose to the source of that burnt smell . . . which turned out to be the trash can.

She expected a burnt lasagna. Or a cake experiment gone awry (Maisey had lately tried baking as a soothing pastime/distraction). Hell, she would have even taken a smoldering cigarette.

She was not prepared for the tattered shards of a cardinal-red T-shirt. With a big, blocky *S* in the center.

It was the shirt they had bought in the Stanford student center when they drove up over summer break to take the college tour. They had hit a few other schools on the way—Caltech, Pepperdine, UC Berkeley, a detour to UC Davis—

and of course, Maisey was familiar with the USC and UCLA campuses already, having been born and raised in Los Angeles. But the moment they had stepped onto the Stanford campus, Maisey's entire being changed. She became excited instead of contemplative. She'd asked a thousand questions of their poor sophomore tour guide, when she usually restricted herself to a hundred. It was like with every step, her feet were taking root in the fertile ground where she would grow.

And now the T-shirt was half burnt, in the trash.

"Maisey . . ." Sophia said, gingerly fishing the T-shirt out of the trash. "What happened?"

A huff and a sigh. Still she scribbled. "My T-shirt caught fire."

"On what?"

"On my Stanford rejection letter."

Cold disappointment shot through Sophia's chest, followed quickly by the heat of anguish for her daughter.

"Oh, sweetie. I'm so sorry."

"It's fine," Maisey said, brushing off her mom's embrace, still refusing to look anywhere other than her papers.

"It's not fine. That's your dream school."

"Yeah, well, they didn't want me. Obviously." Maisey kept her eyes on the page, but her voice quavered. Sophia had to resist the urge to throw her arms around her daughter again. "I have to work on these other school applications."

"Not right now you don't," Sophia replied. "Come on. Let's find some chocolate, and a bad movie featuring gory death, and we can pretend every time someone dies it's the Stanford admissions person."

"No. I'm good."

"Oh! Or better yet, I'll call Sebastian," Sophia said, whipping out her phone. "He can grab us some of those amazing macarons—I think the bakery's open? It's only . . . crap, it's midnight . . ."

"NO, MOM." The words were like cannons in the air. Booming and definite. Sophia froze with her finger on the Send button.

A rush of air left Maisey's body. Like she was too tired, too vulnerable to keep up the pretense. Then, she straightened her shoulders, gathered her papers.

"I'll keep working on these in my room."

"Maisey, you don't have to do everything right now. Let's just . . . talk, okay?"

But Maisey gave a firm shake of her head as she brushed past her mother.

"Dad's coming to get me tomorrow early to drive down to his parents. So if I don't see you when I get up . . . have a good time in Baja."

"I'll be up," Sophia said, quietly. "You'll need pancakes—your dad will forget to feed you, I'd lay money on it."

Maisey gave a half smile, turned to meet her mom's eyes for the first time since Sophia had gotten home.

"Sure, but if not—I'll make him stop at a diner on the way. I know how to feed myself now."

"Of course you do."

"And you know . . . have a good Christmas."

And with that, Maisey shut her door, and left Sophia alone, in the middle of the silent kitchen, knowing that at some point in the last seventeen years, she had lost the right to burst into her daughter's room and hug her, just to try and make everything better.

CHAPTER 9

 "OH MY GOD! IT'S LITTLE NATHALIE! YOU look amazing!" squealed the older woman who opened the door. "How are you feeling?"

Two days after Christmas, the holiday decorations in Dad and Kathy's condo were gone, replaced by a myriad of pink and blue streamers, pink and blue balloons, pink and blue table decorations, pink and blue foods, pink and blue EV-ERYTHING.

Nathalie stepped into the living room, noting that at least the tree was still up . . . but its usual decorations were gone, and it was now covered in pink and blue ornaments.

Where on earth did Kathy get all of those pink and blue ornaments?

This could only mean one thing: someone had shown Kathy the internet.

"Wow," David said, a step behind Nathalie, as he hung up his cell. "This is . . . surreal."

"And this must be Daddy-to-be!" the older woman said. She wore her hair in the hard shell of a bouffant that reminded Nathalie strongly of her eighth-grade French teacher.

"I'm Cecily—or Madame Craig, as Nathalie called me in eighth grade," the woman trilled.

Ah. That explained that.

"Of course, now, I'm in her stepmama's book club, and we were just so thrilled when we heard your news! And your sister's! Family is the most amazing thing!"

Nathalie was still staring at the room, so David stepped up, pasted his "I'm a genial lawyer" smile on his face, and held out his hand. "David. And yes, Daddy-to-be."

"Call me Cecily," she simpered, melting under David's smile.

Madame Craig—Nathalie would never be able to think of her as Cecily—took their coats, and exclaimed as she assessed Nathalie's body. "Well, you're hardly showing at all!" She put out her hand and Nathalie thought she was trying to shake her own . . . but then the hand landed on her stomach. "Just a little pooch! Lucky you! One would think it's just holiday weight!"

Nathalie was slowly getting used to people knowing about her pregnancy. She had told her department head at the school, and was heartily congratulated right before she was given a timetable for scheduling a sub for the last few weeks of school (her due date at the end of May meant that she would be abandoning her students a hair before the end of the year, and a lot of sub lesson planning for herself beforehand).

Word made it around her department before she could believe it, and she was congratulated and hugged by people she'd worked with for several years who she'd barely ever shaken hands with. Everyone got very touchy when you were pregnant.

But this was the first time that someone had actually reached out and touched her stomach.

It was a bit of a shock to have your abdomen felt up by your eighth-grade French teacher. Even David seemed kind of stunned by it. He took a step forward, and half stood in front of Nathalie, shielding her from Madame Craig.

And she did *not* have a pooch! She was currently only eighteen weeks along . . . and granted her pants were getting tighter, but they still buttoned.

Kinda.

In truth, she was spending more and more time in her yoga pants. She'd even preliminarily perused the maternity section of Target while shopping for Christmas decorations, knowing that the time was going to come that she would have to invest in some work appropriate clothes with stretchy parts.

The maternity section kind of shocked her, actually. Usually, she averted her eyes when she went past, blinkered by never needing that section before. But now, she was drawn to it like a moth to a flame.

First, she was pleasantly surprised. The muumuus she'd feared were not in attendance. Instead there were stretchy sweaters, tailored shirts . . . the kind of things she would definitely be comfortable teaching in. Except . . .

Everything came in stripes. Horizontal stripes.

Now, Nathalie was not a fashionista by any means, but she'd lived with boobs and hips long enough to have ingrained upon her one of the central tenets of fashion: horizontal stripes are for teeny tiny skinny models and the occasional prisoner. For the rest of the masses, especially those with even a modicum of width anywhere on their bodies, horizontal stripes were verboten.

But now that a widening was expected and even encouraged, she guessed everyone was expected to gorge themselves on horizontal stripes for once in their lives. Might as well show it off, right?

She told David this when she got home, arms laden with strings of lights and garlands, but he was once again killing aliens on Xbox and barely noticed.

It was becoming a constant that if David wasn't on his phone dealing with overseas billing issues, he was on the Xbox, trying to destroy creatures from a hostile blue civilization. In fact, he'd basically had his phone glued to his ear ever since he supposedly got off from work the Friday before Christmas.

Since it was their first Christmas in their new house, Nathalie had wanted to do it right. She'd bought her outside lights from Target, and was all set to hang them, until David pointed out they didn't have an external outlet. They'd have to run an extension cord through an open window, and given that their neighborhood wasn't the best and that it actually got cold in the winter, he wasn't willing to do that. Garlands would have to suffice for the outside.

But inside the house, she went nuts. She got her tree up, decorated, tinseled (she figured tinsel would be out for the next several Christmases, as it was a likely baby-will-try-to-eat item), bought wreaths for every door, inside and out, and put out her mother's collection of nutcrackers in prominent locations.

David had said the place looked like an elf vomitorium.

David hadn't really been in the Christmas spirit. The foreign deal he was working on was dragging on with detail after detail having to be rehammered out every time someone found a typo. He was moody, and distant, but Nathalie knew that once she gave him his gift, all the tired would melt off of him.

Christmas Day, they'd spent the morning at home, in their pajamas. David even left his phone on its charger next to the bed while they traded presents and drank hot cocoa, enjoying their few hours before they had to drive the two hours north to Santa Barbara to have Christmas lunch with Nathalie's dad and Kathy. It was the most blissful Nathalie had felt in a long time, the most at peace, and the most connected. After she finished opening her gift from David's mom, Dr. Russo-Chen (socks, as per usual. This time with purple polka dots. Which, given the polka dots on David's new pajama pants, must be all the rage in Italy), Nathalie handed David the envelope with her present in it to him.

He opened it . . . and his face fell.

"Monterey?"

"Three days, after Christmas." She nodded eagerly. "We can leave right from the gender reveal party at my dad's place. Your office is closed that week. And we never got to have the Monterey experience last time, so I say let's go see some seaside cliffs. Just us."

"I don't . . ." David stopped and started again. "Can you get the deposit back?"

The whole of Nathalie's body froze.

"I can't go back to Monterey."

Nathalie's face fell. "You can't?"

". . . because of work. I was just told on Friday. They, the foreign company we're buying—the deal needs to be finalized before the start of the new fiscal term."

"And the new fiscal term starts . . ."

"January first. Next week."

"Oh." It was all she could manage to say. "And you can't make overseas phone calls from Monterey."

David looked back down at the envelope. The carefully

crafted card, the printout of their itinerary (she'd spent hours agonizing over the font choices), the pamphlet from the resort where they'd be staying. It was meant to be more than a getaway, a stress reducer for David. It was meant to be a babymoon for them—a way to get back to what was important.

"I'm sorry, hon," he said, and to his credit, it truly sounded like he was. "If I help make this deal, it will be really good for us."

"Yeah, okay." Nathalie shook her head. "I don't know about the deposit, but I'll try."

The rest of the day had been subdued, to say the least. Nathalie was almost glad when they came into Kathy's kitchen later that afternoon to be feted and fed and exchange presents.

Kathy's inane chattering kept everyone—Dad, Marcus, David, Lyndi, and Nathalie—from having to talk about anything substantial. And during the drive home that night, Nathalie could claim exhaustion, and avoid bringing up her disappointment about their trip.

And now, two days later, they had taken the drive up to Santa Barbara again, with David on the phone the whole time. By this time, her feelings about the Monterey trip had morphed from disappointed to rationalized. There was no point in being wistful for what she couldn't have. David was obviously working very hard. And hey, she'd gotten half the security deposit back.

She was lucky that he'd been able to come to the gender reveal party, she told herself. He hadn't intended to—too much to do, his paralegal was out of town and time was ticking down—but Nathalie put her foot down.

"We are finding out the gender of our child, via cake,"

she'd said in her best Don't-Mess-with-Teacher voice. "You are coming."

No one, not even David, could deny the Don't-Mess-with-Teacher voice.

However, it didn't seem to work on other teachers, or if it did, Madame Craig would have recognized it when Nathalie said, "Please don't do that," regarding the French teacher's presumptuous physical exam.

But Madame Craig didn't seem to notice that she had overstepped by molesting her former student. Instead, she turned and called out to the room, "Kathy! They're here!"

A parting of the book club seas, and Kathy emerged.

"Finally!" Kathy said, elbowing past other guests to come embrace Nathalie and David. "I was afraid you'd forgotten where we lived!"

"We were here two days ago," Nathalie deadpanned.

"Then there's no reason for you to be so late!" Kathy replied. "Your sister made the right decision, staying with us the past few days. That way she wouldn't miss a thing!"

Nathalie's eyes narrowed. "We're not late—you said eleven, it's eleven oh sev—"

"My fault," David said, again putting his body between Nathalie and a late-middle aged woman. "I got stuck on a work call."

Kathy's brittle smile turned aghast. "Working? Through the holidays? Oh, David, you certainly are dedicated."

"I know," David said, shaking his head. "It's my curse."

"It sure is," Nathalie said, forcing a smile.

"Oh but look at you! I told you to dress like the guest of honor, and you're wearing that?"

Nathalie looked down. "This is my best dress." Of the

ones that still fit, anyway. It was a loose green sheath made of stretchy fabric that looked amazing with tights and boots and a belt. She had just left off the belt, for possible pooch-related reasons. In fact, the dress was cut so well, it might last her the whole pregnancy.

"Guest of *honor*, Nathalie. Did you not have anything in pink and blue?"

"No," Nathalie said, through gritted teeth. "I guess not."

"I swear you're almost as bad as your sister." Kathy shook her head. "But luckily I got to take her shopping. Now, we're going to do the big reveal at noon."

"The big reveal?" David asked. "You mean cutting the cake. Finding out what color is on the inside?"

"Oh, don't get me started on the reveal. I wanted to do these adorable smoke bombs in the condo complex's courtyard, but the association nixed it. Then I wanted to do a big balloon release, but this one committee member—Frances Watson, horrible—was concerned about the balloon scraps choking seagulls. Seagulls, honestly. Like we need more of those.

"So yes, we are cutting cakes, but . . . we also have something special planned!" Kathy declared, clapping along with every word like a preschooler who was about to get cake.

To be fair, they were all about to get cake.

"And there's your sister! Doesn't she look amazing?" Kathy said, practically skipping the three steps to where Lyndi was clasped tight to Marcus's side.

Nathalie had to admit, Lyndi did look amazing. She had the glow of pregnancy without the waistline of it. She wore a pink flowy minidress with a blue vest over it, discreet gold jewelry, and her hair in milkmaid braids. She looked like she was about to attend Coachella, not her own gender reveal party.

She glanced down at Lyndi's hands. Good lord, she'd even had her manicure done in pink and blue, with gold accents.

Suddenly Nathalie's green dress and boots didn't seem so fashionable anymore.

"Oh, I absolutely adore this outfit! And I'm so glad we got matching manicures. It was such a fun day. Nathalie, you should have been there."

Lyndi gave a shy smile. "I'm just glad the dress is loose so it will fit me for a while."

"Oh, honey, with your figure, that dress will last through the pregnancy and beyond. And besides, you're young enough that your body will bounce back so easily after the baby comes. You watch."

Lyndi blushed. Meanwhile, Nathalie felt her pooch growing by the minute.

"And don't worry, I'll take you shopping again for more maternity clothes when the time comes," Kathy said, her eyes sparkling as she patted a stray hair back into place on Lyndi's braids.

"Mom, you don't have to—"

"Nonsense, like I would allow my baby and her baby to ever want for anything!" Kathy trilled, turning to face everyone else. Then her eyes caught something else. "Cecily! What are you doing? The blue deviled eggs are meant to go on the pink platter and vice versa!"

As Kathy moved away, the burn in Nathalie's throat—from holding her tongue, not from heartburn—subsided. She turned to face Lyndi and Marcus.

And couldn't think of a damn thing to say.

"Marcus, how's it going?" David extended his hand.

"Oh, you know—same as two days ago, just . . . pinker,"

Marcus replied, indicating the paper pompom that was directly above his head.

"Indeed. I assume you and Lyndi's dad got roped into putting all the decorations up?" Marcus nodded with chagrin. David held up his left thumb. "I got this scar my second Christmas with Nat. Kathy made me get all her holiday shopping out of the car and then closed the trunk on my hand. Welcome to the family. We have hats."

As Marcus laughed, so did Nathalie and Lyndi. It was times like this that she remembered just how much easier David made everything. He made parties easier, he made family easier. When she was clueless about what to say or how to act, he was her constant steadfast force.

She leaned into him, grateful. He squeezed her shoulder.

Then, his phone rang.

He glanced at it. "Sorry, hon, I have to take this."

"No problem, I get it." Nathalie nodded. Once he was gone, she turned to Lyndi and Marcus. "He's got a lot of work."

They nodded in time. Then, from across the room, Kathy's voice rang out. "Marcus, can you come help Cecily? Show her how you made these perfect cauliflower florets! Marcus is very *creative*, Cecily."

Marcus shrugged as he moved away, leaving Lyndi and Nathalie by themselves.

They hadn't been able to get a word in edgewise Christmas afternoon, so this was their first real chance to talk, face-to-face, since Thanksgiving.

Now all they had to do was actually talk.

"How do you think Kathy made pink and blue deviled eggs?" Nathalie finally said.

"Blue and pink chickens, duh," Lyndi replied, earning a

look of scorn, followed by the crack of a smile. "Hey—that lady Marcus is with . . . is that Madame Craig?"

"Yes—she's in Kathy's book club. Did she feel up your stomach?"

"No . . . oh my God did she feel up yours?"

Nathalie nodded gravely.

"Are people just going to do that?"

Nathalie shrugged. "Maybe not to you. Your stomach's still flat as a gluten-free pancake."

"Not it's not," Lyndi said, looking down. "Dr. Keen said I'd already gained five pounds."

"Right, how did your appointment go?"

"Great!" Lyndi said brightly. "Very thorough, like you said. Got my bloodwork done that day. And . . . Marcus and I got to see the baby. It was amazing."

The thrill of seeing the first ultrasound danced in her sister's eyes. Nathalie understood that thrill, and she was so happy she got to do her small part in providing it. "Well then," she said, "you're welcome."

Lyndi cocked her head to the side. "What's that supposed to mean?"

"Just, you know . . . for the introduction."

Not just an introduction. She'd *made* the damn appointment for Lyndi. Got her sister—and her little niece or nephew—the medical supervision that was so clearly needed.

"Right," Lyndi said, shaking her head as she pulled out her phone. Her face fell as she read a text.

"What is it?"

"Nothing—just, Elizabeth can't make it."

"That sucks," Nathalie said sympathetically.

"Yeah, she says she has to work."

She glanced over to where David was on the patio, still talking on his phone. "There seems to be a lot of that going around. But at least you've got the rest of the Vowel Brigade coming, right? Olivia and Allison?"

But Lyndi shook her head. "They . . . also have work."

"Right," Nathalie said, awkwardly. "Well, this is mostly Kathy's friends. Who do we still know that lives in Santa Barbara anyway?"

"Well, you know a couple at least."

Nathalie's head swiveled to where Lyndi was looking. At the door, two younger women (well, younger than the book club crowd) were having their coats taken by Madame Craig.

A grin broke out over Nathalie's face as they saw her. "Vicki! Kelly!"

They waved and broke their way through the crowd. The squealing was incessant and immediately lifted her spirits.

"I didn't know you guys were coming!" Nathalie said. "I haven't seen you in forever!"

"Not since—"

"Brunch! With those—"

"Mimosas!" All three of them chimed together.

"Well, that's the bummer of having kids," Kelly replied, as she pushed Vicki aside to give Nathalie a squeeze. Kelly was the shortest of them all but she was also the strongest, having been a dancer for years and a mother for half a decade. "I haven't left the house without someone small clinging to me in four years."

"I told Ron as soon as we got the invite," Vicki chimed in, "that he was taking Luke on a boys' day out and I was going to a party and I dared him to tell me otherwise." Vicki's face split into a wide smile, showing off the Lauren Hutton gap in her teeth that Nathalie had always found mesmerizing. "Oh, we are soooooo happy for you! It's about time you joined the Mom Club!"

Nathalie let the warm glow of their congratulations settle over her.

"Lynds, you remember my best friends from high sch—Lynds?"

But Lyndi had moved away, and was currently being chatted up and petted by some of Kathy's friends.

"You're right to do it younger," one of the ladies was saying to Lyndi. "You'll still be young enough to have a life when they leave the house!"

"I know—that's certainly one upside," Lyndi replied politely.

"These girls," the lady sighed, her eyes glancing in Nathalie's direction, "waiting and waiting these days . . ."

Nathalie's eyes narrowed; she gritted her teeth. She knew exactly what that was—a dig at anyone who had the audacity to have a child over the age of thirty . . . regardless of how long it had taken them to get there.

She turned resolutely back to *her* friends.

"Your sister is pregnant too, right?" Vicki said in low, conspiratorial tones. "That must be . . . interesting."

It was on the tip of Nathalie's tongue to say "It sure is." But for some reason, she couldn't fall back into catty high school patterns. As much as she wanted to bemoan Lyndi's overt fertility, she wouldn't do that. At least, not without a couple of mimosas, and she wasn't about to have one of those.

Plus, the way Lyndi's head stilled, she wondered if she could hear them.

"Kathy's over the moon about it," Nathalie said instead.

"Hmm." Vicki's lips pressed together. She looked like she

was about to say something, but then Kelly bounced into the fray and took Nathalie by the arm.

"Come on, let's get some pink and blue grub—and those pink and blue cocktails—and you can fill us in on all things LA."

As Vicki took her other arm, she asked, "So . . . how are you feeling?"

Nathalie was feeling fine—as she told them. As she told everyone.

Strangely, no one seemed to believe her.

"Really? No swelling?" Vicki said, a blue-and-pink cocktail in hand, as they settled onto the recently unoccupied couch. "God, I remember I was so bloated with Luke, I looked like I'd died in the bathtub and they found my body three days later."

"Ugh, the weirdest for me was the carpal tunnel," Kelly chimed in. "Had it with both kids. I would be working and suddenly my hands would just go completely numb."

"I remember you telling me about that." Vicki laughed. "I said we'd get you one of those beer drinking hats so you didn't have to worry about dropping your mocktinis."

"Well, I did have morning sickness . . ." Nathalie began, but Vicki shook her head.

"Everyone has that."

"I didn't!" Kelly piped up.

"Wait till you get to the truly weird stuff. The restless leg syndrome. The way your skin changes. Your gums will bleed. The stuffed-up nose and the snoring. The gas. Oh my goodness—the gas!" Vicki laughed loudly, causing heads to turn.

"Basically, anything that can leak out of you, will leak out of you," Kelly added, sage wisdom permeating every word.

Suddenly, one of the older women hovering near the couch turned to them. "My worst was in the eighth month—my Jeremy started sitting on my sciatic nerve. I could barely get off the couch the last month of pregnancy!"

"Ohhh, my first pregnancy, my little girl got her foot stuck up under my ribs. I haven't felt pain like that since."

"I just remember drooling all the time. My husband said it was like I was a Great Dane," another book club member said.

"My hormones were so all over the place. I broke down in tears over conjugating verbs." This from Madame Craig.

Then, Kathy found her way into the group. "I had edema so badly with Lyndi. My feet and hands were swollen—the worst was my genitals. It was like trying to walk with a water balloon between my legs!"

Everyone laughed. Everyone that is, except Nathalie. Instead, her head spun.

Aside from the forced imagery of Kathy's swollen genitals—dear God, that was something she could have gone several lifetimes without knowing—the sheer list of potential symptoms always made her a little queasy.

She'd read them before, in her research. But that didn't help prepare Nathalie for what was to come . . . because she didn't know *which* ones were to come.

"Excuse me for a second, ladies," she said, standing.

"Have to pee?" Vicki said knowingly. "That's just going to get worse, too."

Nathalie walked away from the group, and headed for the bathroom, but ended up loitering in the empty hall, taking a moment to breathe.

If she knew what to specifically expect symptom-wise, she could make a plan. Was she going to get leg cramps at night?

If so, she'd be prepared with a body pillow. Was she going to have swollen feet? Then, she'd have old lady orthopedic shoes in her Amazon cart today. Stuffy nose? Saline spray. Etc. so on and so forth.

But she didn't know the likelihood of her getting any or all of these symptoms. And as she passed the mantel, she saw the picture of the only person who could have given her a clue.

Her mom.

In the picture, Nathalie's mother looked about Nathalie's age now, in her early thirties. . . young and bright and full of energy. She had her arms around Nathalie, who was about five. They were standing in front of Sleeping Beauty's Castle in Disneyland, Nathalie grinning so much because she'd already had a candy apple and was riding a sugar high. She knew she was trying to escape her mother's embrace in the picture, trying to go running off to see something, ANYTHING, because they were at Disney so why waste time taking photos?

Nathalie loved this picture. It was one of the few concrete memories she had of "before." Her mother's dark hair hung long down her back. She had a tan and a healthy amount of flesh on her body. Too many of Nathalie's memories of her mother were of someone tired, and skeletal, and in pain.

This was the one picture in the house of Nathalie's mom. She didn't blame her dad for this. She didn't even really blame the move from the house they grew up in to the 1500-square-foot smaller condo. They'd been slowly disappearing long before that, replaced by ones of Kathy, Lyndi, and a growing Nathalie as time went on.

This picture used to be in Nathalie's room growing up. But for some reason, she didn't take it with her to college. When she got home for break, and discovered her room had been converted into a sewing room/yoga relaxation lounge, she was panicked until she discovered the picture on her dad's desk in his office.

This one, it seemed, he wouldn't let go of.

"Hey, kiddo," she heard from behind her. "You hiding out, too?"

She turned to find her father's head sticking out of the den. He held his fingers up to his lips, as if to keep his presence in his own home a secret.

"Hey, Dad," she said. "I was wondering where you were. You aren't into all the pink and blue?"

"It's a little over the top, I know, but Kathy was so excited for you girls," her father said with a shrug as she walked through the door and into the den. The door slid shut. "I figured I'd let her have her fun and I could watch a bowl game in here."

"So you're okay not knowing the sex of your grandchildren?" she said, muting the TV. "How could you possibly live with the suspense?"

"Oh, I'll come out for the cake cutting. But when Kathy's book club is over I find it easiest to . . . stay out of the way."

"Understandable."

"So we didn't really get a chance to talk on Christmas." He threw an arm around her shoulder. "But just want to make sure you're doing okay. How you holding up?"

"How you holding up" was the Dad equivalent of "how are you feeling," she guessed.

"Fine. You know. Morning sickness pretty much gone."

"And David—how's he doing with it all?"

"Great!" she replied, a little taken aback. "Great—he's just stuck on a big project at work right now, but that will be over soon."

And things will get back to normal—at least, that was what she hoped.

"Good. I remember when your mom was pregnant with you. I spent the first couple months certain that I couldn't handle the gig. Pretty much panicking over every little thing."

"You handled the gig just fine, Dad," Nathalie replied softly.

"I was better when Lyndi came around. I figured you were doing all right, I couldn't be that terrible."

"Not one bit. Is Lyndi holding up okay, too?" she asked, cautiously. "In your opinion?"

"I wouldn't worry about your sister," her dad said. "Kathy and I won't let her stumble."

Right. Because, Kathy and Dad would always catch Lyndi when she fell. She'd never had to worry about anything in her whole life.

But rather than give in to the pettiness of her thoughts, inspiration struck. A question she had meant to ask long ago, but only now found the opportunity. "Actually . . . I was wondering something. What do you remember about Mom being pregnant with me?"

"Other than my ongoing panic, you mean?"

"I mean, did she have any specific symptoms? Did I come early, or late, or were there complications? How did she prepare for all the changes?"

Her dad frowned, looked away. Then, after a moment . . . "When it came to stuff like that, your mother was a pretty private person. She didn't complain about things, she would just . . . deal with them. I don't know if you remember when she got sick, but—"

Nathalie looked down to her toes, determined not to let

the shine in her eyes give her away. "I remember. I know what you mean."

"I'm sorry, kiddo. But I can tell you your mom was so happy to be pregnant. That I do remember. And I was just so relieved when you came out with twelve fingers and toes. We just had the extra ones removed."

"Ha ha," she deadpanned. Then . . . "You're kidding right? I know you're kidding."

He smirked, but before he could give an answer, the door to the den slid open, and Kathy burst through. "There you are! Nathalie, it's almost noon! Time for the big reveal!"

"Of course, I'll be right th—"

But before she could finish the sentence, Kathy's perfectly blue-and-pink-manicured hand grabbed Nathalie's, and dragged her out of the den.

"Okay, okay, I'm coming! Kathy, the cake is just sitting there, right? It's not like it's got an appointment after this and needs to be cut exactly at noon."

Kathy rolled her eyes. "Honestly, I don't understand your humor sometimes. No, the cake is not on a timer. But the glitter balloons are."

"The glitter balloons?" This from Lyndi, who appeared at Nathalie's side. Marcus slid in right next to her.

Kathy pointed up. There, in the middle of the living room ceiling, hovering above their heads this entire time, were two large white balloons. Attached to each was a mousetrap-like contraption with a sharp, shiny needle at one end, inches way from pricking the balloons.

"Kathy asked me to set it up last night. It's synced to an app on her phone, set to go off just as you two cut into your cakes."

Marcus waved toward the refreshment table, where two plain white cakes—one marked "Lyndi and Marcus," one marked "Natalie and David" (her name spelled incorrectly, of course)—had emerged.

"No!" Kathy cried. "Cecily, the cakes are meant to go in the center! Marcus, help me!"

As Kathy stalked off to deal with the positioning of the cakes, Marcus was dragged along as if by an invisible thread.

"I don't think Marcus's Kathy-fu is very strong yet," Nathalie said, wryly.

"He's spent the last three days here, I think he's going to turn the experience into his next article for the website."

"Well, that's not good."

"Why not?"

"As evidenced by this party, Kathy has discovered the internet."

Lyndi swallowed a laugh. "He's doing really well though. I remember when you brought David home. I thought Dad was going to crush his hand with the handshake."

Nathalie's eyes slid over to where David was still talking on the phone on the balcony. He gripped the railing, his shoulders sagging. He looked tired.

"Yes, well . . . he broke Dad in, so you and Marcus have it easier." Her eyes went back to Kathy, and now her dad, who had appeared—as predicted—near the cakes. He was being roped into moving them along with Marcus.

The men in the family, all gathered around to celebrate the women.

All except one.

"But then again," she said on a sigh. "You always have it easier."

A queer look crossed Lyndi's face again. "What makes you say that?"

Uh, the fact that you got pregnant without even trying? That our parents are going to carry you and your baby? That people think you're doing this at your age for a reason? That everyone thinks you're going to be fine and nobody's worried about you being able to manage a pregnancy let alone a baby and all anyone will tell me is about how awful the next six months will be?

"No reason," she said, pasting a placid smile on her face. "This is just . . . overwhelming, that's all."

"No kidding," Lyndi agreed.

And she'd been alone in facing it. She knew none of this would have gotten to her the way it did if David hadn't spent the last hour on the phone on the balcony.

"Okay everyone! Everyone!"

"Attention, s'il vous plaît!" called out Madame Craig. Which weirdly worked. Everyone in the room quieted down.

"It's time for the cake cutting!" Kathy said, going pink under the attention from all her friends. "Marcus, the countdown please!"

Marcus looked like he had no idea if he was supposed to just count down from ten or begin a nuclear launch sequence, but before he could decide Nathalie took a step forward.

"Hold on—just let me get David."

"Nathalie, the time!" Kathy panicked, grabbing her arm. "I don't know how to stop the app for the glitter balloons!"

"It's his baby too, Kathy," she said as she wrenched her arm away and moved quickly to the balcony. Before she made her escape, she heard Marcus saying, "If you give me your phone Kathy, I'll see what I can do . . ."

It was frigid outside. Usually, the balcony afforded a thin

view between other buildings of the Santa Barbara coastline, about a mile away. But today, it was cold and gray and wind whipped through the buildings like a sea snake on a mission. But David didn't seem to feel the cold. He was too intent on what was happening on the phone.

"Yes, I agree completely with Brian," he was saying. "But I would also add that if we amortize the cost of acquisition over a decade, we can—no, that's okay, go ahead, Brian."

He turned, and noticed Nathalie for the first time.

"Hey," she said in a stage whisper. "I'm sorry to interrupt, but they are going to do the reveal now."

He held the phone to his chest, muffling the sound.

"Can it wait a couple minutes? It's already evening in China, we are almost done."

"Right, but there's a thing with glitter on a timer . . ."

David glanced up through the sliding glass doors, appearing helpless. "Okay, well, then do it without me."

Nathalie blinked. "What?"

"Do it without me, you can just . . . tell me what it is, boy or girl."

"David—it's the big reveal. Kathy threw this party for *us*. Can't you just mute the call and step inside for thirty seconds—"

"No I can't." He brought the phone back up to his ear. "I have to—yes, Brian, I'm here. Of course Mr. Lee, I know the concerns voiced by the company about amortization, but—"

"DAVID!" Nathalie said, unable to hold back. He looked down at her with such an expression of "what?" that she was momentarily shaken. He never looked at her like that. Not in almost fifteen years of being together. He wasn't even apologetic. He was just . . . annoyed.

"Fine," she said. "Just . . . fine. You do what you have to do, David. I'll go find out the sex of our child, by myself."

She turned away from him, reached for the sliding glass door, when . . .

BANG!

Inside the party, a curtain of glitter rained down on the partygoers.

Pink glitter.

Muffled squeals of delight vibrated past the glass, where Nathalie and David were on the outside looking in.

Then, the door slid open, and the noise and cheering—and glitter—reached her at full volume.

It was Vicki and Kelly, both with pink sparkles covering their hair and shoulders. They quickly pulled her inside.

"Oh, Nathalie! We are so sorry, but Marcus wasn't able to fix the app in time, and the balloons went off!" Vicki said.

"But come on, let's celebrate!" Kelly grinned, then shook out her hair. "Ugh, I have no idea how your stepmom is going to get all this glitter out of the carpet."

"Is David coming?" Vicki asked, her face flushed. It was possible she'd had more than one pink-and-blue cocktail.

Nathalie glanced back at David, who had stepped around the corner, half hiding himself for more privacy.

The coward.

"He's . . . it's okay." She shook her head. Then. "Wait . . . both balloons went off?" Nathalie asked. "But there's only one color."

"Duh!" said Kelly. "Because you're both having girls!"

A prickling sensation ran from Nathalie's scalp down her spine. "A girl," she breathed.

"Come on. Let's cut the cake—although, it's not a big surprise now, but I could use the carbs," Vicki said.

A little baby girl. With pink socks and black hair and Nathalie's green eyes. That's what they were going to have.

That was who their family would be.

But the image that came so quickly fled just as fast, when Vicki and Kelly moved ahead of her to grab slices of cake waiting on the table.

And Nathalie was left alone again, in a sea of pink glitter. Meanwhile, her eyes fell to where Lyndi stood. She was next to her cake, which was sliced up to reveal its inner pinkness. She was in the center of it all, being congratulated by everyone, Madame Craig, the book club ladies, even Vicki and Kelly.

And surrounding her, celebrating *her*, was Kathy, their dad, and Marcus—the newly minted member of the family—right there by her side.

JANUARY

SUNDAY   MONDAY   TUESDAY   WEDNESDAY   THURSDAY   FRIDAY   SATURDAY

CHAPTER 10

JANUARY MOVED LIKE A FREIGHT TRAIN, ONE that had been too long delayed and now needed to make up for lost time. Everyone seemed in a hurry. This was no doubt because most people justified holding off on doing things until "after the holidays." And now that it was "after the holidays," everyone was suddenly overwhelmed by what needed to get done.

And when you're having a baby, Nathalie thought, the amount of stuff you need to get done is exponential.

She'd made no progress on the nursery. Oh, she had cribs and changing tables and layettes and WubbaNubs bookmarked on her computer. She'd swung by the hardware store and selected a dozen or so carefully curated paint chips. But no actual decisions had been made. This was because she couldn't make these decisions without David's input.

After the debacle of the gender reveal party, David had apologized profusely for missing the big moment. He was even super excited for a little girl. He'd gotten a little misty when he was on the phone to his parents in Italy (whether or not his parents were misty, was unknown—but unlikely).

And since the Big Deal had managed to be finalized before the end of the fiscal year, David had taken a much-needed New Year's Day off. They watched football and ate popcorn and didn't clean anything.

But when Nathalie tried to bring up baby stuff later that day, David just hummed, and said, "We have time to think about it, right?"

And she said yes, sure, and they went back to watching football.

In Nathalie's estimation, "time to think about it" was a day—a couple days, tops. But apparently to David it meant weeks—or perhaps never. Because on January 2nd, David was back in the office an hour earlier than normal, and home late.

"I'm sorry, hon," he'd said, seeing the cold dinner she'd labored over (well, the dinner she'd taken out of the box and heated up—her culinary bravado had been tempered by the events of Thanksgiving). "They loved the work I did on the foreign acquisition, so they handed me a new one . . . it's smaller but I'm taking point."

He'd said it with excitement. And he deserved to be excited. It was a big deal that they gave him this kind of responsibility, considering he'd only been in-house counsel a couple months, he'd told her.

And she'd kissed him, and told him she was happy for him.

And she was left holding the paint chips a little while longer.

Honestly, it wasn't a big deal . . . but it would be, soon. Because they needed *a plan*. If she couldn't get his attention when it came to the color of the nursery, what was she supposed to do with the stuff that actually mattered—like writing a will and trust? Like how they should go about saving for the baby's college plan?

But all of this took a backseat while school started up again, and time began to speed forward for Nathalie, too. Most of her students, who had been so lackadaisical in the last few days of December, had suddenly awoken to the new calendar year with a panic. Her juniors were panicked about the SATs. Her seniors—those that had not gotten in early admission—were panicked about college applications and the impending AP exams (a mere four months away!). Their panic translated into more test prep, more after-school counseling, more student hand-holding. So much so, that even Nathalie was tired enough at the end of the day to not want to come home and discuss the baby.

But that didn't mean the baby wasn't there, and growing, and making herself known in the most, er, *audible* of ways.

This was most readily apparent during the super in-depth ultrasound, where she had to drink all the water and then hold it while a technician spent half an hour grinding a detector into her uterus, to get high-resolution photos of every conceivable part of the baby.

When the tech was done she'd peed for longer than Tom Hanks in *A League of Their Own.*

The screening went well—the baby was growing beautifully—and Nathalie was given a sleeve of pictures to take home of their little girl, Shirley. At least, Shirley was her name today. The day before it had been Madison, and tomorrow it would probably be Sarah.

Just another decision she couldn't make without David.

Yes, the screening went well . . . except for one, surprisingly loud thing.

"Oops! It's okay." The technician smiled, while she covered her nose. "Gas happens."

"I'm so sorry," Nathalie replied, beyond embarrassed.

"Seriously, don't worry about it," the technician said. "I've had worse on my table. But I'll be more gentle with the detector, okay?"

"Honestly? It's been really bad," Nathalie had replied. "I feel like a hot air balloon."

"I'm not supposed to advise you medically—I'm just an ultrasound tech," the technician replied. "But I can tell you with my pregnancy, it sorted itself out eventually. Your body's just rearranging itself to make more space. But if it's causing you pain, you should talk to your doctor."

"Thanks," she'd said. "I will."

And she did, at the next appointment.

And was given the same answer.

"It's a fun symptom," Dr. Duque said. "You could start your own section at the symphony." Which made Nathalie crack a smile. "Here are some things you can do to relieve gas . . ."

As she left Dr. Duque's office she felt marginally better, but was once again confronted by the dreaded feeling of Not Knowing.

Not knowing what else to expect. Not knowing what would likely happen, or come next.

After that appointment, Nathalie went home in a funk. And amazingly, David was there.

"Hey!" she said as she opened the door. "I didn't know you'd be here."

She shook out her umbrella as she took in the sweet, warm smell of onions cooking. January in Los Angeles meant winter—and winter in Los Angeles meant rain, if they were lucky. And this January was luckier than most.

"We sent out the paperwork this afternoon, the client

won't get it until they get into the office in the morning, so I thought I'd spend some time with my wife."

Nathalie smiled, running forward to embrace her husband. "What's that marvelous smell?"

"The one thing I found in the cupboard that I thought I could reasonably make," David answered with an irrepressible glee. "Franks and beans!"

Nathalie's smile froze on her face. Considering what by-products her intestines were currently manufacturing, franks and beans were not an ideal dinner.

But David looked so proud of himself. Like a puppy who just figured out how to fetch. So she swallowed, and kept her smile up as she said, "Great! I'll grab us drinks."

Water, she thought. Dr. Duque had prescribed lots and lots of water.

Dinner was served quickly, and they settled into the IKEA table, still with their old metal folding chairs—David had been so busy, he hadn't had time to assemble the new ones that Nathalie had finally chosen.

"Pretty soon there will be a high chair sitting right there," Nathalie said, as she took a bite of beans. And a big sip of water. "We have to start getting this place ready."

"Hm. Yeah. It's really coming down out there," David said, tilting his ear toward the dining room window. Raindrops pelleted the glass in angry fistfuls. Being a SoCal native, Nathalie loved rain like this—it was so rare, and always so, so necessary. And when it cleared, the air would be crisp and you could see the mountains clearly for miles beyond miles. But right now, she was happy to just be in her little house, safe and warm with her dinner-making husband.

Blllllllllurrrrrrffffftttt . . .

And a disturbing amount of gas, she thought as she shifted in her seat uncomfortably.

"What was that?" David asked, whipping his head back, concerned.

"Nothing!" she replied quickly. "I'm just a little . . . gassy."

"What did you eat?" he asked, doing his best to not breathe through his nose.

Nathalie felt inexplicably embarrassed. It was kind of ridiculous. She and David had been together since they were in their late teens. She'd farted in front of him before. *Millions* of times.

But for some reason, she felt the need to maintain the ladylike fiction that the pregnancy was not causing her any form of discomfort. Which was equally ridiculous, because it wasn't as if she hadn't spent her first trimester puking up breakfast every morning.

"It's not me, it's the baby," she said, defiant. There. She was going through this pregnancy, so he had to go through it, too.

"Oh," David said, a pained look crossing his face. "Is that . . . normal? Nothing's wrong, right?"

"Completely normal," she said, nodding fervently.

"Good," David said. Then, looking down at his food, "Good."

Water, Nathalie thought. More water.

"We should also talk about some stuff," Nathalie said, breaking the silence.

"Like what?"

"Like . . . what's the plan for saving for college? Do we want to put the baby under your health care or mine? Estate planning. Whether we want your parents to visit when the baby comes, and if so, where we're gonna put them. When should I go back to work—tangentially, I am planning on breast-feeding but I have no idea what kind of pump to get for when I go back to work."

He blinked twice. "Is that stuff we have to decide now?"

Yes. Her mind screamed. *Yes, let me start planning this.* "Well, not this second. But sometime in the next nineteen weeks might be good."

"Okay. We've got time then."

Time. Time tick ticking down. It was already the New Year. January speeding by, soon it would be February, then March, then . . .

"I don't get it," she finally said. "Why don't you want to talk about any of this stuff? It's important, and we need to—"

Brrrrfffffftttttt . . .

David choked on a laugh.

"I'm sorry," he said immediately. "But—" and he was laughing again, as the *brffffttttt* echoed out again.

And then, Nathalie, ruefully, was laughing with him.

After a solid minute of enjoying the giggles, David slid his folding chair over to Nathalie, the chair making its own *brffff-tttt* noise, which set them to giggling again.

"It's not that I don't want to talk," he said, once they'd calmed down. "I just didn't expect to be talking about wills and estate planning. I came home tonight to spend some time with you," David said, closing his eyes. "Because I was a shitheel at the gender party thing, and this is the first chance I've had to do anything about it."

"Okay, okay . . ." she said, holding up her hands.

"I'm sorry. I promise, we'll talk about all that stuff. To-night, even," he said, taking her hand. "But for now, let's turn down these overheads . . ."

David flicked the lights off.

"Maybe light a candle to take care of that smell . . ."

She smothered a reluctant chuckle, wrapped her arms around his waist. But he'd gone completely still.

"Oh, shit," David said, looking out the window.

"What?" Nathalie said, standing immediately and rushing to the window.

"Our driveway," David said. "It's flooded."

Nathalie squinted out the window, into their driveway. With the lights out, she could see out into what was now a bona fide *river* in their driveway.

"The pump stopped working," David said, as he rushed to put on shoes, a raincoat.

The pump, rarely employed in their desert climate, was installed at the base of their driveway next to their house. The land their home sat on was flat, and drainage was bad, so when it *did* rain, the water pooled and collected at the back door of the house, next to the driveway. The pump collected it and sent it via pipes underneath the driveway to the street, where it could flow into a gutter.

Without that pump, they basically had an aboveground pool for their backyard.

"Oh shit," David said again, as he rushed out the door and into the dark, cold wet. "Stay inside! I don't want you getting sick."

"I'll call a plumber," she said, reaching for her phone.

As she dialed the number, all thoughts of 529 plans and breastfeeding—heck, even a candlelit franks-and-beans dinner with her husband—fled her mind.

LATER THAT NIGHT, as she lay awake, unable to sleep from what the few bites of beans were doing to her intestines, Nathalie snuck out of bed and to the guest bathroom. Last second, she grabbed her phone. Seriously, who knew how long she'd be in there?

She knew she had every right to use her own en suite bathroom, but she didn't want to wake David with her . . . er, midnight musical endeavors. At the moment, it just felt like . . . like she didn't have the right to burden him with anything.

Not even flatulence.

After David had rushed out to try and adjust the pump, she'd called the emergency plumbers. Together, the guys had gotten the pump working again, and David spent a freezing cold hour shoving water with a broom down the driveway and away from the house.

When he'd finally come in, he immediately took a long hot shower to get feeling back into his extremities, and then promptly went to bed.

They didn't talk. Not about college plans, or paint chips, or even share any more jokes about Nathalie's current most persistent pregnancy symptom.

Which was fine. The last thing she wanted for David was for him to be spending his one night off in forever dealing with her questions on top of dealing with a household emergency.

But she did have questions—planning the future, about what to expect in her pregnancy . . . about all of it. And no one to talk to.

She couldn't talk to her dad, he didn't remember how her mom dealt with her symptoms. She couldn't talk to Lyndi, who no doubt was wrapped in the blissful cocoon of being completely taken care of by their parents and therefore not having to worry about a thing. Even her friends who'd had kids, like Vicki and Kelly . . . she couldn't imagine calling them up with questions about college savings plans and breastfeeding pumps.

Brrrrrfffftttt.

Or asking them anything about . . . that.

At some point in time, she knew that all pretense would fall away, and she would gladly discuss her boobs and body fluids at the top of her lungs in public places with complete strangers.

But damn it, today was not that day.

However, she would happily do it anonymously. There had to be *something* on the internet to help her deal with this particular grievance, she thought.

She pulled up the mommy forums on her phone, and typed her query into the question box.

Which yielded immediate results.

- *Don't worry! Magnesium will get things moving down there! Just don't take too much . . .*

- *Oh, the gas I had with my first . . . doing yoga helped realign my gut. My best friend teaches prenatal yoga at the Silver Lake Center . . .*

- *OMG if it's really bad go to the hospital immediately! My sister's sister-in-law's cousin had gas and it turned out to be a ballooning intestine! It almost perforated and they had to do laparoscopic surgery! Luckily she wasn't pregnant at the time, but that would just make me doubly cautious!*

Overwhelmed, she quickly shut the web browser on her phone. All of that was conflicting and absolutely none of it was helpful. Every single time she went on the mommy forums, she felt more confused than when she entered them.

Really, as a teacher, she knew the vagaries of the internet and how it could warp any argument or question. What on earth was she doing on a forum that didn't even cite sources beyond some random person's sister's sister-in-law's cousin?

She was about to shut her phone entirely, when an email notification popped up. By rote, she clicked over.

Weird. It was a Twitter notification.

Nathalie *had* Twitter. As far as she could figure, everyone had Twitter—at least, that was what Lyndi told her when she signed Nathalie up. She just didn't really *use* Twitter. She didn't tweet. She had students, and a responsibility to model correct behavior online, so basically that meant not being on social media ever (ironically, the only 100 percent foolproof method of avoiding accidental overexposure was social media abstinence). But she did maintain a Twitter handle to follow one of her favorite TV shows, *Fargone*. Every week the cast and crew would tweet out behind-the-scenes info while the episode aired, and it was a delightful additional experience. Like those old VH1 pop-up videos, but with fewer random factoids and more photos of the stars being goofy on set. The actress who played Billie was particularly delightful.

The email was one of those "People You May Know" notifications. Twitter prompting you to follow more accounts, engage with more people (and presumably, be online longer and exposed to more ads). But this time, the people she may have known were not official *Fargone* accounts, or devoted fans. This time, it was for an account called @WTFPreg.

First of all, Nathalie was vaguely weirded out that Twitter had figured out that she would be interested in something to do with pregnancy. Her posts on the mommy forums were sporadic, and unassociated with Twitter. Unless *Fargone* had a pregnancy story line she was unaware of (ooohhh!! Please let *Fargone* have a pregnancy story line!) they should have no reason to place a pregnancy Twitter feed in her path.

But, the vague weirdness subsided when curiosity got the better of her and she clicked on the link.

Then complete freak-out weirdness set in.

> @WTFPreg—I could set my house on fire from all the methane in the atmosphere. #pregnancygas

The most recent post had gone up only a few hours ago. Trepidatiously, she scrolled down the feed.

> @WTFPreg—Horizontal stripes—verboten except for the extremely vertical or extremely pregnant.

A strange tingling sensation darted through her body. Like recognizing like.

> @WTFPreg—The Peanut isn't a peanut anymore! It's more of an awkward legume. #anotherdayanotherultrasound

The peanut . . . she'd called their daughter a peanut when she saw the first ultrasound. And *she'd* noticed the uncanny amount of horizontal stripes in maternity fashion. And *she* could no doubt explode her house with the methane content it currently held!

And the very first tweet posted within a week of them finding out they were expecting . . .

> @WTFPreg—We did not expect this baby, even though we were trying for it. So obviously, we are alarmingly stupid people who should not procreate.

Holy shit. It was as if she could have posted every single one of these tweets *herself.*

But she didn't.

But that could only mean . . .

Someone, somewhere, was having the exact same pregnancy she was.

But who?

CHAPTER 11

"IT'S REALLY COMING DOWN OUT THERE, isn't it?" Vanessa said, her eyes shifting to the window.

"Look at me, Vanessa?" Sophia said gently. Vanessa's eyes automatically moved forward, then up, allowing Sophia to finely apply the smoky gray shadow along her lower lids.

"Sorry," Vanessa said, her voice a little breathy—no doubt from nerves. After all, one didn't go to the Golden Globes every day. "Today is just too important for rain! It's like I'm being punished!"

It was 3:30 in the afternoon. The Golden Globes show began at 5 PM West Coast time. The red carpet procession began around four, with massive stars, newcomers, Hollywood power players, and the occasional briefcased accountant all posing for the hundreds of cameras, trying not to be disconcerted by the explosion of flashbulbs and Ryan Seacrest's probing questions.

The car would be coming for Vanessa any minute, along with her hand-holding publicist from the movie. Her sprawling bungalow in West Hollywood was only a few minutes from the Beverly Hills Hilton, where the Globes were held, but she didn't want to miss her chance to walk the red carpet.

Although, the weather might have other ideas.

Vanessa stood in the middle of her living room in her couture gown, a bronze-peach shade of satin that would no doubt wrinkle the second she sat down, but at the moment looked flawless against her white skin and chocolate hair. She had a few hundred thousand dollars in jewelry dangling from her ears and her wrist, borrowed from a Beverly Hills jeweler who had sent a security team when they delivered the box. Her hair was set in loose 1940s finger waves that Kip had worked diligently on. Now, it was Sophia's turn. Paper tucked into the dress's high collar and a T-shirt smock protected the gown as Sophia applied the last of the shadow and mascara to Vanessa's eyes, bringing out their bright green irises, and set off perfectly by the meticulous arch of her brows, and the tiny mole at the corner of her eye.

Vanessa was an exceptionally beautiful woman. She knew it. It was part of her job. But today . . . today her beauty had to be unparalleled. She knew that, too.

And it was Sophia's job to make that happen.

Unfortunately, at the moment Vanessa wasn't really cooperating. And neither was the weather. The former was a complete bundle of nerves, the latter, merely a huge annoyance to a town used to temperate winter sunshine.

"It is totally punishment! I should have listened to my spiritualist," Vanessa was saying, "and done a complete cleanse of my body's aura *weeks* ago. An offer to the weather-gods."

If Vanessa was being punished, so was George Clooney, Steven Spielberg, and a couple hundred other people with a lot more sway in Hollywood, and presumably, with the weather-gods.

But Sophia didn't say that. Instead, she traded her shadow brush for a mascara wand, and began to apply the final layer to Vanessa's eye look. "Don't worry, the rain has been in the forecast for ages, I'm sure the Golden Globes people are prepared for this," Sophia said soothingly. She glanced over at Kip, who, with a nod, fetched a bottle of purified volcanic spring water from Vanessa's assistant, and brought it over. (Volcanic spring water being much like mountain spring water, only much more expensive.)

"And this mascara is waterproof, so at least we don't have to worry about that."

"What would I do without you, Sophia?" Vanessa said, reaching out to grab Sophia's hand. "Oh!"

Vanessa retracted her hand, as if she'd touched flame. In reality, all she had done was screw up Sophia's concentration, and knock her brush hand, centimeters from Vanessa's eye, into Vanessa's cheek.

"Sophia!" Vanessa cried, flinching back. "Oh God, my eye—is my eye okay?"

Kip and Vanessa's personal assistant—a recently acquired employee, an early twenties phone addict who dressed more fashionably than her salary surely allowed and who Sophia was pretty sure was named Marjorie—rushed over to attend to the drama.

"Everything's fine," Sophia said soothingly. "Just a smudge on the cheek. Entirely fixable."

"You didn't get my eye?" Vanessa asked weakly, reaching for a hand mirror.

"No, your eye is perfect." She took a wipe and carefully blotted the slash of black off Vanessa's cheek.

"Good . . ." Vanessa said, taking a deep breath. "I'm so

glad you're going to be with me tonight. Especially if I start crying."

Sophia smiled. Vanessa was not only nominated, but she was presenting an award—best supporting actor in a TV movie, series, or miniseries—so she got to have a select crew of people to attend to her needs backstage in the greenroom. Touch-ups, dress issues, etc. Especially useful if she won, and started bawling her eyes out.

Sophia was excited. The only time she'd ever been backstage anywhere, was when Alan, her first husband, had gotten them tickets to see *NSYNC at the Coliseum back when they were dating. Of course, he got scalped tickets and it was for the wrong date, so there was no concert to attend, but they did sneak around the backstage of the theater, diving behind boxes and speakers to avoid security guards with no peripheral vision.

"I think the black smudge could work," Kip joked. "It looks very *Clockwork Orange*." He knew that Kubrick was Vanessa's favorite, and knew this would make her laugh.

"Or it looks like Sebastian after he got that fish to the face," Sophia added, and Vanessa let go into a full-on fit of the giggles.

"Oh my goodness, when he showed me that picture, I nearly lost it!"

Sophia's smile faded into surprise. "Sebastian showed you that picture?"

"When he was over here yesterday," Vanessa said after a moment. "He was dropping off some of my stuff from Deegan's."

Sophia nodded. That made sense. Vanessa and Sebastian were friends, but they weren't stop-over-anytime friends. But Vanessa and Deegan, the band's lead singer, were still working through their breakup-slash-divorce, and Sebastian sometimes played go-between. To Sophia it sounded like being in eighth grade, passing messages between warring parties.

"It looked like you guys had a blast in Baja," Vanessa said, as Sophia returned to fixing her cheek and finishing up her eyes.

"We did." And they had.

Baja had been exactly what Sophia and Sebastian had needed—a dream of a vacation, four days, five nights lazing about the beach and pool, being pampered.

They had gotten a bungalow of their own. And since Sebastian had dropped Vanessa's name, and the name of the band, they got upgraded to having their own concierge—aka, their own butler. It was a silly amount of indulgence that Sophia was not about to say no to.

"I don't want you to worry about anything," he'd told her. Well, he'd told her stomach. "Hear that, little person? There's nothing here that's going to stress out mommy at all."

Yes, Sebastian was stomach-talking intense about the baby. But it wasn't that surprising to Sophia—he was always intense. When Sebastian turned his bright-eyed focus on you, you felt like the only person in the world. It was beyond seductive.

The problem was when he *wasn't* with you. Things tended to slip his mind, and other things—people, gigs—suddenly took priority.

But Sebastian knew this about himself, and he was trying to improve upon it. Hence Baja. Nothing but sun and each other to wrap themselves up in.

Sebastian had even told her to not pack anything—he would take care of it. And she was greeted by their butler, a glass of sparkling apple cider, and an entire wardrobe filled with bikinis and filmy wraps.

In fact, the only things he had insisted Sophia bring were the period costume from the wardrobe department, and the blood pressure machine he had presented her with at Christmas.

It was really too bad she spent most of their time together silently worrying about Maisey.

She'd told Sebastian about the Stanford rejection. She expected him to be appropriately livid. To feel the unjustness of the decision the same way that she did. Because she *had* been livid. After the initial heartbreak of watching her daughter shut herself away into her bedroom, Sophia spent the entire next day (once Maisey had left with her dad for Christmas having had a minimum number of sympathy pancakes that Sophia had woken up early enough to make) poring over the internet for clues about Stanford's admissions guidelines and the average test scores, school transcripts, extracurricular activities of those admitted.

If anything, Maisey was OVERqualified, her mother-brain determined. Sure, it seemed like being on a robotics team and having won a Westinghouse science competition would have been ideal . . . but Maisey wrote beautifully! She had basically done AP English–level work as a sophomore! She gave back to her school via tutoring! Surely, Stanford had just mixed her daughter up with a different, lesser, Maisey Alvarez.

It took everything in her power to not call the school in an angry rage. First, because she didn't want to be one of those helicopter parents who has controlled everything to the point the kid gets to college without knowing how to do laundry or make a peanut-butter-and-jelly sandwich. And second, because it was the holidays and Stanford's admissions office was closed, according to their voice mail.

But Sebastian hadn't reacted with the same vehemence that Sophia had. Instead, he'd just shrugged one lazy, sun-bronzed shoulder and said, "Well, that's how it goes, you know?"

"How it goes?" Sophia had repeated.

"I mean, she's swimming in a bigger pool now. Same thing happened to the band when we tried to move from our hometown to the city. No one wanted us. We had to go to Europe to train. You know, like the Beatles."

"What on earth do the Beatles have to do with my daughter not getting into her dream school?"

"Nothing," Sebastian answered. "Just . . . I mean, I could have told you Stanford wasn't for her. She'll get over it. Figure out what level she's supposed to be."

"Level?"

"Not everyone is supposed to hit the *Billboard* charts, is all," Sebastian said, and flipped over in his lounge chair. "Next time the butler comes around can you ask him for another Corona?"

But having known her daughter for seventeen years, Sophia wasn't as able to let go of the problem quite that nonchalantly. And she spent the vast majority of the vacation worrying about it.

So much so, that the Fish-to-the-Face incident occurred mostly because of it.

Sebastian had always wanted to try deep-sea fishing. So, as his Christmas present, Sophia had chartered a boat, complete with an experienced fisherman to take him out. Sebastian's face had lit up like a little boy getting his first bike.

"When do we leave?" he'd asked.

"We? Hon, this trip is just for you."

She'd actually been looking forward to not going. Not that she didn't want to be around Sebastian all the time, but she needed a couple hours on the phone. She wanted to confirm with Vanessa's publicist the dates she'd be needed for awards shows. She wanted to get the schedule for the first week back on *Fargone* after break.

And she really, really wanted to call Maisey.

But Sebastian had looked at her with those puppy-dog eyes as if she was his entire world, and leaned into her in that way she couldn't resist. She knew she was going to give in to him. And he knew it, too. It was just the way he was. And so, instead of spending the morning on the phone, she spent it on the high seas.

Bent over the railing, trying to not lose her breakfast.

It had nothing to do with morning sickness. The last time she had gotten on a boat, she'd been a chaperone on a whale-watching trip with Maisey's Girl Scout troop.

Everyone saw whales except for Sophia. She saw her lunch mixed with Dramamine hit the water.

But Sebastian had been so happy, thus she sucked it up, and tried to be happy with him. But her mind kept going back to Maisey. How she must be feeling. What she was doing.

What she was telling her father.

Sophia knew that Maisey had told Alan about Sebastian, long ago. But did he know about the baby? It's not as if she owed him any explanation—their lives were only intertwined because of Maisey now, and they'd rooted themselves in a solid script of co-parenting for several years. Heck, Alan had remarried and had toddlers running around! He couldn't judge her on getting pregnant.

But she knew he would.

She knew that in some eyes, because of this baby, she would be seen as a lesser parent.

But surely her pregnancy wasn't Maisey's first concern right now. Surely, she'd told her dad about Stanford, and he cajoled her out of her stoic silence on the matter and got her ice cream and talked to her logically about next steps.

There was a silver lining. There had to be.

Because Maisey was a remarkable person, who no doubt would find what she needed to do and . . .

She'd find . . .

"Hey, babe?" she'd called out to Sebastian.

"Hold on, hon, I think I've got something on the line!"

"I wanted to ask you . . . we were talking about Maisey, and you said she'd find her level. What did you mean by that?"

"Huh? Just what I said, babe. Can you grab that net? I want to be ready."

"You said some people aren't meant to hit the *Billboard* charts."

"Uh-huh . . ."

"You didn't. Hit the *Billboard* charts, that is. Your first album flopped in the States."

"Wow, harsh much?" The line tightened. "Oh shit! I've got one—it's trying to escape!"

"If you'd stayed at that level, you wouldn't have ever found success. But you went to Europe and got better, and got recognized for it. It took work. So . . . why should Maisey try and find a 'level' to settle for?"

"Um, I don't know, hon," Sebastian replied, now actively in a tug-of-war with what must have been a gargantuan fish, judging by the way his arms were straining. "I was just saying that she's a smart kid, you know? But there are a lot of smart kids. But . . . she'll be fine."

"Right . . . right," Sophia said, dubious as she thought over his answer.

"It's coming! It's coming!" Sebastian cried, winding up the reel. Their hired fisherman guide rushed over to help steady Sebastian. "Babe, the net! The net!"

But she had still been contemplating Maisey, and as such, the net in her hand was long forgotten. She snapped out of it just in time to rush over, and see Sebastian reel in a really big reddish fish, which they were to later learn was a mullet snapper. However, it wasn't the fisherman who told them that, nor was it the chef who was waiting on shore to prepare their catch for lunch. Instead, it was Google, who also informed them that the mullet snapper was a strong, fighting fish. And fight it did.

With a slapped tail to the side of Sebastian's face, the snapper managed to break the line, do two flops on the deck of the boat, and jump itself back into the sea.

So, instead of having a fish by which to tell the story, Sebastian ended up having a black eye.

Luckily, he had a sense of humor about it . . . eventually.

The period costume from wardrobe might have helped soothe his hurt feelings.

All in all, Sophia was glad to have had the vacation, but was equally glad to get back to her life, and get to work.

If only Vanessa would let her work.

"There," she said, finally finishing up Vanessa's eyes. Vanessa immediately grabbed the hand mirror again, and examined her reflection. Sophia held her breath.

"Great," Vanessa said. "Perfect."

"All right!" Sophia said, pulling up a stool. "Sorry, I just need to sit down a second."

"Oh! Of course!" she said, her perfectly done eyes going wide. "I never thought—of course you should sit down. I know nothing about being pregnant. I don't want to be the cause of your blood pressure going crazy."

Sophia blinked twice. She'd never told Vanessa about the risk of preeclampsia. She didn't necessarily want to tell anyone that didn't need to know. Not only was it personal, at this point, it was entirely theoretical. And it would automatically make people treat her differently, as if she were a fragile flower, instead of a woman whose body was doing what it was meant to do.

Sebastian, obviously, did not have the same concerns.

But as Sophia settled onto the kitchen stool in front of Vanessa, she couldn't help but be grateful that at least Vanessa understood. If the blood pressure machine taught them anything on the Baja trip, it was that afternoons saw a (slight) spike, so best to take a minute, get a glass of water, and breathe.

"Oh no! How are you going to be able to sit at the awards?" she worried. "It's not like you have a seat at the table."

"They have chairs in the greenroom," Sophia replied. She assumed. She didn't actually know. "But I'll be fine. Don't worry about me. Now, all we need is the lips and you are going to destroy everyone tonight."

"Hmm . . . I don't know if 'destroy' is the right word."

"Slay?" Sophia tried.

"Conquer!" Kip said, and Vanessa clapped her hands.

"Conquer! I like it. Oh, but not in that shade."

Sophia looked down at the lip palette in her hand, full of bold reds. Earlier, she and Vanessa had picked out a shade that coordinated with the rest of her face but also contrasted beautifully with the peach of her dress. It made her face stand out, while the satiny nature of the gown made her look like a nearly naked sylph.

"You want a different red?" A slight difference in shade

wouldn't make too big a difference. "Maybe something with a bit more wine?"

"No—no red at all. Let's go with . . . this!"

Vanessa had grabbed a tube of gloss. Not lipstick, not a paint—but a gloss with such a high frosted shimmer it might as well have been a trip on X from the late '90s.

In fact, it might have been from that '90s episode of *Fargone* they did.

"That's . . . that's a peach lip gloss," was really all Sophia could say.

"Right—peach! It will go with the dress."

"It will make the bottom half of your face merge with the rest of your body and disappear," she said before she could stop herself. "We need a bold lip color for balance."

"So, that just means my eyes will stand out more," Vanessa said, and flipped the lip gloss to Sophia.

"Vanessa, I really think—"

Vanessa's exuberance shuttered, her face going full ice queen in less than a second.

"You think I don't know my own face?"

"Of course not," Sophia said gently.

"I'm sorry." Vanessa softened immediately, back to her sweetheart self. "This is too important to screw up, is all. But . . . you do what you think is best."

Vanessa held out the tube of lip gloss to Sophia.

The room was completely silent. Kip watched everything closely. Even Marjorie had glanced up from her phone.

Vanessa had told her to do what was best. And what was best at the moment, was *not* putting on the right deep red shade of lipstick . . . but instead preventing a total Golden Globes pressure-cooked meltdown.

She took the tube of lip gloss, and sat down across from Vanessa in the chair.

As she applied the horrible, frosted peach abomination, she thought about how she could persuade and assuage Vanessa in the car on the way to the show. If she showed it to her in different light, perhaps—maybe she could argue it didn't get enough sheen with the lack of sunlight on the rainy red carpet.

This was only temporary, she decided. There was no way she would let Vanessa hit the red carpet looking like an old-school Britney Spears. Surely she had enough time to—

"That's Blake," Marjorie said, as her phone dinged. "The car's here."

Almost simultaneously, there was a knock on the door.

"Hello, hello, hello!" a sharply suited man of about thirty said as Kip swung the door open for him. "There she is!" he said as soon as he spied Vanessa. "You look incredible. Amazing!"

"Blake," Vanessa simpered, and slunk over to give him air kisses. "You always say I look amazing."

"This is a special level of amazing. This is something as of yet unachieved."

Vanessa transformed under the attention of the young but-not-too-young publicist, who scrutinized her appearance with the eye of a connoisseur. And a salesman.

"Are we ready to go?" he asked. "I have your ticket packet, of course. And everyone's badges." He held out lanyards for the three of them. Kip and Sophia took theirs and placed them around their necks. Marjorie glanced at hers, uttered a brief "cool," and let it dangle from her fingers as she went back to texting.

"We are all set," Vanessa said. "Just let me grab my bag . . .

ugh, Swarovski crystals are so heavy . . . do you guys have everything?"

Sophia and Kip nodded. Sophia was just putting the last brush back in her kit when she heard Blake's low hum of concern.

"Mmmm . . . what about your lips? Are we doing color?"

". . . color?" Vanessa said. "We went with peach, right, Sophia?"

Sophia looked from Vanessa to Blake. And somehow, barely managed an answer.

"Well . . . we talked about a red—"

"You should have gone with it. This peach—it's not going to pop in pictures. And you *need* to pop."

Vanessa glanced over at the mirror by the door, and gave herself a long hard look.

"Yes. You're right. God, Sophia—I can't believe you were going to let me out the door like this!"

"I . . ."

"Ugh, just fix it, okay?"

"Absolutely," Sophia said, and hopped off the kitchen stool so fast, she got slightly dizzy as she stood.

It was only a moment. She didn't even wobble. But it was enough that Kip took her arm to steady her.

"Sophia! Are you okay?" Vanessa cried out.

"I'm fine. Thank you, Kip. Just stood up too fast."

"Have you been drinking?" Blake asked, sharp. According to Vanessa, Blake hadn't wanted her to hire Sophia. He'd wanted her to use a makeup artist the PR firm had on retainer for awards season. But Vanessa refused, because of how close they were.

"No!" Sophia cried.

"She hasn't been drinking—she's pregnant, Blake," Vanessa

said, harsh. Then, she glanced at the clock. "Oh, we have to get in the car. Kip—can you do my lips on the way?"

"I can—" Sophia began, but was immediately cut off by a shake of the head.

"Sophia, I'm sorry—I should have realized this would be too stressful for you. You can't even stand up without getting light-headed—I don't want to worry about you passing out in the greenroom when I have so many other things going through my head. And with this lip color? I have to wonder if your eyesight is affected."

Sophia's jaw dropped open. It's possible she made a series of sounds. But it was also possible that they in no way resembled words.

"So? Kip? Can you do my lips?"

Kip, shocked, looked from Vanessa to Sophia. "Uh . . . sure."

"Then let's go!" Vanessa put on her best starlet smile, and threw her shoulders back. Blake opened a wide umbrella, and threw open the door.

"Oh thank goodness!" Vanessa said. "It looks like the rain is clearing."

And with that, she swept out the door, Blake and Marjorie in tow. Kip looked down at Sophia. Quietly, she handed him her kit with all the paints, powders, brushes, and emergency supplies Vanessa might need.

"Go," she whispered.

He hesitated.

"It's okay. Just go."

And with that, Kip was out the door.

Leaving Sophia in the middle of Vanessa's living room, wondering if she would ever be able to get an Uber in this close proximity to the Golden Globes.

CHAPTER 12

"Lyndi, what the hell are you doing?"

Lyndi looked up and saw Paula peering down from the loft offices' windows. Lyndi had just finished loading up her bike with Stan's delivery route of flowers, and was about to flip up the kickstand.

"I'm about to learn a tap routine for my Broadway debut," Lyndi said sarcastically. "What does it look like I'm doing?"

"You can't take your bike out."

"Stan's not here—again. Someone has to take his run."

"Not you," Paula replied.

"We'll walk the floor of the market as soon as I get back, scout tomorrow's flowers. I won't be long, I promise."

"No you won't, because you're not going. Come upstairs. Now."

Rarely had Paula taken the "I'm the boss do as I say" tone with Lyndi. But when she did, it was worth heeding. So, Lyndi unbuckled the backpack full of bouquets from her body, and quickly moved up the stairs.

Paula was sitting behind her desk, and had put on her best stern boss face, her hands laced in front of her.

"Lyndi, I can't have you taking runs anymore. It's not appropriate."

Lyndi sighed. "Listen, I know you want me more in the warehouse, but desperate times call for desperate measures. Honestly, I think we need to let Stan go, he's become too unreliable. I can cover his runs until we get someone new, and I won't be neglecting my duties as your second in command. I'm already half done with the new website skins, and our Instagram is booming . . ."

"That's not why. Although, you're right, we do need to let Stan go," Paula mused. Then, she shook her head, got back to what she wanted to say. "We can't have you doing bicycle deliveries while you're pregnant."

Lyndi felt her stomach flip over. And no, it wasn't the baby moving. She wasn't even showing yet, so she certainly couldn't feel the baby kicking—at least according to Dr. Keen. No, it just turned out her stomach flipped over a lot these days, as she wondered.

Not *worried*, just . . . wondered.

Wondered what it would be like to have the baby in their tiny apartment. Wondered where the crib would go. Wondered if their little girl would have Marcus's eyes or hers. Wondered if Marcus was ever going to stop giving her foot rubs, since she was suddenly ticklish and it didn't exactly relax her.

Wondered if the fact that her gums bled every time she brushed her teeth was a pregnancy symptom or a reason to buy stock in gingivitis mouthwash.

Turns out, it was a pregnancy symptom.

Turns out, a lot was a pregnancy symptom. Like, basically everything.

Twitchy legs? Symptom.

Bloated and gassy? Symptom.

Carpal tunnel? Symptom.

Drooling like a basset hound? Symptom.

Weird darkening patches of skin on your face? Yeah, it's called melasma, and it was a symptom, too.

Lyndi had not been trained to expect any of this. Television had really only told her about morning sickness, and she thought that once that was done, she'd be free and clear, with only the occasional craving for odd foods (her desire for eggs Benedict had gone from a whiny want to a freakish obsession), and a gleefully expanding waistline.

However, so far, the gums were really the only symptom—other than the aforementioned morning sickness—that she'd experienced. But thanks to those pastel emails she still continued to get, and still continued to open with the pathological need of the morbidly curious, she knew what to expect in the nearish future.

But it was also one of those emails that betrayed her to the Favorite Flower.

Well, it wasn't really the email's fault. It was very much her own. But she'd been walking the floor with Paula and one of their arrangers, Judy. Judy was taking pictures of all the flowers that Paula and Lyndi pointed out that they wanted to earmark for arrangements for the next day. Unfortunately, while Lyndi was negotiating the price for wholesale roses (Valentine's Day was only a few weeks off and if they didn't have a good relationship with a rose supplier they were screwed, as she'd convinced Paula to do a special preorder link on the website for the Big V) Lyndi motioned Judy over to take some pictures of the fat English rose varieties.

"Oh damn, my phone died," Judy said. "I didn't get the pink or red hybrids."

"Here, use my phone," Lyndi said, absentmindedly typing in her code to unlock it before handing it over, before even looking at it.

"Oh my God! You're pregnant?"

And wouldn't you know it, but one of those pastel emails was open on her phone. (Congratulating her on having reached the eighteenth week of pregnancy, with a video comparing her fetus in size to the latest in a long line of incrementally sized vegetables—this one a bell pepper.)

Lyndi snatched the phone back as fast as she could, but the damage was already done. Judy was gawking at her with wide, unblinking eyes. And all of Lyndi's protestations of "that's um . . . I mean, it's only . . ." did nothing to help her case.

"Paula!" Judy had called out. "Did you know our little Lyndi's expecting??"

And that was that. If it had been Paula who had found the email on the phone, Lyndi guessed that she would have been discreet about it, but since it was Judy, who spent her mornings arranging flowers and spreading gossip, news of Lyndi's pregnancy had lapped the LA flower district by the very next morning.

It wasn't that Lyndi didn't *want* to tell people about her pregnancy. It was simply that, whenever she did, she wasn't really met with any kind of enthusiasm. She had endured the glitter-covered gender reveal party, where everyone kept telling her she was *so smart* to have her baby while she was young. As if a rebounding body was the only potential silver lining they could think of.

Not to mention, her own friends didn't even bother to show up. In fact, these days Allison, Olivia, and Elizabeth were barely texting her back. All her "hey wassup?" and "We are so overdue for brunch!" missives were either met with silence or with a banal "OMG I'm so busy! Let's try and hang next week!" type response.

However, Judy and the other arrangers were incredibly enthusiastic, wondering when the wedding would be. When Lyndi made it clear that there wouldn't be a wedding, their ardor cooled considerably.

And her boss, Paula, hadn't mentioned it once.

Until now.

"I'm not incapacitated, Paula," Lyndi said, testily. "I can ride my bike. I rode my bike here this morning, didn't I?"

"True, and unfortunately, I can't stop you doing that— how you get to work is your own business," Paula said, taking off her horn-rimmed glasses, a sign of her exhaustion. "But deliveries come under the company's umbrella, and if something happened while making a delivery . . . it would be a big liability."

"Oh." Because what else was there to say? Not only was her baby a shock and occasional inconvenience, she was now a liability.

"Doing deliveries isn't in your job description anyway," Paula said, not unkindly. "Believe me, you have plenty to do."

Lyndi's eyes flew up to Paula's. "I do? I'm sorry, I thought I had a handle on all of my new responsibilities . . ."

"You do." Paula practically laughed. "So much so, I'd like to shuffle some of the stuff on my plate to yours. Especially with Valentine's coming up, I'm going to need all the help I can get. Inventory of the wrapping materials, double-checking the website to make sure it's processing orders correctly— ever since that update it's been buggy—I need a new spreadsheet template tracking our monthly profit margins . . ."

"Wow," Lyndi said, blinking. That was a lot of work—but it was all stuff that Lyndi knew she could do. Paula trusting her with this much was a huge vote of confidence.

Or, she wondered as a peal of unbridled laughter drifted up from Judy and the other arrangers below, was it a way to keep her sidelined?

Either way, she was capable. And her boss was asking her to step up.

"Okay," Lyndi said finally. "I can manage that. But who's going to take Stan's run this morning?"

"Guess I'm getting back on the bike." Paula sighed, taking her massive ring of boss-related keys out of her pocket and handing them to Lyndi. "I'd love a full accounting of the decorative ribbons, especially the pinks, reds, and whites for V-Day, by the time I get back. But first things first . . . we need to make a job listing."

"A job listing?" Lyndi felt her insides freeze with worry.

"Yeah—we need to hire a new Stan."

ONCE LYNDI WAS done with work, it was still barely two o'clock in the afternoon. When she'd been just an arranger and occasional delivery person, she used to love these golden hours. She could spend the afternoon going to a movie, or riding her bike over the little hills of Echo Park, looping around the man-made Echo Park Lake, letting ideas run through her head for new floral arrangements while she idly watched dog walkers, out-of-work actors, yoga devotees—and sometimes, all three at once—take the same pleasure in their free time.

But today, she didn't head that way once she climbed onto her bike. Instead, she found herself cutting across Silver Lake, then enduring the grueling hills of Griffith Park to cross into the San Fernando Valley and the city of Burbank, where her sister Nathalie lived and worked.

Movie studios gave way to big-box stores, then gave way to restaurants and diners, that then gave way to neat little 1950s bungalows on rectangular sixteenth of an acre lots. It was the cookie-cutter life Nathalie had always wanted and that always bewildered Lyndi.

It had always felt like life was muted here. The colors just weren't as strong as they were in Echo Park.

But as she rode through the neighborhoods, Lyndi couldn't help but notice the number of kids. School had just gotten out. Elementary-aged kids were walking home, wearing backpacks bigger than themselves, escorted by parents or in gaggles of friends. One mom was riding alongside a kid, a toddler strapped into a bike seat on the back of her old-school beach cruiser.

Would Lyndi be able to put her daughter on the back of her bike?

Could she do that in Echo Park? With all the hills and the, er, characters that populated the streets and doorways, and occasionally peed in her stairwell?

Or would she have to turn to the cookie-cutter life?

Nathalie would probably say yes.

Or maybe she wouldn't. Nathalie had always been the person who told Lyndi she could do anything. That didn't judge her on trying to find her path to what made her happy.

At least, the old Nathalie did that.

Current Nathalie seemed to have judgment coming off of her in waves.

But maybe, just maybe she had shifted a little bit. The shock of Lyndi being pregnant threw her, but at the gender reveal party, they seemed to get along pretty well. They had something to bond over, after all—mutual horror of being molested by your French teacher would do that. (Oh yeah, Madame Craig got to Lyndi's stomach too by the time the party was over, and the pink-and-blue cocktails were running low.)

And Lyndi really needed someone to talk to at the moment. About what was happening at work. About feeling sidelined. About her hormones being completely out of control—seriously, Marcus must have whiplash from her overt horniness one second and her revulsion at being touched the next.

About whether or not she could ride her bike with her daughter behind her in Echo Park.

In the midst of all the cookie-cutter bungalows was Nathalie's school. The bell had rung probably about a half hour ago, but there were still some kids milling around the front, waiting for rides. Or they were in team uniforms, heading out to the field for various sports practices. The smallest high schooler Lyndi had ever seen was hauling a tuba over her shoulder like it weighed nothing, headed for the marching band in a far field.

Lyndi knew Nathalie usually stayed an hour or two after the school day ended, grading papers and meeting with students. She could only hope that she did today, too. But if she wasn't there, she had an excuse all prepared. She had brought tear-off flyers for the Favorite Flower, looking to hire a new Stan—or rather, a new bicycle delivery person. Lyndi had visited the school before, and knew there was a bulletin board near Nathalie's room for posting things like this. Last time she was here, there had been an advertisement for a photography service that took pictures of you with your cats (and they would lend you some cats, if so desired).

Of course they had also posted listings online, and she

would hit the coffee shops of Echo Park and Silver Lake with more flyers after this visit. But just in case anyone questioned a twenty-four-year-old pregnant woman (who didn't really look pregnant yet, at least not in her blousy shirt) walking into a high school, she had things covered.

She made her way through the halls and found her way to the English department wing, where she had to glance from room to room to remember which one was Nathalie's—pausing only to put up her flyer.

The more she searched, the more sure she felt that talking to Nathalie could help. Not *solve* her problems per se, but at least she would be able to understand them.

Nathalie had always been the one she turned to when she needed to understand.

But when she finally peeked into the right room, she found that Nathalie was not alone. She was speaking to a dark-haired woman around the same age as Nathalie, and they were laughing.

Laughing hard.

Laughing . . . about Lyndi.

"My sister is so irresponsible, she got knocked up by her bisexual roommate, I don't think she's the one I need."

The other woman's eyes went wide with shock, and she covered her mouth to keep the laughter from overwhelming her.

Lyndi felt her stomach sink to the floor.

Well. Guess the gender reveal party didn't mend as many fences as she thought.

Because once again, while Nathalie was the one everyone treated like an adult, Lyndi was on the outside looking in.

CHAPTER 13

"Ms. Kneller?"

Nathalie looked up. Class had ended about ten minutes ago, and the last student had finally left the room, after hanging behind to ask question after breathlessly worried question about the AP Literature exam.

Nathalie loved all her students, but she loved her AP students best . . . probably because they all worked so hard. But the seriousness with which they took the test had caused more than one anxiety attack over the years. She wished she could tell them to take a deep breath and chill out. To go to the beach for the weekend, and *enjoy* a book instead of trying to analyze it. But she had learned over the years that for hypercompetitive kids raised in a dog-eat-dogma of achievement, that usually fell on deaf ears.

If only she could transfer a smidgeon of their drive to some of her more maddeningly lackadaisical non-AP students, the world would be a much more pleasant place.

Well, at least she managed to get them to laugh at Shakespeare's jokes along the way.

But today she had been dying to get that last kid out of there, because she hadn't been able to check Twitter since that morning.

And when she finally got on her phone, she was rewarded with two new tweets.

@WTFPreg—so people molesting a pregnant woman's stomach is just a given then? Cool. Cool cool cool.

@WTFPreg—I swear, if I get ONE MORE pregnancy marketing email, I might actually buy something. Yeah. That'll shut them up.

Nathalie felt that little pool of warmth in the middle of her body every time she read the Twitter feed. Finally, there was someone out there she could relate to! She'd been complaining about the pregnancy marketing emails just that morning. They popped up ever since she set up their baby registry online.

Of course, she was the one to set up the registry. David barely acknowledged that they'd need to get anything beyond a couple of onesies and some diapers.

She'd been dying to get on her phone because over the past couple days, she'd noticed a pattern—the tweeter of @WTFPreg tended to post her thoughts around lunchtime. So invariably, there was a little treat waiting for her at the end of the school day, a gift for getting through another round of teaching overeager AP kids and some of their more apathetic counterparts.

But who—*who*—could possibly be writing them?

"I'm Sophia Nunez—Maisey Alvarez's mom?"

"Of . . . of course!" Nathalie said, realizing she had been staring blankly at the woman who was in her doorway for some seconds, not comprehending anyone was there—her mind still on the tweets and their mysterious author. "Hi, please, have a seat."

"We've met before," Sophia said, as she pulled one of the desk chairs around and brought it in front of Nathalie's larger teacher desk. "At the—"

"At the Los Angeles County poetry recital. Yes, Maisey did amazing that day. How have you been since?"

"Oh," Sophia said with a crooked smile. "You know. Busy. Life keeps us on our toes. Yourself?"

"Much the same," Nathalie said with a corresponding smile. She remembered Sophia. Remembered mostly being struck by how young she was—it was one of the first times she encountered a parent as a peer instead of seeing them as she would her own parents or older, more seasoned co-workers. (It could just be proof she was getting old.) She also remembered just how freakin' gorgeous Sophia was, wearing clothes and makeup with a confidence that one usually found in magazines. Maisey was the kind of kid who didn't broadcast her beauty—although she was a lovely young woman who would no doubt have all the boys in her pocket the minute she decided to notice them. Looking at Sophia was like looking at future Maisey, and being blown away by the sheer power of it.

"You didn't have to come by," Nathalie said abruptly, to stop herself staring. "We could have done this over the phone, especially if this interferes with work..."

"No, we're doing night shoots this week, so I don't have to be at work until later this afternoon."

"Right," Nathalie replied. "And I swear, I won't ask you for *Fargone* spoilers."

Sophia gave a small laugh. But they both knew this chit-chat was nothing but stalling.

So best to get down to it.

"Ms. Kneller, we both know that parents don't get calls from the teacher without a reason. That's why I wanted to come in and do this in person. Maisey's never been in trouble before."

"And she's not now!" Nathalie was quick to reassure. She set her shoulders. "As you know, I'm Maisey's faculty advisor, and I . . . I just wanted to ask if things are okay at home these days."

Sophia's expression stilled. She sat up in the chair. "Did something happen?"

"Well . . . yes and no," Nathalie said. "Maisey didn't turn in her paper this week." For Nathalie's AP class, the only home-work she assigned—other than extensive reading—was one paper a week, ten pages long. It was grueling (and no pic-nic to grade), but it taught the students how to interpret lit-erature on their own terms—and more importantly, it taught them how to argue, how to persuade, and how to write.

Sophia sat up straighter. "That's not like her."

"No, it's not." This was the second year in a row Nathalie had Maisey as her student and it was definitely not like her. "The Maisey I know often hands in her homework a few days early."

"Well . . . it is second semester senior year," Sophia ven-tured. "Senioritis?"

"I thought it might be that, although, senioritis doesn't usually strike my AP students until after the AP exam in a couple months. I offered to cut her some slack, asked if she'd like to turn in her paper late for a grade markdown but still she'd get credit. If it was an A paper, she'd get a B, for ex-ample." The first B Maisey had ever gotten in her class, but better than nothing. "But when I made the offer, she just shrugged and said, 'Why? It doesn't really matter, does it?'"

Sophia sucked in her breath.

"Okay," Sophia said eventually. "Okay, I'll have a talk with her. Thank you."

"Ms. Nunez—"

"Sophia, please."

"Sophia—I don't bring this up to get Maisey in any trouble. It's just very out of character for her."

"Yes it is. I just . . . I've never had to have this talk with her before. She's never . . . Reading and writing are her favorite things in the world. She's never been disrespectful to a teacher."

"And she wasn't now," Nathalie replied. "Trust me. I could tell you horror stories about students so gifted with insults you pray that they'd one day use their powers for good instead of evil. But I thought if Maisey was having difficulty at home . . . I know she was severely disappointed to not get into Stanford."

"Yes." Sophia nodded obliquely.

"And I worry that that was enough for her to question her entire future. I spoke with the guidance counselor, and she said that Maisey hadn't applied to any other schools yet either. Deadlines are fast approaching and—"

"She hasn't?" Sophia said abruptly. "But . . . I saw her, filling out applications. Right after she heard about Stanford. She had stacks of them, to UC Davis, San Diego . . . even UCLA and Berkeley."

"According to the guidance office, she hasn't requested any transcripts for applications, so . . ."

Sophia put a hand to her forehead, leaning on her elbow.

Her eyes fell to the surface of the desk, no doubt her mind running a million miles a minute, trying to figure out the mind of a brilliant but lost teenager.

Then she took a deep breath. "It's not just Stanford. It goes back earlier than that."

"Earlier?"

"Ever since she found out about the baby, I feel like she's been pulling away."

Nathalie nearly choked. "Maisey's pregnant?"

"What? No!" Sophia replied. Then, she laughed. "God, if Maisey was seeing a boy, I'd know where to place the blame for her behavior, because that's what I was like when I was her age. No . . . *I'm* pregnant."

"Oh. Oh!" Nathalie blinked. "Congratulations!"

"Thank you," Sophia said kindly. "It's an adjustment for us. Me, Maisey, Sebastian—that's my boyfriend."

"Understandably."

"Still. I would have thought Maisey would have been past the age of jealousy over a baby brother or sister."

"I've been teaching for a decade now, and kids at this age aren't quite adults yet, no matter how much they pretend to be. Big changes still throw them—and they are facing down one of the biggest with college looming."

"Do you have any kids yourself?" Sophia asked.

"Not yet," Nathalie replied. Then, a hand went automatically to her stomach. "Although, give it four months or so, and I will."

"You're pregnant, too?"

Nathalie nodded.

"Well, congratulations to you as well then!" Sophia smiled. "You don't look it."

"That's because I'm sitting and wearing this loose blouse."

But Sophia shook her head. "You don't look pregnant, you just look—"

"Lumpy?"

"I was going to say 'glowing.'"

"Now there's a classic descriptor. For what it's worth, you don't look pregnant either."

"Thanks—but I'm not as far along as you. I'm barely out of the first trimester. The only clothing I've outgrown so far are my bras." Sophia looked down at her own boobs—Nathalie couldn't help it, she looked, too. "It's obscene. Come on, we're reaching seventies porno levels here."

Nathalie couldn't help it. She laughed. Long and loud. It just . . . felt really good to laugh at something. Anything—but especially something that had to do with pregnancy. It just felt like everything that had to do with the baby lately had been so stressful. Doc's appointments, 529 plans, whether or not she should do a water birth . . . Every little thing was so very, very important. And she was the only one paying any attention, so that just made it more stressful. So to be able to laugh at something . . . well, perhaps she was laughing a little too hard, because between the tears streaming out of her eyes, she could see a shocked expression on Sophia's face.

"Sorry, that might be a little TMI," Sophia said by way of apology. "I don't think I'm supposed to be discussing my boobs with my daughter's literature teacher."

"No, please! That is the *least* TMI thing anyone has said to me in so long. I cannot tell you the number of personal stories of body fluids and functions that I've been subjected to when people find out I'm pregnant. It's like the scene in *The Shining* when the elevator doors open—just a flood of horror people can't wait to share with you."

"Well, I could tell you some, if you wanted," Sophia said, on the fade of a laugh. "But honestly, all that stuff becomes a blur. At least it did for me anyway. Once the baby's here—none of that really matters."

Nathalie sobered, then studied Sophia.

"What does matter?"

Sophia looked to the side, pulling from way back in her memory. "Well, for the first couple months, you spend most of your time trying to keep the baby fed, and clean, and comfortable—basically you focus all your energy on keeping the baby alive."

"And then?"

"And then . . . they are alive. They start to become real people. They have their own way of looking at the world, and it's truly amazing what they know. I remember so many little things that add up to the big thing that's Maisey. Scribbles on paper that are drawings of whole worlds. Recited stories about every detail of what happened at the park. I remember " Sophia gave a small laugh to herself. "Oh God, I remember 'eat soup.'"

"Eat soup?"

"When Maisey was about two, she started asking me every day to 'eat soup.' So I made her every kind of soup imaginable. Chicken Noodle, Minestrone, Tortilla, New England Clam Chowder. If Campbell's made it, I bought it. But she would take one bite and then not eat it any more. It took me *weeks* to realize that 'eat soup' was actually," she held her arms wide and started singing, "Iiiiiiiiit's Supercalifragilistic-expialidocious!"

"Excuse me?"

"You know, from *Mary Poppins*—which she'd seen at her grandmother's house and fallen madly in love with. We watched *Mary Poppins* once a week after that for an entire year. To this day I have that damn movie memorized."

Sophia was lost in the memory, thus, she didn't notice as Nathalie began to tear up again. But this time, it wasn't caused by extreme laughter.

All the little things that make up the big thing. They were so much more important than anything she was going through now. Any worries, any wondering. Any little annoyance at her stepmother or her little sister . . . or even at David . . .

WHUMP.

Nathalie's eyes went wide. Her hand flew to her stomach.

"Oh!" she said, surprised.

"What is it?" Sophia asked immediately.

"I think . . . I think she just kicked me."

Nathalie looked down at her lumpy stomach in wonder. The belly she'd been gaining wasn't flabby, it felt like a small medicine ball sitting beneath her skin—solid and full. And now, it felt like there was something moving *in* that medicine ball.

She'd felt little flutters the past couple days. Mostly, she thought it was related to the anxiety she'd been feeling about, well, everything (and possibly also, her favorite Mexican food she picked up for dinner). But this wasn't a flutter. This was a definite kick—or punch. Whatever it was, it was made independently of Nathalie's body, and it had actual impact.

It was her daughter, saying hello.

She was there. She was real.

She would have Nathalie's eyes and David's dark hair and his soccer skills—

. . . David.

And suddenly, Nathalie started tearing up again. But this time, she couldn't stop it.

She didn't know why—it just opened up a flood of emotions that she'd been keeping below the surface. And she was doing it all in front of a student's mother—who had the grace to not look too alarmed.

Just a little bit alarmed.

"Are you okay?" Sophia asked, leaning over the desk and pulling tissues from the box that Nathalie kept nearby, handing them to her.

"Th–thank you." Nathalie sniffled. "I don't know what's wrong with me today."

"Might I suggest hormones?" Sophia said wryly.

Nathalie choked on a laugh. "I was . . . She kicked me, and the only thing I could think was that my husband wasn't here to feel it."

Sophia nodded. Although, she would probably nod at anything to deal with the hysterical crying pregnant lady. "Understandable."

"He's been so distant lately, I can't explain why—we've been together forever, I thought we were on the same page about having a baby. But now that we actually are . . . God, I'm so sorry, this is deeply unprofessional. If we weren't a teacher and a parent, and if we weren't pregnant, I'd offer you a drink."

Sophia paused. Then . . . "Would you like some pregnant lady contraband?"

Nathalie's eyebrow went up between dying sniffles. "What do you got?"

Sophia reached into her bag, and drew out the most beautiful thing Nathalie had ever seen in her life.

It was glistening. Just out of the fridge, it looked like, from the slow beads of sweat sliding down the most beautiful silhouette market testing had ever managed to produce. Sixteen ounces of heaven, the deep amber color of a whiskey held up to firelight.

Diet Coke.

Nathalie's mouth watered. Soda wasn't *really* on the Do Not Consume If Pregnant list. But caffeine was best limited, if not outright avoided, and all the (wonderful, delicious) artificial colors and sweeteners in a Diet Coke surely were not great for a developing fetus. And as Nathalie wasn't about to do anything that could harm the baby, she hadn't had a soda in ages.

She'd tried to assuage her cravings for carbonated beverages with seltzer water, mixed with fruit juice, but it wasn't the same. It couldn't be. It didn't slide down the throat and spread across the chest in the same way. It didn't offer anything close to the satisfaction.

She must have taken an inordinate amount of time staring longingly at that bottle, because Sophia finally interrupted her nearly pornographic daydream about swimming in a pool of soda.

"If it's any help, I drank a little soda here and there with Maisey, and she turned out fine. Minor issues with doing her homework lately aside, of course."

Nathalie bit her lip. Then, gave a quick nod.

Sophia handed over the bottle. She cracked it open (that sound!) and took a deep swig.

"That's amazing," Nathalie finally said. She took one more long gulp, then handed the bottle back to Sophia—like they were sharing a flask.

"I bet your husband is more tuned in than you think," Sophia said, but Nathalie just shook her head.

"He's always working. And if he's not, he's de-stressing

with video games. I can't get him to focus long enough on the baby for him to realize we only have a short period of time before she's here. It's like he doesn't pay attention to the fact that things are happening *now*."

"I get it, you know," Sophia said, taking a swig of her own. "Sometimes it feels like you're the only person who is pregnant. Like this is only happening to you—and everyone else around you is just going about their lives as normal."

Nathalie could only nod . . . and hold out her hand for the bottle.

"My daughter's not exactly into having a little sibling," Sophia admitted. "And while Sebastian is much better than Alan was—Alan being Maisey's dad—he's still . . . clueless. Worries over every little thing I tell him, then that concern disappears as soon as he thinks it's been solved with a blood pressure machine. Goes back about his life. Don't get me wrong, I love him, and when he's there, he's *there*. But he's . . . well, he's younger than me. And sometimes that really shows." Sophia sighed, and looked to the ceiling. "They have no idea about the upheaval a baby will cause. Because their lives aren't upheaved yet. You and me, we can see it coming, because it's growing and kicking inside us every day."

Nathalie's hand went to her stomach again, the spot where she had felt the quickening.

"I just wish I knew what to expect," she said finally. "Everyone has a pregnancy story, but none of them are my story, none of them are a map for what is going to happen to me."

"Not knowing what to expect is great training for having a kid." Sophia smiled ruefully.

"I have over a hundred students every semester, I wouldn't be able to handle them without having a plan."

"It also helps to have someone to talk about this stuff with."

"Do you? Have someone, I mean."

Sophia waved a dismissive hand in the air. "I just talk. I don't care who's listening. Kip, my co-worker, knows more about my body than any gay man should. My mother, she's the same mold as me, oversharer, so we just talk over each other. When Sebastian is in town he tries to keep up but I can tell he's panicking sometimes and just wants me to take care of everything. Maisey might never have sex in her life thanks to all she's heard me say."

Nathalie shook her head. "Maisey's going to bloom in college. I hope you're ready for that."

"No mother is ready for that. But I can't wait to see it." Sophia smiled, her eyes getting a little watery herself. Hormones, no doubt.

"But what about you?" Sophia continued. "Do you have anyone to talk to? Parents? Siblings?"

"My stepmother is . . . a bit much sometimes. And my sister—well, my little sister is pregnant, too."

"Well, there you go!" Sophia cried. "Someone who's going through it."

"My sister is so irresponsible, she got knocked up by her bisexual roommate, I don't think she's the one I need."

Sophia's eyes went wide, a hand covered her mouth. "Seriously?"

Nathalie nodded.

"How did that happen?"

"I assume she tripped over something. She's only twenty-four."

Sophia blinked. "Twenty-four's not that young. My mother was married and had me by twenty-four."

"My mom, too. But . . . it's different. Lyndi's a young twenty-four—she doesn't know what she wants out of life, bounces from job to job. She's basically a kid herself."

Nathalie gave a little, hysterical giggle. Sophia followed suit. But then . . .

A shuffle. She heard it, by the door. Probably a student, Nathalie thought. Although, something prickled along the back of her neck. The same feeling she used to get when Lyndi was a kid and hovering outside her bedroom door, hoping to borrow lip gloss.

But when she turned around no one was there.

She frowned. She could have sworn . . .

But then, Sophia's giggle had died down. And she'd grown reflective.

"I was nineteen when I had Maisey. It's . . . it's hard. You hardly know yourself, and you're about to have another person you need to know, inside and out. Once you get to our ages, you have the benefit of knowing who you are and how you're going to take care of everything."

Nathalie's smile fell immediately from her face.

"I'm sorry, I didn't mean to infer anything—"

"No, I know," Sophia said, waving her hand. "Trust me, I got used to speculation about my life when Maisey was little more than a baby. But it's never easy. Even though I had a support system in my mom. Your sister, she's going to need the same thing. Even if it's just someone to talk to about how hard it is." She cocked her head to one side. "You guys are lucky to have each other."

Nathalie let that settle in her stomach, next to the pop and fizz of the half-drunk soda.

She was lucky to have her little sister in her life. Lyndi's immaturity may be aggravating in the extreme, but she'd also always been the one to make everything better. Just her existence—her being born—made living with Kathy tolerable. And she deserved more than the annoyed scorn Nathalie felt every time she looked in her direction recently.

But it was damned hard sometimes.

"You know what?" Nathalie said finally. "Maisey is incredibly lucky to have you, too."

Sophia chuckled. "I don't know how she turned out to be such a good kid. When I was her age I was obsessed with whatever boy I was dating and getting my eyeliner wings perfect."

Nathalie leaned forward in her chair. "Can I ask something?"

"Shoot."

"How *do* you get your eyeliner wings perfect?" She'd been dying to know since Sophia had walked into the room how she managed to look so flawless.

Sophia blinked. Then, she reached into her voluminous bag, and pulled out a makeup bag, and a rolled-up set of brushes. Then she took one final swig of the Diet Coke, finishing off the bottle.

"Okay, but if we're doing this," Sophia said, "I'm going to need more soda."

FEBRUARY

The stomachs have eyes.

Literally. Also, I'm starving.

CHAPTER 14

I'M LUCKY TO HAVE HER, I'M LUCKY TO HAVE HER, I'm lucky to have her.

Sophia had repeated that phrase to herself in her head more times in the last week than she had in the entirety of the previous seventeen years—and that included the fiasco preteen era when Maisey had been scarily intent on setting Sophia up with her then-best friend's recently divorced dad.

But ever since Sophia had gone to see Ms. Kneller—Nathalie, as she'd been told to call her after having given her a smoky-eye look that would no doubt tantalize her husband and high school sophomore boys alike—Maisey had gone from acting like an aloof but levelheaded responsible teenager to a . . . well, to a complete and utter Teenager.

The shift had happened almost immediately. Sophia had made a concerted effort to get up early the next morning (night shoots had them not finishing up until nearly 3 AM) and talk to Maisey before she left for school. She was going on less than two hours of sleep, but she knew it was important enough to warrant a little bit of a sleep schedule interruption.

It was also important enough to warrant waffles, she thought. For Maisey. It had nothing to do with the fact Sophia was craving carbs covered in maple syrup.

The waffles were made and on the table before Maisey even emerged from her room, her school bag slung over her shoulder.

"There you are!" Sophia had said brightly, as she quickly swallowed the bite of waffle she had just taken.

"What's all this?" Maisey asked, as she headed to the fridge.

"Waffles. And talking."

Maisey's eyebrow went up. "Talking?"

"Come on kiddo, I texted you yesterday that I wanted to talk today."

"I figured you meant after school," Maisey replied, nonchalantly grabbing a yogurt squeeze pouch and readjusting the heavy school bag on her shoulder. "You know that night shoots do a number on you."

"Well, this is too important to wait until after school. Or after night shoots. I had a conversation with Ms. Kneller yesterday."

Maisey hesitated for just a second. But then sighed. "Yeah, so?"

Sophia blinked. "So? So . . . I hope there are some finished college applications in that overloaded backpack. And the paper you owe in your lit class from last week."

It only took a second. A fraction thereof. But Sophia's eyes were glued to Maisey's face, so she saw it. She saw the shift. From wary and aloof, to combative. To spoiling for a fight.

"God, Mom, you have one conversation with a teacher and suddenly you're a helicopter parent. Nice of you to show up."

Show up? Like she hadn't shown up to every recital, soccer game, and parent-teacher night in seventeen years.

"Hey now," Sophia said, warning. "Ms. Kneller is just concerned about you. As am I."

"What's the big deal? I didn't turn in a paper? I assure you, my grades can take it."

Sophia felt her frustration rising. What her mother used to call "her blood getting up" whenever she had to deal with a teenage Sophia. "It's the attitude that accompanied the lack of paper. Not to mention your college applications."

"My attitude is the problem? Okay then, I'll smile and be super-duper cheerful and then you won't care that I didn't do my paper or my college applications."

"Maisey! This is your future we're talking about—now is not the time to devolve into a spoiled brat!"

"Right, Mom, I'm so incredibly spoiled."

"Maisey—" Sophia's voice had taken on a warning tone. One that she knew only too well, from having heard it employed against her during her own teenage years.

God, she needed to call her own mother and apologize for . . . everything.

She took a deeeeeeeeep breath, and tried to dredge up the memory of how close she and Maisey were.

"This is important. I don't care about the lit paper. You're right, your grades can take it.

"But these colleges—they don't know you. They're not going to wait for you, or give you leeway. I know you're still disappointed about Stanford. And maybe, after a year or two at a different school, you can transfer. But right now, you need to finish your other applications so you can *go* to school in the fall."

During her (rational, well thought out, good job, Mom!) speech, Maisey had dropped her eyes to her bag, begun fiddling with the zippers. And when Sophia was done there was a long pause, the only sound Maisey's breathing. She hoped that she got through to her. She crossed her fingers behind her back.

But then, Maisey looked up, and if possible the edges of her eyes had gotten even harder.

"Why? Eager to have me out of the house so you can paint my room blue?"

And with that, Maisey stormed out of the room, out of the house, and off to school, in a perfect teenager huff.

Oh, yes. Sophia had learned in her last doctor's appointment that she was having a boy. She could only hope that seventeen years from now, he was less stubborn than his sister.

Over the course of the next week, it was as if Maisey, ever the overachiever, was determined to work through all the steps of stereotypical teenager-dom in rapid succession. Her interactions with Maisey ran the gamut from sullen silences, to disdainful sarcasm, to slammed doors and even to missing curfew. Not that Maisey had ever had a curfew, as she'd never tested the upper limits of what was allowed.

But when Sophia came home one morning at 3 AM from night shoots, and discovered that Maisey was *not* in her room, she had called two police stations and one hospital before Maisey responded to her texts, saying that she had gone over to her dad's for dinner, and decided to spend the night.

Her phone call with Maisey's father the next morning was in no way productive.

"If you're going to be working nights, Maisey *should* stay with me," Alan barked, irritated. "She's still a kid, you know."

"I have no problem with her staying with you," Sophia said, trying to keep her calm with the man who'd only decided to be a parent a handful of years ago. "If she's going to go out, she needs to *tell me*. But she's being a brat right now, because she's mad at me."

"Why?" Alan asked without sympathy. "What did you do?"

Had a sex life, apparently.

The fact that *Fargone* was on night shoots didn't help. When Maisey was home in the afternoon, Sophia wasn't. When she and Maisey overlapped for those brief few minutes in the morning, she was practically brain-dead and couldn't find the energy to face off against her newfound teenager.

But she was brain-dead most of the time to begin with. The flipping night-and-day schedule of sleeping until noon and working until dawn had been doable when she was in her twenties, but now that she was thirty-six, and pregnant, it was beyond exhausting.

Not to mention, ever since the Golden Globes peach lip gloss incident, work itself had not been her oasis of calm, creative expression amid chaos that she normally enjoyed.

Vanessa had been glowing at the awards. She was featured in all the glossy checkout line magazines and online awards show fashion roundups. But she had become remarkably frosty toward Sophia, blaming her no doubt for the almost catastrophe of the peach lip gloss.

It was on the first night of the night shoots that it all came to a head.

"No, I want Kip to do my makeup," Vanessa said, as soon as Sophia sat down in her ergonomic rolling stool (usually she worked on her feet, but once she told the producers about the pregnancy it had shown up in the makeup trailer with no other explanation). "I'm sorry, Sophia, but this is such a pivotal episode, and Kip and I talked over the exact look I wanted when we were in the limo to the Globes."

Sophia's eyebrows went up as she shot a look to Kip, who seemed both frozen and guilty at the same time.

". . . okay. You know we had long discussions in the production meetings about what the look for this episode would be. We showed you sketches. I'm sure Kip's ideas are great—"

"Exactly, Kip's great," Vanessa replied, keeping her face neutral in the mirror. "I loved the sketches, and Kip is just going to add that little extra oomph. You understand, don't you, Sophia?"

Sophia had bit her lip. "Sure. But Kip has a lot of other people to prep, too . . ."

"And now you have time to help him with that! Come on, Kip, let's go."

Then Vanessa actually clapped her hands, and Sophia had no choice but to scoot away.

Kip mouthed an *I'm sorry* as they traded spots.

"Just . . . stick to what was approved?" Sophia whispered back, and Kip nodded vigorously.

Immediately, Sophia felt this total loss of intimacy, being taken away from her work, her canvas, and her friend, as Vanessa laughed and began reminding Kip exactly what kind of look they had talked about.

The next touch-up on Vanessa's co-star this episode wasn't scheduled for a half hour, and rather than sit around and watch, Sophia slid out of the trailer. She found her way to the office of Roger, the executive producer, and told him what had happened. Leaving out the peach lip gloss, of course. She tried to be as neutral as possible, but if Kip was going to be co-opted the production needed to know, especially if they had to hire on an extra hairdresser for the episode.

"I'm sorry." Roger sighed. "Ever since the movie came out, she's gotten more demanding with wardrobe, too. It'll blow over. In the meantime, do what you can to keep the ship steady—no one's better at that than you."

So she focused on the co-stars, the guest stars. They'd never had better makeup in their lives. But still, watching Vanessa and Kip every day (or rather, night) was like a knife to the gut.

"Well, is it really that big of a surprise?" Kip had said, after one particularly excruciating night as they put their trailer back in order, readying it for the next day of shooting. "Vanessa is crazy jealous of you."

"Jealous? Of me?" Sophia said in utter disbelief.

"You know how all the entertainment blogs write about her. That she and her rock star hubby broke up because she wanted kids and he didn't. That she's baby crazy."

"There's no truth to that though." Sophia grunted. "You didn't put her in this Pale Moon foundation, did you? You know the way the DP lights the scene."

The director of photography was an Australian gentleman with a keen eye for framing a shot—but no idea about how lighting and makeup worked together. The one time that Sophia had used the Pale Moon foundation on an actor, she saw one frame from the video feed from the camera and forced the crew to stop shooting for an hour while she took the actor back and made him not look like a translucent zombie.

Roger had thanked her for it . . . eventually. Once he saw the dailies.

"Of course I didn't, you've taught me better than that. And isn't there?" Kip said. "You're not only pregnant, you're pregnant by her friend and her ex's bandmate. Like, it's okay for the band if Sebastian the bass player has a kid but not the lead singer? And all of this happens as she's under massive pressure from doing the awards circuit and her marriage is ending."

Sophia took a moment, let that settle under her skin.

"I'm not saying she's right," Kip said. "I'm just saying . . . give her a break. This will blow over."

But as the week progressed, and the drudgery at home and work continued, Sophia had to wonder—which would blow over first? Maisey or Vanessa?

The only thing that kept her sane was the thought of Sebastian. But unfortunately, at the moment, that's all he was—a thought. And the occasional phone call.

As much as Sebastian said he had promised to force the band to cut back and play only local gigs, those local gigs hadn't transpired. In fact, they had instead decided to join another couple indie bands on the road through the Southwest to Texas—the tickets were all presold, they were filling in for a band that had been told by their label they couldn't tour, it was a great opportunity! At least, that's how Sebastian had put it.

"Look at it this way—better to get all the touring done before the baby gets here, right?" he'd said as he packed. A little too enthusiastically, to Sophia's suspicious mind. "And this way, it'll give the manager time to get us local gigs for the fall, when the baby's here. Once that happens, I'm never leaving your side."

She couldn't do anything but agree with that. But it meant that the only person Sophia could lean on in that time was reachable only by phone, and he was on as sporadic and crazy a schedule as she was.

"HEY HON WE'RE IN PHOENIX."

"Sebastian! Oh, it's so good to hear your voice. I'm having the longest day. Still at work past midnight, of course, and I just put lipstick on my 100th pig—literally pigs, we're on a farm and it's a plot point—but you won't believe the craziness I've been dealing with. Maisey is *still*—"

"IT'S CRAZY HERE, TOO. THE SHOW IS PACKED. WE'VE NEVER PLAYED CROWDS LIKE THIS."

"It sounds like it."

"WHAT?"

Sophia took a deep breath. "I SAID IT SOUNDS LIKE IT."

"LISTEN, GOING BACK OUT FOR AN ENCORE. WE'RE GONNA DO ANOTHER SET WITH THE GUYS FROM THE OTHER BANDS. LOVE YOU!"

That was how their phone calls tended to go. It was no wonder Sophia's blood pressure had spiked slightly.

She took her blood pressure every morning (or rather, every afternoon once she woke up) with the machine Sebastian had given her. And steadily, over the course of her night shift/teenage Maisey week, it inched up.

Not crazily, but whereas her blood pressure was usually in the 110s or 120s over 70s, for the past few days it had been in the 130s. A slight uptick. She called her doctor, who told her that 1. She probably shouldn't be taking her blood pressure every day, as it was likely added pressure and stress and threw the results a bit, and 2. It was good information to have, and she should come in and they would record the results so they could keep an eye on it properly.

She went in. The doctor ordered her to pee in a cup for the next twenty-four hours (it was a very big cup) to test her protein levels.

Like that didn't add to her stress, too.

The tests came back negative. The doctor reassured her, quelled her fears. And she didn't mention any of it to Sebastian.

He would ask her if she wanted him to come home. And God help her, she would say yes, and he would. But it would be a lot to tear him away from the band. And he was working so hard to arrange things so he could be there when the baby came. Besides, the crazy was dying down. Night shoots were done by the end of the week, and they returned to a normal schedule on Monday. Once her sleep schedule flipped back around over the weekend, her blood pressure went down five points.

And once she settled things with Maisey, it would go down another five, she was sure of it.

So come Monday morning, when she was getting ready for work in the predawn hours, she also got the waffle iron out, and whipped up a new batch of delicious carbs by which to interrogate one's teenage daughter.

But this time, she would do it better. It would be Waffles Take Two.

She would go into Maisey's room, and wake her up by rubbing her back and singing softly, the way she had since she was a little girl. Then the smell of maple syrup would no doubt make her pliable enough to get an honest conversation out of her. The subsequent meal would, no doubt, make everything normal again.

But two things turned that hope into a pipe dream. While Sophia was waiting for the waffle iron to ding, a similar ding came from her pocket.

It was a web notification. Which Sophia got all the time. She had a notification set up for the show, and every morning after an episode aired her phone sounded like a pinball machine lighting up with all the watercooler articles being written. But she also had a notification set up for the band, and ever since they had been on tour, those notifications were building in frequency. In fact, she had gotten so many notifications for them recently she was about to ignore this one, but she didn't.

Although she sort of wished she had.

It was an article in the online edition of one of those glossy rags she only ever got to read when she got a manicure. It wasn't exactly a think piece—it was little more than a gushing blog post about "Hanging Out Backstage with the Hottest Band!" And there was a picture of a group of young enthusiastic groupies with Deegan, Mick, all the guys . . . and Sebastian.

The guys all had their arms around the groupies' (tiny) waists as they posed for the pic. Sophia knew—she *knew*—it wasn't any more than a photo. But Sebastian wasn't looking at the camera. He was staring deep into the eyes of one of the groupies.

Sophia knew that look.

It was the one that made her feel like the only woman in the world.

So . . . that waffle got a little burned.

However, Waffles Take Two could still be salvaged. She would just get Maisey up, and they would commence with the bonding.

But when she gently knocked on Maisey's door and poked her head in, it was to find Maisey already up and dressed with her headphones on and packing her bag.

"Where are you going?" Sophia blurted, the smell of waffles forgotten.

Maisey pulled an earbud out of her ear. "To work."

Sophia blinked twice. Twice again. "Work?"

"Yeah—I got a job."

". . . what? Where?" Sophia stuttered. What kind of job did a high school student get that started at five-thirty in the morning?

"At a florist. I'm a delivery girl."

"You can't be a delivery girl—school starts at eight AM!"

"Not for me it doesn't," Maisey said.

A cold panic shot through Sophia's chest. "You didn't . . . you can't drop out of school!"

"Oh Jesus, Mom, chill out. I didn't drop out of school. I have first period free this semester, remember? Dad signed a waiver so I can use that time for a job—an "externship" is what the school called it. So, I don't have to be at school until nine, at which time, I'm done with morning deliveries."

Sophia put a hand to her chest, to calm her racing heart. Thank God, she hadn't dropped out. In fact, it was ludicrous she'd even thought it. Maisey, for all her week's worth of temper, loved school. And probably, considering all the extra courses she'd taken over the years, she could skip the rest of the year and still get her diploma. Not that Sophia would ever want that to happen. But falling down a rabbit hole of self-pity was not Maisey's way.

Still . . . she had a lot of questions. And she asked them all at once.

"Where is this florist? How are you getting there? How are you allowed to get a job without your parents' permission? Why do you want a job? I thought you used your free period for tutoring!"

Maisey shouldered past her mother, leading them into the kitchen where the waffles sat, still steaming.

"The florist is located in the flower district downtown. I'm taking Dad's old car—he says I can use it from now on because they just got the minivan. And since Dad knows about the job, I do have parental permission, not that it's required by law. And I wanted a job, because . . . because I don't want to be here."

Those words echoed across the small kitchen, as Maisey

grabbed one waffle off the table, and took a bite, before slamming the door on her way out. The only sound louder was Sophia's heart breaking.

Sophia managed to sit at the table before her knees gave out. Her daughter didn't want to be there. Didn't want to be anywhere near her mother.

So much for Waffles Take Two.

Sophia's eyes fell to the plate on the table. The last swirls of steam rising from the golden beveled circles.

It only took a second for the plate to go flying. Crashing and breaking against the cabinets on the other side of the kitchen. The maple syrup was going to be hell to get out of the hinges.

Yup, everything would be back to normal, Sophia thought as her nose stung with held-back tears. Soon.

CHAPTER 15

"MAISEY! THANK GOODNESS YOU'RE EARLY!"

Maisey's head whipped up as she shuffled into the chaos that was the Favorite Flower. Her new boss, Lyndi, was neck deep in roses, as was everyone else. Red roses, pink roses, white roses, yellow roses, and for some reason, a small pocket of blue roses that didn't seem to be getting as much play as the others.

Maisey's eyes went wide; awake for the first time that morning. "Holy crap," she said.

"Holy crap is right," Lyndi said, on a small disbelieving laugh. "We got thirty percent more last-minute orders overnight than we were expecting. We had to beg our suppliers for emergency stock."

"Wow." They knew there might be a last-minute rush... but thirty percent more orders than they had planned for?

"Never underestimate the ability of guys to completely forget that it's Valentine's Day. Can you join the line? Throw some bouquets together?"

Maisey nodded. She'd only been on the job for a week—and granted, only as a delivery girl—but she had the basics of arranging down. She joined the assembly line right behind the head arranger, Judy, who showed her the order and sketch for the day's arrangement, and led her through her first bouquet.

And she worked like that, intensely, mindlessly, focused, for a solid forty minutes assembling bouquets. And to be honest, it was a complete relief to have that time without having to think about . . . anything.

Without having to think about her mom, or her college applications, or how she just wanted to go to the library and read for the next four to six months. Lose herself in story after story so she wouldn't have to focus on her own.

Her mother had been so . . . earnest lately. The week of night shoots—usually a really dull time for Maisey where she used the quiet time at home to either read a couple of manga she got from the library or watch the latest cool sci-fi show with hot midtwenties "teenagers" staring longingly at each other—were suddenly fraught with tension. She was wary at all times that her mom would come home from work unexpectedly, and want to *talk* more. That she would want an explanation for why Maisey hadn't done her college applications yet.

The problem was, Maisey didn't have a reason. Not a good one anyway.

Her intentions had been strong. The second she read the rejection email she got from Stanford, she immediately printed it out, reread it, set it on fire along with her Stanford T-shirt (if they were gonna crush her dreams they weren't gonna get free advertising out of her) and set about downloading and printing out the application forms for all the other schools they visited.

But as she began the tedious task of going through all

those applications—filling out the same information over and over again—her name, her birthdate, her unending desire to attend [INSERT SCHOOL NAME HERE]—she began to feel tired.

Physically, emotionally. Her body felt like it was seventy-one, and not seventeen. She just didn't want to look at the papers anymore after a while.

And so, she didn't.

For far too many weeks now.

Because why get your hopes up for an application to somewhere you didn't even know if you wanted to be?

Stanford . . . she had *known* she wanted it. The minute they walked onto campus, she'd felt this "oomph" in her stomach. She didn't feel that at UC Davis, UC San Diego (she was the only Southern Californian she knew that hated the beach with a passion bordering on fury), or Sacramento State. Just thinking about those other, lesser schools made her heart ache.

To be fair, there were two other schools that gave her a modicum of the same "oomph" as Stanford: Cal Berkeley, and UCLA. Both of which were just as difficult to get into, just as much of long shots. And if Stanford didn't want her, with her 4.5 GPA, her county-wide poetry and essay contest wins, her before- and-after-school tutoring, and her frankly amazing personal essay, then why on earth would the other two?

So she shelved her applications. And then, she found herself sitting in her classes, and her mind would wander to the same point that the applications had painted in neon: What did it matter? If she wasn't going to have the future she wanted, why was she still working so hard to achieve it?

So she sort of . . . stopped. Not entirely of course, that just wasn't in her. But she stopped doing extra. Stopped reading beyond the assigned chapters or trying to find out context. She would simply learn what they wanted her to learn, and nothing more.

Part of her just wanted to blow everything off. To ignore everything, and lose herself in trolling through her new favorite YouTube star's Instagram, or in reading a book that wasn't assigned coursework. To hole up in her room and stake that claim to it.

Because dammit, it was *her* room. She'd made that little two-bedroom apartment a home as much as her mom had. She'd chosen the colors, they'd done the painting together. It was hers. This was her home! Why should she make any effort to be anywhere else?

Because part of her—a much smaller part—knew that her mom was going to need her.

After all, she always had. A long time ago, it was Maisey who had taken over the organizing of their lives. It was Maisey who figured out their weekly schedules, where she had to be and when she had to be picked up—if she would spend the afternoon hours of the day studying in her mom's makeup trailer or if she would have soccer practice or Spanish club. It was Maisey who had put a pad of paper on the refrigerator and begun to keep a grocery list. And it was Maisey who showed her mom how to set up automatic bill pay via her bank's website.

Whether or not Sophia would have gotten around to figuring out these things eventually wasn't the point. It was Maisey who had made their lives run easier.

Was Sebastian, with his musician's priorities and unwashed hair, going to be able to fill that role? Did Sebastian even have any idea what kind of Drano to buy to deal with their problematic bathtub drain?

Would he even give a shit?

Surely, it was better if she stayed right where she was, and helped take care of her mom.

But then . . . an even smaller part—an insidious little swirl in her brain—would whisper that her mom *wouldn't* need her. That she and Sebastian and their new bouncing baby boy would be just fine without her. Building a new life without Maisey in it.

No doubt they'd move into their own place. And Sebastian would insist that Sophia hire help—someone else to keep track of the groceries, the schedule, the web bill pay feature on her bank app. Her mother—her creative, free-spirited, determined mother—would transmogrify into this new person, who would survive and succeed without Maisey's help.

And Maisey would be alone in the world.

Maybe that was why she was spending more and more time at her dad's. He *didn't* need her, but then again, he never had. It was kind of nice to not have that expectation of yourself. That you didn't have to be the responsible one. You could just be the kid, and hang out.

But even though her dad welcomed her, he didn't have much room for her either, not with toddlers running around. And Christy—his wife—was nice enough, but she had never found the ability to talk to Maisey about anything more substantial than the weather, which made her feel like a perpetual guest, and not a member of the family.

So when she saw the posting at school looking to hire delivery drivers for a florist, Maisey took the little flyer tag on impulse. She wouldn't be in the house in the mornings when her mother would try to ambush her with waffles. She would be making money. She could . . . be something else for a little while. Not Maisey the high-achieving high school student, or the failed Stanford applicant. And definitely not Maisey the responsible daughter. Just, Maisey: here to deliver your flowers.

The job had turned out to be pretty chill, with the exception of the crazy of Valentine's Day prep. Lyndi had told her she was being hired to replace someone named Stan, but since she drove a car, and his route was through downtown and better suited to a bike, they switched her out with someone else, so she had a route that took her back up to Burbank and North Hollywood. Meaning she did her deliveries, and would pull into the parking lot of school with whole minutes to spare before she had her first class of the day.

At least, that's how it had been for the first week. Now that she saw the boxes and boxes of Valentine's bouquets beginning to pile up as they went down the assembly line, she wondered if she was even going to make it to school by lunch.

She was just reaching for a stem of pink striated tea roses when another hand reached in from her left for the same stem.

"Sorry!" he said, immediately, drawing back his hand, then turning to squint at the bouquet instructions written on the big whiteboard on the wall. "I think I'm out of order."

". . . Foz?"

The mop top of perpetual bed head whipped around. "Hey, Maisey," he said, blinking behind heavy-rimmed hipster glasses. "What are you doing here?"

The last time Maisey had seen Foz, it had been in her English Lit class last semester. But he didn't have the same class with her this semester, so the tuft of hair sticking out from a folded-over set of arms, virtually asleep on the desk, had been a missing feature in her daily life.

Normally, she would have wondered what had happened

to him. AP English was a yearlong course—you didn't take it one semester and then drop it when it came time to take the actual test. Not to mention, they'd been in almost every upper level class together since the beginning of ninth grade.

But then again, she'd been preoccupied. And the whereabouts of Foz Craley were not foremost in her mind.

But now, he was standing in front of her, not slouched over, not half-asleep in class. Instead he looked very tall, very awake, and very sweaty.

"I work here," she said, once she came to her senses. "I'm the new delivery driver."

A confused look crinkled his brow. "No . . . I thought I was the new delivery driver."

"Actually, you are both the new delivery drivers," Lyndi said, coming up behind them. "We needed a new Stan, but we decided with all the extra work we'd had since Christmas to put on another. Foz is the new Stan, you're the new Diaz, who used to drive the North Hollywood route, and Diaz is now our swing driver, taking on whichever route needs extra help. Today, that's the west side."

Lyndi then checked her clipboard, then the clock, and with a "Judy, we need to start loading!" she moved off.

"Can you show me what I'm doing wrong?" Foz said, indicating the bouquet in his hand, which was, to put it kindly, lopsided. "I'm not an arranger."

"Neither am I, but I figured it out," Maisey snorted.

"Okay, fine," Foz grumbled, holding his hands up. "It's not like we're getting graded on it."

Maisey let out a long sigh. "You missed the base leaves in the beginning. They act as a cradle for the rest of the bouquet. And you have to line up the stems correctly, crisscross them, or else it looks all—"

"Like it got chewed by a dog?"

Maisey stifled a laugh. "Maybe not a dog. Maybe a vigorous gerbil."

Foz snorted at that. "Might as well start over then." He put the lumpy half arrangement in an unused bucket under the table.

"Might as well," she conceded. Then, a bit more kind, "Just follow me and do what I do."

They worked like that, side by side, quietly, for another fifteen minutes or so. Foz watched Maisey like a hawk for the first couple bouquets, but then he seemed to have it down enough to hum a song under his breath as he worked. And Maisey found it to be kind of nice. She was strangely used to Foz's presence, since he'd always been within her peripheral vision at school. It lent a normalcy to the weirdness of the new job, the new spaces she found herself in.

After a while, she found her voice enough to ask casually, "So how come I haven't seen you in AP English Lit this semester?"

He paused in his arranging. Gave her a funny look, which she caught out of the corner of her eye before continuing his latest bouquet. "I transferred schools."

She looked up. "You did?"

"Yeah. Seriously, it took you this long to notice? Man, there goes my ego."

"I . . . I didn't just notice, I just didn't know," she fumbled. "If you've transferred, it's not like we run into each other in the halls and I can ask, you know? Or that we ever really talked to begin with."

"True," he said with a nod. "We never really have talked." Then turned back to his bouquet.

They worked a little while longer in silence. But this time, instead of the silence being comfortable, Maisey was burning with questions.

"Why?" she finally asked.

"Why?"

"Why did you transfer," she clarified.

He didn't look up this time. "I wanted to be closer to my grandfather. He lives in Whittier."

Whittier was a suburb of Los Angeles to the east of downtown. "I've never been there. What's it like?" she asked.

"Same as anywhere." He shrugged.

"Still . . . sucks you transferred second semester senior year. That's practically cruel and unusual punishment."

He looked up at her then, and she had this weird feeling in her gut. Like his eyes were a really peculiar color green, and she had to keep holding his gaze to figure out if she'd ever seen this particular color green before.

"Life's full of changes, Maisey," he said, his voice softening. "You just have to roll with them."

"Still," she said, her breath strangely catching.

He shook his head. "It's not so bad. I basically have enough credits to graduate anyway, the only classes I'm taking are mandatory gym and computer tech credits. That leaves me half the day to ride my bike around delivering flowers."

"But, you're not getting your AP credits."

"Actually, I'll still be able to sit for the tests—technically you don't have to be in the class to take them."

"Oh," Maisey said. Why on earth didn't she know that? She wondered if she could register for a couple extra AP tests before end of semester . . . she'd had to sacrifice AP US History because the class was the same time as AP Spanish . . .

No. No, she told herself. She didn't care about that stuff, remember?

"Ms. Kneller is letting me keep up with the coursework on the side, too—I do the readings, turn in a paper once a week. In fact, I was dropping off a paper when I saw the job listing on the bulletin board for the delivery job. It seemed like a good way to make use of my mornings."

So Foz had been the one to tear the other tag on the flyer sheet. It was almost too perfect.

They'd always been matched pretty evenly, ever since freshman year.

"You dropped off a paper? You didn't email it?" she questioned.

He gave a quizzical little smile. "You with the logic. You're like Sherlock Holmes."

She simply blinked at him, waiting for an answer.

"Hey, maybe it's nice to visit the old stomping grounds every now and then. The principal said I can even walk the stage at graduation, since I did most of my coursework there. And I already got early admission to USC, so I'm not too worried about my transcripts."

Maisey felt that flip in her stomach again. But this time it was due not to Foz's strangely green eyes, but to the acid that had begun churning.

"USC," she said, choking the words down. "Awesome."

"What about you?" he asked. "You were applying to Stanford early admission, right?"

He was watching her carefully. And she could have made some flippant answer, brushed off her rejection. Or just have lied outright and said she was keeping her options open. But mercifully, before she could open her mouth to answer, Lyndi's voice rang out from her position on the stairs.

"All bouquets are accounted for—that should do it, everyone!"

They began moving the heavy boxes of bouquets from their assembly line on the floor to the back loading dock where the delivery drivers were lining up. Maisey had parked her dad's old Corolla there when she came in early, so naturally she was first in line. She popped the trunk, and opened the back doors, and began sorting through the boxes to find the ones with the Burbank/North Hollywood code that let her know they were hers to deliver.

She found the right pallet. Then, she looked at it.

Maybe her Dad's Corolla wasn't built for the flower delivery service.

There were boxes on boxes on boxes. And somehow, they had to all fit inside the four-door sedan.

"Welp," Foz said, coming up beside her. "This is going to take some physics. Or you could just do two runs. That's what I did this morning."

So, Foz had already gone on one bike run this morning. No wonder he had been all sweaty and, er . . . glistening when he came in.

Maisey shook her head. "I have to be in class after this."

"Well, then let's start playing our game of car Tetris."

They worked side by side, trying to fit the boxes into the Corolla's trunk, then the backseat, and finally the front passenger seat.

By the time they were done, Maisey was as sweaty as Foz.

"Never let it be said that two overachieving kids can't accomplish anything together," she said between heavy breaths.

"Oh no, you're not all loaded already?" Lyndi said, coming up behind them, making Maisey jump. Seriously, how did she do that? Lyndi was like this little sprite hovering over your shoulder—you don't realize it's there until your conscience needs a poke.

"These three boxes were on the wrong pallet—they belong on your route, Maisey," Lyndi said, indicating the triple stack next to her.

Foz and Maisey looked from the three boxes, to the overstuffed car, then back to Lyndi.

"You might have to do two runs after all," Foz said.

"School, remember?"

"No worries, Maisey, you'll make it to school, I promise," Lyndi said. "I can take some of the route, ride my bike up—"

"No you can't, Lyndi!" Judy's voice rang out. "You know what Paula said about riding in your condition."

"Condition?" Maisey asked, trying not to notice the crestfallen look on her immediate superior's face.

"I'm pregnant," Lyndi said, matter-of-factly.

Well. There seemed to be nothing but pregnant people around her these days, Maisey thought.

She wasn't the only one who felt the awkwardness of knowing more about her boss's reproductive health than she should. Foz ducked it entirely, grabbing one of the boxes and saying, "Let me see what I can do."

Maisey and Lyndi stood, watching Foz bend and twist and find a way to fit three extra boxes of flowers in the already jam-packed car.

"So . . . how far along are you?" Maisey asked. She'd been around her mother long enough to know this was a question that pregnant ladies got asked.

"Twenty-one weeks," she replied. "Halfway there."

"And . . . how are you feeling?"

Lyndi snorted. "Annoyed, mostly. Like the only thing important about me at the moment is what's in my uterus."

She'd directed this comment at the passing Judy, who ignored her with her nose in the air.

"Can I ask you a question?" Maisey said suddenly.

"Sure."

"Is it weird?"

Lyndi regarded her. "Yes. But it's also weirdly normal. This is something that happens all the time. You just gotta roll with it."

Roll with it.

Was that what her mom was doing—rolling with it? Working, trying to keep Maisey in check, taking her blood pressure daily, and making all those incremental adjustments that led to the big one?

It sounded exhausting.

"And . . . how do you roll with it?" she asked.

A smile softened Lyndi's face. "I haven't quite figured that out yet."

"That's what happens when your roommate makes you his baby mama." Judy clucked her tongue as she passed. "Confusion."

"He's not my roommate, he's my boyfriend," Lyndi said through gritted teeth.

"Not according to him," Judy singsonged as she pushed a new pallet of bouquets.

"Wait . . . what did you say?" Lyndi said, immediately frowning as she followed after. "Judy!"

But Judy was giggling with the other arrangers as they helped the drivers load their flowers, looking at something on their phones.

Just then, Foz ducked back out of the car, breathing heavy, but triumphant.

"Okay!" he said, brushing imaginary dust off his hands. "You are all set. I have no idea how you're going to deliver all of these before class starts, but good luck."

He flipped her car keys around his fingers, catching them in his hand before holding them out to her.

"Thanks," she said. "And thanks for loading my car."

"No problem. Oh, and happy Valentine's Day. To that end . . ." Foz reached behind him, and into a bucket that she hadn't noticed by the car. "Here. You deserve these."

He held out the abandoned lopsided bouquet, his first attempt at flower arranging.

"For teaching me."

She took the flowers, gingerly. Uncertain what to do with them, she held them between herself and Foz, like a barricade made of petals and missing thorns.

"Well, I should . . . get going," she said.

"Me, too. I have to load my bike for my next run."

She climbed into the driver's seat. She turned the engine on (once she shoved back the flowers that were blocking the ignition)—then, abruptly turned it off.

"What's wrong?" Foz asked immediately.

"Nothing. Hey—if you went on a run this morning, did you go to the LA Center Studios?"

He shook his head. "I don't have any deliveries there today."

"But my moth—I mean, isn't there usually a delivery to one of the shows? *Fargone?*"

"Yeah, but that's on Mondays." Foz shrugged. "It's not Monday."

As he moved off, Maisey chewed her lip.

Her mom wasn't getting any flowers today. Which meant Sebastian had forgotten Valentine's Day.

It took Maisey the better part of three hours to make all of her deliveries in the North Hollywood/Burbank route. Thankfully, she didn't have to be in school until second period, but she was still so late when she pulled into the school parking lot, she had already missed half of AP Spanish.

So, she could either sit in her car for another twenty minutes, waiting for the school bell to ring, or she could try and sneak in the back of class.

Or, she could make one last delivery.

After all, the lopsided flowers Foz had given her couldn't sit in her car all day. And home was mere blocks away.

A vase, spread out the arrangement in some water, and it wouldn't look so lumpy anymore. It might even look like something that Sebastian had special ordered.

Because as much as she hated to admit it, she *had* seen her mother these past few weeks. No matter how much she tried to ignore her, and stay in her own, angsty headspace, she could still see Sophia out of her peripheral vision. Worried. Waiting. Wanting.

And just yesterday, red-nosed from crying.

That had almost made Maisey stay home that morning. Instead, coward that she was, she ran out the door even earlier, to avoid seeing any more evidence of her parent's pain.

She parked on the street, trotted up the steps, and unlocked the door to their apartment. She would just pop these on the kitchen table in the bright Fiestaware vase she'd given her mother as a Christmas gift when she was six. That way, the flowers could be credited to both of them—her and Sebastian.

That lanky idiot was lucky she was there to cover for him.

But the moment she walked into the kitchen, she was assaulted by the realization that said lanky idiot didn't require her to cover for him.

Because he was there.

And he was basically *licking* her mother.

"Oh—oh, Maisey!" her mom said in between giggles. "Sebastian—stop that!" She gently pushed Sebastian on the chest and got him to retract his tongue from her ear. "What are you doing home?"

"I . . . I had a free period and I needed to grab something I forgot. For class," she finished lamely. "What are you doing home?"

"Well, I was on my way to work when I opened the door, and found this magnificent gentleman on our doorstep," her mother cooed into Sebastian's adoring (. . . gak . . .) face.

"I drove all night from our gig in Phoenix. I wasn't going to let this little lady spend V-Day without her baby daddy. So I told her to call in sick."

Considering her mother was not in work clothes and wearing her flowered satin bathrobe—and Sebastian was wearing her blue polka-dotted one—Maisey did not like to guess what had happened in the interim between her mother leaving for work and Maisey walking in the door.

But something else irked Maisey more. "You *told* her? To compromise her job?" The last time her mother had ever taken sick days was when Maisey had mono in eighth grade. That game of spin the bottle had taken down half the class.

"They don't need me today anyway." Sophia sighed. "There are no department meetings, and it's just the principals filming, and Vanessa won't let me touch her with a ten-foot pole."

"Nessa's just been bitchy because her movie got completely shut out for Oscar noms, so she doesn't get to go to the awards," Sebastian said. "I'll talk to her, baby, don't you worry."

"Oh, Sebastian," her mother sniffled. The tears were welling again. No doubt a great deal of emotions and hormones and endorphins were rushing through her body, making her horribly sentimental and girly.

That was the only excuse for the sappy look she had on her face. And the fact that she would ever, ever let this guy intervene in her work.

"I have no doubt my mom can handle it, Sebastian," Maisey said, hard.

"Maisey's right, babe," Sophia said, looking between her absolutely correct daughter and her overstepping boyfriend. "Although I appreciate it. Just like I appreciate your Valentine's Day present."

"What present?" Maisey asked, kicking herself for letting her curiosity get the better of her, because now she was subject to Sebastian taking off the robe (gak!) and exposing his shoulder.

Where there was a fresh, shiny tattoo, with the name *Sophia* in elaborate script.

"What do you think, Maisey?" he asked. "Got it last week. Couldn't stop thinking about your mom when we were in San Antonio, so I decided to give my thoughts some permanence."

San Antonio. If memory served, that was where the groupie pic from that article was taken. Her mom didn't think she knew about it, but she wasn't the only one with web notifications.

"Cool," Maisey said through clenched teeth.

Then her mom's gaze fell to the flowers in Maisey's hand.

"Where did you get the flowers, honey?" Then her eyes lit up. "Are they from a boy?"

Technically, yes. But . . . "Um, no. They are from work. Extras. Here. Put them in a vase, would you?"

She handed them lamely to her mom.

"Thank you, honey!" she said, burying her nose in them, then took in their half-formed arrangement. "They're . . . er . . . gorgeous."

"Need to work on your flower arranging skills," Sebastian said. "If you want to keep your job, kid."

"Sebastian!" her mother said in mock outrage. "Maisey can do anything she sets her mind to."

"Right. Totally. Except flower arranging. And she works at a flower shop."

As her mother swatted Sebastian playfully, and he wrapped himself around her again like the octopus he was, Maisey cleared her throat.

"ANYWAY." Her mom glanced her way, but Sebastian's tongue was aiming for the right ear again. "I'm just gonna grab that thing from my room."

"Okay, hon. You want anything? I made waffles . . . well I made them a while ago but they can be nuked."

"Nope, I'm good," Maisey said, stalking away to her room before she vomited.

"Yeah, we sort of forgot about the waffles, didn't we?" she heard Sebastian purr, and her mother's corresponding giggle.

Once safely in her room, Maisey pushed her back against the door in relief. The walls of their apartment were just getting more and more stifling. Then, her eyes fell to her little desk.

And the pile of college applications sitting on top.

Before she could change her mind, she grabbed them all, and stuffed them into her bag.

Time to get this done, she decided.

Every single rationalization she had for avoiding it had fled as she watched her mother only have eyes for Sebastian. And Maisey would be damned if she stuck around to watch out of fear or spite or whatever it was that had her acting like such a coward.

No. She was going to get the hell out of there.

CHAPTER 16

THE AMOUNT OF CRAP LYNDI HAD TO PUT UP with at work the week of Valentine's Day should have earned her a six-day, seven-night all-inclusive spa vacation with cabana boys who could double for Ryan Reynolds feeding her plate after plate of eggs Benedict.

Instead, she'd gotten to deal with delayed orders of flowers, last-minute reorganizing to accommodate extra orders, a minor website crash, and taking on customer service duties the day after the Big V, which meant she mostly dealt with first and/or sole time customers completely flummoxed by the return policy, when their declarations of love didn't go how they had hoped.

On the one hand, this was invigorating—she handled everything with grace and aplomb, and in a timely fashion. She didn't back down with their wholesalers. She held her ground with the arrangers. She got in and got her hands dirty, showing everyone what she was capable of doing, even if her stomach was starting to poke out a bit and her boobs leaking ever so slightly. (Seriously, how did that happen?

There wasn't going to be a baby for another four and a half months, but by God, there would be milk ready for it.)

On the other, it also allowed Lyndi—or forced her, depending on your perspective—to ignore Marcus for the time being.

And what he had done.

He had not done anything as banal as forgetting Valentine's Day—indeed, with Lyndi stressing about rose orders, he could hardly forget. In fact, they had promised each other no gifts—Lyndi was thoroughly hearted-out, and Marcus had been so busy putting the finishing touches on a new article that he'd only had time to rub Lyndi's feet twice a day instead of the usual five.

And then, Valentine's Day arrived.

And Lyndi finally got to read the article Marcus had been working on.

So did the rest of the world.

TELLING MY EX-BOYFRIEND I GOT MY ROOMMATE PREGNANT

It had been a small article, intended for the listicle website's cynical, millennial-focused Valentine's Day coverage. It was buried among a dozen other articles by the website's usual late-twentysomething contributors, most about the hazards of modern dating, the perils of swiping left or right, and the bewilderment of parents who had helicoptered their children's entire lives, but somehow could not helicopter them into long-term satisfying relationships.

Needless to say, Marcus's article had stood out.

And stood out far enough to end up on the phones of her co-workers, as they loaded bouquets into cars and onto bikes.

Exactly what she needed to be dealing with on such a crazy day.

When she took the phone from Judy and she saw the title of the article, it was like she couldn't remember how to read. She knew she was looking at letters, and words, but they didn't translate in her brain. For the first time that day, she didn't know what to do.

Luckily it only lasted a few seconds. Then she handed the phone back to Judy and said, "If you ladies have so much time on your hands these deliveries should already be loaded."

She'd said it in her best Paula-inspired Boss voice, her best Nathalie-teacher voice. And it worked. Everyone went back to loading up the deliveries. And if they shot Lyndi the occasional hooded look, well, that's what the boss got, right? No point in making a big deal out of it. It would blow over. Much like everything else on the internet, Marcus's article would be forgotten and replaced with the next thing . . . likely a timely article written by another millennial about how St. Patrick's Day is *really* about community and green artisanal beer and not about that month's excuse to drink yourself stupid.

(That was an unkind thought, Lyndi said. But she was a little disappointed that she was going to have to sit out her friends' green beer meet-up this year. Not that she'd gotten the invite yet.)

Yes, she was convinced the article would be forgotten. So when she got home that night, she let Marcus rub her feet, and tell her excitedly about how the article had been received. About how it had gotten more clicks than any other Valentine's Day article they posted that day. And about how he'd gotten such positive feedback on his writing.

"An agent even called me! A literary agent!" he'd said,

unable to hide his grin. She let him clink his glass of sparkling apple cider up against hers, as he leaned in for a kiss.

And she knew what type of kiss it was.

Usually, she was reciprocal, if not actively initiating sex. For real, since she'd gotten pregnant (and past the constant-nausea stage) her main pregnancy symptom was unending randiness. A circumstance which Marcus was bemusedly more than happy to take advantage of.

But at that moment, she really couldn't celebrate with him.

"Sorry, babe," she'd said, gently pushing him back. "I'm exhausted from today."

She knew they'd get their groove back, just as she knew *Telling My Ex-Boyfriend I Got My Roommate Pregnant* would disappear into the ether, before anyone in her family or friends circle could find it. No one read Marcus's listicle website— or at least, they didn't admit to it.

Then, it got picked up for the *New York Times'* Modern Romance column.

And suddenly, everyone had read it.

"Lyndi!" her sister exclaimed when she called. "I just read Marcus's article. It's, um . . . very honest. I didn't know he'd been in such a long-term relationship."

"Oh, honey!" This from her mom. "I'm just so proud of that boy of yours—the *New York Times!* I've told all my friends . . . although you think they would have fixed that typo in the title! It's the *New York Times,* after all."

Lyndi did not have to guess what her mother thought the typo was.

But hey, at least it got her friends—or at least Elizabeth— to reach out to her via text.

OMG just read Marcus's article in NYT! So brave!

You must be so proud!

Yup. Proud. That was totally what she was.

It was only at this point that she could bring herself to read the article.

There was nothing in it that wasn't true. It detailed a lunch Marcus had had with Frankie, his ex-boyfriend. A lunch she'd even known about. Marcus and Frankie had been together all through college, and for a little while after. When Marcus made the move to LA, Frankie made the move to the East Coast. They'd decided to split, but still remained close friends.

When Frankie was coming through town, Marcus had been so excited. Lyndi had been, too—she'd wanted to meet Frankie ever since she learned about his existence. But Marcus had suggested, with a glance at Lyndi's slightly expanded waistline, that he go and see Frankie on his own. Their relationship was pretty complicated, after all. Which Lyndi accepted.

Sure, she might be curious about the man who had loved Marcus before she did. And that curiosity might have led her to do a couple of Google searches in the past, but she wasn't jealous. There was no reason to be. She knew that now she and the baby were the center of Marcus's life.

At least, that's what she'd thought, until she read the article.

Of course, she couldn't say this to Marcus. Because Marcus was riding an unanticipated career high.

"I can't believe it," he said, as he threw shirts onto their bed, trying to figure out which ones were fashionable enough for his purposes. "I thought they were going to read the book proposal and laugh their heads off. And not in a good way."

Marcus had indeed talked to that literary agent. And that

literary agent had convinced him to put together a book proposal based on his two memoir-ish articles about his life. A twenty-something writing his memoirs was laughable, as Marcus himself said, but this literary agent seemed adamant that he had a voice that needed to be heard.

So, he took a week off of listicle writing, and pounded out a ten-page document outlining the basic shape of the book, as well as a sample first chapter. That, along with his two articles, was submitted to the agent. Who apparently submitted it immediately to a few publishers. And now, the agent was flying him to New York to meet with the publishers individually, to "see if they clicked," as the agent put it.

"I'm just sad that I'm going to have to miss the baby shower," Marcus said. He was planning on being in New York for a week. Unfortunately, it was the week that her mom had planned—down to the last pink napkin—to have her baby shower.

Invitations had gone out formally in January. Like, real invitations. On paper. Lyndi hadn't gotten a paper invitation to a party . . . ever, that she could remember. Even her one friend who got married right out of college had sent the invites via Instagram to the masses. And held the event in a bar.

The baby shower—rather, the joint baby shower with Nathalie—would be held in a bar, too. The Ora Café, to cater to Lyndi's vegan-esque pregnancy tastes. While glad that they wouldn't have to trek all the way up to Santa Barbara again, she was a little worried that none of her friends would have the easy excuse of the party being too far away, so they would have to come up with something even more lame to avoid her.

And since Marcus would be in New York, Lyndi was 100

percent certain she would be standing at her baby shower alone.

"I know, it sucks," she said, picking out her favorite red shirt of his, folding it, and putting it in his suitcase. "But you have a really good reason. Not even Kathy could argue against it."

Marcus grinned. "But she tried."

"She did," Lyndi agreed. Now that she was building her own family, it felt like her mom saw her differently—and she was starting to get some of the frustration Nathalie was always complaining about. "But I'm so jealous you're getting a week in New York! If I was going I would spend the entire week just walking around Brooklyn."

"Sounds like something you wouldn't want to do in winter."

"Ugh, I always forget it isn't seventy-five degrees and perfect everywhere."

"I wish you could come with me," Marcus said, wrapping his arms around her and kissing her on the nose. She let herself slide into his embrace. Time had passed, and she was feeling a little bit more sentimental. Maybe not back into their groove, per se, but well on their way.

"Me, too. But can't miss the shower—not to mention work." Ever since Valentine's Day, they had kept a surprising amount of their new customers, which meant more work, which meant Paula needed her more than ever. "But I was thinking . . . I could come over the next weekend? We could change your tickets, you could stay another couple days. I did glance at flights, and they're pretty reasonable this time of year."

"That's an idea," Marcus said. "I'll ask Frankie."

Lyndi froze. "Frankie?"

"Yeah—ask if he's willing to put up with the two of us for a day or two."

"You're . . . you're staying with Frankie?"

"Of course. The agent is covering my tickets, but I couldn't let her put me up in a hotel, especially when Frankie's couch is right there."

And with those words, something in Lyndi—something that usually kept her quiet, and kept the peace—broke. The pain that had been fomenting inside of her ever since she read that article a week ago spilled out.

"Are you serious? You're staying with Frankie?"

"Well, yeah," Marcus said, finally looking up at her distraught tone. "He's basically my best friend."

"The best friend you used to sleep with." The spite dripped from her words in ways she didn't mean it to.

But it certainly got his attention.

"Yes. Are you telling me you're not friends with any of your exes?"

"Not *best* friends. Not 'stay on their couch' friends. Not write an entire article about having lunch with said *friend*."

"Okay," Marcus said, closing his suitcase with a forceful *thud*. "Let's do it."

"Do what?"

"You've been weird since the article came out in the *Times*. What the hell is bothering you about it?"

"Nothing."

"Sure doesn't feel like nothing. I've seen you swallow the congratulations I've been getting. You turn the conversation away every time it comes up."

"Maybe I've got other things on my mind, ever think of that?"

Apparently he had thought of that, or more so, he didn't care, because he laughed in a broken, harsh way.

"Come off it. You know what's bothering you, and so do I."

"Oh really? If you knew what was bothering me about the article, I doubt you would have written it that way."

"You know, I can't change the fact that Frankie was the first person I ever loved. And that loving him changed my life. But the fact that you would rather I hide that about myself is really, really disappointing."

"What?" she replied, blinking in shock. "That has nothing to do with it."

"You pretend to be this open-minded, thoughtful person, but really, you're just a sheltered suburban little girl at heart."

"Wow." She couldn't contain her shock. "It's almost like you expected this fight. Dare I say you're spoiling for it? Could it be that this trip to New York is a chance to rekindle an old romance?"

"Don't be ridiculous. If I were going to be with Frankie I'd be with Frankie. We didn't work out. But Frankie was and is important to me! You don't get to be mad that I'm seeing him!"

"I'm not mad that you're seeing him!" Lyndi replied, hot. "I'm angry that you decided to tell the whole world that—"

"That what? That I'm bisexual? I wrote my first article about that, too! I'm not hiding it. But now that everyone you know knows it, suddenly it's shameful!"

"Don't you dare put those words in my mouth!"

"I'm not going to say I'm sorry that I loved him because it makes you more comfortable. I'm not going to say I'm sorry for writing it, either!"

"I don't hate the article you wrote because of what you said about Frankie. I hate what you wrote about *me*!"

Marcus's hands went to his hair, nearly pulling it out. "What on earth did I say about you in the article?"

"Nothing!" she cried. "And that's the problem. Nothing beyond calling me your 'roommate.'"

Marcus opened his mouth to reply, but something stopped him. Perhaps, Lyndi thought between gulping breaths, he had finally heard her.

"The entire article, I'm your roommate. Not your girl-friend. Not even your 'baby mama' as much as I despise that term. That's what Nathalie calls us—roommates. Never to my face. But she does. I could take it from her because I thought she just didn't get it. But I never expected to hear it from you."

Again, nothing from Marcus.

"*That's* what you told the world. What you told my family and friends. I thought I was more than that."

"You are." He moved toward her, his arms open.

"Since when?" she asked, stopping him in his tracks. "When in your mind, did we stop being roommates and start being together?"

". . . I . . . I dunno. Around the time—"

"Around the time I told you I was pregnant?"

His silence was all the answer he needed to give.

"I thought we'd been more a lot longer than that," she said sadly. "I guess Nathalie was right. I guess you were always just my roommate."

"Lynds—I wasn't sleeping with anyone else. Before the baby I mean. I just . . . it's hard for me to place my trust in a relationship. Any relationship."

"Would we even be together without the baby?" she asked.

"Yes!" he answered immediately.

"You seem awfully sure for someone who thinks I'm a closed-minded suburbanite at heart."

"Lyndi." He sighed. "I'm sorry, I shouldn't have said that. I do want you. I want this baby. I want us."

"Which do you want most?" she asked. It was an unfair question. But it was one by God she needed an answer to.

And it was an answer he apparently could not give, because he remained heartbreakingly silent.

"You know what, have fun in New York," she said, defeated. "I'll see you when you get back."

"Where are you going?" he asked, as she moved to the door to grab her jacket and her helmet.

"I'm just going for a ride. Clear my head."

"Are you sure you should—"

But before he could get the worried sentence out, she was through the door.

And she made it all the way down the stairs, out the front door, and nearly onto her bike before she burst into tears.

MARCH

The nesting. Oh God, the nesting.

CHAPTER 17

 ANOTHER DAY, ANOTHER TRIP TO IKEA, Nathalie thought, as she followed by rote its amiable arrow-lit paths. Since becoming pregnant, there was something so soothing about the big blue box that dominated downtown Burbank. She had come here after work more often than she liked to admit, enjoying the meatballs and the affordably priced modernity. Even the plethora of Allen wrenches. But really, she knew the reason she found IKEA so delightful at the moment was it had everything she needed, for each and every room, and lots of it.

Which for someone who felt time creeping up and her preparedness sliding away, was more relaxing than a coma.

But this trip was not destined to be soothing. No . . . this trip was already fraught with assembled-furniture-related tension. Because this time, Nathalie had David in tow.

"I thought you said we had all this stuff on the registry?" David said, as he kept a foot behind her, lollygagging as she beelined straight for the nursery section.

"We have a lot of things on the registry," she replied, her teeth unconsciously gritting. He would know what they had on the registry if he'd ever *looked* on the registry. She'd signed him up for it, too, he could just log on anytime. But no . . . that didn't happen. "But stuff like storage bins, and oh! These cute little night-lights! They are just finishing touches for the nursery."

Part of Nathalie realized she was in a hard-core nesting phase. But that didn't mean that David wasn't driving her crazy. If he wasn't asking her relentless *why-do-we-need-this* questions, he was ignoring her and her extremely necessary preparations completely. The spare room, which currently was a catch-all office/guest room/place where David's dumb-bells went to die was scheduled to be turned into the perfect nursery for their little girl, who at this point, was only thir-teen short weeks from joining them.

But David didn't seem to feel the immediacy of this. He ig-nored every single attempt Nathalie made to get him to move his stuff out of the spare room so they could start painting the walls. Meanwhile, Nathalie spent hours agonizing over paint chips, coming up with a shade called Blue Iris for their daughter's room.

"Blue?" Kathy had asked when Nathalie explained her design scheme. "But you're having a girl!"

"It's a very feminine blue," she had replied, but Kathy con-tinued on, sputtering objections, and plotting out ways to incorporate pinks into the curtains and linens.

But David wasn't objecting to her designs, and her femi-nine blues. He was putting up barriers to *any* change what-soever.

"Do we really need bins and night-lights?" he replied, de-feat evident in his voice.

"*YES*," she replied. "We do."

"Fine. Then why are we looking at cribs?"

Nathalie blinked at him. "Because I told you we are getting the crib today."

"It's not on the registry?"

She took his phone out of his hand, and queued it up to their registry website. "Why don't you look at the registry and tell me what's on there."

David took the phone from her, gingerly, like it was a time bomb. Good, maybe a little more irritating and a little less teacher-patience was required in the present situation. Especially considering how crowded IKEA got on a Saturday afternoon. Her bastion of peace and tranquility was quickly becoming overstuffed with people here for KALLAX bookshelves and Swedish Fish.

Really, if it wasn't for her anonymous Twitter friend, she would have lost her temper with David long ago.

> @WTFPreg—"We're having a baby so we have to get rid of all this stuff." "I'm giving you a baby and you're taking my stuff?!?!?"

The latest series of tweets actually gave her a small amount of sympathy for David's position. He didn't have the kind of keen baby-focus that Nathalie had, if simply because she was reminded of it every minute of every day, now that the baby was tap-dancing on her abdomen.

But still, he wasn't the only one giving up their stuff. She'd lost her office space, too, to make room for their daughter. She'd already dragged her little desk out of the spare room and into a tight corner in the bedroom, and put all of her extra stuff in storage. Why David, who didn't have the burden of working on his feet all day *and* being pregnant, couldn't bring himself to do the same was . . . well, it was heartbreaking.

She knew he was stressed and just wanted to play video games. She knew he was under pressure. But she also came to understand—quite recently—that he had put a lot of that pressure on himself.

As she stared hard at him, and he avoided her eyes by seemingly scrolling through the baby registry on his phone, the phone miraculously buzzed in his hand.

He couldn't hide his relief as he answered it.

"Hey, Brian. Yes . . . yes I sent the documents . . . Hello? . . . hello, I'm losing you . . ."

And then the line went dead.

David blew out a breath, frustrated. "Okay, I'm going to go stand outside, call him back."

Nathalie reared back, livid. "No you're not!"

"I can't not reply. And I have no reception in here."

"This place is twenty-two acres big—if you leave you'll never find me again."

"I'll call you."

"Not if there's no reception," she countered immediately.

David's mouth hung open, stopped by sound logic. Then he shook it off, and was back to being able to argue in his lawyerly fashion. "Then let's go. We can come back another day. This place is too crowded anyway."

Nathalie found herself breathing like a bull in the ring. "David, we have to do this today! Because you haven't wanted to come and do it any other day."

"I haven't been *able* to come and do it any other time. You know how crazy work is right now."

Her eyes narrowed, her hands went to her hips.

"Yes, David, I know exactly how busy you've been. Dinner last night clarified that point very accurately."

David's eyes went stony. In retrospect, perhaps IKEA

wasn't the ideal place for a couple who had an unfinished fight simmering from the night before. But then again, not mentioning to your wife that no one at your office knew she was pregnant was a bit of a faux pas, too.

Nathalie had been looking forward to last night's dinner since David had told her about it a week before. His immediate boss, Brian, had invited them to meet him and his wife at Burbank's finest steakhouse, a fancy-enough place to throw Nathalie into a tizzy of clothes-related panic.

The difficulty was none of her fancy dresses accommodated her belly anymore, and all of her maternity clothes were meant for school—professional, but not exactly cocktail attire.

"I could wear the red one, I suppose? It's empire-waisted, and I think I'll be okay in heels still . . ." she had said to David as she pulled out every single article of clothing in her closet that fit. He sat on the bed, in his suit, looking miserable. But hey, that was the husband's role in this particular situation, wasn't it? "I could wear the black skirt and a top if I dress it up a little with accessories? Or there's the green sheath dress . . . it's not very fancy, but I look the least pregnant in it "

"The green dress," David said immediately.

"Why?" she asked, suddenly suspicious.

He shrugged a little and said, "It's my favorite."

She felt a suffuse glow of pleasure as she put the green dress on, happy that David had a favorite of hers from her new temporary wardrobe. However, that sneaking suspicion didn't let go of the back of her brain. And she should have paid more attention to it.

Brian was a ruddy-faced man with hair several shades lighter than his complexion. His wife was small with a wide, welcoming smile. Nathalie liked them immediately. Odd, considering how much she had been prepared to be intimidated by the man whose dictates had been keeping her husband on his work-toes for the last six months.

"So Dave here says you're an English teacher!" Brian said, as they sat down to dinner. "You must give my wife recommendations for books, she can't get enough—three book clubs!"

"Oh, not before cocktails!" his wife replied. "Two drinks in and I'll be telling you all about how much I detested *The Road*."

"It's a Cormac McCarthy script you're doing all those contracts on, isn't it Davy-boy?" Brian said, turning to David, who did not, for once in his life, seem to mind being called Dave or Davy-boy.

"Pfft," his wife said, winking at Nathalie. "My husband never listens to my opinion on books."

"Hey, he sells tickets and wins Oscars," her husband replied.

"That was last month's adventure in lit acquisition," David replied with a good-natured smile. "Long hours. But it all turned out in our favor."

"Then what have you been doing this month?" Nathalie asked her husband. He had been coming home just as late, playing just as many alien-blowing-up video games, taking just as many after-hours phone calls. If he didn't have a huge project . . .

"I'd love to know that, too! Seriously, I've never met anyone more dedicated to get his desk cleared by the end of business," Brian said. "You've got a go-getter there, Nathalie."

"I've been working on ironing out those last wrinkles in the terms for the new development from our Japanese acquisition," David replied judiciously.

"Oh good," Brian's wife exclaimed as the waiter approached

to take their drinks order. "I'll have a double martini, my husband will have a manhattan. Nathalie, what would you like?"

"Nothing for me, thanks," she demurred, and turned her attention back to David and Brian.

"That? We don't need those done until next business quarter! My goodness, you are a showstopper."

Nathalie watched David's face closely. His good-natured smile was becoming strained, his posture stiff. He usually reveled in being praised for his hard work.

But this . . . this sounded like he was trying to put as much distance between himself and his work as possible—even though he never stopped doing it.

"Oh, but you must have something!" Brian's wife butted into her thoughts again. "A glass of wine, perhaps?"

"Oh, she's not—er, that is . . ." David stuttered.

"I'm not drinking," she said easily. "I'm pregnant."

The sound that came out of Brian's wife's mouth could only be described as a Muppet squeal. Then, she swatted her husband's arm. "You sly dog, why didn't you tell me!"

"I didn't know myself," Brian said, with a slow smile of awareness. "Davy-boy, you've been playing things close to the vest, haven't you? No wonder you're getting next quarter's work done now."

"Oh you lucky girl! We never had kids ourselves, Brian's work always made timing impossible, and then my life just got so crazy, and well . . . we made do."

"Yep, with all the extra income and time to travel and go enjoying life," Brian guffawed. Nathalie saw David's jaw twitch.

As Brian's wife had inundated her with the usual questions ("When are you due?" "Boy or girl?" "How are you feeeeeeeeeling?"), Nathalie glanced at her husband, who would not meet her eye. On the inside, she festered. But oddly, she could tell that David was, too. What on earth did he have to fester about? He wasn't the one ambushed by people not knowing about their growing family—a family he seemed to be in complete denial of if he hadn't even told his closest associate at work!

After that, dinner had taken on a false lightness. While Brian and his wife took on the full delights of the bar, David didn't drink more than a glass of wine. Still his face was red with the effort it took to keep Brian talking, and off the subject of their child. Meanwhile, Nathalie listened to the conversations, tried to contribute with personal and humanizing stories about her husband to cast him in the best light, all the while she was roiling on the inside.

And now, they stood in the middle of IKEA, at a détente over a phone call and bad reception.

"You don't need me to pick out a crib," David said dismissively. "You can do what you want."

"We should be doing this stuff together." Nathalie sighed. But when David remained silent, she huffed out a breath. "*Fine.* I'll pick out the crib on my own. Just like I'll paint the nursery on my own, and move all your stupid dumbbells out on my own, and do *everything* on my own!"

David didn't seem aware of the people that had begun to give them a wide berth as they stood in the nursery section, because he came to loom over her, his voice raised. "Well, we wouldn't have to be doing any of this if you hadn't insisted on getting pregnant!"

Sound rushed out and back in again like waves on the shore, while Nathalie made sure she'd heard what she'd heard. Then . . .

"*WHAT?*" she screeched.

And just like that, they had become that couple. The one having a fight in the middle of IKEA. But she had stopped caring—or possibly stopped seeing everyone's stares. The only thing she could see was David's face, and the naked truth he was finally revealing.

"I don't recall getting pregnant *on my own.* You were a willing and enthusiastic participant!" she yelled. "We've talked about a family for *years.*"

"And then it took us *years* to get here," David yelled. "I finally got settled in a new job, we finally paid off student loans. You know what I was going to do if we didn't get pregnant when we did? I was going to ask if we could take a break from trying. We could have saved money, and just been David and Nathalie again. I was going to take you to Italy to visit my parents. Instead, we have a house, and we are going to have to replace the air-conditioning system soon because it's a thousand years old and we will *never* get ahead now. How are we supposed to save for college? Why should I make up a will and trust if we have nothing to leave our kid?"

Nathalie watched him, oddly dispassionate. She had to stay cold. Because otherwise she would have disintegrated into tears from his overheated words.

"So excuse me, if I'm late home from work occasionally, or need to take a call, while I try to make myself so indispensable to my bosses that I'll have a job so we can stay on this insane and stupid roller coaster!" he finished through gritted teeth.

She waited one second. Two. Stared him down. And finally he seemed to realize that not only had he lost his temper.

He'd lost it in the middle of IKEA.

Then, Nathalie—the Nathalie who dealt with ninety-seven students on a daily basis as well as administrators and parents and Kathy and her dad and Lyndi—emerged.

"So let's just not have the baby," she said, utterly dispassionate.

"Don't be ridiculous."

"I'm not the one being ridiculous."

He threw up his hands. "I can't talk about this now."

"No, you don't get to testify without hearing counterarguments, counselor," she replied, rounding on him. "You don't get to have buyer's remorse. You don't get to pretend that this isn't happening, by 'neglecting' to mention to your boss that we're pregnant. It is. Nor do you get to pretend that you never wanted it. I'm not having this baby alone, no matter how much you seem to wish that was the case."

David opened his mouth and closed it, unable to come up with words. But then, luckily to him at least, he didn't have to. Because at that moment, the cell reception stars aligned and his phone buzzed again.

"I have to take this," he said.

"No you don't," she pleaded.

"Just . . . just stay right here. I'll step outside to take the call, and then we'll pick out a crib. Okay."

"David," she said, her heart and voice cracking. "If you take that call, not only will I not be here when you get back, I won't be home when you get home."

But he'd already raised the phone to his ear. With one last look back at her, and a mouthed *I'm sorry* he walked away.

"I'LL GET IT!" Sophia called out as she stepped toward the door. Not that Maisey was going to raise herself from her cocoon of her bedroom. She wasn't expecting anyone—Sebastian was back out on the road—so maybe it was for Maisey. Sophia had caught her texting with someone named "Foz" more than once, and the only explanation she could get out of her daughter was that he was from work.

God, she hoped it was this Foz person, so she didn't have

to stalk her own newly reticent daughter at the flower co-op to be updated on her life.

But when she opened the door, it was to find that it was most definitely not for Maisey, but for her.

"Hey, Sophia," Nathalie said, putting on a brave face, but it was obvious she had been crying. "Um, do you mind if I come in?"

Ever since their parent-teacher meeting, Nathalie and Sophia had been texting like fiends. At first it had been about Maisey, Sophia happy to learn that her daughter had filled out all of her college applications (because she certainly didn't tell Sophia about it). Then, it segued into talking about pregnancy (they had a running tab of how many people asked "how are you feeling" of them that day—Sophia was ahead, if only because she worked with so many different people on a daily basis) and then just silly jokes and memes and sighing over the same actors. They'd even snuck away a couple of times for brunch or a movie—always with a contraband Diet Coke, of course. It was not simple making friends with other women in your thirties, so it seemed precious to have begun to do so.

But now, Nathalie was on her doorstep. And that was a huge leap ahead in their nascent friendship.

"I . . . I'm sorry. I know it's weird I'm here."

"No, it's okay—"

"It's totally weird, but I just had a huge fight with my husband, and didn't know where to go." She gulped and forced a watery smile. "It was either this or a hotel, and I hate hotels."

Leaps of friendship be damned. She felt oddly touched that Nathalie had come to her. Because whether Nathalie was aware of it or not, Sophia had been there when it came to having fights with one's husband while pregnant.

"Of course!" she exclaimed, and pulled Nathalie inside. Then, she called out, "Maisey, you'd better finish up your English homework, because Ms. Kneller is staying for dinner!"

NATHALIE MIGHT NOT have felt very celebratory when she walked into the restaurant the next day for the joint Nathalie and Lyndi Kneller Baby Shower, but she sure as hell looked good.

"Thank you so much for doing my makeup," Nathalie said, sotto voce to Sophia who stood by her side, as they entered the unbearably cool Ora Café. "And thank you for coming with me."

"Are you kidding?" Sophia said with a wide smile. "You promised a pregnant lady all the canapés she could eat—I wouldn't miss this for the world!"

"There will be food . . . although I cannot vouch for its edibility," Nathalie said. "The last time Lyndi brought me here I ordered something that turned out to be eighteen-dollar sliced cucumber, served by a guy who took his man bun more seriously than I have ever taken my hair."

But for the first time in practically ever, Nathalie did not feel hopelessly untrendy in Lyndi's favorite Echo Park restaurant. Nor did she feel judged for what she was sure was an obvious love of cheese, meat, and other nonvegan treats. This was credited to the perfect winged eyeliner, sculpted brows, and gently contoured cheekbones that she sported, thanks to Sophia's expert hand.

And as she scanned the room, looking for some sign of a Kathy-devised baby shower, it was almost enough to forget that the one person she hoped to see was nowhere in sight.

He was supposed to be here.

She hadn't seen David since yesterday in the IKEA. She had, at least, spoken to him—or whatever you called texting.

THE BABY PLAN

Like rational, sane people who love each other despite being in the middle of a fight, she'd sent him a message to let him know where she was and that she was okay.

> staying with my friend Sophia tonight.

> . . . okay. I'm at home. RU all right?

> yes. A little sad. You?

> The same.

Then, after several breath-holding seconds . . .

> Sleep well.

She and David had been together for fifteen years. He knew well enough when to give her some space. And vice versa.

The difficulty was, they had never needed this much space before.

Their fights were usually small, more like discussions wherein they took opposite sides and tried to convince an unseen jury of the virtues of their own point of view—civilized, like debate club. Everyone shook hands at the end, as there was no doubt in either of their minds that the right decision had been made on the kind of dishwasher they should buy, and whether or not they needed to hire a gardener to keep their drought-tolerant front yard weed-free. They were after all, not just adults, but partners in their lives.

And if they did have a larger-scale decision to make, usually the spouse who was less affected deferred to the thought process of the other. Like when Nathalie chose which school for her master's in education, or when David lost his job and had to decide next steps.

The difficulty was, this baby—their daughter—affected them both, equally. And to hear the anger and disinterest coming from David yesterday in the middle of IKEA made her heart hurt like it never had before.

She'd told Sophia all about it last night, while making up the couch. And Sophia upped her new friend game by being both sympathetic to Nathalie *and* thoughtful about David.

"Unbelievable—like he's under some huge burden," she had said. "Like he's the one who has swollen feet."

"And weird leg cramps at night."

"And a uterus that feels like a basketball."

"You guys are so weird," Maisey had said, shaking her head and removing herself from the conversation by redirecting her attention to a text on her phone.

"You'll be weird, too, when it happens to you, honey. But not for another decade, please."

"At least," Maisey snorted as she walked away.

"Say hi to Foz for me," Sophia singsonged.

An exasperated "God, Mom!" was followed by a slammed door.

Nathalie's eyes followed the trail Maisey had left. "Foz Craley?"

"I . . . I actually don't know. My daughter has become much too secretive for my liking. It's someone she works with."

"Well, if it is Foz Craley, he used to be in my classes. Great kid. It was a shame he had to leave school."

Sophia's eyes had gone wide. "My daughter is texting with someone who dropped out of school?"

"No—not like that. He had to relocate for his family. His grandfather . . . well, I don't want to tell tales out of turn, but suffice to say, he had to take on way more responsibility than anyone his age should."

"Hmm . . ." Sophia said, looking back at her daughter's closed door. "Responsibility is such a double-edged knife. Especially between the sexes."

"What do you mean?"

"Well, look at you and your husband. He's freaking out because of the responsibility of the upcoming baby. Grasping for a way to handle it. But you—it's already real to you in a way it can't be to him. Because you have swollen feet and weird leg cramps and a basketball uterus. So you feel the responsibility in a different way. And handle it differently."

Nathalie was silent, letting Sophia's words sink in.

"What about you?" she said finally, nodding to Sophia's slightly rounded belly. "How are you handling it?"

"It's getting harder," she replied after a few moments. "Sebastian's been on the road for a while now. He says he's doing it so he can have time once the baby's born, but . . . I don't know. I don't actually have a lot of experience with relationships."

"You don't?" Nathalie asked, utterly shocked.

"I spent the last seventeen years focused on Maisey. So it's been a struggle finding the right balance with Sebastian, which is even harder when he's not here. I don't know what I'm doing half the time, and I just want it to work. But sometimes it feels like this is happening to me and only me, not to all of us."

"All?"

Sophia nodded her head toward Maisey's door. "But . . . I

just have to tell myself constantly that it will be better tomorrow. As always, as women . . . we handle it. Don't we?"

"Yes," Nathalie agreed, holding up her contraband Diet Coke to clink glasses with Sophia's. "That we do."

It would be better tomorrow, Nathalie had decided. She and David would talk. They would remember that they were best friends and not only needed each other, but wanted each other. They would be able to figure out how to handle it—together.

She had regretted not going home to David as soon as her head hit the pillow on Sophia's couch.

And when tomorrow arrived, she and Sophia drove over the mountain to Echo Park and the baby shower, ready to do just that.

But now that she was here, and she could see David wasn't, she felt adrift all over again.

But then again, it didn't seem like the baby shower was there either.

There wasn't a hint of pink. No baby booties in sight.

Did they have the right place?

Finally, after standing there awkwardly for what seemed like an eternity, a man-bunned server (potentially the same man bun that had alarmed her before?) shoved them through the Sunday brunch rush and pointed them to a set of doors at the back.

"I guess the party's on the patio."

"So what should I expect?" Sophia asked, as they wedged their pregnant bellies past vegan diners. "Outside of cucumber canapés?"

"My stepmom is throwing it, so . . . slightly cheesy décor, some low-pressure crafting . . . basic baby shower stuff, I assume. She went a little overboard for the gender reveal party, so my dad told her that she should scale it back for—"

The first thing that assaulted Nathalie was an ultrasound photo.

Her ultrasound photo.

Blown up on a canvas so the baby in the picture was roughly the size of a motorcycle.

Opposite was a separate canvas, with another ultrasound photo, equally disturbing in size. And in between, was a banner with the words "Happy Babies Shower #Lyndalie!"

"Wow," Sophia said.

"I just remembered something," Nathalie breathed, unable to take her eyes off the . . . everything.

"What?"

"Kathy rarely actually listens to my dad."

Moving past the banner—and the looming photos of her unborn daughter and (presumably) her niece—Nathalie was assaulted by a sea of pink. Now that the sex of both babies was known, Kathy had dedicated herself to the color scheme. But whereas most people would have just had some streamers and tablecloths in their chosen color, Kathy had imported pink everything. The chairs were painted pink. The stones of the patio floor had been given a pink wash that made Nathalie pray for rain—and unfortunately, the rainy season in LA was decidedly over. The patio fence had been wrapped in pink tulle. There was even a pink step-and-repeat—a pink wall canvas that you could take pictures in front of—emblazoned with the phrase #lyndaliebabies!

"It's like the inside of my old Barbie Dream House, isn't it?"

Nathalie turned, and saw her sister, ethereal as always. It took all of the power of her wingtipped eyeliner to overcome her jealousy over how buoyant she looked. Her belly now protruding gently underneath her flowy, flowery gown that hung off her frame like a maternity model. Like her pregnant stomach was filled with little more than wisps of air, instead of the sloshing weight that Nathalie felt in her own belly.

"Let me introduce you to Sophia," Nathalie said after greeting her sister.

"Wow, you look so much like someone I work with, it's uncanny," Lyndi said, as she shook Sophia's hand. "You have the exact same eyes and mouth. Do you have a little sister?"

"No, I have a daughter, Maisey."

"Oh my goodness!" Lyndi cried, clasping Sophia's hand. "You're Maisey's mom! That's not possible!"

"I got an early start." Sophia shrugged.

"She talks about you all the time. Says you're an amazing makeup artist." Lyndi looked between Sophia and Nathalie, her mouth forming a perfect O. "You must have done Nathalie's makeup! It looks fabulous. I love the wingtips. I could never get those right."

"I'd be happy to show you—" Sophia began, but Nathalie cleared her throat.

"Sophia's not here to work, Lyndi."

"It's all right," Sophia said. "If you don't enjoy your work, what's the point? I did bring my makeup bag."

Nathalie felt annoyance—however unjustly—rise in her throat and sting at her eyes. She knew it was petty, but she wanted *her* makeup to look this good—not Lyndi's, too.

God, she would give anything for a distraction. A celebrity sighting. A minor earthquake. Anything.

"Yoo-hoo! Nathalie!"

As if on cue, Kathy parted the seas of the patio and trotted up to the new arrivals.

"Honey, you look marvelous!" she said, embracing Nathalie, bussing her cheek, and coming away with no doubt half the contouring. "Pregnancy agrees with you! My goodness you look better than you did on your wedding day!" She turned to Lyndi. "You remember I told her she should have hired a professional makeup person, but your sister was all about 'saving money.' Oh here honey! Have a 'momosa'! Nonalcoholic, delicious . . ."

Kathy had pulled one of the servers into her orbit, and grabbed three champagne glasses off the tray.

"And pink," Nathalie commented.

"Yes, well, I had a difficult time finding any decorations in a 'feminine blue.' And your sister approved of the décor, didn't you Lyndi?"

"It's great Mom," Lyndi said judiciously. "Thank you so much for doing this."

Nathalie cleared her throat. "Sophia, this is my sister Lyndi, and my stepmom Kathy."

Kathy's smile froze on her face as she turned to Sophia.

"Welcome Sophia," Kathy said. "So glad Nathalie brought a friend . . . even though I wish she would have told me."

Nathalie decided to ignore the dig.

"Kathy, what's #Lyndalie?"

"It's your names, silly! Lyndi and Nathalie!" Kathy replied.

"You couldn't have written 'Lyndi and Nathalie'? Instead of Lyndalie?" Which sounded like Lyndi swallowed Nathalie, and merely burped up the last syllable.

"It's a *hashtag*," Kathy said. "The blog I read said that everyone hashtags their events. I suppose it's for good luck, but I have no idea."

"No, it's for social media, Mom," Lyndi began, but Kathy just smiled at her blankly. "So people can follow the tag and see what's happening at an event?"

"Why would anyone want to follow a tag? Why not just come to the party?"

Rather than for Lyndi to explain why the entire world might not *want* to come to a party, but would take thirty seconds to peruse the pictures on Facebook, Nathalie stepped into the fray.

"Speaking of people coming, where's David?"

Kathy just blinked at her. "Honey, he's your husband. Where did you leave him?"

"I . . . I thought he was coming," she answered lamely. "From work." It was a Sunday, but he had been working so much recently it was entirely probable that Kathy wouldn't blink twice at this lie. And she didn't.

"Honey, this is a baby shower! Purely female space. No boys allowed!"

"I . . . I don't think that's been the case since the mid-eighties."

Kathy just waved her hand dismissively, spilling a little of her pink "momosa" as she did so. "Call him and have him come if you want, but it would just be so strange. Marcus isn't even here—and we have crafting, and you'll love the baby games . . . Pin the Baby on the Uterus is supposed to be a real hoot!"

"I imagine it is," Sophia said, when Nathalie couldn't muster an answer.

"Kathy, I thought you were going to keep this more low-key—WHAT IN THE HELL IS THAT?"

They had migrated over to the food table, where there were the expensive sliced cucumber and other no doubt vegan delights . . . but there was also something that looked like a dark red gelatinous mass balanced atop a short column of confection.

And it was bleeding.

"Placenta cupcakes!" Kathy cried out, delighted. She picked one up, showed it off. "I read on that blog that lots of new mothers are eating the placenta . . . it's supposed to be wildly healthy."

"That's not . . . It's not really—" Lyndi said, looking a little wan.

"No, it's just Jell-O," Kathy replied, her disappointment obvious. "I couldn't find real placenta anywhere."

Well, there was really no response for that.

Luckily, Kathy was easily distracted by new arrivals coming in behind them. "Hello! Welcome! Gifts go on the gift table. The pink one. No, the other pink one!"

As Kathy moved off, that left three pregnant women staring at a table of placenta cupcakes and each other.

"Do you think anyone is going to eat those?"

"David would," Lyndi said. "If he were here."

It was true. David would try almost any food at least once. It was one of Nathalie's favorite things about him. His willingness to step into the unknown and give it a shot.

Maybe . . . maybe he could give this a shot, too?

"Give me a sec, Sophia, I just have to send a text," she said, taking two steps away.

"So you work with Maisey at the flower shop?" she heard Sophia say.

"It's a floral co-op. Let me introduce you to Paula, she's the owner . . ."

As Lyndi and Sophia continued to chat, Nathalie took out her phone. Kathy was right about one thing. If she wanted David there, she should invite him.

Want to come to a baby shower?

She typed the message, hit Send. Waited.

Nothing.

No little loading dots, nothing to indicate that he'd gotten the message.

He was probably just away from his phone. No doubt, he would get the message in a couple minutes. She turned on her ringer, so the phone would audibly ding when he texted back.

She kept the phone in her hand as she turned, and scanned the crowd for Sophia—her emotional support person. And the spike of petty jealousy rose from her stomach to her throat, when she saw, near the pink-encrusted hashtagged step-and-repeat, Sophia applying eyeliner to Lyndi's lids.

Once again, nothing was Nathalie's own. Not even her friends.

She checked the phone clutched in her hand.

Still nothing from David.

This was going to be a long baby shower, Nathalie thought.

And she was very quickly proven right.

Nathalie had noticed a distinct change in how people reacted to her, ever since her belly became decidedly oversized. No one asked "how are you feeeeeeeeeeling" anymore. It was assumed you felt pretty darn pregnant. No, the comments became far more . . . observational.

"You're having a big one, aren't you?"

"My goodness, your baby looks ready to drop!"

"Aren't you hot with all that weight?"

"I can tell by the way you're carrying that you're having a boy."

That last one was from one of her own co-workers, who must have been blind, considering their Pepto-colored surroundings.

But she was a trouper, Nathalie told herself, and she could handle overly personal comments with people she usually only saw in the teachers' lounge.

It would just be a lot easier if she didn't feel the need to check her phone every five seconds.

But David . . . he wasn't responding. By now, he had to have seen the text. There was only one explanation—he didn't want to see her. He didn't want to talk.

He was still angry and sad about yesterday's fight.

And it just made Nathalie angrier and sadder.

Add to that Sophia had disappeared with Lyndi and set up a makeup station in the corner, with a line of ladies waiting to have their makeup done, Nathalie's mood was becoming a murky mix of frustration and sadness that could have only been compounded by her hormones.

"Oh what a fabulous idea!" Kathy cried out, her voice carrying across the patio. "A makeup artist at the party; Lyndi you think of everything."

Sophia wasn't there to be put to *work*, Nathalie fumed. She was there to enjoy placenta cupcakes and roll her eyes with Nathalie at the decorations. She was about to cross the room and intervene when Kathy called out, "Everyone! It's time for the games!"

So Lyndi and Nathalie were trotted to the front of the patio, where chairs had been set up for them, displayed to the (now very nicely wingtipped) crowd.

Nathalie slid Lyndi a glance. Lyndi's face was shining with her smile, practically glowing from all the attention.

"Any idea what we are in for?" Nathalie muttered.

"Mom told me a bunch of different games," Lyndi said. "They all sort of sounded like fun."

"Okay, everyone! The first game is called Guess the

Weight!" Kathy said, clapping her hands. "It's pretty self-explanatory."

Oh, hell.

After a casual round where the partygoers constantly thought she weighed more than she did—and of course thought that Lyndi weighed less—it was time for the next round of Compare Lyndi to Nathalie, which took the form of . . .

"Old Mom vs. Young Mom!" Kathy called out, to the titters of the crowd. "As many of you know, my Lyndi is a wee bit younger than her sister. So I have a list of things an old mom might do, versus what a young mom might do—and we get to guess which is which! First up: watching Disney movies vs. making a YouTube channel of minimovies you make with your child!"

But that wasn't the worst of it. No, the straw that broke the pregnant lady's back came when the games were finally dispensed with and the presents were opened.

By this time, Nathalie had grown weary of checking every phantom buzz of her phone, only to find blankness staring back at her. Her face hurt from grimacing through the humiliation of the games.

And she was freaking *starving*, because the only thing served at the party that wasn't raw cucumber was placenta cupcakes.

So by the time she and Lyndi moved on to the pastel-wrapped pile of boxes and bags with soft elephants or bunnies on them, Nathalie just wanted the whole thing over with.

But as they opened each gift, the oohing and aahing over onesie sets or a baby bathtub, Nathalie began to feel a little bit better. Sure it was an endurance test, but she was enduring it for her baby. She couldn't help imagining her daughter playing with that toy, or in that particular outfit.

Or possibly, Lyndi's daughter in that particular outfit, because . . .

"It's weird how people keep giving us the same stuff," Nathalie whispered to her sister.

"I figure all babies basically need the same things," Lyndi replied with a shrug.

"Yes, but . . . not the *exact* same stuff." They had just opened a pair of gifts from Aunt Carol—who had flown down from Seattle for the occasion and was currently consuming a bloody cupcake and a non-nonalcoholic momosa near the back of the crowd—and had each received a set of purple printed crib sheets.

The exact same crib sheets.

"It's like they think we are having twins. Did you let Kathy know how to find your registry?"

"Oh, I didn't do a registry," Lyndi said, looking up from opening a big stuffed bear—no doubt exactly the same as the bear Nathalie was currently opening.

"You didn't?" Nathalie asked, alarmed.

"I didn't really have any idea what the baby would need. I figured you would know better, so I told Mom just to tell everyone to work off of yours."

Nathalie's hand froze in pulling the bow off the oversized bear. And suddenly, she couldn't take it anymore.

"You can't do anything on your own, can you?" she said, her voice shaking.

". . . what are you talking about?" Lyndi replied.

"You couldn't even have a different registry?" Her voice was a harsh whisper. "Couldn't think for yourself on that one?"

Now Lyndi stilled. "I didn't think it was that big a deal."

"No, of course not, because nothing is that big a deal. Not stealing my registry. Not making my friend do your makeup. Not having a shower at your favorite restaurant where they apparently don't serve actual food." Nathalie shook her head, letting the bear fall to the ground as she stood, brushed out her skirt. "It's like I have nothing of my own. Not my own pregnancy, because I have to share it with you."

"It's not like I planned it!" Lyndi said, rising to meet Nathalie. There was a decided pause in the oohs and aahs of the roundtable of women passing the presents from one to the other. "You're the one who was always going on and on about your plans! You used to tell me you were going to be pregnant when you were thirty."

"Yes, I'm so terribly *sorry* that it took me three years to have a healthy pregnancy, Lyndi. And meanwhile, you manage to get knocked up the first time you trip over your roommate's penis!"

Lyndi drew back as if struck. "That's not what happened!"

"Really? Because that's basically what he wrote in his article!"

The crowd gasped and shuddered. There was no pretense anymore from their guests. Everyone was riveted, watching the sparring sisters like Ali/Foreman.

"Why are you acting like this?" Lyndi said, hurt. "It's our baby shower."

"No, it's *Lyndalie*'s baby shower, whoever the hell that is. Certainly not me. Because I wouldn't have done all—" she waved her hand at the sea of pink they were mired in "—*this*."

"Now there's no call for that, Nathalie." Kathy stepped forward from where she was organizing the gifts. "I tried very hard . . ."

"Not really. You never asked me what kind of shower I would like. Never thought that maybe what I want would be different than what Lyndi wants."

"Well, of course you would want something different," Kathy said, throwing up her hands. "You never like anything I've ever done. Lyndi likes everything. So I went with the one person I knew could be pleased."

"You went with your daughter. Shocking," Nathalie said. The edges of her vision were getting blurry with red. "Unfortunately my mom isn't here, so I don't get a shower."

"Now, that's enough!" Kathy cried. Lyndi reached out and placed a hand on her mother's shoulder, but Kathy held firm. "I long ago accepted the fact that you would never call me mom, but I have been your mom for the last twenty-five years! She was only your mom for ten!"

Cold settled across Nathalie's skin, while heat fell down her cheeks—tears. She hadn't even realized she was crying.

"*She* will always be my mother."

Nathalie couldn't see Kathy's face anymore. Whether or not it was because her eyes were filled or because she didn't want to, she could not say. But she turned as quickly as she could, and moved through the crowd, which parted for her like she had an infectious disease.

She threw open the doors of the patio, and was nearly running when she ran directly into a familiar form.

"Hey," David said, steadying her by her shoulders. "What's going on here?"

Nathalie looked up into his face, and his expression changed immediately. "What's wrong?"

"What are you doing here?"

"You invited me," David replied. Then, forcing her eyes to meet his. "What's happened?"

"Nothing," she said, wiping her face. "Can you just . . . take me home? Please?"

David looked down into his wife's face, then into the over-pink patio beyond. She knew exactly what he saw. The frozen crowd. The hurt on Lyndi's face. The pain on Kathy's.

Then he looked down at her, and saw the shame on Nathalie's.

Then David, smart man that he was, simply nodded, and ushered Nathalie out the door.

CHAPTER 18

"LYNDI, CAN YOU COME IN HERE, PLEASE?"

Paula's voice echoed down from the lofted office space, above the flower assembly area. Lyndi was busying herself with sweeping up the last remnants of cut stems and errant leaves. Everyone else had already gone.

It had been a brisk morning for work. Their orders had been ruthlessly organized, the assembly stations well stocked and laid out with military precision. The bouquets were wrapped and loaded into the cars and on the bikes before morning rush hour had even had time to clog the freeways. Lyndi had even assembled over fifty of the bouquets herself.

Which wasn't much of a surprise, as all of this was Lyndi's doing.

For the past three days, she had gotten into work early, partially because she was unable to sleep, and partially because Marcus—following Paula's advice—didn't let her take her bike in to work anymore.

"Let" her take her bike. God, she hated that. As if she wasn't an independent adult, and had to be given permission to do anything. But she wasn't strong enough to be defiant right now, even with Marcus still away in New York. Instead, she deferred to his and Paula's wishes, and took an Uber, cutting her commute time into fractions.

But ever since the capital *D* Disaster of a baby shower, she'd made it her mission to make the Favorite Flower more efficient, more profitable—and more in her control.

She'd basically banned idle chitchat on the assembly floor, keeping a steady supply of peppy house music on the stereo (a trick she learned from the one SoulCycle class she ever took) to keep people moving at a respectable pace. Even Judy, who usually was the chattiest of them all, was bopping along to the music, as if they were all in a race for both speed and bouquet-perfection.

Indeed, it was, if Lyndi said so herself, a vast improvement over the way things usually went.

So why did Paula's command sound so . . . commanding?

Lyndi abandoned her broom, and trotted up the steps to the office, her expression as neutral as her expectations. After all, maybe she wasn't about to get scolded for her choice in motivational music. Maybe it was about something benign, like spreadsheets or carnations (although she had strong feelings about carnations).

Turned out she was right—and wrong, on both counts.

"Lyndi, are you seriously playing house music to get people to work faster?"

"Yes." Lyndi kept her hands behind her back so Paula wouldn't see her nervously picking her nails while she answered. "That, and it helps keep me awake this early in the morning."

"You have never had trouble staying awake at work." Paula shook her head with a hint of a smile.

"I'm told sleepiness is a symptom of pregnancy."

Lyndi had meant it as a joke. If anything, she had more energy than before—and a driving need to accomplish things before the baby arrived, which her pastel emails told her was a nesting instinct. But the way Paula blanched had her rushing in with reassurances.

"Don't worry, I'm not sleepy. I was just making a quip. And I suck at making quips."

"Good. Good," Paula said, holding a hand to her chest. "I'm sorry, I just know *nothing* about pregnancy, and babies. The very idea of it . . ." Paula wriggled her shoulders, shaking off her queasiness.

"That's okay." Lyndi nodded. She was more used to than she'd ever acknowledge the reaction her peer group had to babies. Their bewilderment was like the anti–biological clock.

"Just keep the volume down a bit on the house music tomorrow, please."

"No problem," Lyndi replied, and stood there awkwardly for a moment. Waiting for something else to do.

"Do you need anything else?" she said eventually.

"No, our flower orders are already in with the wholesalers for the rest of the week," Paula said, shaking her head. "I can't believe how fast and thoroughly you put your lists together."

"Did you get the lilacs?"

"Yes," she replied, "although I'm still not sure about the scent. Lilacs can be overpowering."

"Oh, but they're special. They only bloom for a few weeks and they are so soft and lovely, the ultimate touchable flower. Trust me on this."

"I do trust you," Paula said offhand. "That's why business has been up twenty percent since your hire."

Lyndi felt herself blushing. It was totally like Paula to say something so complimentary, in such a vaguely disgruntled way.

"Unless you want to help me go through these résumés," Paula continued, "you should get out of here. Enjoy an afternoon of freedom before you have a small creature to constantly worry about keeping alive." She waved vaguely at Lyndi's stomach.

"What are the résumés for?"

"For our new managerial position," Paula said, flipping through the papers, seemingly bored and bewildered at the same time.

Lyndi stilled. Confusion trickled across her skin. "We have a new managerial position?"

"We will."

"But I . . ." Lyndi hesitated. Paula looked up from the pile of résumés.

"But what?"

She took a deep breath. "But I thought I was already in the new managerial position."

Paula's eyebrow went up, but she said nothing.

So it was up to Lyndi to say something.

Which took more guts than she knew she had—and dipping into the long dormant language she'd learned in her business classes.

It was terrifying.

"I know the title is only assistant manager," Lyndi said in a rush, "but I've been working super hard—I mean, extremely hard—to learn the business side of the Favorite Flower and to streamline our inventory, clean up our website and boost its capacity for traffic, and work creatively to make new product categories. That, at least, was my intention."

Paula's second eyebrow rose, but again she said nothing.

"And I think I've done all these things."

"You have," Paula said. "And very well."

"So, if there's going to be a new managerial position, what are they going to be doing?"

Paula let the papers in her hand fall gently to the desk. "They are going to be doing everything you just said."

Lyndi gaped for a split second. Then . . . "Well, then certainly I would think that I would be the one to . . . that I could be your new manager."

"I would think so, too—but you can't," Paula replied. "Because this person is going to be doing all of these things in Boston."

It took a moment for Lyndi to register what Paula was saying.

"Boston?" she repeated.

"The Favorite Flower is expanding," Paula explained. "We've been doing great business in Los Angeles, and we are about to launch shipping services. Our setup here allows us to ship overnight to the West Coast, but we need a similar setup on the East Coast to penetrate that market. So, we are opening up a Favorite Flower distribution center in Boston."

"That's . . . awesome," Lyndi said. "Congrats. So, does that mean you are going to shift your bulk buying? Because I've had my eye on a new source for our wrapping materials but we aren't at a quantity yet that makes it cheaper than our current—"

"Lyndi," Paula said firmly, stopping her before she could go too far down that road. Then, Paula shook her head, a rueful smile playing over her face. "Man, I really wish you weren't pregnant."

"What?" Lyndi replied. "Why?"

"If I had my druthers, you would be great as the East Coast version of me. You've excelled at the administrative aspects of the job, as well as being a kick-ass floral designer. But . . ."

"But . . . you didn't think I would want to move across the country when I'm about to have a baby."

Paula's eyebrow went up. "Well, do you?"

Lyndi let her eyes drift down. Her hand came to rest on her rounded belly. The permanence of it. The reality.

"No," she said quietly. "I guess not."

LYNDI DRIFTED TO a stop at the corner of Sunset and Echo Park Drive, lost in a haze of her own thinking. The honking horns of rush hour traffic winding through the packed and crumbly streets barely penetrated her mind. A place packed with oddball shops and mural-covered buildings (and a Walgreens), it was one of the few areas of Los Angeles that could claim to be pedestrian, and as such, cars tended to be a little bit more aware of people on foot.

And people on their bikes.

It felt so good to be on her bike again—it had been weeks and her legs were stiff from lack of pedaling. She knew Marcus would be livid if he found out—but Marcus wasn't home yet. She still had another few hours before his flight was scheduled to land from New York. She still had that precious little bit of freedom that came without someone watching you, making sure you didn't break the pregnancy rules.

Besides, she needed to think. And the only place she had ever been able to do that was on her bike.

A week ago, everything in her life had been fine. On track, even. She had a boyfriend she loved. She had a family that supported her. And she had a job that she felt good about. Now, she didn't know if she even got to call Marcus her boyfriend anymore, given he hadn't really considered her his girlfriend, just his baby mama. Now, she knew just how much resentment her sister held toward her. How much Nathalie— her favorite person in the world—hated her for being pregnant. And it turns out it wasn't enough to like your job—not when you suddenly realized you wanted to excel at it.

The light changed, horns honked behind her. She headed across the intersection. A few blocks down was Echo Park Lake, Lyndi's favorite place in the city, and she set her pedals on that course.

A man-made oasis, Echo Park Lake beckoned to people young or old, rich or poor, dog lovers or cat (although most of the cat people left their felines at home). Nathalie, of course, would make fun of her if she knew she loved it.

"It's so dirty!" she could hear her sister saying, as if anything slightly less than perfect wasn't worth enjoying.

Marcus didn't understand her love of the place either.

"It's just not . . . authentic, babe," he'd said to her more than once, when she'd invited him to come with her.

But Marcus wasn't there at the moment. So screw him and his authenticity.

She loved the lake. It was always alive. People came out, congregating near the water they knew to be precious in the desert, feeling the sun on their skin. There were health nuts running in circles around the lake, the more lethargic hanging out on the shore under the palm trees. Sure, there was the requisite homeless population, but didn't they deserve a little bit of paradise, too?

If it wasn't for the skyline of downtown Los Angeles looming in the background—and the fact that you could easily see the other side of the lake—you could pretend you were on an island in the Pacific far from the worries of the world.

Lyndi's favorite thing about Echo Park Lake was the pedal boats, which you could ride to the fountains in the center of the lake. Not that Lyndi ever had taken one of the pedal boats. She'd always wanted to—it was like riding a bike on water!—she just hadn't.

Somehow, she was afraid that was going to be the theme of her life from now on.

Something that she wanted . . . some adventure she should be on . . . she'd have to shrug, and let it pass her by. Because now she had the baby to consider.

And she suddenly had so many things she wanted to do.

She wanted to go skydiving—okay, she was not super keen on flying. Or heights. Or falling. But that was more reason to do it—to overcome those fears! But when on earth was she going to get to go skydiving?

She wanted to road trip to Alaska. She wanted to try a pottery class. Heck, she wanted to try pot! She hadn't ever really felt the desire to do so in college, but now . . . okay, she didn't really *want* to now, but the choice was being taken from her. She would have a kid, she wouldn't be able to experiment with quasi-legal drugs.

She wanted to go to Boston.

She wanted to be the person that Paula relied on, that she sent across the country to open up a new arm of their business. But . . .

She couldn't go 3,000 miles away from her family, from everything she knew. Because she would need them. She would have a kid.

For the very first time since she peed on that stick, she felt the pinprick of regret.

She was almost happy that the sunset hit her full in the face as she turned a corner and came to see the reflective waters of Echo Park Lake. Since she'd forgotten to grab her sunglasses, it would give an excuse for the tears in her eyes.

But it also made it so that she completely missed the car that was trying to make a left turn. She'd had no idea it was there—until she heard the horn, the screech of brakes, and the screams.

CHAPTER 19

 "Hello, can you help me? My sister is here?"

Nathalie said the sentence she had been practicing in her mind since she'd gotten the phone call a half hour ago, jumped in her car, and sped to the hospital on Sunset Boulevard.

"Ms. Nathalie Kneller?" the nasal voice on the other end of the line said. "You are listed as Ms. Lyndi Kneller's emergency contact on her insurance . . ."

It had been hard to hear any words after that, but Nathalie did manage to make out that there had been an accident, and her sister was in the hospital. What unit, Nathalie didn't know. What the injuries were, Nathalie didn't know. And she wouldn't let herself speculate. Instead, all she did on the (way too long, what the hell was with traffic today?!?) ride down was practice her first sentence.

She would take every moment after as it came.

Of course, it would be helpful if the veritable *sloth* manning the front desk was able to hang up the phone long enough to hear one complete sentence.

"Yeah—no, she said that's what the eggplant emoji was for. I didn't get it either—"

"EXCUSE ME."

Nathalie didn't have time for her teacher voice to take effect. She went right to holy-hell-my-sister's-been-hurt-and-your-emoji-cluelessness-is-stopping-me-from-seeing-her voice.

"I was called. My sister was in an accident. She's pregnant. Where. Is. She."

It might have been the snarl. The gritted teeth. The Do Not Mess with Me Belly. But something got the hospital receptionist off the phone and onto the computer, asking how to spell "Kneller."

With her visitor sticker slapped on her suit jacket, Nathalie broke into a run to the elevators, stabbing at the button marked "4th floor, Labor and Delivery."

The nurse on the desk in Labor and Delivery was a lot more helpful. But then again, it might have been because it looked like she was a pregnant lady with labored breathing who was freaking out in the Labor and Delivery department.

Once they figured out they didn't need to hook up Nathalie to a monitor, they led her to the hospital room where she finally, *finally*, got to see her sister.

The room was dim, the curtains pulled across the windows and the encroaching twilight. The only sound in the room was the beep of a monitor, hooked up to the still and quiet form of Nathalie's little sister.

The last time Nathalie had been in a hospital room like this was when she was eight. When she had visited her mother.

Her mother had never let her come unless she was awake and able to play with Nathalie. She wouldn't let her daughter see her weak. Toward the end, Nathalie wasn't allowed to come visit at all.

So to see Lyndi so lifeless . . . so vulnerable . . .

She reached out and took her sister's hand. It was alarmingly cold. So much so that only the steady beeps from the monitor and the visible in-and-out of Lyndi's breath reassured her. That, and the harness-looking contraption that encased her other arm from elbow to knuckle. It was so stiff and had so many different buckles that Nathalie wondered that it wasn't a torture device instead of a healing one.

At that moment, Nathalie didn't know what to do. She had come to the hospital, she had said the line she had practiced over and over in the car, which had taken her here. But now that she *was* here, she didn't know if she was supposed to do any more than hold her sister's hand.

Was she supposed to hold Lyndi's hand? Was that allowed?

Was she supposed to flag down a doctor and force them to tell her Lyndi's status? Was she supposed to sign forms? Was she supposed to notify loved ones? Make medical decisions?

Was she supposed to feel anything other than horrible and regretful and as if she was the worst person on the planet?

"Are you holding my hand because you're going to propose? Or is this just a weird hospital thing people do?"

"Oh my God!"

Nathalie actually jumped in the air when her sister's sardonic voice interrupted her own unfocused thoughts. But instead of dropping her sister's hand, she ended up squeezing it tighter.

"Ow! Nat, are you trying to break my other hand?"

"No! Sorry! God . . . I thought you were . . ."

"Comatose?"

"No . . . although your hands are really cold."

"They're always cold." Lyndi frowned at her icy fingers. "I have Mom's circulation."

"Right," Nathalie said, and immediately felt a rush of guilt at any thought of Kathy. She had been studiously avoiding letting her mind tend in that direction for the past few days.

"What are you doing here?" Lyndi asked, breaking the awkward silence.

"I was called."

"Oh . . . I didn't realize they called you," Lyndi replied dully.

"Lyndi." She hesitated. Then she asked, "You . . . you listed me as your emergency contact on your insurance?" The *why* was implied.

"Well, of course I did," Lyndi replied, looking at Nathalie as if she were stupid—and in this instance she probably was. "I always put you down."

Nathalie felt heat coming to her cheeks, oddly affected by Lyndi's words.

But then, of course, was the awkward silence again. Bred by two sisters who hadn't been able to talk to each other in months.

"So, er, what happened?" Nathalie said. "Are you okay?"

"I'm fine."

"Come on. If you were fine, you wouldn't be in the hospital," she argued, putting her hands on her hips. "They wouldn't have called your emergency contact."

"I'm certain you were only called because I'm pregnant. It seems to be the reason for everything nowadays."

"Didn't you ask the doctor?"

"No, I was unconscious when I came in."

"Lyndi!" Nathalie cried.

Lyndi sighed the sigh of the deeply suffering. "I was riding my bike . . ."

"You were RIDING YOUR BIKE?" Her heart practically stopped beating. "How could you be so stupid? Riding your bike? In LA traffic? When you're six months pregnant?"

"Okay, can you let me get through the story, and then berate me?" Lyndi said. "It would save a lot of time."

"Fine. But, Lyndi—" One look from Lyndi shut Nathalie up. "Fine."

"I was riding my bike, turned right into the sunset. I didn't have my sunglasses on me so my eyes took a minute to adjust. By the time they did, I was in a car's blind spot. It swerved into me, I swerved away from it and into a pole."

"You hit a pole?" Nathalie tried very, very hard to keep the judgment out of her voice. "Are you okay? Is the baby okay?"

"I broke my wrist," she said, holding up her splint-covered hand. "And they're monitoring the baby." She lifted up her hospital gown, showing two sensors strapped to her belly— one low and one high. "One's for fetal movement, the other's the heartbeat. So far so good, but they're going to keep me overnight."

"Good." Nathalie took a deep breath. "Good. But, um . . . that doesn't explain why you were unconscious. And why they called me."

"When I came in they drew my blood and you know how the sight of blood makes me pass out, so I . . ."

"You passed out."

"That must have been why they called you. Because I was out for a little bit." Lyndi cleared her throat, resettled herself in her hospital bed. "So, as you can see, everything's good. You don't have to stick around."

And with that, Nathalie lost it. And by *it*, she meant the top of her head, because it practically exploded.

"I'm sorry, I don't have to stick around? Oh okay, I'll just leave my pregnant little sister in the hospital. Never mind that I rushed all the way here afraid she was *dying*. Never mind that she was a total idiot riding her bike and hit a freakin' pole. Never mind that obviously someone is going to have to help her because she broke her wrist and can't take care of herself."

Lyndi turned shocked eyes to Nathalie, but Nathalie didn't see them. She wouldn't see them until they had gone as steely as Lyndi's voice.

"Okay, you really can go now."

The low control in her words made Nathalie stop pacing.

"You didn't mean that I can't take care of myself because I've got a broken wrist." Lyndi's eyes narrowed. "You meant I can't take care of myself, period. So how am I going to take care of a baby if I can't take care of myself? That's what you're really saying, isn't it? That's what you meant to say at the baby shower and that's what you meant to say now."

Nathalie was caught. She could lie. Deflect. Not kick up any dust, and bring everything back to a state of even. But suddenly, after the last however many months of tight smiles and keeping things even, and one colossally disastrous baby shower, Nathalie didn't want to keep things even. She wanted to do what came naturally to sisters.

She wanted to finally have it out.

"Okay, Lyndi," Nathalie said, throwing her hands up in the air. "Yes—you've always had someone taking care of you. Dad, Kathy, me. Now Marcus. Although Marcus obviously isn't taking very good care of you if he isn't even here right now."

"Marcus is on a plane. Coming back from New York. And I'm sure that I'm going to get the same lecture from him that you're giving me, so don't worry about me being 'taken care of.' Your version of care is well covered."

"You've never had to worry about anything the way we worry about you," Nathalie replied. "For heaven's sake, I had to schedule your OB appointments!"

"Only the first one. And you didn't *have* to—you just did! Because that's what you do. You take over. Because you don't think I can stand on my own two feet. Just like Mom and Dad. And you know what," she rushed through before Nathalie could counter, "you can be mad at me for 'stealing your pregnancy'—whatever the hell that means—but I didn't do this *to* you. It honestly has nothing to do with you. Maybe, just maybe, you could consider the possibility that it's *you* who is stealing *my* pregnancy."

Nathalie gaped. "That's ridiculous!"

"It's not ridiculous. People actually want you to be pregnant. They're happy for you—no one is happy for me."

Nathalie was about to retort . . . but something stopped her. Something had broken in Lyndi's voice. Something raw and true and little.

"You really feel that way?" she asked, quieter.

"Come on—I hear what people say about me. All of Mom's friends at the gender reveal party? And what they say about you."

"About me?"

"Everyone is so happy for you." Lyndi swiped at the corner of her eye.

"Everyone is happy for you, too," Nathalie tried, gently sitting on the edge of the bed.

"No, everyone wants to 'help' me. Mom, Dad . . . everyone tries to 'guide' me. And all that talk about how having a baby earlier is so great! My body will just spring back!" Lyndi rolled her eyes. "They're trying to think of *something* good to say. Because saying 'you don't have your life together enough to have a baby' doesn't really fit on a Hallmark card."

Nathalie stared at her sister. Minutes ago, she had been struck by how young and vulnerable she had seemed. Now, she was struck by how smart and forceful she could be.

"You're right," Nathalie said. "I'm sorry. I've been a total, selfish bitch."

"It's not just you. It's like no one can believe I *do* see how hard it's going to be and that things are going to change," Lyndi finished. "It's as if I'm not allowed to want my own child."

"You do want her, don't you," Nathalie said with wonder.

"I do." She turned her head and met her sister's gaze. At some point, Nathalie had taken Lyndi's hand. Held it. "I really do. And so does Marcus. Say what you will about him, but at least Marcus wants this baby. Sometimes it feels like he's the only one who does."

"Well, at least you have that going for you." Nathalie sighed, allowing herself to indulge in a little self-pity.

"What do you mean?" Lyndi asked. "Everyone is happy for you."

"Right," Nathalie agreed. "Everyone, except the one person who really matters."

Lyndi blinked twice. "David?" Then, her eyes narrowed. "I'll kill him."

"What? No, come on." Over the course of David and Nathalie's fifteen-year relationship, Lyndi had looked up to David like a big brother. There were times Nathalie had thought Lyndi liked David better than her.

"I'm serious. He's dead to me," Lyndi said through a stern face.

Nathalie nearly laughed. "Lyndi, you've known David since you were a kid."

"Doesn't matter."

"He taught you to drive."

"Dead. To. Me."

"You were maid of honor at our wedding."

"Yeah, and do you know what I told him ten minutes before you got married?" Lyndi said, struggling to a sitting position. "That if he ever did anything to hurt you, I would travel to South America, buy an authentic machete, bring it back, and hack him to pieces with it. I know whose side I'm on."

"You said that?" Nathalie blinked. "You were thirteen."

"I was precocious." Lyndi shrugged. Then she frowned. "And I was in my horror-movie-watching phase."

A giggle burst forth from Nathalie's lips. And then another, and another. And along with it, came the sweetest relief she'd felt in some time.

"I've missed this," Nathalie said, holding her belly as she laughed. The baby kicked (or was it hiccups?) in time with her chuckles.

"Aw, Nat. I've missed you, too."

Slowly, Nathalie's chuckles turned to sniffles, although the smile stayed wide on her face.

"Okay. Tell me everything," Lyndi said.

"Everything about what?"

"Being pregnant, dummy! I've been dying to compare notes."

AND SO THEY did. And they did not limit themselves to their pregnancy symptoms. Although when Lyndi described how her little girl had once gotten her foot stuck in Lyndi's ribs, Nathalie was silently grateful for her far more banal hip stretching symptoms, flatulence, and overriding desire to pee all the time.

No, they talked about everything. They talked about the baby shower, about the strange freedom of being allowed to be large. They talked about the latest episode of *Fargone* and how they were decorating their nurseries (although, for

Lyndi, it was more how she was decorating the corner of the living room that was going to be the nursery). It was wonderful, and it was necessary.

Because they each had their sister back.

They talked so long, by the time Dr. Keen came in on rounds to check on her patient, she discovered not one but two pregnant women in bed, sitting side by side.

"I'm sorry you had to come in, but I'm glad you did," Dr. Keen chirped. "I always feel better when my patients have family around."

"Not a problem," Nathalie said, waving away the concern. "On the plus side now I don't have to worry about going on a hospital tour—I've got down where I'm supposed to go now."

The doctor palpated Lyndi's abdomen, and asked all the right questions, to which Lyndi gave all the hoped-for answers.

"No bleeding. And yes, she's been kicking."

"Quite a bit," the doctor said, reviewing the printout from the monitor. "Well, you look good. I'll be back in a little bit with the ultrasound machine, so we can make absolutely sure, but I think you have dodged a bullet."

"I didn't dodge anything. I hit a pole," Lyndi said, as Dr. Keen left.

"David would be appalled at your lack of peripheral attention. He'd never have let you drive out of our driveway."

"What's up with him anyway?"

Nathalie told Lyndi all about David—about his outburst at IKEA and how it had seemingly come out of nowhere, but in truth it had been building brick by brick every day since she'd announced she was pregnant.

"He's been killing himself at work, even though his own boss says he shouldn't be. And when he does come home, all he does is play video games," Nathalie said. "It's like pulling teeth to get him to do anything baby-related . . . or even talk about it."

"Sounds like someone needs a serious sister-in-law knock upside the head."

Nathalie's brow came down. "You have become surprisingly violent while pregnant."

"And hungry. And horny. And angry. And weepy. And uncoordinated," she finished, holding up her splinted wrist. "But seriously. I crave some of that standoffishness. Marcus wants to make sure I'm doing everything right all the time. Every day when I come home he's there, ready to rub my feet and force-feed me a prenatal vitamin."

"That's . . . good?" Nathalie said.

"Yeah, it's hard to be pissed off when he's so good at being good to me."

"But you were right to be pissed off. About that article."

"Thanks. The only thing I feel I can trust is my daily pastel email."

"Your what?"

Lyndi took out her phone and showed her.

"'*How to Give In to the Bloat, and Nine Other Ways to be Gleefully Pregnant*,'" Nathalie read. "That's . . . cheering."

"And it tells me how big my baby is by comparing it to produce. Look, this week it's an eggplant."

"This gives a whole new definition to an eggplant emoji," Nathalie mused, and then cracked up while she told Lyndi about how she had nearly leaped across the check-in desk at the hospital, and why.

"I'll have to see what . . ." Nathalie whipped out her own phone. Then, she was suddenly self-conscious. "Never mind."

"No—no, never mind," Lyndi replied automatically. "What is it?"

Hesitantly, she handed over her phone. "I've got my own online guide for pregnancy," Nathalie admitted, and Lyndi's eyebrow perked up.

"Please tell me it's not pastel. I would kill to have a non-pastel baby app."

"It's not. And it's not an app. It's a Twitter feed."

As she guided Lyndi to the @WTFPreg feed, she told her how completely eerie it was. How everything that she was thinking or feeling would turn up on this person's feed. Every symptom—hell, even every tiny observation! How they always made her feel better, to know someone out there was having the same difficulties she was.

"But who is it?" Lyndi asked, scrolling down and occasionally laughing at what she read.

"I don't know. It has to be someone who's about as far along as I am, right? Our pregnancies line up. You know for a while there, I thought it might be you."

Lyndi smiled at her sweetly. "Sorry to disappoint. I'm overloaded just keeping the Favorite Flower's Instagram going. Did you know we have over a hundred thousand followers now?"

"Wow . . . is that a lot? It sounds like a lot."

"It's enough to make me exhausted just thinking about doing more on social media. So, not me."

"Yeah, I figured that out. For one thing, you've never shied away from wearing horizontal stripes." Then, she hesitated. "Actually, I thought it might be my mom."

"You thought it was Mom?"

"Not Kathy. *My* mom. I know it's crazy," she said immediately. "But I thought that . . . maybe she was showing me that I wasn't alone in this. Stupid, right?"

"No," Lyndi said, soft. "Not stupid."

"I know it's impossible. It's probably some sarcastic mom-to-be, venting her frustrations to three Twitter followers from the middle of nowhere Kansas."

"I don't think so." Lyndi frowned. "The things she talks about? And the times they post? I think she's on the West Coast. In the Pacific time zone, at least."

"How can you tell?" Nathalie leaned in, and was promptly schooled like a noob by her younger sister on the archiving aspects of Twitter—i.e. she showed her where to find the time and date stamp on the individual tweets.

"How do you know all this?"

"A hundred thousand Instagram followers, remember? I may not be on Twitter, but I have to know how to use it to do my job."

"You're really good at it," Nathalie said softly. "Aren't you?"

"I am," Lyndi replied, but there was a hint of bleakness to her voice. "It's the first thing I've ever been really good at."

"But . . ."

"But. I just wish I had figured out how good I was at it a little earlier." Then, Lyndi proceeded to tell Nathalie all about her work. About how she had ruthlessly organized and streamlined their orders. How she'd figured out how to opti-mize their website and online presence without ever taking a programming course. How she loved getting to be creative and build beautiful arrangements, like a chef built his menu from the fresh ingredients at the market.

And she told Nathalie about Boston. And how she wasn't going to be going there.

"That's outrageous!" Nathalie cried. "That's workplace dis-crimination. You could sue!"

"I don't think so," Lyndi replied. "If I went to Paula to-morrow and said I wanted the job in Boston, baby and all, I think—hell, I *know*—she'd give it to me. But come on. I can't do that."

"Why can't you?" Nathalie asked. But apparently it wasn't a question Lyndi was prepared to answer. Instead, she stared at her fingers for a while, before finally looking back up.

"I just feel like there's a lot I'm not going to get to do now."

She told Nathalie about what she had been doing down at Echo Park Lake. How she always saw runners and sunbathers and pedal boats, and how those people all seemed so carefree.

"And I'm not going to get to be carefree anymore."

Nathalie thought for a second before patting her sister's hand. "I'm sorry but that's bullshit."

Lyndi blinked at her.

"I'm serious. If you looked at those runners, I'd bet you'd see that every third one is pushing a stroller. And those picnickers? Half of them have kids with them, I'm sure." Nathalie shrugged. "So what if you won't be able to be carefree and do stuff on a whim? You'll still be able to do stuff. The only person stopping you from riding a pedal boat is you."

Lyndi seemed to take that in, as a knock on the door sounded the arrival of Dr. Keen, pushing the ultrasound machine.

"Let's see how she's doing!" Dr. Keen declared, as she lubed up Lyndi's belly, and rubbed the detector over her abdomen.

"Hey, there's my wiggly little eggplant," Lyndi said.

"And my wiggly little niece," Nathalie added, all eyes on the white-and-gray blob on-screen, outlining the head, the spine, the perfectly beating heart of Lyndi's baby.

"Baby's moving great," the doctor said, moving the detector across Lyndi's belly. "Heartbeat is strong, your fluid looks good. We want to keep you monitored for a little while longer, just in case, but I would say you and baby are A-OK."

"Thank God," Nathalie said.

"Thank God," Lyndi whispered.

"Thank God," came the voice from the doorway.

"Marcus." Lyndi's voice broke when she saw him. He looked like he was one big wrinkle. His usually neat clothes were a mess, his hair tufted and askew, like he'd been pulling on it out of stress. And his face was lined with worry beyond worry.

"I got the message when I landed at LAX. I just jumped in the car . . . my bags are still at baggage claim, I think."

Nathalie glanced toward her sister, who held her breath, every ounce of her being entirely focused on Marcus. Slowly, Nathalie slid out of the hospital bed. Marcus filled the space she left, coming to stand by Lyndi's bedside.

". . . How was New York?" she asked.

"Well." He took a deep breath. "Looks like I'm going to be writing a book."

"Really?" Lyndi smiled warmly. "Congratulations."

"Yeah." He rubbed the back of his head. "It's not going to be a lot of money, I'll still have to keep my job. But . . . I'm going to be an author. And I wouldn't be doing this without you, Lynds."

As Lyndi began to sniffle, Nathalie started to get the impression she probably shouldn't be here to witness this.

"How . . . how was Frankie?" Lyndi finally said.

"Frankie was . . . Frankie," Marcus replied. "It was actually really good to see him."

"It was?"

"Yes. Because seeing him in New York kind of illuminated just how amazing my life is right now. With you. The person I'm in love with."

Yeah, definitely shouldn't be witnessing this, Nathalie thought as she tiptoed to the door.

"Nat," her sister called after her.

She turned.

"Thank you."

"Yes, thank you for being here," Marcus said, the look in his eyes pretty much a full-bodied hug from across the room.

"Anytime. Well, not *any* time, because I don't want you running into a pole again. But . . . anytime."

"Love you," Lyndi said.

It was so damn good to have her sister back, Nathalie realized. This was what she had been missing most. How could she have ever let her selfishness get in the way of that?

"Love you, too."

As the door eased shut behind her, Nathalie heard Marcus's gentle whisper. "So . . . how are my girls?"

APRIL

SUNDAY   MONDAY   TUESDAY   WEDNESDAY   THURSDAY   FRIDAY   SATURDAY

This is really happening.

CHAPTER 20

"HOW MANY SCENES DO WE HAVE LEFT?"

Sophia plopped herself down in her wheelie chair, and took a long, well-deserved swig of water. She'd been on her feet far too long already today, and it felt like they had just started. Usually she tried to make as much use of the chair as possible, especially considering the way her back hurt now that her stomach was tipping her forward at every given opportunity. It might have been seventeen years in between pregnancies, but the conventional wisdom was true—you did show sooner and bigger with the second child. Right now, at about twenty-six weeks, Sophia felt as heavy as she had when Maisey had been born.

The wheelie chair had taken on the widening imprint of her butt—at once comforting and alarming.

But she hadn't been able to avail herself of that butt imprint yet today, because she'd been out in the sun, turning thirty extras into frost giants for a medieval-set episode that was in no way a rip-off of *Game of Thrones*.

"Four," said Kip. "Mostly touch-ups though, no new makeup work. So at least we have that going for us."

"Don't count chickens," Sophia replied. "We still have to prep for tomorrow's battle scene."

"*Uhhhhnnnnnnggghhh . . .*" Kip sighed dramatically, flinging himself over the back of his makeup chair. "I swear the writers are trying to kill us."

"Oh, like you've never staged a medieval time travel battle with magic demons before." Sophia snorted.

"I do take some solace in the fact that I'm sure the writers are also trying to kill themselves."

"Come on—it's the season finale. These last couple episodes are always a doozy."

"Even without a diva to appease."

Sophia said nothing, but knew exactly what Kip was talking about. She had hoped that after awards season was over, and the slight of not being nominated for an Oscar had passed, Vanessa would return to being Vanessa. A little obsessive about how she presented herself, but ultimately a kind person with a job she loved and was good at.

Sadly, she had been disappointed.

Oh, Vanessa wasn't off the deep end by any means. She'd even been nice to Sophia, happy to smile and make small talk . . . as she went to sit in Kip's chair. For his part, Kip was mortified but a professional. Sophia told him to make sure he got a bump in salary along with his new duties as Vanessa's key makeup artist.

Her diva behavior wasn't limited to the makeup trailer, though. She'd begun taking a deeper interest in the scripts. Asking for her character to have certain lines or scenes to play. Making a casting suggestion or two. Demanding a story line that had her fighting a horde of frost giants and ultimately sacrificing herself (until she was revived next season, natch) in an emotional blaze of glory.

"I overheard Roger saying her latest changes put the finale over budget by a cool million."

"That will be forgiven just as soon as they get the ratings on the episode," Sophia said.

Yes, the producers might hate it, but the bitch of it was, the fans would love it.

Personally, as a TV watcher, Sophia preferred the smaller, more emotional scenes. The ones where the characters got to reveal something true about themselves. But those scenes had been replaced with a fantastical shoot-'em-up extravaganza at the cost of millions of dollars, and her aching back.

At least she found making extras into frost giants to be a challenge creatively.

"Three more weeks." Sophia sighed. "Three more weeks and we're free."

"Amen," Kip said, giving the sign of the cross—obviously not raised Catholic, else he would know better. "I've got to go. The prep meeting for tomorrow's big scene is in fifteen minutes."

"Go." Sophia waved him away. "Have fun."

"Hey—you designed some beautiful frost giants today," he said, his hand on the door handle. "Everyone says they look amazing."

"Thanks—just don't sing my praises too loud," she replied. "She might not like it if—"

"If . . . you were acknowledged as being damn good at your job and necessary to the show? No worries, your secret is safe with me."

And with that Kip let himself out of the trailer.

Finally alone, Sophia sank down into her wheelie chair, and put her throbbing feet up on Kip's makeup chair.

Usually, she would have been the one going to the meeting. She was the head makeup artist, after all. But somehow, not only had Vanessa maneuvered Kip into position as her personal makeup artist, but she'd apparently mentioned that he should be having more involvement with the production than Sophia. Vanessa had come to Roger, deeply concerned that "in her current condition, Sophia shouldn't have to run across the lot to make a meeting" . . . nor should she have to tax herself to be the creative voice of the show.

Roger saw through this, of course. And Roger had a delicate position to negotiate. He couldn't fire Sophia—she hadn't done anything to warrant it, and there was a union behind her to make trouble if she complained. But he needed to keep Vanessa's feathers unruffled, keep her happy, keep her *working*. Because when you are literally the only person who can do your (very important) job, you hold all the power.

Sophia knew how to handle this. She would keep her head down, do her work, and in three weeks' time, take a nice long vacation.

Working in television wasn't a fifty-two-week-a-year type gig, with two weeks off paid vacation. It was contractual and transient. Meaning, you worked for as long as the show shot, where it shot, then your contract ended. If the show was coming back for another season (and no doubt *Fargone* was going to be coming back, they had the ratings and the magazine covers to do so) you got a nice few months off.

Lots of people used the hiatus to work on other projects— to do a movie, or a short cable series that shot off-cycle. But this year, Sophia would be using the hiatus to have a baby.

She couldn't wait.

To not have to deal with the stress involved in simply showing up to work. To not have to make polite small talk when

Vanessa was in the chair, being worked on by Kip. To be able to have normal hours on a daily basis could only be good for her.

And this stress at work hadn't been good for the baby. Her last appointment, her doctor had said her blood pressure was slightly elevated again. Not outside the range of normal, but at the very top of it. Of course, Sophia knew this already, because she'd been taking her blood pressure daily. And every morning that she strapped that band around her arm, she wondered if this would be the morning that the numbers would read so high that she felt compelled to tell Roger and Kip that she should stop working . . . and then she wondered if she would feel anything other than sweet relief.

So yes, she looked forward to the hiatus. To the future.

Best of all would be that she would finally be able to set up house with Sebastian.

That was the plan at least. Although, it had been hard to nail Sebastian down for specifics. He was still out on the road—the impromptu tour had turned into something less impromptu when it was extended to fifteen more cities. The band was no longer just the show openers, they were considered co-headliners, and had signed contracts that, according to Sebastian, were going to put them on the national map.

And according to the tabloids and the blogs and now the *Billboard* charts—yes, they were very much on the national map.

The last time she'd managed to bring up the subject with him, his response was an enthusiastic "absolutely!" before he had to get back on the bus for another eighteen-hour drive through the middle of the night.

The poor boy sounded so exhausted. So, Sophia determined that she would make it so when he came home, everything would be done, and he wouldn't have to worry about it.

While the offer to live with Sebastian at the Hollywood Hills house was generous, the idea of bringing a newborn into the middle of a house intermittently occupied by five guys was laughable. Plus, it was a short-term rental. And while Sophia would ideally love to simply move Sebastian and the baby into her apartment, she knew that he thought it would be a little tight with all of them, and Maisey when she came home from school. So, she'd begun looking at new places online.

Another bit of stress to add to the pile, the idea of moving house.

But it had to be done once the hiatus came—ideally before she became too whale-like.

Even though it was incredibly stressful, daydreaming about her upcoming perfect life with Sebastian and perfect living situation made the time pass during hard days on set . . . which lately was every day.

In fact, she was daydreaming about what color the tile backsplash of the new chef's kitchen in her mythical future house would be at the very moment that the makeup trailer door swung open, and the stomp of stilettos brought Sophia out of her chair and on her feet.

"No, I can't just go and . . . Kip tell him . . . oh," Vanessa said, as she entered the trailer. Behind her a young yet weary set PA kept pace, a walkie glued to his hand as he dogged her steps.

"Vanessa," Sophia said, as evenly as she could manage. "Kip just left for the production meeting."

"But my scar—" Vanessa grumbled. She lifted her hair and showed the long (mercifully fake) scar that ran from her earlobe down the length of her neck. It was caused by a time travel warlord trying to stop the alternate reality Vanessa's character creates. It was also caused by Kip every morning in the makeup chair. Right now, the putty that scar was made of hung loose along her face.

"Where's Eva?" Sophia asked.

Eva was the on-set makeup artist. There to do the tiny touch-ups in between takes to make sure everything was consistent and perfect.

"Eva sent us back here," Vanessa said. "She didn't have the right glue with her."

"Can we get eyes on Kip from makeup?" the PA said, low into his walkie. "We need him back for a touch-up on Vanessa."

"No, it's fine," Vanessa said, suddenly, her eyes on Sophia. "Sophia can do it."

"I can?" she asked, unable to stop herself.

"Of course you can," Vanessa said. "Unless . . . you don't know the design?"

"No, I know it," Sophia said. In fact, she had made the design and showed Kip how to cast the mold for it. Not that she was going to tell Vanessa that.

Sophia hopped to her feet, crossed to her makeup kit, and pulled out the glue. By the time she turned around Vanessa was sitting in the chair, the wide-eyed PA quietly calling off the search for Kip into his walkie.

"So . . . putting your feet up?" Vanessa asked, as Sophia approached the scar, delicately lifting it, to see where to apply the glue.

"Just for a minute," she replied. "It's been a long morning."

"Has it?" Vanessa asked. "You weren't in here when I was getting my makeup done at six AM."

"You're right, I wasn't," Sophia murmured. No, she had been outside in the extras tent, creating thirty frost giants out of people who worked for fifty dollars a day and free lunch.

But it wasn't worth mentioning. All she had to do was glue this scar back into place, and continue to go about her day.

"I'm glad you're putting your feet up," Vanessa said, not unkindly. "You need your rest. That's why I'm so glad Kip's able to ease your burden, so to speak."

"Mm-hmm," Sophia replied. "Lift your jaw a bit, please? Thank you."

"And you should know he's doing great. Really creative, has a lot of talent. And you're the one who discovered that. You should get some credit."

"Thanks. A little to the left now?"

Vanessa shifted her face, professional that she was. "In fact, I recommended Kip to be key makeup on this movie I'm doing over the hiatus. It's an ensemble historical sci-fi rom-com, absolutely everyone is in it. The director is just visionary."

"Hmmm . . ." was really the only reply Sophia could make.

"It's going to be such good exposure for Kip. You should be really proud of him."

"I am," Sophia replied with a smile. A genuine smile. And it was that genuineness that set Vanessa's jaw tighter. And as Sophia was currently gluing a scar to the jawline, she could tell.

"I don't suppose you have anything exciting planned for the hiatus?" Vanessa asked, unable to keep the brittleness from shining through. "Throwing yourself a baby shower?"

"No," Sophia said, suppressing a smile. "I went to a friend's baby shower recently, and it kind of put me off them for a while."

Sophia had left Nathalie's baby shower shortly after Nathalie did. Honestly, most people made a quick escape, because when the hostess was crying in the bathroom and the placenta cupcakes were wilting in the sun, it stopped being any fun.

Nathalie, to her credit, had called Sophia the next day, and apologized profusely for leaving her there, and for her behavior. They'd texted multiple times since, mostly about how their hormones were out of whack, and it could only be solved by mutual commiseration over Diet Coke.

However, as nice as it would be to get a bunch of baby presents, it was better for Sophia's health if she avoided the inherent drama of a baby shower of her own.

"I'm taking a break this time," she said. "I want to spend some time with Maisey before she goes off to school."

"Of course," was the softer reply. "Where's she going to school?"

"Don't know—we expect to hear any day now," Sophia said. "And I'm going to spend it prepping for the baby. Sebastian and I are looking at new places."

"You are? He never said anything about that to me," Vanessa replied, her brow coming down.

Much of Sophia's relationship with Vanessa was knowing when to keep her mouth shut and not ask questions. However, in this instance, the words just popped.

"Why would he?"

Vanessa went frostily still. "Because we're friends, Sophia. We've been friends a lot longer than he's known you."

"Right," Sophia said, immediately backtracking. "I just meant . . . *when* would he tell you? He barely has time to call me, they're constantly working."

"Oh." Vanessa relaxed. "When I went to their gig last weekend."

The brush stilled in Sophia's hand. "You went to their gig? In Atlanta?"

"I flew out. Just for the night. The show was amazing, you should have seen it."

Sophia would have loved to have seen it. But with work, Maisey, and the blood pressure situation . . . having her fly out was something she and Sebastian had never even talked about. Her jealousy was heavy, like a sleeping bear sitting on her chest. And there was nothing she could do about it.

"I'm sure it was," was all she could muster saying.

"And you don't need to worry about Sebastian."

"Why would I worry?"

"He told me you were mad about that tabloid picture you saw. But that's just fan service, we stars have to do it all the time," Vanessa said breezily.

Sophia felt a shot of hot anger shoot through her body. Sebastian had told her about their private, personal conversation? One that Sophia had thought was long resolved . . . even though those same tabloids kept following the tour and speculating about each of the band members' love lives. She'd read one article where Mick had said Sebastian was the only one off the market because "he's got an amazing girl and a baby on the way" and Sophia wanted to have that printed out and plastered on billboards.

"When I was there, he was a very good boy, and he didn't so much as look at another woman. And don't worry, if he ever does, I will talk to him and set him straight."

"No," Sophia said.

Vanessa's eyebrow shot up. "No?"

"Vanessa, thank you, but if Sebastian ever needs to be set straight, I will be the one to do it."

"I'm sorry. I thought I could just approach him as a friend."

"Right. You're his friend. But he's my boyfriend. And the

father of my child. So it's better if you leave our relationship to us."

Vanessa turned her eyes to Sophia, cold.

"I see. And here I thought I was helping." She shook her head. "Sebastian can't be here and asked me to look out for you, you know. He told me that you needed to be careful about your health. So I told Roger to give you less work, I asked Kip to help out. I'm concerned about you. And you could say thank you."

"Vanessa, I—"

"Are we done?" she asked.

"What?"

"With my scar, is it fixed?"

". . . yes. You're camera ready. Give this to Eva," she said, handing a small vial of glue to the PA who was still watching this exchange nervously. "She should have it in her kit."

"Especially if this falls off again," Vanessa added. "God knows that's extremely likely, too. Let's have Kip come to set, just to double-check it."

And with that, Vanessa exited the trailer, the PA on his walkie, again calling for someone, anyone to find him Kip.

Sophia exhaled a long breath. There were only three weeks to go until the hiatus, and somehow, some way, she knew that she had just made them a whole lot worse.

"SEBASTIAN, YOU SHOULD have heard her. I know she's a friend of yours but . . . yes I know."

Maisey didn't mean to eavesdrop. But it was hard not to. She'd been in her room, patiently waiting for her mom to get home from work, only checking the clock every fifteen seconds or so.

"I know she's been a big supporter of the band. Well, she was married to one of you for a while, remember? . . ."

But when she heard the front door open, she paused before hopping out of her room. Chalk it up to nerves. But that pause was just long enough for her mother to answer her cell, and for Maisey to hear her mom's voice soften with relief as she said, "Sebastian."

"I'm just saying, it's stressing me out is all . . . When are you coming home? . . ."

Of course, now that her mom was five minutes into the conversation, telling Sebastian about her day, she didn't sound so relaxed anymore.

And that was a problem. Because Maisey wanted her mom relaxed. Happy, and without distraction, when Maisey told her the news.

It had begun that morning. She had woken up predawn as per usual. These days, she didn't even bother tiptoeing or rushing out of the house—the early morning was routine now, and her mother knew she wasn't going to get any substantive mother-daughter exchanges out of her. But as she was putting some peanut butter on toast to shove into her mouth before heading to the flower district, Maisey's phone dinged.

Maisey didn't get a ton of emails. She mostly texted with her mom, her dad, and her friends—or God forbid, someone called her and she had to speak to them verbally. The emails she did get were in general school assignments, or coupons from the grocery store. But that morning, her phone dinged with the unmistakable sound of incoming email.

At first, she didn't recognize the address. Then, she couldn't believe what she was reading in the text.

Dear Maisey Alvarez—Congratulations, you have been accepted to Pomona College, class of 2022! An acceptance packet will be sent to your home in the coming days . . .

If the peanut butter weren't gluing her mouth shut, she would have no doubt screamed.

Pomona was a great school. Heck, it was one of the best in Southern California. She'd applied in her rush of applications, determined to get in somewhere, *anywhere*, to escape the upcoming household transition to . . . wherever her mom decided to move. Maisey knew her mother was looking at new houses, even though Sophia tried to keep it under wraps. Saved Google searches were the tattletale.

It twisted Maisey's gut every time she thought about their little place not being their little place anymore. But with an acceptance from Pomona sitting in her inbox, she began to feel a slight tingle of excitement for the future, instead of dread.

She almost woke up her mom to show her then. Almost. But she was already running late, and Sophia had been on set very late the night before, barely making it home before Maisey went to sleep. And knowing Sophia, if she got this news she would demand a full accounting of it, the school, and celebratory waffles.

So she drove to work. And when she got there, she got her second surprise of the morning.

Another email dinged on her phone. This one from Sacramento State.

Congratulations, Maisey! You have been accepted to . . .

She'd nearly had to sit down, her knees were so weak. As it was, she was leaning on the assembly table, tears in her eyes, when Foz walked into their stall, flipping his keys around his fingers. The flipping immediately stopped when he saw Maisey.

"What is it?" he asked immediately. "What's wrong?"

She could have said that nothing was wrong. She could have gleefully told him about her news. The problem was, she didn't know if gleeful was how she felt. So instead, she just handed him her phone, and let him read it.

"You got into college?" he said. It wasn't said with shock, more plain puzzlement. Like he was shocked she was shocked.

"I got another one, too. Pomona."

"Maisey, that's awesome! Congrats!" he said as his face split into a grin and he pulled her into a hug.

This . . . was a little more shocking.

"Come on, you can't honestly be surprised, can you?" he said, as he let her go. His hand lingered on her wrist for a moment longer than she was used to.

"I'm not surprised, I'm just . . ." And then, it all came pouring out. How she had been so devastated by Stanford's rejection, she'd decided she wouldn't even go to college. How her life was in so much crazy upheaval at home, it forced her hand. And how now, she had a choice to make, and a plan to follow for her future. And that she didn't know how to handle it all.

"It's like I'm suddenly an adult, you know? And there's a difference between being the responsible kid people marvel at and applaud for being so levelheaded, and being an adult, where you're expected to just know how to handle things."

"I get it," Foz replied, nodding. "It can be overwhelming. For what it's worth though, not taking you is Stanford's loss."

She rolled her eyes, but still could feel the pink starting up in her cheeks.

"So, who's it going to be?" he asked. "Pomona or Sacramento?"

"I don't know. I've got a couple more to hear from. UCLA, Berkeley."

"You'll get into both. I have no doubt."

"You think?"

"Maisey, you're the best student in AP Lit class."

She blushed deeper at the matter of factness of his statement. As if he couldn't believe this wasn't common knowledge. "I thought you were the best student in AP Lit class?"

"I'm not in AP Lit class anymore, remember?" He smiled at her.

"Yeah, you're just going to have to kick my ass academically from USC."

"By the time I get to USC you'll be so far ahead of me I'll be in the dust."

Her brow came down. "What do you mean? I thought you were going to USC in the fall?"

Foz's grin faltered. "I got accepted for the fall, yeah. But I'm going to have to defer it for a while."

"Why?" she asked. Then, when he shrugged, looking into the middle distance, she decided enough was enough with being enigmatic. "Why did you have to leave school? I know you said it's because you wanted to be closer to your grandfather . . ."

"I had to move in with him," he said finally. "A relative or caretaker had to be willing to live with him, or else we would have had to move him into a facility. He's . . . he's not well."

"Oh," Maisey replied. "I'm sorry."

"This is my dad's dad. My father died in Afghanistan. My

mom remarried, I've got two little brothers still in elementary school. She couldn't uproot their lives and move to Whittier. I had already turned eighteen, so I decided I would do it." He sighed deep, keeping his eyes firmly over Maisey's shoulder, refusing to look at her. "I thought I'd be able to commute to USC in the fall, but . . . he's gotten worse. I'm going to have to stick closer to him."

"I'm sorry," she said again. Because there was nothing else to say.

"Don't be," he said. "USC will still be there. This is what you do for family."

He looked at her then, searched her face. And damned if she didn't feel like there was something pulling her by her belt buckle, tugging at her, urging her to lean into him.

"I wanted to ask you something . . ." he said, his voice the only thing she could hear. His face was the only thing she could see. There were no flowers. No deliveries to make. No Lyndi moving down the steps from the office at a pace way too fast for a pregnant woman, and heading right for them.

"Guys, come on, we have a lot to load up today!" Lyndi said. Whatever inches had disappeared between them came rushing back in as they stepped away from each other. To the far left, Judy hissed, "Sheesh! Lyndi, what are you doing!"

Apparently, as much as the world felt as if it had fallen away, it hadn't, and the teenaged couple was the morning entertainment at the Favorite Flower.

"Sorry, but we are so behind today," Lyndi said, oblivious to the ire of the arrangers who had been spying on them. "Foz, you might have to take two runs today—too many orders to fit in your car otherwise."

The Favorite Flower had become so successful most of the

bike deliverers had transferred to cars if they had access to one. According to Lyndi delivery capacity was becoming a real issue.

"Oh, I think you'll be surprised by my car's capabilities," Foz said, winking at Maisey as he moved toward Lyndi, those keys flipping around his hand again. "Let's see what we can do."

Nothing more was said between Maisey and Foz for the rest of the morning. Instead they loaded his car—packed it to the gills with all of his deliveries. Luckily his car did have hidden talents, and all of his deliveries could fit. The downside was that it took so long he had to hop in his car immediately and drive off. No wink to her, no smile, not even a wave goodbye.

And certainly no finding out what he was going to ask her.

"You ready? We have to get you loaded up, too. If you miss class my sister will kill me."

Yes, finding out that Ms. Kneller and Lyndi were sisters was an interesting side effect of having her teacher have a random sleepover with her mom last week. Inevitably, Ms. Kneller had talked about her sister, who was also pregnant, and Maisey had managed to put the pieces together. The upshot of which was that Lyndi now felt personally responsible for making sure Maisey's job did not get in the way of her school obligations.

Maybe she didn't feel personally responsible . . . maybe she was just as scared of Ms. Kneller as the rest of her class was.

They began putting the boxes filled with bouquets into the trunk and backseat of Maisey's car, Lyndi doing so one-handed, as her right hand was in a wrist splint.

"Let me do that," Maisey said, taking one of the boxes from her.

"Thanks," Lyndi said, her face twisting into a grimace. "I hate asking for help, but—"

"Come on, you're rocking a cast right now. It's no problem."

"You know I was just thinking I don't know how your mom does it, but now I know," Lyndi said, smiling. "She's got you looking out for her."

"What do you mean?" Maisey asked. "Does what?"

"Life," Lyndi said, waving her hand. "When I met her at my baby shower, she ended up doing half a dozen people's makeup, was on her feet the entire time, and never once complained."

"She loves doing that, though," she replied, confused. "Why would she complain?"

"Right, and I love doing this. But even the stuff you love gets hard sometimes. This," she indicated her belly, "can be difficult. Just trying to do normal stuff. Job, home, all of it changing around you. Anything small can compound the crazy. I just broke my wrist. Your mom's got preeclampsia hanging over her head—that's seriously scary."

"I never thought . . ." Maisey said, and then stopped. She really hadn't thought. She hadn't really been thinking about her mom's stress level lately—she'd been a bit more focused on her own. "Stuff like that doesn't faze my mom."

"Trust me," Lyndi said. "She's human. She's fazed. I'm just saying, having a good kid like you around, it probably really helps."

Maisey thought about Lyndi's words throughout all of her deliveries. She thought about them all day at school, too, when she should have been freaking out about the AP exams next week, or prom the weekend after. And she thought about it when she got home . . . right up until the moment she checked the mail.

And there was an enormous packet inside, addressed to her. Berkeley, it seemed, liked to do things old-school.

Her heart was pounding so hard, the words on the first page of the packet barely registered. The usual *congratulations* and *class of 2022* floated across her eyes, but then she came across three little words.

Three little words that seduced, and made dreams come true: *financial aid package.*

Her mom had always said she could apply to any school she wanted. And she knew her mom had some savings, and her dad had some savings. But she also knew that their savings were nowhere near enough to cover four years of tuition without some help.

That was one of the many reasons as a California resident she was focusing solely on California schools. Going to a school in-state was usually much cheaper . . . but probably not cheap enough.

Suddenly, with a financial aid package, Berkeley—one of the best schools in the country, not just in California— seemed like a real possibility.

The flutters in her stomach wouldn't subside, no matter how much she told herself to calm down. She wanted to jump around. She wanted to yell it from the rooftops, from Facebook, from everywhere.

She wanted to tell her mom.

She nearly texted with the news that she had gotten into three (!) schools that day. But something told her to wait. To do it in person. Because . . . because they hadn't talked in a while.

Not really. Not about the things that mattered.

Of course they talked about their schedules, and what they wanted at the grocery store, Maisey's homework, and what to watch on TV that night. But they didn't talk about how they *felt* about the TV show. Maisey hadn't told her mom anything about which schools she chose to apply to. How stressed she was about the AP tests. About how much she was enjoying work, and how much Foz might have to do with that.

And Maisey knew that was her doing. She'd needed the space. To figure out how to be the person who came next. And for it to not hurt so much when her mom moved on to her new life. But at that moment, with all of the hard work she had done to get into college, she wanted to share the moment with her mom.

So she waited. The clock ticking on her desk. Pins and needles, all that stuff. And finally, finally, her mother walked through the door.

And Maisey had paused.

"I thought you said you'd be back by the end of the week," her mom was saying, the sadness in her voice apparent. "No, I can handle another couple days, but . . . I don't mean to unload on you, sweetie . . . yes, I know you're busy . . . Work is just so stressful right now . . ."

Maisey froze. She didn't know what could be making her mom's life so hard at work—she loved her job, usually. But if the show was getting to be too much, there was no way it was good for the baby.

I don't know how she does it. Lyndi's voice rang in her head. *Trust me, she's fazed.*

Maisey peeked out the door. Her mom was putting her bag down on the kitchen table as she collapsed into a chair. Her posture spoke of her exhaustion. Her voice spoke of her sadness.

But it was sadness Sebastian apparently wasn't able to hear. Because after another few seconds she asked, "Is there someone there with you? I thought I heard . . . oh, the television. Right, that makes sense."

Having a good kid like you around, it probably really helps.

"Well, I'll let you go. I know you've got a show in a little bit. Break a leg. I love—" Her mom pulled the phone away from her ear, the line obviously dead. "You," she finished ruefully. Then, she turned, and gave a small smile. "Hey, honey."

"Hey, Mom." Maisey suddenly felt very young, and very unsure of herself. "Sorry you're having a hard time at work."

"Don't worry about it, Maize." Her mom shook her head. "It'll be over soon enough."

"Can I . . . can I get you anything?"

"You know what? I'd really like to not do anything. To just veg out with you and a bowl of popcorn and not have to worry about anything serious . . . or even anything not serious for a little bit."

Maisey nodded. "Okay. We can do that."

"We can?" she asked. "You don't have homework?"

"Did it already." Maisey shrugged. "What's on tonight? There's that British cooking show you like for some unexplained reason."

"It's a *baking* show, and it's very soothing," her mom replied, laughter coming back into her voice. "And I know I must be hard up if you're willing to watch that with me."

"It's not so bad. Soothing, like you said. If nothing else, I'll get a nap out of it."

"Great. I'll start the popcorn," her mom said. "What's that?" Her eyes had fallen to Maisey's hand, holding the Berkeley packet. Her future.

"Nothing," she said, flipping the packet back into her room. "It can wait."

CHAPTER 21

"Nat! Are you sitting down?"

"I'm thirty-four weeks pregnant, I'm always sitting down," Nathalie snorted into the phone, as her tired eyes glazed over another student essay. It was a beautiful day at the end of April, spring was in full flower in Los Angeles and Nathalie couldn't get off the couch.

It had only happened recently, this need to ABC—Always Be Couching. One day she was completely fine, practically trotting down the halls at school, around the house as she cleaned, and in IKEA as she finally picked out the crib and the furniture she wanted after the previous aborted trip. Then, all of a sudden, her body was just done. It said, "Nope! No putting up wall decals or assembling that combination dresser and changing table for you! Have a seat. Rewatching last season of *Fargone* is a much better use of your time."

She should have known it was coming. Dr. Duque had warned her after all.

"The baby shifted. She's head down and you're starting to carry her lower," she had said at their latest appointment—she was seeing Dr. Duque weekly at this point. Nathalie felt like she should ask if they were going steady. "It's starting to get exciting."

For someone who still had six weeks to go, exciting was not something you wanted.

But her ABC motto wasn't the only thing that had her stuck on the couch at the moment. No, what had her placed in the center of the microsuede not paying attention to her papers was the terrible trip she had just returned from, and the weight it left her with.

Nathalie hadn't spoken to Kathy since the baby shower. She had no illusions as to why. But it was incredibly jarring to have no contact from her stepmom—the woman was not prone to giving the silent treatment. In fact, this was the longest Nathalie had gone without hearing from Kathy in the entire history of their relationship. So, when her dad called and invited her up to see them, she was a little relieved. She burned one of her sick days (when she called her department head and told her she had a cold coming on, she was treated to a list of symptoms she'd had just previous to going into labor with her own kid ten years ago—seems like Dr. Duque wasn't the only one who thought things were getting exciting) and drove the two hours up to Santa Barbara.

Only to be met by her dad—and just her dad—at the door.

"Where's Kathy?" she asked, as her dad took her jacket, and led her into his den. She was expecting Kathy to be fussing in the kitchen as per usual, but there was no one there.

"She's visiting her friends in San Luis Obispo," her dad replied.

"So . . . she doesn't know I'm here?"

Her dad looked at his shoes. "She told me she'd already arranged to see friends when I invited you."

"Oh," Nathalie replied, feeling the blow like a punch to the chest.

"Yeah . . ." her father said, sighing. "You know I don't like to get in between you and Kathy. You two have always had to find your own balance. But she worked really hard putting that baby shower together for you girls. And she was hurt by what you said."

"I know," Nathalie said.

"I think you have to fix this one, kiddo."

"Don't you think I've tried? I've called to apologize a dozen times. I'm so, so sorry I insulted the shower."

"She doesn't want an apology." Her dad shook her head. "Not for that."

"Then for what?"

"You . . . you've never been able to think of Kathy as a parent. And that really hurts. She made you lunches. She explained your first period. She attended band concerts. She put in the work."

"What does she want then?" Nathalie asked, her voice cracking. "Does she want me to forget my mother?"

"Of course not."

"Good, because I'm holding on to the few memories I have for dear life! I don't need somebody to make my lunch right now. Or attend a concert." Nathalie's eyes fell to the one picture of her mom on the mantel, as tears began to fall. "My entire pregnancy, the only person I wanted to talk to, I can't. I want to ask her what it was like when she held me for the first time. I want to know what I'm going to feel when I have my daughter. And I'm sorry, but Kathy can't help me with that."

Her dad's voice was choked with emotion when he finally spoke. "I'm sorry I can't help you. I . . . Your mother would be so proud of you. Kathy and I are proud of you. I think Kathy just wants you to recognize her."

"And I wish she would have recognized me!" Nathalie cried. "And you, too."

"What do you mean?"

"I'm not Lyndi. And Lyndi's not me. You—both of you—have been treating us like the same person with the same pregnancy. And we're not. It was really hard for me to get pregnant. I know every baby is special, but this one is special to me. I just think my mom . . . my mom wouldn't have done that."

By now, her dad was openly crying. She hadn't seen her father cry in nearly twenty-five years.

"I'm sorry, Dad." She sniffed. "Tell Kathy I'm sorry, too."

"You're leaving?" her dad asked, surprised. "You don't have to go, kiddo. We can hang out. Talk."

"Thanks, but . . . if Kathy doesn't want to see me, I don't want to risk being here when she gets back."

She came over, squeezed her father's arm, and gave him a perfunctory kiss on the cheek. He didn't move. "I'll talk to you soon."

And she'd cried the entire two-hour drive back.

By the time she arrived home, her emotional exhaustion matched her physical exhaustion, and she collapsed on the couch.

Which was not uncommon.

After all, she had begun to do everything from the couch. She graded papers from the couch. She ate dinner on the couch. She burst into tears at pictures of kittens from the couch. She had very strained, very polite conversations with David from the couch.

Another reason her heart felt so heavy.

They had been unbelievably polite with each other, ever since the fight in IKEA. When he'd picked her up from the baby shower, they hadn't talked much on the way home. David had tried to broach the subject, by saying he was glad to see her, and that she was okay, but as Nathalie was busy trying to not burst into tears in the car, she didn't really respond.

Since then, they had begun their dance of politeness. The fight, and all the emotions therein lay just below the surface of every "good morning," and "should we get pizza for dinner?", but neither of them dared to mention it. Because neither of them wanted to risk the fragile state of affairs, where everything was okay, as long as one didn't look too closely.

Even when Lyndi had had her accident, David's relief that she was okay was palpable, but he didn't take her sister's near-death experience as the sign it obviously was to clear the air between them.

It was getting worse than unbearable. It was getting livable.

Part of Nathalie felt like it was up to him to approach her. Because he was the one who was fighting against the reality of their situation, he was the one regretting that they were pregnant. But another part of Nathalie—the small, female, constant-calm-waters part, felt like this was her fault. She was too busy getting back together with her sister to spend the time to get back together with her husband.

However, it was hard to regret that. Ever since Lyndi's accident, the two of them had been in near constant contact—when Lyndi wasn't busy making up with Marcus, that is. But they were constantly on text, on email, or on the phone with each other—the last of which Nathalie was now doing from the couch, of course.

"I'm glad you're sitting down," Lyndi singsonged, "because

I have a surprise for you." Nathalie could practically hear the sunshine in her sister's voice.

"What's the surprise?" Nathalie asked. Unless it was a transferrable reserve of twenty-something energy, a repaired relationship with her stepmother and/or husband, or a sneak peek at the next season of *Fargone*, Nathalie didn't think she much cared. "And where are you? You sound like you're in an echo chamber."

"I'm at Marcus's office at the website. I've never been here before, it's very . . . industrial," Lyndi replied. "As for the surprise . . . How would you like to meet @WTFPreg?"

Nathalie sat up. Twenty essays about the poetry of Dylan Thomas spilled off her lap. "What?"

"I found her!" Lyndi cheered triumphantly. "Well, Marcus found her. Okay, actually, it was Marcus's friend at work George who found her. Or we think he did."

"Hi, Nathalie," she could hear Marcus say in the background. "For legal purposes I'm telling you it wasn't me or anyone at the website who did this."

"Lyndi," Nathalie said, warning in her voice. "What did you do?"

"Nothing illegal."

"That's not gonna make her feel better," she heard in the background, from someone she assumed was George-from-Marcus's-work.

"It's totally legal and in no way an invasion of privacy. Anyway, ever since you told me about the Twitter feed, I've been following it. It's pretty funny."

Nathalie blinked. "Okay. But she didn't put her name or location on there—believe me I looked. Or is there some secret social media thing I, as an old, do not know?"

"No there isn't. But you know that tweet she posted last week? The one about being tired all the time?"

Nathalie looked down at her couch-prone body. Of course she remembered the tweet. She was currently living it.

> @WTFPreg—Discovered pretty much all work can be done from a prone position on the couch. Plus don't have to deal with marathon traffic. Score!

"What about it?"

"Marathon traffic!" Lyndi crowed triumphantly. "When that posted, I started looking up major marathons, and when they are run, trying to narrow down where she might be. Nathalie—she's *here*."

"Here. In Los Angeles?" Nathalie said. There was a decided note of panic in her voice; where did that come from? But then, "Hold on—the LA Marathon was a month ago."

"Yes, so I initially dismissed it. But then when I couldn't find any place with a traffic-causing marathon, I remembered. Last Friday, the morning that posted? One of our drivers Foz had a terrible time making his deliveries because of a half marathon in Hollywood! It couldn't be a coincidence."

"Okay . . ." Nathalie said, trying to keep her heart from beating out of her chest. "So, she's in Los Angeles. So are four million other people. How would I meet her?"

"Because we know *where* she's tweeting from!" Lyndi crowed, triumphant. "At least, we know where she tweets from on Friday mornings."

"This is going to give me a headache, but . . . how do you know that?"

"Marcus noticed this pattern in the tweets. On Friday

morning, she'll usually send a tweet or two between the hours of eight and nine. Every other day of the week, tweets are midday, lunchtime. We figured, Fridays . . . she has a little extra time in the morning.

"Then, a couple months ago there's a tweet on a Friday morning with that photo, remember?"

"Which photo?" @WTFPreg often posted pictures—memes usually, of annoyed pets or zen-like places. Basic internet amusements, but nothing that would ever tell you who someone was.

"The one of the pregnant lady from afar."

Nathalie remembered that one. It had been a zoomed-in shot of a pregnant woman in a horizontal striped shirt, standing on a street corner, about to cross. The pic was tagged: #eerilyfamiliar #horizontalstripes.

Yes, it was eerily familiar. Especially because Nathalie had bought that exact same shirt at Target.

"She posted that photo on a Friday!" Lyndi said.

". . . But that doesn't mean she took the photo on a Friday," Nathalie replied, dubious.

"Actually . . . hold on, I'll let George explain it."

"Hi Lyndi's sister," said George. He spoke matter-of-factly, like he was explaining how to boil rice, instead of internet-stalking someone. "Basically, knowing they were in Los Angeles, we used the shadows in the original picture to determine time of day. That picture was taken right before it was posted, likely 8:30 in the morning."

Then, some noises as Lyndi took back the phone. "And behind the pregnant lady there's a blurry billboard. So, using an internet image search, we found other shots of that corner—one of which was geotagged. Using map features we could figure out where the picture was taken *from* . . .

"Nat—that picture was taken in front of a Starbucks, about ten minutes from you!"

It took Nathalie a moment to realize what Lyndi was saying. "She's . . . she's here? She's not only here, she's ten minutes away?"

"I figure she gives herself a weekly treat on Fridays before she goes into the office," Lyndi reasoned. "So, if you find yourself at that Starbucks on Friday morning, between the hours of eight and nine . . . chances are good you'll meet your pregnancy Twitter twin."

"But . . . but tomorrow is Friday!" Nathalie cried. Then she looked around at herself, fat butt glued to beige microsuede, sitting in a sea of ungraded Dylan Thomas papers. "I have school, and papers to return . . . and if I went how would I even figure out who she is?"

"She'll be the one who's super pregnant," Lyndi said, flatly. The *duh* was implied. "Nathalie, you have to do this—and if you don't I will."

And with that ultimatum, Nathalie knew she would be spending tomorrow playing hooky from school.

Once the decision was made, a strange awareness tingled across her body. Destiny coming to shove her off the couch. It took all the energy she had, but she went along with destiny.

The next morning, she took extra care with her hair and makeup. She flossed. She contemplated giving her eyebrows a quick pluck. It wasn't because she was nervous, oh no . . . but somehow, today felt monumentally important.

"You look nice," David said, his mouth full of toothpaste. "Assembly at school today?"

"Hmm? No," Nathalie said quickly, smoothing her hand over her green dress, the one outfit she still felt like she looked decent in. She had long since gone past the point of trying to appear glowing and vibrant. Now, most days she opted for "covered." But the stretchy green sheath dress, that old workhorse, had survived early and middle pregnancy, and now was her go-to for anytime she wanted to look presentable. "I . . . I'm not going to work."

"Why?" He looked immediately concerned.

"I have a doctor's appointment this morning," she lied easily. "Just my regular checkup," she added to appease his worried look. She had doctor's appointments so often now there was no way David could keep track of them all.

In reality, she had let her department head know that her cold was lingering another day. She was again met with a litany of signs of early labor—what was it about pregnancy that made people share personal medical information? "And it's a half day at school for . . . testing . . . so I'm just taking the whole day."

David met her eyes in the mirror, his toothbrush paused in midbrushing. Then he shrugged, rinsed out his mouth, and moved on in sleepy unawareness to get ready for his day.

Usually, Nathalie was the first one out of the house, what with school hours starting so early. But with her lie, she would have to wait out David—because the doctor's office wouldn't be open until normal hours and she was nothing if not committed to the details of her lie. He moved *ridiculously* slowly. Tying and retying his tie. Brushing his hair into place—which was always going to stick up in the back, there really was no use in trying. Slurping his cereal. Nathalie kept a small, patient smile plastered on her face, all the while her insides were screaming.

Finally, *finally*, David went out the front door.

Immediately, Nathalie dashed back to the bedroom. One last check in the mirror. Hair was still good. Brush her teeth again, just to be extra fresh. Maybe she really should pluck her brows? Sophia would know, but . . . No—no time to call. She had a date with a decaf mocha latte, and possibly with someone she knew very well, but had never met.

The entire drive to Starbucks, she wondered who @WTFPreg could be. Not that she hadn't been wondering that for months, but now that they would meet, face-to-face . . .

Would it be a complete stranger? Someone who would no doubt be alarmed by the other pregnant lady who had cyber-stalked her to her Friday mocha ritual? Or could it possibly be someone she knew?

Not Lyndi—but what about Sophia? She was the other pregnant person in Nathalie's life—other than Ms. Hicks in the math department, but both seemed unlikely. Ms. Hicks only announced her pregnancy last week, and Sophia's work schedule made it so it was unlikely she was able to keep a standard Starbucks date. No . . . there was no possibility it was someone she knew.

But it *felt* so close to her. Like there was this mirrored version of herself, sitting just inside the Starbucks, taking a moment for herself in the morning, before life began.

Her hand fell on the tinted glass of Starbucks's door. And she froze.

She wondered if anyone would be there. She wondered—briefly, crazily—if she would see her mother there. Young, and healthy. Exactly the same as she had been in the picture that lived in Dad's office.

She almost didn't want to walk in—because doing so would destroy that fiction.

But she had come this far. She would regret it if she didn't open the door.

Besides, Lyndi would kill her if she didn't.

The smell of coffee embraced her like an old friend. The Starbucks was in what was surely its usual morning chaos. Long line of cranky uncaffeinated people waiting as patiently as they could to make their orders, and a half-dozen baristas scrambling to meet their needs while wordless indie pop played over the sound system.

She looked around for another third-trimester pregnant woman. But there was no one. Only people in suits, or tired moms in yoga pants carting preschoolers around. No pregnant woman.

Maybe she had beaten her here, she thought as she joined the line, and eventually ordered a decaf mocha. But then, her phone dinged—a notification from Twitter.

@WTFPreg had just posted.

Coffee is a deeply held religious belief.

Okay, she was *definitely* here. But where? The bathroom? Maybe she was on the patio outside, or tucked into a corner table—if she was sitting down Nathalie wouldn't be able to see her belly. She scanned the tables. But there were no women sitting. Just a bunch of young twenty-something guys, typists that populated LA coffee shops, heads in their computers while they worked on their screenplays. Her eyes scanned over to the left where two grandfather-aged men talked about baseball, and an Asian man in a suit with his eyes on his phone—

An Asian man in a suit who looked achingly familiar.

Suddenly, everything clicked into place. The tweets . . . everything feeling so familiar, lining up with her pregnancy . . .

Because it was her pregnancy.

Or rather, it was *their* pregnancy.

Slowly, she approached the table. "Is this seat taken?"

David looked up. At first, blinking, unable to realize what he was seeing. Then it dawned on him that his wife was smiling down at him.

"What are you doing here?" he asked. "I thought you had a doctor's appointment?"

"That was a lie. I lied," she said, as she sat down. Then she slid the phone across the table, opened to the latest @WTFPreg tweet. "I'm not the only one."

He stared down at the phone for several seconds, total confusion on his face.

"How did you find it?" he finally asked.

"Twitter recommended you. Because they thought I might know you. Those predictive algorithms are really scary. You didn't notice that I was following you?" He shook his head. "Well, I have been," she said. "For months. Suffice to say I'm your biggest fan."

They sat there, the bustle of Starbucks around them. David watched her, lost.

"I'm sorry," she said eventually. "I thought . . . I thought you weren't interested in the baby. I thought when I talked about the pregnancy and how I was feeling, that you just tuned me out."

"I was listening," he said.

"I know that now." She nodded. "You heard everything. You don't know how much that means to me, because I thought . . . I thought I was alone in this. I just wish you would have talked to me about it."

"I didn't know how. And I didn't think you wanted me to."

"Why not?"

"I don't know. We never talked about the first pregnancy.

The one we lost," David admitted. "I know you were devastated. But I . . ."

She reached out and took his hand. His breath shuddered.

"I thought I was going to lose you. When you were in so much pain and we didn't know what was going on, before they diagnosed it as ectopic. I thought, 'This is it. She's going to die and my life is going to end because I can't do it without her.' It's why I didn't want to go back to Monterey over Christmas. I can't think about that place without thinking about that time."

"You never told me that," she whispered.

"So, I was scared when we got pregnant again. And I guess I started distancing myself. Tried to provide for my family, because that's what men do, but leaving everything having to do with the baby up to you. But I had all these feelings and thoughts about it—you're right, all pregnant women wear horizontal stripes, I've never noticed that before—I had to put them somewhere."

"So you made the Twitter feed," she concluded.

"The Twitter feed helped. But then as you've gotten bigger, all those old fears have started to come back, and I finally . . . just lost it. In IKEA, of all places." He smiled ruefully.

"There's something about pictorial-only directions that just drives people to their limits," she joked gently.

"I'm so sorry about what I said that day. I didn't mean any of it. I've wanted to have a family with you since the day we met."

"It's all right to be scared," she said. "I'm scared, too. But it would be a lot easier to handle if we had talked to each other about it."

"You're right," he agreed. "So let's talk."

"Now?" She blinked. "Don't you have to go to work?"

"I'm thinking about playing hooky," he said, his eyebrow going up in that way that had made Nathalie's heart zing since she was nineteen years old. It was still there, she realized. Her love for this man.

And it always would be.

"I've already called in sick," she replied.

"Great. So, let's talk. I'm really curious to know how you knew I'd be here. At this Starbucks."

Nathalie let out a bubble of laughter. "I'll let Lyndi explain that to you. She's never going to believe me when I tell her about this."

CHAPTER 22

"DELIVERY FOR SOPHIA NUNEZ, FROM THE Favorite Flower!"

Maisey had driven onto the lot that Monday morning practically buzzing. She felt as if she'd had a triple espresso followed by a 5-hour Energy chaser. But her current high had nothing to do with caffeine.

It had to do with a conversation she'd had not an hour before. And her bubbling need to tell someone about it.

And that someone was going to be her mom.

It had been a couple days since the Berkeley letter and Maisey still hadn't told her about getting into college. She haunted the mailbox every day, making sure she intercepted any letters from higher institutions that could come in before her mother got home.

She would tell her mom about it, she told herself. Once her mom was less stressed. Maybe when the hiatus began. Certainly before she enrolled.

Besides, she reasoned, in actuality she had months to tell her mom about Berkeley—it didn't start until the fall.

The prom, on the other hand, was a little over a week away.

It had happened before she even made it into the Favorite Flower that morning. When she pulled into the parking lot behind their stall, she was surprised to see Foz there, hanging out beside his car, flipping his keys over in his hand.

Usually, she beat Foz in to work. Partially out of a latent sense of competition with him, but mostly because since he was in Whittier now, she lived closer to downtown. But she was more surprised to see him because he hadn't been in to work the past few days.

"Hey," she said, as she climbed out of her car.

"Hey," he replied, coming off the wall he was leaning against, and headed toward her. He fell into step beside her as they walked to the market's doors.

"Were you waiting for me?" she asked, eyeing him.

"Kinda."

"Why?" She was certainly feeling bold that morning. Although she hadn't a clue the reason.

He stopped walking. She waited. He opened his mouth to speak, but then nothing came out.

"You've been out the past couple days," she began, slightly hesitant. "Were you sick?"

"No. Nothing like that. I had AP exams."

"Oh." She felt oddly relieved. So he hadn't been avoiding her. Not that he had any reason to avoid her. But there had been a certain awkwardness to the last time they saw each other. They started walking again.

"I don't have any until next week. Which did you—"

"Computer science and biology," he said automatically.

"Not my subjects," she said ruefully.

"Not mine either."

They walked on in silence for a few steps. Something was definitely up with Foz. She just had no idea what it was. But it kept making her glance at him out of the corner of her eye, curious.

"So listen . . ." he said, slowing his steps. Her body became alert and strangely uneasy.

"Yes?"

"I was going to ask you something."

Her heart leaped into her throat. Last time at work. As they were talking about college. The last thing he said before Lyndi came and roped them into loading their cars, he'd said he wanted to ask her something.

"I was going to ask you to prom."

Her eyes shot up to his face. "You were?"

"Yeah, but then I realized, I can't ask you to prom."

"Why not?" Did he have a girlfriend? You would think sometime in all of their working together and all of their texting that he would have mentioned a girlfriend in an off-hand, casual way . . .

"Because we don't go to the same school anymore."

"Oh," she said. Then, realizing, *"ohhhhhhhh . . ."*

"Yeah," he said, rubbing the back of his head, making his hair stick up even more than usual. "Apparently, I missed my new school's window for buying tickets . . . and besides, you probably have a date to your prom already. But just know, that if I could have . . . I would have asked you to prom."

". . . Okay," was her reply. Her utterly dumbstruck reply.

He waited a second, to see if she had anything more to say, but when she didn't, he just shuffled his feet forward, and tried to cover up the awkward big talk with awkward small talk.

"So . . . ready for work?"

But instead, she reached out and grabbed his hand. He stopped, turned back to her.

And she took a breath, and dove in.

Kissing Foz was not what she expected it to be. She'd kissed guys before. She was a senior in high school, there had been the occasional game of spin the bottle in her friend Jennifer's basement in middle school. And that one time she'd gone to sleepaway writing camp for a week, and a boy asked if he could kiss her so he would be able to write about it in their composition class—he turned out to be gay and when he read his composition aloud, she learned that her kiss confirmed it. But this was the first time she'd ever kissed anyone she'd spent a decent amount of time thinking about kissing beforehand.

And it lived up to her imagination.

Foz, for his part, seemed to be taken by surprise. So much so, he didn't respond at first. But once he clued in to what was happening, he smiled against her mouth, his hand snaking into her hair.

Her kiss quickly became *their* kiss. And it lasted far longer than a predawn Monday morning moment in a parking lot probably should.

When they broke it off, it was with gasps of breath and tingling skin.

"Wow," Foz said.

"Yeah," she breathed. Then . . . "Hey Foz?"

"Hmm?"

"Wanna go to prom with me?"

He smirked. Then, it exploded into a full-on grin. "Yes, I do."

"Good," she said. "So . . . it's a date."

"It's a date."

They walked in silence into the Favorite Flower, sneaking peeks at each other out of the corners of their eyes.

Judy and the other arrangers were already there, their

heads whipping around to see them enter. But instead of beckoning them over to get them to work in the assembly line making bouquets, they froze, then started whispering and giggling all at once.

"Do you think they know?" Foz asked, bewildered.

Maisey scoped Judy. She had her eyes deadlocked on the two teenagers, and she wasn't even hiding her massive grin and whispering to the others.

"They absolutely know."

"Man, what if I had said no?" Foz whispered. "That would have been so embarrassing for you."

"Considering you said you were gonna ask me, I was reasonably sure of your answer."

"That, and the kissing," he said, making her turn bright red.

"And the . . . that," she agreed.

"Hey, so since you asked me, does that mean you have to buy the flowers, and the limo, and stuff?"

Maisey snorted. "I think we've got our flowers covered. And as for a ride—don't worry your pretty little head about it. I'll get my dad's Corolla washed for the occasion. I'll honk the horn outside your place, when I come to pick you up."

Foz practically choked on his laughter, as they both dissolved into giggles. And that's what they were like the rest of the morning. They worked side by side putting together the last of the bouquets, stealing glances, making silly jokes, and giggling. And then, as they loaded up their cars, Foz would find excuses to step just a little closer to Maisey, to let the side of his hand graze the side of hers. It was like being really, really awake—but only able to see the incredibly minute. The big stuff around you didn't matter one whit.

Which was, no doubt, why they misloaded one box of bouquets.

"Hold on," Paula said, looking down at Maisey's loaded Corolla. "Lyndi, wasn't this box supposed to go on Foz's run?"

Lyndi trotted over as fast as her pregnant belly would let her. She checked the label.

"Yep. Don't worry, I'll call him back." Foz's car had already left the lot.

"I'm sorry, it's my fault, Lyndi," Maisey said. "I wasn't paying attention."

"And we know why!" came the cry from Judy, twenty feet away.

Maisey determinedly ignored her as she checked the box, saw the addresses on the labels. "Don't worry about it, I can take them."

"Are you sure?" Lyndi asked. "You won't be late for school?"

"It's not out of the way," Maisey said, and threw herself into the car, and took off up the road.

And that was how she ended up on the studio lot, delivering her mother's weekly flowers from Sebastian.

Unfortunately, her mother was nowhere to be seen.

"Hey, Maisey!" Kip cried, coming over from rearranging brushes to throw a bear hug around her shoulders. "Good to see you! How's everything? What's going on at school?"

"Hey, Kip—sorry I don't have a lot of time," she said as she slipped out of the bear hug. Normally, she would have gossiped with Kip for hours, but she really didn't have a ton of time that morning. And she *had* to see her mom, to tell her her news. "Where's Mom?"

Kip grimaced. "They have her in the extras' tent today, creating more frost giants out of thin air in less than an hour and a half. You can leave the flowers here, sweetie. I'll tell her you came by, she'll be touched."

"No, I . . . I kinda wanted to talk to her. Where's the extras' tent?"

Kip pointed Maisey in the right direction, but it only took her thirty seconds and two wrong turns in the sea of trailers to get lost.

Maisey had been on the lot before. When she was in middle school, she was in her mom's makeup trailer all the time, doing homework in the corner while her mom crafted characters out of paint and hairspray for whatever show she happened to be working on. She'd spent plenty of time in the last three years on *Fargone*'s set, too. But they must have rearranged the trailer layout on the backlot since she was last here, because she was so turned around, she accidentally wandered over to where a sitcom was shooting, and was quickly chased off by a harried PA.

She found her way back to the *Fargone* area, but still didn't see a tent anywhere. However, she did see a trailer that had its door wide open.

While she knew it was not exactly a good idea to go jumping into other people's trailers—it was akin to stepping inside their office, or house, uninvited—Maisey was lost enough now she didn't know where her car was, let alone her mom. And she *did* have a bunch of other deliveries to do before school.

Besides, their door was wide open. And there was someone in there. She could hear them working out. Or maybe lifting stuff.

"Hello?" Maisey asked tentatively as she knocked on the door and took one step inside. "Can you point me to—"

The words died on her lips.

At first, Maisey didn't quite comprehend what she was

seeing. It just looked like two faceless bodies, wrestling. Oh, she *knew* what she was looking at. She knew what sex looked like, she'd seen a movie. But to see it happening live, and so unexpectedly . . .

And then, to realize that the guy in the equation, with his back to her, had familiar lanky hair.

And an even more familiar *Sophia* tattoo on his shoulder.

"Maisey!" Sebastian cried, just a blur of movement as he dove for something to cover himself with.

"Jesus—Sebastian! Mom!" Maisey said, ducking her gaze and squeezing her eyes shut. This was something no child should ever see. She was going to be scarred for life. She would send all of her therapy bills to Sebastian in perpetuity—

"Mom?" came the sultry voice from behind Sebastian. "Whose mom?"

Maisey didn't want to look. But she knew she had to. And there, paying lip service to the idea of covering herself, was Vanessa Faire.

Biggest rising star in Hollywood.

Her mom's supposed friend.

"Oh . . . Maisey, right?" Vanessa said, her face taking on a look of pure innocence. Hell, maybe she had deserved that Golden Globe after all. "You're . . . you're Sophia's daughter? Oh, dear."

"Maisey, it's not what it looks like," Sebastian said in a rush, pulling his pants on. "I'm not . . . I didn't mean for this—"

But Maisey was out the door before Sebastian could get his second leg in his jeans. She was nearly back to the makeup trailer—if only she could find it!—before Sebastian caught up to her.

"Maisey, wait!" Sebastian said, out of breath, as he grabbed her arm. "You can't tell your mom."

"Are you crazy?" Maisey replied. "I'm telling her right now."

"It will only hurt her!" They were in an alley of trailers—which ones Maisey had no idea. But two people came around the corner, and Sebastian's hand tightened on her arm.

"Give me a chance to explain," he said, as he pulled her in between two trailer bumpers, pulling the hood of his hastily thrown on sweatshirt up over his head.

". . . she doesn't know you're here," Maisey realized.

"Of course she doesn't."

"I don't mean on set. She doesn't know you're even in the state. You're not supposed to be back for another two days. Trust me, she's been counting them down."

It was marked in big red marker on the wall calendar in the kitchen. "Sebastian Home!" was right before "AP Exams!" "Hiatus!" and "Graduation!" All had equal exclamation marks, each massive events worthy of excitement.

"I . . . We got done early, and . . ."

"You don't 'get done early' with concerts. It's not like working in a stockroom," Maisey argued. "You told my mom weeks ago that you'd be back two days from now, but you knew then that you'd be done already. You didn't want her to know."

"Okay!" Sebastian exploded. "I bought myself a little alone time—is that so wrong?"

"You weren't exactly alone back there."

He sighed. "Your mom . . . she can be real needy, you know? She didn't used to be, but lately . . ."

"Lately she's been pregnant with your baby and is trying to plan for the future. That's not 'needy.' That's normal."

"Well, it's not normal for me, okay? I love your mom, but it can be a lot," Sebastian said, running a hand over his wispy beard.

"So, your answer to that is to fuck—" he cringed as she

said the word that so accurately described what he had been doing "—Vanessa Faire? Who, correct me if I'm wrong, has been making my mom's life hell on this show?"

"Nessa and I go way back. She's a friend. And she's not making Sophia's job hard on purpose, she's—" He stopped himself, when he seemed to realize that defending the woman he was cheating on Maisey's mom with was probably not the best way to win Maisey over. "It only happened once."

"You expect me to believe that?"

"It's the truth!"

She stared at him, hard. And he seemed to realize there was no point in lying about the situation. At least not so obviously. "Okay—it might have happened more than once. But it's not going to happen again. I promise."

"I don't care if it happens again," Maisey replied. "And neither will my mother. Because she is going to kick you to the curb."

"Maisey, please . . ."

But she was already walking away.

"What about her blood pressure?" Sebastian called out.

Maisey paused. That was about the only thing that could make her do so.

"The doctor said she needs to keep it under control, right?" Sebastian continued. "Or else it could hurt the baby. She could end up in the hospital like she did with you."

He was right. The doctor had commented that her blood pressure was slightly elevated. This . . . on top of everything going on at work . . . the stress her mother let slide off her every night when she got home. This was going to devastate her. And normally, Maisey knew her mother could handle it—there wasn't a person on earth stronger than Sophia Nunez.

But it wasn't just her she had to worry about anymore.

"I will tell your mom, I swear," Sebastian said, coming toward her. "But you have to let me do it right, so it doesn't put her in the hospital. Because that's what would happen if you burst in there right now, and told her."

Sebastian leaned over her, his voice pitched to seduce, to persuade. And it was working.

Because he wasn't wrong. Springing this on her mom . . . she could end up in the hospital again. And it would be all Maisey's fault.

"Thank you," Sebastian said, when Maisey hesitated. "I'll make everything right, you'll see. Thank you. Thank you."

Sebastian pulled Maisey into a hug, but before he could get his arms around her, she pushed him away, skeeved at the very thought of being touched by him.

"Right," he said, edging up to the precipice between them. "I should get back . . . talk to Vanessa. Don't you have school?"

She nodded dumbly. Then, without anything more to say, Sebastian hesitated a bare second, then backed away. Careful to keep his hood up, lest he be spotted.

Leaving Maisey in the byzantine maze of trailers, a forgotten and now crushed bouquet of flowers falling to the pavement at her feet.

"SOMETHING IS UP with Maisey."

Maisey was eavesdropping again. From behind her bedroom door again. And this time, she was trying really, really hard not to shake with rage.

Because Sebastian was in their kitchen, pretending for all the world like nothing had happened two days ago.

It made Maisey wonder, how often had he pretended like that?

After leaving the lot, studiously avoiding seeing her mother, Maisey spent the rest of that day in kind of a fog. Most of her friends wrote it off as the kind of grim focus that comes with freaking out about the AP tests next week, but Ms. Kneller pulled her aside and asked if everything was okay.

"Um . . . you're friends with my mom, right?" Maisey said, awkward as the rest of class filed out of the room.

"Yes," Ms. Kneller replied, nonplussed. "I've slept on your couch, Maisey."

"Right," she replied. Like that wasn't weird enough. "Did she tell you about her predisposition to preeclampsia?"

Ms. Kneller blinked. "No. I didn't know that. Is she okay?"

"Yes, she's fine. But . . . if there was something that could affect her blood pressure—even if it was better for her to know in the long term, should she know?"

Her teacher leaned forward on her elbows. "If it's worrying you this much, I think your mom would want to know, whatever it is. Is this about school?"

". . . yeah. I'm just, er, stressing about AP tests next week."

Ms. Kneller relaxed a little. "I have no doubt that your mom already knows how much these tests mean to you. This time of year they put so much pressure on you kids. AP exams, the prom, graduation, college. It seems like the future is coming at you like water from a fire hydrant, doesn't it?"

Maisey nodded slowly.

"But you don't need to stress out so much. You're going to do great. You'll get through the next couple weeks. Just try not to let extraneous stuff distract you in the meantime."

Try not to let extraneous stuff distract her in the meantime. Great advice. If only that extraneous stuff wasn't her mother's love life and her unborn baby brother's entire future.

With Foz she was much less cagey, and told him every-thing. Down to the tattoo on Sebastian's shoulder.

"Ew," Foz said. "Oh my God, that's traumatizing!" Then, "You have to tell your mom. She deserves to know, even with her blood pressure."

Part of Maisey knew he was right. But another part of her didn't want to risk it.

To risk . . . not being believed.

Because it was entirely possible her mom wouldn't believe her. Her mom was head over heels about Sebastian. She hadn't been able to see straight since he came into her life. Their relationship was complicated, complex, and bewildering to Maisey . . . but it was also this bright and shining thing that lit her mother up in ways Maisey had never seen.

Her mom might not be willing to give that up.

"I can't," she said, eventually. "I told Sebastian I would let him tell her."

"And has he?"

No. No he had not. After school that day, Maisey waited for her mom to come home. She tried to act casual as she asked her mom about her day. She waited a full thirty sec-onds before asking if she'd heard from Sebastian.

"Not today," her mom said glumly. Then she brightened. "But he'll be home in thirty-six hours. Besides, we don't need to talk every second of every day."

"Glad to hear it," Maisey mumbled, the "your mom is needy" defense of his actions crumbling. Then she impulsively reached out, and squeezed her mother's arm. "You're totally capable of standing on your own two feet, you know."

"Oh trust me, I know," her mom said, on a laugh. "I've been doing it forever. But sometimes it's nice not to have to."

She wanted to prepare her mom for what was to come. Because if Sebastian hadn't told her that day, surely he would tell her the next.

Except he hadn't. No call on the following day. And then, he showed up on her mom's doorstep, with his duffel in hand, as if he had just stepped off the tour bus.

Her mom had been full of squeals of delight and expansive displays of affection when she opened the door. This continued into the living room, her mom talking a mile a minute about how happy she was to see him, about all the planning she'd been doing.

Meanwhile, Maisey stood, arms crossed over her chest, watching Sebastian, and waiting.

Finally his eyes met hers. Then he turned to her mom and said, "Soph, let's sit down, okay. I've got some stuff to tell you."

It was about that time that Maisey excused herself to go to her room. And left her door open just enough so she would hear when her mother needed her.

But then . . . Sebastian never said ANYTHING.

"Some stuff" to tell Sophia turned out to be just . . . stuff. Stupid stories about being on a tour bus with a bunch of other guys. Recounting crowd size at their last gig.

"Wow . . . I didn't know there were that many people in Omaha, period!" her mom said. Then, "But wasn't Omaha last week?"

"Mmm hmm."

"So, if that was your last gig, what have you been doing for the past week?"

Maisey braced herself against the door frame. Surely this was the time. He would tell her. He had to.

"Oh! No, that was our last *big* gig. We had a couple of studio gigs last week. With like, local radio stations. They were small, invite-only shows."

Oh, they were small, invite-only shows, all right, thought Maisey. She had been the only uninvited guest.

But as her mother made small sounds of acquiescence to Sebastian's obvious lie, Maisey's frustration boiled over. Couldn't she see that her boyfriend was being annoyingly cagey? Couldn't she tell that this lanky less-than was keeping something from her? These were the thoughts that swirled in her head as her foot—entirely of its own accord—lashed out and kicked her door.

The whole apartment froze at the sound of the *thud!* of her boot.

"What was that?" Sebastian said.

"Nothing," her mom replied. "Something is up with Maisey." Maisey could practically hear her shaking her head.

"What do you mean?" Sebastian asked.

"I just feel like she's keeping things from me." Sophia sighed. "She hasn't told me a thing about prom, or plans for graduation, or colleges—and I know that they've been sending out their acceptances. Maybe you can get it out of her?"

She could feel Sebastian's discomfort. "I dunno. I always felt like . . . Maisey doesn't like me that much."

"Babe, don't say that," Sophia replied. "She's got a lot going on right now is all."

"If you say so," he said on a big sigh. "I just think she doesn't want me around . . . but I don't want to cause any problems between you two."

Maisey felt a cold sense of dread run down her spine. She didn't know what he was doing . . . but it wasn't good. And it certainly wasn't telling her mom about his infidelity.

"Don't worry about Maisey, that's my job. Now, I've got your favorite ready in the fridge . . ." her mom singsonged.

"My favorite is sitting on this couch," he replied. "But if you're talking about your famous cherry lemonade, I've been dreaming about it for weeks."

Maisey peeked her head out of her room, in time to see her six months pregnant mother jump up from the couch, have her ass playfully slapped by Sebastian as she crossed to the kitchen door to fetch and carry for him.

For this guy.

This wet, wispy-bearded, cheating guy.

She was done hiding behind doors. She stomped into the living room. Sebastian didn't even turn around.

"Hey, babe, don't forget the lemon wedges," he said, resting his head against the back of the couch.

"Sorry, fresh out of lemon wedges," Maisey said.

He sat straight up, whirled around in his seat. Then, he tried to relax. "Hey, kid," he said, loud enough for her mom to hear. "What's up?"

"What's up?" she replied. "Oh, I don't know. Your penis up Vanessa's vag?"

"Sssshhhhhhhhhhhh!" he said, leaping out of his seat. "You . . . wow, you're blunt."

"These are blunt times," Maisey shot back.

"Come on, Maisey, I'm working my way up to it," he said, this time even lower. They both had their ears pricked for movement from the kitchen. The prevalence of slamming cabinet doors told them that Sophia was too busy trying to find the Fiestaware pitcher and that she hadn't heard a thing.

"No you're not. You're just going to pretend that nothing happened?" Maisey hissed. "That everything is normal?"

"Yes," Sebastian hissed back. "Because your mom doesn't

need to know about it. Not right now, with the baby. In fact, I was thinking I probably shouldn't tell her until after the baby comes."

"What?" Maisey nearly screeched. "That's three months away! By then it will be too late!"

"Too late for what?" he asked, his voice becoming a sneer. "Too late to get rid of me?"

"Too late for her to make a decision about it," Maisey said. Her heart was pounding, and she could feel the stinging inside her nose that told her tears were imminent. She wasn't good at this. Confrontation. She was only a kid, for chrissakes, she wasn't used to squaring off with adults—even adults as unadult-like as Sebastian. But it was too important to back down now.

"You'll just . . . you'll never tell her, will you?" she said, keeping her breaths short to prevent any tears from falling. "You're such a child. You think that if she doesn't know, it will just go away. That it will just be this thing in the past that doesn't matter."

"It's already this thing in the past that doesn't matter!" Sebastian said, swinging from angry to desperate. "I broke it off with Vanessa. Nothing like that will ever happen again."

"Yes it will—you'll do this every time you go away on tour." It was times like this that Maisey was thankful for debate class.

Sebastian scoffed. "The road is a crazy place, I can't predict what's going to happen. I'm trying to do the right thing by your mom—be the decent guy."

"Then do the right thing and tell her."

"No, dammit!" Sebastian swore under his breath. "I'm not going to tell her. And neither are you."

"Why not?"

"Because she won't believe it."

Maisey stayed silent, but kept her eyes locked on Sebastian's.

"You could have told her anytime in the last two days. If you didn't tell her when it happened, why would she believe you now?" he said. "It's not like you and your mom have been getting along lately. She relies on *me*. She trusts me. She needs me. Don't take that from her."

"She deserves to know."

"Know what?" Sophia said, standing in the doorway from the kitchen, the tray with the pitcher of cherry lemonade in her hands. A bowl of lemon wedges on the side.

"Nothing, babe," Sebastian said, crossing to her. "Let me get that. You shouldn't be on your feet."

That was what did it. Sebastian's false concern. His jumping up to help her mom now that she was done doing all the work. And the way he smirked when he said, "Maisey, you should be helping out more."

"Mom, I have something to tell you." Her voice was louder than expected. A couple of octaves higher than normal. But she got the words out.

"Maisey, not now okay?" Sebastian said smoothly. "Let your mom relax."

Sophia turned to her immediately. "Honey, what is it?"

She took one breath. Two. Then set her feet, and said it.

"Sebastian . . . Sebastian's been lying to you."

"Maisey . . ." His growl warned, but she persevered.

"He wasn't on the road. I saw him two days ago."

"You . . . saw him two days ago?" Her mom looked from Maisey to Sebastian. "Here, in Los Angeles?"

"In Vanessa Faire's trailer."

Sophia took one step back from Sebastian. Two. "Is that true?" she asked him, her voice cold.

". . . Yes," Sebastian admitted. And Maisey felt this massive relief. Finally, her mom would know. "But it was supposed to be a surprise."

"A surprise?" both Maisey and her mother said at the same time.

"Vanessa . . . was helping me."

"Do what?"

Yes, do what exactly? Maisey thought.

"Pick out a new place. For the two of us. I mean, the three of us." Sebastian placed a gentle hand on her mother's belly. "Vanessa knows how much you're looking forward to us being together, so she wanted to help."

"You . . . found a new place for us?" Sophia said, her eyes turning to water.

"No, Mom—"

"We haven't found anything yet, but I've been looking."

"That's wonderful . . . but—"

"Mom, please listen—"

"A nice big place? Maybe down by the beach?"

"I'd love to be by the beach—"

"Dammit, Mom, they weren't looking at houses, they were having sex!"

You could hear a pin drop. Sophia turned to face Maisey, her expression blank.

"I was delivering flowers to you, and I couldn't find you," she explained in a stumble. "But I found them . . . in the middle of it. In Vanessa's trailer."

The room vibrated with the words. Then, it exploded.

Rather, Sebastian exploded.

"That's . . . that's totally ridiculous!" he said, his face turning a particularly deep red. "I would never do that. I told you, Maisey hates me—and this proves it. She just wants me gone, and wants you alone and having to deal with a baby all on your own. It's beyond selfish! Who are you going to believe? Me, or your daughter who hates me?"

Maisey remained gravely silent, focused on her mother's face. *Please believe me*, she begged silently. *Please don't believe him.*

But he was telling the truth. She did hate him. She did want him gone. She *was* selfish for her mother.

And her greatest fear was that Sebastian had enough truth behind him to make her mother believe him . . . because she wanted to believe him.

But as Sebastian sputtered and raged, Sophia shushed him gently. Maisey felt her heart sink as she watched her mother place a soft hand on her boyfriend's chest.

"Oh, Sebastian," she murmured, the words tender and easy.

"Babe," he sighed, bringing the hand to his mouth to kiss it.

But she slipped her hand out of his before it could reach his lips.

"I am going to absolutely believe my daughter."

The smile fell from his face. His body became ramrod straight—a wire of fury.

"She's a little bitch—" He stepped toward Maisey. And suddenly, Sophia wasn't being kind anymore.

She stepped in front of him, holding her belly in one hand with the other on Maisey's arm. "You need to get out of my house," she said, her voice a growl. "Before I call the police."

"You wouldn't—"

"A domestic charge from your pregnant girlfriend will look really good to your record label, don't you think?"

Finally, he seemed to get it. Grabbing his duffel bag, he

slammed his hand against the door frame on his way out, rattling the small space to its foundation.

But then, just as quickly as it had happened, the apartment stopped shaking, and everything settled down again.

"Mom . . ."

But her mom had already wrapped herself around Maisey, buried her head in her daughter's shoulder.

"You're taller than me." Her mother's words were muffled against Maisey's shirt. "When did you get taller than me?"

"Eighth grade?"

"I don't mean like that." Sophia pulled away, looked Maisey in the eye.

"Now . . . is there anything else you haven't told me?" her mom asked through sniffles, pulling away from her daughter's embrace to dry her eyes. "Any other life-altering things I should know?"

"I got into Berkeley."

Sophia coughed out a laugh. Then another. "You did? Oh, honey!" She pulled Maisey back into her arms.

"And a couple other places." The UCLA acceptance had come in the mail just yesterday.

"That's amazing! Why didn't you tell me!"

Maisey could only shrug, ashamed of the convoluted train of thought that had her keeping secrets.

"Well, for the record, that is the kind of thing that can only help my blood pressure. Oh, Maisey, I knew you could do it."

"Also, I'm going to prom."

This time, Sophia didn't even bother with restraint. She threw her head back in full-throated joyous laughter. "That's wonderful! Foz asked you, I assume?"

"Technically, I asked him."

"Atta girl."

Then her mom paused, hand to her belly. Maisey went on full alert.

"Are you okay? Is it your blood pressure? Do we need to go to the hospital?"

"No, sweetie. None of that. Just your brother giving Sebastian an extra kick out the door."

"Oh," Maisey said, her heart settling back down. "So, things . . . feel good?"

"No. But things feel right for the first time in a while." Sophia moved to the kitchen, to the fridge, and pulled out of the back a hidden bottle of Diet Coke.

"Come on. I think we have a lot of catching up to do."

CHAPTER 23

"SOPHIA! YOU HAVE TO HIDE! SHE'S COMING!"

Sophia looked up from the count. She was doing inventory on her stock. They would be on hiatus in the blink of an eye, she had to account for everything they had, everything they used over the course of the season. Her stock and her receipts needed to match up. And she was halfway through counting up their supply of false eyelashes when Kip came bursting into the makeup trailer.

"Dammit, Kip, you made me lose count!"

"Girl, give it up—she's on her way here now!"

There was no need to ask who *she* was. Nor was there a need to ask why Kip was all aflutter.

Vanessa always did know how to command attention.

"This is my makeup trailer," Sophia said quietly. "I'm not hiding from her."

"Well, do you mind if I do?" Kip said.

Sophia quirked up a brow. "You're her key makeup artist. She's coming to see you, not me."

"I can't even stand to touch that woman's hair. Out of solidarity."

"Uh-huh," Sophia replied. "Solidarity, and not an abject fear of her lashing out at you?"

"That, too."

It had been two days since Sophia had unceremoniously kicked Sebastian out of her home. Yesterday, Sophia had come in to work with rage in her heart and her head held high. She had the right to her anger, she knew. Because Vanessa was a lying little snake. It was one thing to have an affair. It was another to bring Sebastian to set, to literally fuck three trailers away from where Sophia was working.

And there were no secrets on set. Everyone knew everyone's business, because you lived on top of each other, and there were PAs whose entire job was to report on people's whereabouts.

It was like a very tight-knit, incestuous family.

However, when she got to set on Thursday, she had completely forgotten that Vanessa wasn't shooting that day. They were filming scenes that didn't involve her, so she got a rare day off.

Sophia was determined to keep their conflict between themselves, and so kept her mouth well shut. But somehow, the news got out anyway.

The blame could only be laid at Kip's door. He was the only person Sophia told. No wonder he wasn't keen to meet with Vanessa.

It started with looks. Eva the on-set makeup artist and Gary the assistant camera operator stopped talking the second she walked by. The extras she turned into frost giants were less circumspect—they gossiped in front of her outright.

"They say Vanessa was banging that guy from her ex-husband's band—the one with the hair! Like, in her trailer."

"I heard he's got a pregnant girlfriend, too."

"No!"

"She's not famous or anything, but still . . ."

But still.

The worst was when Roger, the producer, brought her into his office.

"So . . . Sophia."

"Roger," she replied.

"We are almost done with the season."

"True."

"I've been told that things have become . . . complicated in your personal life. And I'm sorry for that. Betrayal . . . is a horrible thing." Roger shook his head, sighing. Sophia raised a brow.

"If you want to take some time . . ."

"No, I want to do my job," Sophia replied. "Like you said, the season is almost done."

"Okay. I just want to make sure that . . . we finish out the season without any extra problems. We're going to have press on set tomorrow, writing a color article on the finale and on Vanessa. And Vanessa's . . . under a lot of pressure." Roger came around the desk, and leaned against it, looming over Sophia. "Let's get through this together."

Sophia looked up at him from beneath her lashes. "Absolutely," she chirped.

So when she came to set this morning, it was with a new resolution. No more rage. No being hurt. Just . . . getting through it.

But that was before Kip decided to dive into the toilet cubicle of the makeup trailer, hiding himself away right before the door swung open and Vanessa Faire made her entrance.

Sniffling up tears, and with red-rimmed eyes.

"Sophia!" she said, her voice breaking. "I . . . I'm so glad you're here."

"Where else would I be?" she asked, surprised to find her voice serene. "This is my workspace."

"Right," Vanessa said. She folded her arms against herself, trying to make herself smaller. More vulnerable.

"Would you like me to find Kip for you?"

"No. You're the one I wanted to see." Vanessa took a deep breath. "I need to apologize to you."

Sophia blinked so hard she was surprised she wasn't accidentally sending Morse code.

"On behalf of both of us. But especially on my own behalf, because . . . because we were friends once." Vanessa sniffled. "Do you mind if I sit down?"

Before Sophia could answer either way, Vanessa slid herself into Sophia's makeup chair.

"It never should have happened. Sebastian and me. I honestly don't know what came over us. I . . ." Vanessa sighed deeply, and turned the chair around, so she was looking at Sophia in the mirror. Their usual positions. Where Sophia was behind her, in servitude, and Vanessa had control.

"I think I was jealous. I had been for a long time. My relationship fell apart, while yours with Sebastian was just starting. And he and I had been friends for so long, we just understood each other, fundamentally, you know?"

"Hmm" was the only reply Sophia could make. It was unreal. She had listened to Vanessa tell morning-after stories before, recounted tales of her breakups and makeups with her ex-husband (or any guy she might be seeing). She could always nod sympathetically and act shocked at the appropriate moments at those, because they didn't personally involve her.

But now, it seemed like Vanessa was expecting the same kind of treatment.

"And then you got pregnant, and everyone was so happy. But Sebastian—he told me that he was conflicted, being out on the road—and I understood that conflict, because my life is nothing if not hectic . . . I mean, when would I have time for a baby, regardless of what the tabloids say?"

Sophia waited. Half-curious to know if Vanessa really did feel badly about her actions.

But then she got her answer.

"I mean, part of me thinks you should be thanking me, because of Sebastian's doubts. Everyone knew about them, and now you do, too."

"Thank you?" she replied in disbelief, but Vanessa seemed to hear it as an actual thanks, since she smiled pityingly at Sophia in the mirror.

"I know, that's so selfish of me to think, but it's true." Vanessa sighed, and brushed her hair off her shoulder. In the mirror, she dropped her gaze from Sophia's eyes, to her own reflection. "I know you're hurt. And you have every right to be. But I know that you'll recover, and when you do, I hope you can find it in your heart to forgive me."

Sophia cocked her head to the side.

"Why?"

The gentle smile slid slightly from Vanessa's face. "Why?"

"You've never done anything without something being in it for you, so . . . why would you come here to beg my forgiveness?"

Vanessa let out a long, rueful sigh.

"Because I need you. In my life. Kip is great and all, but he's not you. You've always gotten me. Understood what I need to do my job. Known exactly how to highlight my cheekbones. You're too important to Team Vanessa to treat this way."

"Team Vanessa?" Sophia managed to say through her incredulity.

"You are a founding member of Team Vanessa!" she said. "And I need you. To do my makeup, to be my confidant. I miss you."

Vanessa let her (admittedly well performed) heartfelt plea hang in the air. Sophia waited until Vanessa was visibly uncomfortable with the silence.

"Which do you miss more, Vanessa?" She raised a brow. "My friendship, or my ability to make you look good?"

Vanessa only hesitated long enough to paste a smile on her face. "Your friendship obviously! I do so hope we can rebuild our bridge of trust."

"Right. Our bridge of trust."

"However, right now, I need your ability to make me look good more."

"What about Kip?"

"Kip is . . . fine." Vanessa shrugged, and Sophia swore she heard a gasp of indignation from the toilet. "But today's the big finale. And there's a bunch of reporters here. *Entertainment Weekly* is going to put me on the cover for the season finale!" She squealed and clapped her hands like an excited child. "I want *you* to do my makeup. Come on, let's show all these gossiping PAs and grips and camera guys that we are bigger and better than our personal differences."

There it was. The looming threat. If Sophia didn't do her makeup, and do it well, the whole crew would know it was because of her own pettiness. That *she* was the problem.

"Okay," Sophia said.

"Okay?" Vanessa repeated. Then leaped out of the chair to hug Sophia.

She managed to keep herself from wrenching herself free.

"Thank you!" Vanessa sniffled. Then she turned back around, flung herself into the chair, and smoothed the crocodile tears away from her eyes. "Oh, I'm so glad we can both be adults. Today is too important to leave to chance. I need to look absolutely amazing. Stunning."

Sophia dug into the plastic drawer organizer that held all the foundations, praying that Kip hadn't gotten rid of what she needed. She managed to keep her smile to herself as her fingers closed around the little compact labeled Pale Moon.

"Don't worry. I will make you look more incredible than you ever have in your life."

SOPHIA DIDN'T OFTEN go to set. Usually she was too busy prepping for the next scene to watch them film the current one. But this time, she just couldn't help herself. She needed to see Vanessa in all her glory.

She tiptoed onto the stage, being sure to keep to the shadows that lined the bright environs of the set—which happened to be a snow cave, built out of foam board and plaster. Here, Vanessa would have her big scene. She, as the impervious Billie, would wail and rend her clothes and cry out in pain for her lost love, who was turned into a frost giant. This of course, was a massive spoiler, so the reporters who currently chatted with one of the writer-producers in the corner had signed NDAs, embargoing the big secret until it was slated to air.

She ignored all the looks, and all the whispers. And she walked straight up to the person she needed to see.

"Hey, Gary," she said, and the camera operator turned

around. Slowly, because he had a heavy steady camera apparatus strapped to his torso. Gary liked to say he was two inches shorter than he had been fifteen years ago when he first took the job as a steady cam operator.

"Sophia," Gary replied with a smile. "What can I do for you?"

"Just wondering . . . how did the DP light this scene?"

Gary looked at her quizzically. "Same as always. Vanessa requested a warm amber glow but the director nixed it since she's supposed to be freezing her balls off in an ice cave."

"Great. That's perfect."

"Perfect for what?" Gary replied. His eyes narrowed shrewdly. "What are you up to?"

"Nothing," Sophia chirped. "Just . . . do me a favor, and let her get one take in first. She always likes her first take best."

Gary looked Sophia up and down, and shook his head. "Only because you deserve better than they treated you."

"Thanks, Gary," she said.

"Don't thank me, thank my union. Hopefully they'll have my back."

Then, Sophia receded to the shadows. She didn't have to wait very long. Vanessa, fresh from the costume department, came striding in, and the entire set jumped to the ready.

"Hello! Good morning!" she called out, waving to various crewmembers without breaking her stride. She only detoured when she got to the reporters.

"Kara! Marc! Wonderful to see you again!" Air kisses were deployed, arms clasped. "Keep your eyes open and your recorders handy—you're about to see a show!"

And she was off to confer with the director.

No one said anything about her makeup, of course. Because in this light, her makeup looked fairly normal. Perhaps slightly paler than usual, but hey, she was supposed to be in an ice cave.

But once she got under the hot lights, and was viewed through a camera . . .

"Gary! Can we go?" Vanessa called out. "I'm ready, I feel it, let's do it!"

When the lead actor was ready, the set accommodated. People scrambled to make sure everything was in place. Grips did final checks of their equipment. Last looks were called.

Sophia went up to Vanessa, gave her one last check. "Knock 'em dead," she said.

And then, the director settled into his chair next to the video monitors. His eyes met Vanessa's. "And . . . action!"

Something shifted in Vanessa with that word. She bent slightly, moved . . . and transformed herself into Billie. She spoke her dialogue in a voice shaking with emotion. She called out to the frost giant/lost love who was frozen in the ice. She railed against the alien race that put him there. She swore her vengeance against their leader. And she cried out for her mother, and for the child (spoiler!) that was growing in her belly.

When the lines were done, when Vanessa's sniffles subsided, the entire set continued to hold their breath. Until . . .

"Cut!"

Then, everyone—*everyone*—burst into applause. Even Sophia. She couldn't deny that Vanessa was damned good.

"Vanessa!" the director called out, rushing up to her. "That was the most amazing thing I've ever seen!"

"It was, wasn't it?" Vanessa said, laughing with relief as the director helped her up off the floor. "I left everything on that floor. I'm spent."

"I'm sure it came through."

"Did you watch it on the monitors?"

"No—I was too enthralled watching you."

"Oh, then let's see it," Vanessa said, clutching his arm. "Now?"

"Absolutely. I want to relive that moment again and again."

As everyone gathered around the monitors, from the lowest PA to the highest producer, to the reporters, Sophia decided now was a good time to start moving toward the doors.

Because as soon as Vanessa's face came up on the monitor, the celebration stopped.

". . . What . . . is . . . *that?*" Vanessa said, stone-faced.

"What do you mean?" the director asked. Then, peering closer, "Oh. Oh my. GARY!"

"What?" Gary replied, feigning innocence as well as Vanessa did. "I thought that was a choice."

"*You think it was my choice to look like a rotting zombie?!*" Vanessa screeched.

"Vanessa, darling," the director said in his most soothing voice. "We will just do it again."

"You think I can do that again? I gave the take everything—everything! And that bitch—"

"Bitch?" It must have been one of the reporters asking.

"She did this to me! Get away from me, you fucking dolt!" Some poor PA had no doubt gotten into her eye line. "Are you deaf as well as stupid? Move!!! I'm so fucking done with this. I'm done! I'm better than this goddamned show, better than stupid frost giants! Better than . . . basic cable!"

Vanessa's meltdown echoed through the stage, and into the reporters' cameras and tape recorders, reaching Sophia's ears as she strode away from this job, toward the outdoors.

And strode toward freedom.

MAY

SUNDAY	MONDAY	TUESDAY	WEDNESDAY	THURSDAY	FRIDAY	SATURDAY

"This was not the plan!"

CHAPTER 24

 As April slid away and May came with the advent of a SoCal summer, the days were beginning to blur together in their scarcity and importance.

The countdown had begun. As Nathalie's calendar flipped to May, all the way at the bottom there was the circled due date—May 31st. And every day before it was packed with events and information. The AP tests. Finals. Doctor's appointments. Getting one last haircut before the baby arrived. Getting her car serviced, and the car seat installed. Placing everything breakable on a high shelf. Putting those little plastic outlet covers in all the lower outlets. Finally transferring all those old home movies from VHS to digital that had been sitting in the closet of what was now the baby's room and wouldn't have anywhere to go.

There was no putting it off anymore. Things had to get done.

But it was also time to start relaxing. Her body was crying out for it. Every day when she got home, she collapsed on the couch, which now bore a deep indentation of her body. She slept hard at night for short stretches, and then woke fitfully.

Things were sore she didn't know could be sore. She was doing all the work she could, trying desperately to finish out the school year for her seniors, but more than once she had to resist the urge to just let her students watch a movie, and use the fifty-five minutes of class time to let her mind stop running.

Back in olden times, they called it one's "confinement"— when one just stayed home, and put her (swollen) feet up, letting her body rest before the stress of having a baby.

And Nathalie was ready for it. Just as soon as she took care of one or two little things.

After all, it wasn't every day a girl went to the senior prom.

"Are you sure you're okay going to prom without me?" David said, watching as Nathalie pulled a silk wrap around her green sheath dress, trying to disguise the well-stretched aspect of the only garment she had left that was vaguely decent. With strappy metallic sandals, large earrings, and some judicious low lighting in the reception hall, she should pass muster.

Of course, nothing could overcome the fact that she had to wear her glasses.

That's right, there was a new symptom to add to the ever-growing list of pregnancy annoyances—her contact lenses no longer fit properly.

As Dr. Duque explained it during her last visit, "your body retains fluid during pregnancy. It retains this fluid everywhere—including your eyes. Sometimes, it subtly changes their shape."

Meaning, her contact lenses felt like a pair of too-tight jeans on her eyeball. The assurance that this was temporary didn't do much to appease when one was trying to hold on to their beauty standards by tooth and nail (and eyeball).

But in this instance, it was workable—the glasses helped distract from the sheath dress.

"Don't pretend for one second that you wanted to put on a suit and come to the high school senior prom," she said, smiling back at him.

"Oh no, don't misunderstand." He came up and wrapped his arms around what remained of her waist. "I am *ecstatic* that you said I didn't have to go to prom. I wear suits all day, I don't need that on my Saturday night. But, I just want to make sure you're okay going without me."

She pecked him on the lips. "I'll be fine. I'm only thirty-six weeks, we still have plenty of time." It was true, even though it didn't feel like it with that circle on the calendar now visible. "I'm not even driving, I'm taking an Uber. And Lyndi will be with me."

"Lyndi's going?" David's brow quirked up.

"Her co-op is doing the flowers. I invited her to stick around after they do the setup, so she's like my junior chaperone."

"Think Lyndi's up to that level of responsibility?" David asked, wryly.

Nathalie thought of the role Lyndi played in uncovering David's secret Twitter confessional. "Of late, I have been nothing but surprised by my sister's ability to solve problems."

Indeed, Lyndi was in problem-solving mode when Nathalie arrived. She found her sister in the ballroom of the rented reception hall, giving instructions to one of the staff.

"No, the crystal beads have to drape from the flowers! Fall like raindrops!"

"Wow," Nathalie said, in complete awe.

Bowers of fat, white flowers greeted her in the entryway. Crystals dripped from them, like diamonds. Tarnished gilt and silver lent a touch of old elegance. Romance mingled with drama and celebration in Lyndi's designs.

This was the tenth prom Nathalie had attended—not including her own—she was used to the prom committee pulling out all the stops. Not to mention a lot of the kids' parents worked in the entertainment industry, so they knew how to create an illusion. But the place looked so good, you could almost forget that they were in the middle of a Burbank rented reception hall, with sound-dampening ceiling tiles and hollow Greek columns. Instead they were transported to the coast of Long Island in the 1920s, attending the party of the summer in style at the mansion of the mysterious Jay Gatsby.

Who seriously knew his flowers.

"These kids aren't going to know what hit them," Nathalie said.

"I hope so," Lyndi replied, satisfied that the staffer was making the crystals fall in the appropriate raindrop-like fashion. "Hey, thanks for convincing the prom committee to hire us. We needed a beta test of our new event services."

"No thanks necessary—this is amazing." Nathalie lightly touched one of the freesia blooms. They moved, arm in arm from the entryway into the main ballroom.

"I love the theme they chose—the Roaring Twenties. Check out the tables! One of our wholesalers had these art deco planters I couldn't pass up and they work perfectly."

"I'm sure they do. Why couldn't you have thrown my baby shower?"

"I got my creative gene from somewhere, you know," Lyndi said, turning to her. "If you called her, I know she'd pick up."

Nathalie felt the heat rise in her cheeks. "She didn't."

Nathalie still hadn't spoken to Kathy. After her conversation with her father, she didn't know who was supposed to reach out first. She'd opened up her email at least once a day, and wrote an email that just said, "I'm sorry."

She just never managed to press Send.

It had been a month. And while every other part of Nathalie's life had markedly improved, there was still this shame, right in the center of it.

She will always be my mother.

But even if she did manage to connect, she was scared to death of what Kathy might say.

That Nathalie was ungrateful. (She was.)

That she was a brat. (Also true.)

That she never wanted to speak to Nathalie again?

"You're right," she said to Lyndi, desperate to change the subject. "I should try her tomorrow. Look, the first arrivals are coming in."

"Awwww . . ." Lyndi turned into a puddle of mush at the sight of the starched and pressed eighteen-year-olds looking more mature and spit-shined than they ever had before. The girls striding forward with confidence, and the boys not quite fitting into their tuxedo shirts. "They're so cute!"

"Yeah—David's going to be sorry he missed this. He could have shown all these boys how to wear a suit."

"What is David doing tonight?" Lyndi asked.

"He's putting together the crib." At long last, David was assembling the IKEA furniture for the nursery. Assisted by a six-pack of his favorite IPA, of course.

"Wow. It's really happening soon, isn't it?" Lyndi replied.

"Not for another four weeks," Nathalie said quickly. "And you will be three weeks after that. Does Marcus have the crib up?"

"Actually, we've been figuring out some of that stuff . . ."

"Where the crib will go? I don't wonder, in your tiny apartment, you're going to have to feng shui the crap out of that place."

"The crib. And the couch," she added enigmatically. "And everything else."

Nathalie's brow came down, but before she could ask what Lyndi meant by "everything else," there was a gasp from behind them.

"Oh wow—this is beautiful!" Sophia said, her eyes on the flowers, the gilt, the long strings of crystals glinting in the candlelight.

"Sophia!" Nathalie cried, coming over to embrace her. "What are you doing here?"

"I'm a chauffeur," Sophia said, winking. "I just dropped Maisey and Foz out front."

"Maisey's taking Foz?" Nathalie's eyes lit up with the delight of gossip.

"He's a very nice young man," Sophia replied, softening. "I know my daughter doesn't have any plans to drink, but I still didn't want them driving, with all the crazies on the road tonight. But I couldn't *not* sneak in for a peek of the place! Lyndi, this is gorgeous."

As Lyndi murmured her thanks, Nathalie saw out of the corner of her eye a veritable goddess enter, towing a familiar curly-haired young man in her wake.

"Holy moly—is that Maisey?"

"Yep," Sophia replied, beaming. "A friend of mine in costumes hooked her up with the dress, and she let me do her makeup for once."

"Foz looks like he got struck by lightning. He's utterly gobsmacked."

"As well he should be," Sophia declared.

"I can't disagree with that," Nathalie said. "And as a chaperone, it is my duty to make sure that he remains respectfully awestruck."

"So, what are our other duties as chaperones?" Lyndi asked. "Do we monitor the drama? Count the votes for prom king and queen?"

"Actually, from this side of things, prom can be pretty boring. You just make sure no one spikes the punch—"

"There's a punch table?"

"Not since movies set in the 1950s. It's metaphorical punch," Nathalie explained, and the other two nodded in understanding. "You're mostly here to make sure that everyone acts appropriately. But honestly, in my ten years of proms, I've never had to break up a fight. Never even had to comfort a crying girl in the bathroom. The most exciting thing I did once was find someone an emergency tampon."

"Well, here's to a boring prom," Sophia said, watching her daughter lead Foz to the dance floor.

"Uh, I think this prom just got a little more exciting," Lyndi said, looking down at the floor. Nathalie followed her gaze. She was looking at the skirt of Nathalie's green dress. Strange, but there was a dark splotch on the front. It was warm, and wet. A long trickle ran down the inside of her leg, pooling in a puddle on the floor beneath her.

"Nathalie. I think your water just broke."

CHAPTER 25

"THIS WAS NOT THE PLAN!"

Nathalie's mind screamed her objections. Or perhaps she was screaming the words aloud—it was difficult to tell in the rushed aftermath of her bodily fluids leaking all over the banquet hall floor. After a stalled second—during which Nathalie ascertained that she really did break her water and hadn't accidentally peed herself—Lyndi and Sophia jumped into action.

"Call an Uber!" Lyndi cried.

"They'll take forever to get here," Sophia said. "You should see the street outside, it's like a parking lot with all the kids arriving. We'll take my car."

"I'll go tell the principal we have to leave."

"I'll go bring the car around. Next stop, hospital!" Sophia said, as she trotted past an incoming group of glammed-up seniors.

Meanwhile, Nathalie stood staring at the puddle currently ruining her strappy sandals.

This was not the plan.

Because of course, Nathalie *had* a plan. It involved going

into labor gently, at home. Making good use of all the aromatherapy candles and soothing mood music she had been researching. When her contractions were five minutes apart, she would calmly tell David it was time to drive her to the hospital, where Dr. Duque would be waiting with a room ready to deliver her daughter into the world.

It was, to be frank, the perfect plan.

And it was one that wasn't meant to be implemented for another four weeks!

But instead, she was standing in the middle of a ballroom floor at a high school prom, with a bunch of high school seniors staring at her in shock and mild horror.

Yeah, not the plan.

Not having a hospital bag packed was not part of her plan.

Also not the plan? The low aches that began spreading rapidly, radiating from the back of her hips down her legs—like period cramps but so, so much worse—before she was loaded into the back of Sophia's car.

"Is this a contraction? Is this what it feels like?" she remembered saying before another wave of aches overtook her.

Lyndi only gave a small unknowing shake of her head, but Sophia nodded as she sped through another turn.

"Granted, it's been a while for me, but yeah, that sounds like a contraction."

"Oh God, this is horrible! Why would anyone do this . . . I mean, it's fine. This is totally fine," Nathalie managed to say, once she saw just how unblinkingly gray her little sister looked in that moment.

Sophia swerving through downtown traffic like a NASCAR driver was also not the plan—but at that moment, Nathalie was grateful for it.

However, getting to the hospital and discovering that Dr.

Duque wasn't coming in, because she was on vacation in Mexico for the weekend? DEFINITELY NOT THE PLAN.

"Hello!" chirped Dr. Keen. "How are we doing?"

"WE ARE IN LABOR," Nathalie gritted out.

"Yes you are," Dr. Keen replied, her smile not even falling a millimeter. "Let's get you set up then!"

They processed Nathalie quickly. When the nurse timed her contractions, Dr. Keen shifted from chipper and unconcerned to chipper and "Let's get you into a room. Now."

Sophia and Lyndi trotted behind her as they wheeled Nathalie into a delivery room, and practically threw her into the bed.

"Go ahead and put on this robe, and then we'll do an exam, see if we need to call anesthesia."

"Fuck yes, we need to call anesthesia."

"Yes, but if you're too far along, we won't have time, so . . . chop chop and get changed!"

"She's too young," Nathalie said, as soon as Dr. Keen was out the door. "It's like she's a kid with a play stethoscope."

"Uh, she's *my* doctor, and I trust her," Lyndi replied, as she helped Nathalie out of her green dress.

"That's because *you* are young. You think your generation knows everything."

"Considering young Dr. Keen is going to deliver your baby, you better hope they do," Sophia said, and Lyndi smirked.

"That's not helping," Nathalie gritted out. Another contraction gripped her, and she buckled on the bed. This baby . . . this baby could be here any moment! And it occurred to her that David wasn't.

"Crap I forgot to call David!" Nathalie gasped, reaching for her phone.

"Relax, I called everyone," Lyndi said.

"I'm not going to relax until he's here!"

"Well, then you can relax now," came a harried voice from the doorway.

David.

He was there. His hair was standing straight up. He was wearing what he affectionately called his "work pants"—a pair of jeans that had survived since college with paint splotches and holes in the knees. His eyes grazed over the other occupants of the room, and honed in on Nathalie. He rushed to her side, kissed her forehead, and took her hand.

"I thought we had four more weeks," he said.

"So did I," she replied weakly.

"I think that's our cue," Sophia whispered to Lyndi, and they shuffled toward the door.

"We'll be in the waiting room . . ."

"No!" Nathalie cried, panic oddly rising in her chest. She didn't know why, she just knew that she didn't want her sister or Sophia to leave. That, as long as she was flanked by these wonderful women, she would be okay. "You guys should stay."

"Really?" Sophia smiled.

"Really?" Lyndi looked a little green.

"Don't worry, Lyndi," she replied. "You can stay on the 'waist-up' side of the line."

"Yeah, kid," David said, smirking. "Think of it like a trial run."

Lyndi shot her brother-in-law a look of mock disgust she had perfected at the age of twelve while he laughed at her. Then, Lyndi came over and took Nathalie's other hand.

"Oh no you don't try and stop me . . ." A voice moved down the corridor outside. "Now WHERE IS MY DAUGHTER???"

Nathalie turned to her sister in shock. "When you say you called everyone . . ."

"Yeah . . . everyone includes Mom," Lyndi affirmed.

"How did she get here so fast?"

"She was at my apartment helping with some stuff," Lyndi replied. "You're going to have to talk to her eventually." Then she called out, "We're in here!"

A quick turn of kitten heels clacked along the linoleum, and suddenly, Kathy burst into the room, trailed meekly by Marcus.

"Kathy," Nathalie said, her voice small. It was incredibly odd to be in a hospital bed about to give birth, but feeling like a little girl caught after breaking something precious. But Kathy just rushed to Nathalie's side, wedging in next to Lyndi.

"Nathalie, honey," she said softly. "You're going to do just great. I know it. Everything you do, you do so well."

She felt the tears welling up in her eyes. She opened her mouth to give what could only be a ham-fisted apology for her behavior, but Kathy spoke first.

"Now, your dad is on his way, but I don't want him to miss a minute. I'm just going to video things until he gets here."

"Oh, no, I don't think—"

"Now, tell me, Nathalie," Kathy said, pulling out her phone and holding it up, "how dilated is your cervix?"

Nathalie looked to Lyndi, who elbowed Marcus, for help.

"Hey, Kathy, let me see if I can make it so your video is high-quality resolution," Marcus said, reaching for her phone.

"Oh thank you, Marcus. I want to make sure I get *every-thing*," Kathy said, as Marcus discreetly turned off the camera.

"I should find the waiting room," Marcus said as he handed the phone back to Kathy.

"No, you should stay," Lyndi said to Marcus. "David said I should, as a trial run."

"Not a bad idea," Marcus replied, eyes on Nathalie.

Before Nathalie could reply, another voice came from the door.

"Mom!"

Odd, because no one should be calling her mom quite yet. Nathalie shot a look to her sister. But Lyndi just threw up her hands. "This one is not on me."

"Maisey, what are you doing here?" Sophia said, rushing over to the door.

"Haley said someone's water broke, and saw you rushing out of the ballroom, saying you were going to the hospital! Is everything okay?"

"Everything is fine," Sophia replied. "With me, at least."

"Jeez you run fast, Maisey." Foz Craley's out-of-breath voice came from the doorway. "Is everything . . . oh. Uh, hey, Ms. Kneller."

"Hi, Foz," Nathalie replied. Because really, what else could she possibly say? "Enjoying prom?"

"Certainly memorable." He nodded, edging his way into the room behind Maisey. "So it was your water that broke on the ballroom floor, I guess?" At her nod, he smirked. "I think you prevented several teenage pregnancies tonight."

"Hey, there's a silver lining." Lyndi smiled at her.

"You're having a baby, Ms. Kneller! This is so cool," Maisey said, looking around the room. "I mean, weird, but cool."

"As long as you're here, you should come in," Nathalie said.

"Really?"

"Why not—we already have six people, what's two more?"

Foz looked at Maisey, as if issuing a dare. "I was considering going pre-med."

And so, surrounded by her husband, her sister, her friend,

386

KATE RORICK

her stepmom, her quasi brother-in-law, her student, and her student's prom date, Nathalie gave birth to a baby girl.

It wasn't as straightforward as it was in the telling, of course. For a time, there was nothing to do but labor and wait for what was to come.

The nurse came in and hooked up the various monitors and IVs she would need. Dr. Keen examined her and said she was at six centimeters . . . just under the wire to get her epidural, thank God.

The handsomest anesthesiologist in the world came in and inserted a line into her spine, making her go pleasantly numb from the waist down.

That was when she *really* managed to relax.

But it seemed like the medication had barely taken effect, before Dr. Keen was back in the room, doing an exam . . . declaring her at ten centimeters. And suddenly . . . everyone in the entire hospital was in her room.

Equipment dropped down from the ceiling, lighting her vaginal cavity like a movie star during her big scene. Nurses and attending doctors crowded in, and crowded out Kathy and her nonfunctioning camera phone.

She was told to push.

She pushed.

She didn't particularly care that a dozen people were currently looking up her well-lit vagina.

More pushing. Quite a bit more pushing. More people coming in. And then . . .

"Are you ready to meet your daughter?" Dr. Keen asked, from somewhere between Nathalie's legs.

Nathalie nodded, clutching David's hand. Then suddenly . . .

She was here.

A very surprised and goo-covered baby was held up by Dr. Keen, and placed on Nathalie's chest.

And everything else faded away.

She peered up at Nathalie with squinty confusion. As if waiting to be introduced.

"Hi," she managed to breathe. The baby had a shock of dark hair, standing up on its ends exactly like her father's. She had ten fingers, ten toes. She was so very small, but somehow managed to be the entire world wrapped up in a six-pound package.

Nathalie barely noticed as the room began to cheer, to cry. Kathy clutching Lyndi's hand. Lyndi clutching Marcus's. Sophia had her arm wrapped around a tired Maisey, while Foz typed busily on his phone.

"You don't mind that I livestreamed this, right, Ms. Kneller?"

She shrugged Foz's query off. Literally nothing else mattered. The banal faded into the background. They took the baby to the baby station on the side of the room to do some basic tests—weight, length—after asking David if he wanted to cut the cord. Dr. Keen and the nurses finished the delivery (she was asked if she wanted to keep her placenta. She said no.) and cleaned Nathalie up, and then the baby was back in her arms again.

Everyone gathered around, wanting a look.

"She's so tiny!"

"Good job, sis."

"Oh dear, she definitely has your father's ears."

"Is anyone hungry?" This last from Marcus.

Nathalie practically got whiplash nodding at Marcus. She had just pushed a baby out of her body, that had to be a couple thousand calories burned, at least. She was starving.

"Is there a cafeteria?" David asked.

"I think I saw it on our way in," Sophia said, hopping to her feet. "I'll show you."

"I could use something to eat, too," Maisey said. "C'mon, Foz, you owe me a bad chicken dinner."

"Technically, you owe me that bad chicken dinner," Foz replied as they headed toward the door.

"No, Mom, you stay," Lyndi said, when Kathy stood to join them. "I'll grab you a sandwich."

"Lynd . . ." Nathalie whispered.

"Like I said, you have to talk to her eventually," Lyndi whispered back, as she left the room as quickly as her pregnant belly would allow.

"While everyone's off getting food—the three-bean salad is delightful—mind if we give the baby a quick listen?" Dr. Keen said, as upbeat as a chipmunk.

Nathalie carefully handed the baby over to the nurse. As the nurse cooed over the baby, and Dr. Keen made notes on a chart, Nathalie turned back to Kathy, who had a nervous, tired smile on her face.

How to apologize? Where to begin?

"You did great, Nathalie," Kathy said. "Just like I knew you would."

Nathalie gazed over at her daughter. "Thank you."

"You know that was the easy part, though."

Nathalie looked up. "The easy part?"

"The birth. The hard part is what's to come. The diapers, the screaming at all hours. The guessing game of whether or not she's hungry. Don't get me started on cracked nipples! Your sister practically bit my left one off, she'd latch on and not let go. I still have phantom pains."

Nathalie felt a little flame of irritation rise up from her exhaustion. "I'm sure we will manage."

"Everyone thinks that, honey," Kathy said, patting her arm.

It was so hard to maintain her intentions to patch things up with Kathy when Kathy couldn't go three sentences without annoying or criticizing. So hard, in fact, that she didn't notice when the concerned nurse called Dr. Keen over to the baby.

"Why don't you let me be a parent for five minutes before you start telling me that I can't do it," Nathalie said, trying to maintain a neutral tone.

"I never said you can't do it, Nathalie," Kathy said, her voice rising. "I said—"

"Excuse me," Dr. Keen interjected. She was no longer chipper. And that was enough to drain any irritation from Nathalie and put her body on full alert.

Dr. Keen conferred with the nurse in low, rushed tones. The only words Nathalie could make out was "on call pediatrician," and "pneumothorax."

The nurse moved to the phone, talked quickly in low tones. She asked for a rapid response team. Then, everything started happening at once.

A half-dozen people—rapid response, true to their name—entered, and surrounded the baby. They started listening with stethoscopes, checking charts, saying letters and numbers in bewildering combinations . . . and those numbers and letters made them work faster.

"What? What is it?" Nathalie asked, frantic. But everyone was still focused on the baby. All except Dr. Keen, who had gotten out of the rapid response team's way. With a nod from one of the team's doctors, Dr. Keen came over to Nathalie, her voice calm, steady.

From Dr. Keen, that was more unnerving than anything.

"Ms. Kneller, we need to take your baby down to NICU for an assessment."

The blood drained from Nathalie's face, coursing down her body, out her frozen feet, and to the floor. Only to be replaced by the horrible, horrible realization that something was wrong.

"Why? What's wrong? Is she okay?"

"Your daughter is not breathing properly."

The words echoed through the room, through Nathalie's head. It was as if she had heard the words, but lost the capacity to understand them. She groped blindly for something, anything to hold on to.

And that was when she found Kathy's hand.

"What does that mean?" Kathy asked, the words Nathalie couldn't form coming out of her stepmother's mouth.

"At thirty-six weeks, your baby's lungs are not fully mature. It's possible she has a collapsed lung," Dr. Keen explained. "We need to give her a chest X-ray."

One of the rapid response team slipped a mask over her baby's face—oxygen.

"And then?"

"Then if the X-ray shows a pneumothorax, we will do a simple procedure to put a tube in her chest and expand the lung."

A procedure. Surgery.

"Okay. Okay," Nathalie said in a rushed breath. "Let's go to NICU. Let's go now."

"Honey," Kathy said, "hold on. You can't get out of bed yet, you just gave birth."

A moment later proved Kathy correct. The epidural hadn't worn off yet—she still couldn't feel anything from the waist

down. And if she could, no doubt her body would be screaming with sore muscles and pain.

But . . . "To hell with that, I need to—"

At that moment, David came back into the room, his arms
loaded down with prepackaged sandwiches.

"I didn't know what you'd want so I got one of everything. I
figured . . ." It took him a second to look up and read the room.
When he did, his body immediately tensed. "What's going on?"

"Something is wrong with the baby's lungs," Nathalie said,
choking back her tears. "Go with her!" She pointed wildly at
the rapid response team who had the baby in a wheeled bassinet. "Now, now, go now!"

David dropped the sandwiches on the floor, and moved to
the baby's side, as they wheeled the bassinet out of the room.

Leaving Nathalie without her baby for the first time in nine
months.

But she wasn't alone. She was still attached to someone,
gripping Kathy's hand for dear life. And Kathy gripping her
back.

"What do I do?" Nathalie's voice cracked. "I can't just sit
here, I have to do something."

"You are doing something," Kathy said, soft and fierce.
"You are healing. You are getting yourself ready."

"Ready?"

"For when she needs you," she replied. "What I was saying earlier, about the hard part being yet to come—this is it.
When you want to do something, but can't. When you have
to wait, and prepare, and hope that everything is going to be
okay. And it *will* be okay, Nathalie. You have to be as ready
for that. Because she is coming out of that X-ray, out of that
surgery, and she is going to need her mother.

"I know you're scared," Kathy continued. "And I know . . . I know you wish your mom was here instead of me. But I am here to tell you that as someone who has known you for the last twenty-five years, you can do this. You can. For that little girl? It'll be the easiest thing in the world."

Nathalie held tighter onto Kathy's hand, tears sliding down her nose. She couldn't look Kathy in the face—she couldn't move her eyes from the door, where David and her daughter had disappeared . . . where they would come back. But Kathy's words managed to find their way into her mind, writing themselves under her skin. And Nathalie knew, without question, that her mother *was* there. Both of her mothers were.

Because no one else but her mother could know exactly what she needed to hear.

They stayed like that, hands gripped together, Nathalie with her eyes locked on the door, Kathy whispering truths and hopes with equal fervor in her ear.

People came in—Lyndi and Marcus back from the cafeteria, a nurse here and there. But none were who she needed to see, so she simply did not see them. She was vaguely aware that Kathy told Lyndi in simple words what was going on, and Lyndi kept the rest of their group at bay.

Seconds ticked into minutes, while everything became focused on a single point. There was only Nathalie, Kathy, and the door.

Finally, the door admitted the one person Nathalie wanted to see. And life came roaring back.

"She's okay," David cried as he burst through the door.

A tingling sensation coursed through Nathalie's body—and not just because the epidural was finally wearing off.

"What happened?"

"They did the X-ray, her left lung was collapsed. They took her immediately to a treatment room, and inserted a chest tube, reinflating the lung. Nat—she gave the loudest scream, you wouldn't believe it. She's a fighter."

Nathalie grabbed David ferociously. Held him tight. She barely noticed the sighs of relief in the room, her sister's tears of joy. Nor did she notice that Kathy had let go of her hand.

"Can we see her?" Nathalie asked.

"The nurse is here with a wheelchair, she'll take us down to the NICU."

Then, Nathalie was wrapped up in blankets, her body sore and floppy, but every nerve pointed toward seeing her baby again. As the nurse wheeled her toward the door, Nathalie made her pause for a moment.

"Kathy," she said. And then she stopped.

There weren't words enough to convey what she wanted to say. How everything had become lost in those harrowing minutes, and the only thing she had to hold on to was Kathy's hand. How much the woman who had aggravated her and raised her meant to her.

"Thank you."

It was so little. But it was enough.

Kathy, tears in her eyes, held a hand to her heart.

"Go on, honey," she said. "Go see your little girl."

EPILOGUE: AKA, BEGINNING

THE FIRST PROUDEST DAY OF SOPHIA'S LIFE had been when Maisey was born. The second proudest day was when she left a young, irresponsible Alan and jumped headfirst into creating a life for herself and her daughter. But jockeying for position was the day that all of the hard work paid off, and Maisey graduated high school, with honors.

"I'm so proud of you, sweetie!" Sophia said when they found each other in the milling crowds on the high school football field after the ceremony. Maisey looked like the adult she would no doubt become in her scarlet cap and gown—poised, confident. A force to be reckoned with. Sophia, already emotional, was barely able to relinquish her daughter to her father for their hugs.

"Great work, kid," Alan said, Christy and their cute, chubby toddlers beside him. "I can take almost no credit for it. It was all your mom."

Sophia gave Alan a surprised look. "Hey, I call it like I see it," he said. Then his wife Christy shot *him* a look. "Or Christy rightly pointed out that all the work she does with our kids you did alone."

"Wow," Sophia said, giving Christy a soft smile.

"No kidding, wow," Maisey added.

"Now, I can't give you a car for your graduation, because I already gave you my car," Alan said. "So, how about I take you and some of your friends to dinner?"

"Oh, thanks Dad," Maisey replied. "But Foz and I already have plans for tonight."

Alan's face went still. "Who's Foz?"

Maisey and Sophia pointed to where Foz was with his mom, stepdad, and grandfather, about twenty feet away through the crowd. He'd been allowed to walk with their graduating class—Ms. Kneller had made sure of it. He'd been seated in the row right behind Maisey, and Sophia had been amused watching them whisper things to each other throughout the long graduation ceremony.

"Uh-huh," Alan deadpanned. "And what are these 'plans'?"

"Alan, relax," Sophia said. "He's a good kid, and I trust our daughter."

Alan made a noise that sounded like a car tire leaking air—which was better than it exploding from pressure, she supposed. "Okay, we are definitely having dinner with this Foz next week."

"Deal," Maisey said.

Then, one of the toddlers tugging at Christy's hand made his escape, causing Christy to duck through the crowds after him, lifting the other child up and balancing him on her hip as she ran.

"Oh crap," Alan said. "Sorry, he's a runner. So proud of you, sweetie." Alan pecked Maisey on the cheek before darting off after his wife and kids.

"Are you ready for that?" Maisey asked, as she watched Christy dive around graduates and their families trying to catch her runaway.

"Not yet," Sophia admitted. "Luckily he won't be mobile for a little bit. But, I know better what to expect this time. You were a great first kid. I learned a lot with you."

"Not a kid anymore though," Maisey said, smiling.

"No you are not. So . . . what are you going to do, my adult child?" Sophia said, taking her daughter's arm. They strolled across the turf, enjoying the pleasant after-ceremony exhilaration.

"I have work tomorrow morning," Maisey said. "And then . . . I have to send in my registration paperwork for UCLA."

"UCLA?" Sophia pulled to a stop. "Not Berkeley?"

"UCLA." Maisey had gotten the acceptance right before prom. While Sophia was dealing with the fallout from her zombie-makeup work at *Fargone*, Maisey had been making the biggest decision of her life thus far.

"Why? I thought you wanted to be in the Bay Area. And Berkeley has such an amazing literature program—"

"I made the decision on prom night," Maisey said. "Yeah, the financial package isn't as good as Berkeley, but if I live at home for the first couple semesters, I think I might be able to get through college debt free. I figure, with the baby, money is going to be tight, and—"

"No, don't you dare," Sophia interrupted. "I don't want you worrying about me—that's not your job. You are not going to sacrifice your future because of decisions I made. This baby and I will be fine. Trust me, I'm going to sue Sebastian for so much child support he's going to rue the day his band ever became successful."

"Well, I definitely approve of that." Maisey smirked. "But that's not why. When Foz and I were in the waiting room, and Ms. Kneller's baby was in surgery, I realized that . . . I don't want to miss him."

"Who?" Sophia asked, eyes wide. "Foz?"

"No . . . my brother," Maisey replied. "I don't want to miss a single second of him."

Tears welled in Sophia's eyes, as her hand fell to her growing baby bump.

"Are you sure?" she asked.

"UCLA's got a pretty kick-ass literature program, too, you know."

"As long as it's not about the money. I told you not to worry about that . . . because I got a new job."

"You did?" Maisey perked up. "Mom that's great! Where?"

Sophia's new job was on a sitcom. A perfect situation for her, because as they only filmed one day a week, her work hours were much more reasonable. Ironically, she was filling in for the last ten weeks of shooting for someone who was on maternity leave. The other makeup artist had stated her intention of not coming back, so, after Sophia's own maternity leave, the job could become permanent.

She had been thrilled to get the work . . . not to mention shocked that anyone wanted to hire her. Usually when you sabotage the lead of your show—no matter how much they deserved it—it's considered bad form.

But it turned out that Vanessa's form was worse.

The reporters on set that day breathlessly rushed to tell the story of her histrionics—and they had audio, too. With a judicious apology, that would have likely been the end of the scandal, but Vanessa didn't manage an apology—not a sincere one, anyway. The public saw right through her, helped by a new leak of rumors about how she hadn't been such a peach to work with on that indie movie they did last summer. This was accompanied by a Twitter rant where she tried to defend herself, and ended up digging the hole deeper. Vanessa had always been tabloid fodder, but lately it had gotten rabid, expecting her to explode at any minute. They always had new photographs of her ducking her head as she came out of a restaurant, or preening in a club . . . and there was Sebastian, somewhere in the background, looking strangely glum under such negative scrutiny.

They deserved each other, Sophia thought.

"I'm sorry about Sebastian," Maisey said after Sophia's re-counting.

"Don't be," Sophia replied. "I am 100 percent better off without him. And there were plenty of problems before Vanessa. It's like he thought a blood pressure machine and a tattoo were what I needed from him."

"Ugh, 'Sebastian,'" her daughter commiserated. "It's like his parents knew he was going to be an asshole, and gave him the most pretentious rock-'n'-roll name to match."

"Oh, Sebastian's not his real name. He chose that—and to be that—for himself," Sophia replied.

"It's not?"

Sophia shook her head. "His real name is Steve."

And then, Maisey laughed. And they didn't stop laughing, until Foz came over, his nervousness trumped by his vague befuddlement.

"What's the joke?" he asked.

"Nothing," Maisey said, wiping away tears. "I wasn't able to hear when they gave you your diploma . . . is your name really Foz?"

"Uh . . . it's short for Alphonse," he replied, eyeing the giggling pair like they had lost their wits.

"Close enough," Maisey allowed, her giggles subsiding.

"Can I borrow Maisey for a second?" Foz asked Sophia. "I wanted to introduce you to my grandfather."

Sophia shooed the pair away. As they came up to Foz's mother and grandfather, it did not go unnoticed as Maisey slipped her hand inside his.

Sophia took a deep breath, turning her face up, letting the California sun warm her. Her hands came to her belly, felt her son kick. He was just as eager to start his journey here. And Sophia was ready to guide him.

What a wonderful, wonderful day.

NATHALIE WAS VERY sorry to miss graduation this year—she had a number of seniors that she was fond of, none more so than Maisey Alvarez. And while she might have yearned to attend the festivities, even if she was on maternity leave, Nathalie had a rather good reason for skipping the chance to wish everyone good luck and listen to what was no doubt a run-of-the-mill valedictorian speech (if you've heard one, you've heard them all). Because that day, ten days after a prom night to remember, Nathalie and David finally brought Margot Kathleen Chen home.

"There she is!" Kathy cried, throwing the door open for them. "Welcome home, Margot!"

They had named the baby after Nathalie's mother. When she thought of it, nothing felt more right. But the middle name had been up for debate—until ten days ago, when the right name became clear as day.

"Now, I've got everything ready," Kathy said, ushering Nathalie in, David following behind with all the bags— diaper bag, Nathalie's clothes bag, the breast pump and breast milk Nathalie had been pumping while Margot had been in NICU, and all the supplies the hospital gave them. "There's lunch and dinner in the fridge—five meals in the freezer, all you have to do is move them to the fridge a day before to defrost. I would put them in the oven for five or ten minutes longer than usual, I think your oven is much more finicky than mine . . ."

Kathy talked a mile a minute. Nathalie felt that old irritation well up, but she was too pleasantly tired to care. She would let Kathy do what she liked. The baby was where Nathalie's attention was now.

Margot was perfect. Even the scar where her chest tube had been was perfect.

The doctors and nurses in the NICU had been amazing. They'd seen to Margot's every need. She was, at six pounds, one of the larger babies in the ward, and one of the loudest. One of the nurses even said that having a strong baby like Margot in there was a good example for all the other babies, making them cry loud, too. Nathalie didn't know if it was true, but it was a nice thing to hear. They'd made Nathalie feel so comfortable, helped her learn her baby, she almost didn't want to leave.

Almost.

Having her home felt right. In their little house, in her feminine blue room, with the finally assembled IKEA furniture.

"May I . . . ?" Kathy asked, her eyes on the baby.

Nathalie tentatively handed Margot over.

"Wait! Did you wash your hands? All visitors are supposed to wash their hands, that's what the nurse said—"

"Yes, David," Kathy singsonged, with a roll of her eyes to Nathalie. "Why don't you go unpack your bags?"

"Right. Right—don't want dirty hospital germs on our stuff. Nat—you should get out of those clothes, shower. Twice."

"Why don't you go first?" Nathalie said, and David, glad to have a task, disappeared into their bedroom.

"He's been like that since the surgery. Caution is one thing, but I swear, he'd burn my clothes if I'd let him."

Kathy eyed the loose T-shirt and sweatpants she was wearing. "Well, perhaps . . . no, I won't say anything. I think they look fine."

Kathy returned her attention to cooing at the baby.

"Have you heard from Lyndi?" Nathalie asked.

"Yes—they're staying the night with your father's college roommate in Kansas City. Your father is having a ball, even though the RV is packed to the gills."

"Already?"

"They want to get to Boston before the end of the week," Kathy replied.

While Nathalie giving birth four weeks early had been quite the surprise in their family, it was nevertheless topped by Lyndi's news.

It was just like her little sister to one-up her.

"Hey," Lyndi had said, as she came into the NICU to see Nathalie a few days earlier. "How's Mom and Margot?"

"Good—recovering more by the minute," Nathalie replied. "Killing my boobs with her milk demands."

"Yeah, she's definitely not a vegan."

"Marcus will be so disappointed."

Lyndi rolled her eyes. "For the hundredth time, he's gluten-free, not vegan. He just likes vegan food." Then, she leaned over, and let a gloved hand run over the top of the baby's head. "I'm so proud of you, Nat."

Nathalie blushed, and let her eyes fall to her daughter. "It's super hard, and incredibly easy at the same time."

"You are my inspiration. Seriously, I don't know how I'm going to do this in seven weeks' time." Lyndi hesitated. "Especially so far from home."

Her eyes shifted to her sister.

"I told Paula that I wanted the job in Boston."

"You did?"

"I did. I'm officially a manager, overseeing the opening of the Favorite Flower's East Coast operations."

"Lyndi, that's—"

"Insane?"

"Amazing. But . . . what about Marcus?"

"He's coming, too. The website will let him go freelance, submit articles and listicles for publication . . . and he can write his book from anywhere, he doesn't need to be in LA for that." Lyndi gave her usual small shrug. "So we are moving in a week. That's what Mom was doing at my place—helping me pack boxes. I'll have six weeks to set up the office, and then six weeks off, and then dive right back in. As the boss."

"Wow," Nathalie replied, in awe. "It sounds like you have it all figured out."

"Hardly," Lyndi scoffed. "I have to get an apartment, and a doctor, and figure out how to transpose our business model onto a new city . . ."

"You can do it," Nathalie interrupted. "I have complete faith in you."

"Thanks . . ." Lyndi said, biting her lip. "I was kind of hoping you would help me make a plan."

"Like you could stop me." Nathalie had laughed—and then the baby, who had been snoozing in the crib so contentedly woke up, and began to bawl.

And Margot was bawling now, wriggling in Kathy's arms, turning her head back and forth, searching.

"Oh, I think this one's hungry," Kathy chortled, as Margot

began to mouth Kathy's chest. "Sorry, baby, this bar's been closed for a while."

Nathalie came over and took her daughter back. "Again? I swear, you never stop eating."

"I remember you were like that—it used to drive your mom crazy."

Nathalie's head shot up. "What?"

"You used to eat day and night. Your mom said she'd feed you in her—and your—sleep. You just chow down, and she'd wake up two hours later, still holding you, and you'd still be sucking away."

"How do you know that?" she asked. Her entire body had gone still, oblivious to Margot's wriggling.

"She told me," Kathy replied simply. Then, after seeing the look on Nathalie's face. "Honey, you know your mom and I were friends."

Yes, they'd been friends, before Kathy had moved away for work. When she moved back, her mother was already gone.

"Of course I knew that. I . . . I didn't know you were friends when she was pregnant with me."

"Sweetie, I threw her baby shower!" Kathy cried. "Oh my, and once you came along? We would meet for coffee once a week, just so she had an excuse to get out of the house. And if you were awake, the only thing you wanted to do was eat. And only from the left side—your mom used to joke that she was a D cup on one side and an A on the other."

Nathalie could only stand there, in complete disbelief. All this time, she'd been searching for someone to give her answers . . . to give her a clue about what to expect during her pregnancy. She'd been so lost, yearning for her mother. And she'd had the answers in front of her the entire time.

"What else did she say?" Nathalie asked. "About . . . about me, as a baby?"

"That you were the most wonderful girl in the world," Kathy said, tweaking her nose.

"Right, but I'm looking for specifics. How many ounces did I drink in a sitting? Did I have reflux, baby acne, did she use the cry-it-out method?"

"Nathalie, I'll tell you everything I can remember." Kathy's eyes flicked down to Margot, whose wriggling had gone from desperate to frantic. "But first why don't you feed that child? We have all the time in the world, I'm staying all week until your dad gets back. Although, do you have anything besides the air mattress or the couch? My back is not what it used to be. I really wish you would have considered getting a *slightly* bigger house, I told you—"

As Kathy chattered away, Nathalie sighed, and her gaze fell to the baby in her arms. Her stepmother was right. They had all the time in the world. Because, while the road might not have been straight, they had made it here at last.

She was home, a baby at her breast. Finally a mother.

Exactly as she had planned.

ACKNOWLEDGMENTS

THIS BOOK'S GESTATION WAS ALMOST EXACTLY nine months long. I know this because I was eleven weeks pregnant when this idea was pitched, and my daughter was about eleven weeks old when I turned in the completed manuscript. And much like with a baby, while I did do most of the work, this book did not come to fruition by my will alone. I have to thank Lucia Macro and Annelise Robey for pushing me to take a risk in a new genre. For my writer friends who cheered the decision, beta read chapters when I was uncertain, and—in one particularly inspired email chain—came up with the unholy confection known as placenta cupcakes. For my doctor sister and my OB, who answered random questions without fail. But most important, my unending gratitude belongs to the numerous women who gave me insight into their pregnancies, their jobs, and their lives . . . then let me co-opt them. Kate, Natalie, Eva, Krystle, and Mom—thank you so much for sharing your stories.

About the author

About the book

Insights,
Interviews
& More . . .

Meet Kate Rorick

KATE RORICK is an Emmy Award–winning writer who has worked on a number of television shows, most recently *The Librarians* on TNT. She was also a writer for the hit web series *The Lizzie Bennet Diaries,* and authored the series' two tie-in novels, *The Secret Diary of Lizzie Bennet* and *The Epic Adventures of Lydia Bennet.* In her other life, she is the bestselling author of historical romance novels under the name Kate Noble. Kate lives in Los Angeles with her family. ᔧ

Research, or Lack Thereof

I love research. It's my favorite part of writing, in that I don't have to be writing to do it. I can be watching TV, reading the internet, visiting a museum, or taking a pole-dancing class, and tell myself that I'm not procrastinating, I'm researching. (Note: I have never taken a pole-dancing class. It looks hard.)

Of course, some books require more research than others. However, *The Baby Plan* was an anomaly for me in that it required almost no documentary watching, no poring through books, no scouring the far corners of the internet for a crucial piece of information. Almost no research at all . . . because I was currently living it.

That's right, I wrote *The Baby Plan* while planning for a baby of my own.

Now, some might think this is a prescient bit of authorial wisdom. *Hey, I know, I'll write a novelization about the experience of being pregnant, and in that way get to write off all my medical expenses!* But I'm not as savvy as that. In reality, this book came about because I was desperately trying to figure out what I was going to write next—and not having much luck—when my agent and editor pitched me the idea of "something to do with modern day pregnancy."

They thought I could speak to this subject, because I had already gone ▶

3

through it with my now three-year-old son. Surely all I had to do was harken back to that time and put to paper what the experience was like.

Little did they know I was currently reliving that time, eleven weeks into gestating my daughter.

At first I was hesitant. Because I couldn't possibly encompass the vastness of what pregnancy is. It's harrowing, it's joyful, it's disgusting, it's beautiful. Everyone experiences it differently. But then a lightbulb went off. Since it's impossible to represent *everyone*'s pregnancy, I didn't have to even try. I just had to represent what it was like for Nathalie, Lyndi, and Sophia to be pregnant.

It can't be too surprising that many of their experiences turned out to be mine?

Like Lyndi, I gave up my beloved poached eggs for breakfast, because undercooked eggs are a no-no and this makes me sad to this day.

Like Sophia, I had some extreme porno-sized boobage.

Like Nathalie, toward the end of my pregnancy, I was retaining so much fluid it changed the shape of my eyeballs, and I had to forgo contact lenses for the last month or so.

I would wake up in the night with my hands numb and tingly, from pregnancy-induced carpal tunnel.

Also, my leg would seize randomly while sleeping, causing me to wake up and freak out my husband while I yelped in pain.

Both my son and daughter sat on my sciatic nerve, making it almost impossible to walk for the last month of pregnancy. When I absolutely had to move, my husband insisted I use a cane.

I did drool like a basset hound.

I did have my mom tell me about her pregnancy induced genital edema, and that's something I could have gone my whole life without knowing, thanks.

I did paint my daughter's room a feminine blue, which required Pinterest links to convince people it would work.

I did take a tumble—on the sidewalk, not on my bike—and ended up in Labor and Delivery under observation for a couple of hours one weekend. (Pro tip: it's pretty boring, so bring a book!)

I have received daily pastel emails.

Way too many people asked me how I was feeling.

In nonpregnancy real life occurrences, my driveway has flooded. I have geo-tracked a specific Starbucks simply by analyzing a picture (or rather, my brother-in-law got way too into figuring out if it could be done and we discovered that it could). I have broken an IKEA chair.

And . . . I had a secret pregnancy Twitter account. I needed a place to marvel at the insanity pregnancy brought into my life, but on social media I chose to keep my first ▶

pregnancy mostly private, for a hundred different reasons. I worried that I wouldn't be seen as myself by my job, by my friends . . . and I also worried about if something horrible happened. If everyone knew about the pregnancy, they would then also have to know about this theoretical tragedy. I couldn't face the idea of having my pain be public. So I kept it to myself as long as possible.

But I still needed to express myself somehow. To put it out into the ether, yell into the void. So, I created a Twitter account that became the place where I vented in 140-character bursts, under the handle @WTFPreg. It still exists, if you want to check out the real time thought processes of a newbie mom-to-be. Which, it turned out, I needed reminding of.

As much as it was a coincidence that I was pregnant while writing this book, it was a really good thing that I was. Because all the tiny annoyances and oddities of the first pregnancy had just become a blur of memory by the time I was growing big with my second.

I cannot emphasize this enough: I had two of the easiest, most run-of-the-mill pregnancies imaginable. No complications. Healthy babies. I also read all the books, was prepared in ways big and small. And yet, the myriad of stuff your body puts you through, that you have to write off as your new normal . . . well, let's just say none of the movies or TV pregnancies I'd seen prepared me for this.

So, no matter how well Nathalie planned, or how much experience Sophia had, in retrospect I have decided that Lyndi had the best approach to pregnancy. Whatever will come, will come, and you just have to accept it as it goes along. ᴥ

Reading Group Discussion Guide

1. The novel opens with a Thanksgiving disaster. What is it about holidays that brings out the worst—and best—in families? Have you ever had a holiday disaster? What happened?

2. In your opinion, has the Baby World gotten out of control with showers, gender reveals, and Facebook reveals? Discuss if you feel this is all over-the-top or a chance to celebrate with friends and family.

3. Tell us some baby shower or baby party horror stories!

4. Lyndi's friends avoid her once she announces her pregnancy. Do you think they are just being "mean girls" or does Lyndi's pregnancy somehow make them feel conflicted and confused?

5. It's been said that "sisters are a shield against life's cruel adversity." How do you think this is true or not true? In what ways could Lyndi and Nathalie be better sisters?

6. In what ways do you feel Nathalie might be too hard on Kathy? Conversely, are there ways that Kathy has been tone-deaf with regard to her stepdaughter's feelings?

7. Sophia's daughter, Maisey, is horrified that her mother is having a baby. In what ways are Maisey's feelings justified? Do you think Sophia proceeded without much consideration for her future or her relationship with her near-grown daughter?

8. David, Marcus, and Sebastian all deal with impending fatherhood in different ways. Do any of them handle it well? What could they do better? Is there ever validity to men feeling "left out" or "pushed aside" during pregnancy?

9. Each woman feels challenged at work during her pregnancy. How do we, as a society, support or not support working pregnant women?